FALLEN SEAL LEGACY

SEAL Brotherhood
Book 2

SHARON HAMILTON

D1377529

SHARON HAMILTON'S BOOK LIST

SEAL BROTHERHOOD SERIES
Accidental SEAL (Book 1)
Fallen SEAL Legacy (Book 2)
SEAL Under Covers (Book 3)
SEAL The Deal (Book 4)
Cruisin' For A SEAL (Book 5)
SEAL My Destiny (Book 6)
SEAL Of My Heart (Book 7)
Fredo's Dream (Book 8)
SEAL My Love (Book 9)
SEAL Brotherhood Box Set 1 (Accidental SEAL & Prequel)
SEAL Brotherhood Box Set 2 (Fallen SEAL & Prequel)
Ultimate SEAL Collection Vol. 1 (Books 1-4 / 2 Prequels)
Ultimate SEAL Collection Vol. 2 (Books 5-7)

BAD BOYS OF SEAL TEAM 3 SERIES
SEAL's Promise (Book 1)
SEAL My Home (Book 2)
SEAL's Code (Book 3)
Big Bad Boys Bundle (Books 1-3 of Bad Boys)

BAND OF BACHELORS SERIES
Lucas (Book 1)
Alex (Book 2)
Jake (Book 3)
Jake 2 (Book 4)
Big Band of Bachelors Bundle

TRUE BLUE SEALS SERIES
True Navy Blue (prequel to Zak)
Zak (Includes novella above)

NASHVILLE SEAL SERIES
Nashville SEAL (Book 1)
Nashville SEAL: Jameson (Books 1 & 2 combined)

SILVER SEALS
SEAL Love's Legacy

SLEEPER SEALS
Bachelor SEAL

STAND ALONE SEALS
SEAL's Goal: The Beautiful Game
Love Me Tender, Love You Hard

BONE FROG BROTHERHOOD SERIES
New Year's SEAL Dream (Book 1)
SEALed At The Altar (Book 2)

PARADISE SERIES
Paradise: In Search of Love

STANDALONE NOVELLAS
SEAL You In My Dreams (Magnolias and Moonshine)
SEAL Of Time (Trident Legacy)

FALL FROM GRACE SERIES (PARANORMAL)
Gideon: Heavenly Fall

GOLDEN VAMPIRES OF TUSCANY SERIES (PARANORMAL)
Honeymoon Bite (Book 1)
Mortal Bite (Book 2)
Christmas Bite (Book 3)
Midnight Bite (Book 4 Coming Summer 2019)

THE GUARDIANS (PARANORMAL)
Heavenly Lover (Book 1)
Underworld Lover (Book 2)
Underworld Queen (Book 3)

AUDIOBOOKS
Sharon Hamilton's books are available as audiobooks narrated by J.D. Hart.

ABOUT THE BOOK

Nebraska born and bred Navy SEAL Calvin "Coop" Cooper, after his own family has perished in a tornado, is ordered to meet the family of a prominent San Diego psychiatrist. The doctor's brother is a fallen SEAL medic who died in Grenada. There, Cooper meets Libby Brownlee, the beautiful niece of this fallen hero. Heavily influenced by her father, "We don't speak military here," is her comment about the military in general, and the SEAL community in particular.

What starts out as a frosty debate between two people privately dealing with their own personal grief, turns into a passionate affair neither expected. Just as Cooper realizes perhaps Libby is the woman he's always been looking for, she is snatched out from under him by a psychopathic killer bent on revenge.

Cooper, along with his buddies in SEAL Team 3, use their training to find Libby, but it might be too late. Will Cooper be able to survive the loss of the woman he loves, or will his duty, honor and self sacrifice be enough to keep her safe?

AUTHOR'S NOTE

I always dedicate my SEAL Brotherhood books to the brave men and women who defend our shores and keep us safe. Without their sacrifice, and that of their families—because a warrior's fight always includes his or her family—I wouldn't have the freedom and opportunity to make a living writing these stories. They sometimes pay the ultimate price so we can debate, argue, go have coffee with friends, raise our children and see them have children of their own.

One of my favorite tributes to warriors resides on many memorials, including one I saw honoring the fallen of WWII on an island in the Pacific:

> "When you go home
> Tell them of us, and say
> For your tomorrow,
> We gave our today."

These are my stories created out of my own imagination. Anything that is inaccurately portrayed is either my mistake, or done intentionally to disguise something I might have overheard over a beer or in the corner of one of the hangouts along the Coronado Strand.

I support two main charities. Navy SEAL/UDT Museum operates in Ft. Pierce, Florida. Please learn about this wonderful museum, all run by active and former SEALs and their friends and families, and who rely on public support, not that of the U.S. Government. www.navysealmuseum.org

IF YOU GOT ANY CLOSER, YOU WOULD HAVE TO ENLIST

I also support Wounded Warriors, who tirelessly bring together the warrior as well as the family members who are just learning to deal with their soldier's condition and have nowhere to turn. It is a long path to becoming well, but I've seen first-hand what this organization does for its warriors and the families who love them. Please give what your heart tells you is right. If you cannot give, volunteer at one of the many service centers all over the United States. Get involved. Do something meaningful for someone who gave so much of themselves, to families who have paid the price for your freedom. You'll find a family there unlike any other on the planet.

www.woundedwarriorproject.org

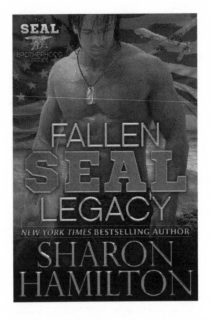

Go to Youtube for the video trailer for

Fallen SEAL Legacy.

youtube.com/watch?v=gvgpI5Ad1tQ

CHAPTER 1

A TORNADO SCRAPED the Nebraska landscape with deadly force, tasting contents of houses and farms, furrowing down fence posts and over pencil-thin crop rows like a tongue from Hell. It seemed to like the flavor of metal and sheetrock as well as the tender green stalks of corn, sunflowers and soybeans. Human and animal body parts spewed out to the sides, detritus from a bored gourmand.

Sirens wailed in the distance. The steamy ground hissed in response.

SPECIAL OPERATOR CALVIN "Coop" Cooper awoke and smelled cherries mixed with crisp morning sea air. He heard running water and then felt the steam, which had filled the entire motor home.

Daisy. In the shower. Slippery and soapy all over.

She'd spent the night in his love cave, which was usually parked by the beach. What a night it had been.

He still wore a handcuff that dangled from his left wrist. Only Daisy had the key. He chuckled to himself.

His other SEAL Team buddies called his place the *Babemobile*. They could call it anything they liked, he thought. Coop was saving a ton of money by pocketing his housing allowance.

He'd have been pissed if it was one of his Team buddies using up all his propane taking a hot shower. But for Daisy he allowed the indulgence, since her qualities and talents made it so worth it. Besides, it was one of the greatest places to fuck. Maybe…

Coop scratched above his forehead as the handcuffs jangled and then slapped against his ear. His sparse light brown hair left his fingers sticky. And smelling of cherries.

That would be the gel she used on me last night. The gel I used on her, all over.

Daisy did have a job to get ready for, and God, yes, they *both* needed a shower.

Coop rolled over and placed his palms behind his head, disentangling the sweaty sheet from his long six-foot-four-inch frame. It had been a wonderful Coronado Island night. Daisy was the best pleasure partner a guy could want. Totally willing. Totally hot. She'd brought her costume bag filled with "cop props" as she liked to call them. She'd arrested him several times last night, and each time he was subjected to fierce interrogation which usually made her wind up in compromising positions. He loved her sex play.

"I have a thing for cops," she'd told him one day when she was working on a new tat.

"I'm not a cop," Coop had said.

"But you wear a uniform. I love uniforms, too. Got a whole closet of them."

He could only guess.

Everyone else wanted to bang her, too. But she, temporarily at least, had secretly chosen Coop to share her bed. Or rather, his bed. Daisy never brought anyone to her place. Cooper had occasionally dated other girls, mostly when they threw themselves at him. He wasn't really looking. They just seemed to find him.

Daisy was the one all his SEAL Team 3 buddies hired to do their tattoos. It was odd, with all the places they'd been sent, all the injuries they'd incurred, his buddies would only let one tattoo artist touch their delicate skin. Daisy was the best. In lots of ways.

Coop rubbed his groin, which was getting interested in chasing down the trail of thoughts his brain wandered through.

Down boy.

He usually parked his motor home at the beach, where the owner of the now-defunct trailer park was happy with the fifty bucks Coop gave him each month for his share of the water and power used. But tonight he'd parked in the lot at Costco so they wouldn't have any visitors. No sense having a sweet young thing calling on his door, thinking he was available, and him being kinda busy. Daisy had followed him there so he wouldn't need to take her home. She was a very practical woman.

"Hey baby," Daisy said as she paraded in front of him, sizing up his exposed torso. "We had some fun last night, didn't we?" She put two fingers in her pink-lipped mouth. Those lips would leave a ring, all right. Her makeup was done, and she was wearing one of those kid's tee shirts that showed off the frog tattoo around her belly button, which was pierced with a gold ring glinting in the morning sun. Her shorts were so short, if Coop slipped a hand up her backside, he'd be in clover before he got three inches in.

"You smell good." *You taste good, too.* Cherry wasn't his favorite flavor. He liked the way she tasted all by her little lonesome, he thought as he scanned her many alluring attributes. And he'd told her that one time, just before she exploded in his arms. Telling her things like that worked real well on Daisy. Like some of the girls in high school he had read scriptures to, especially the Love Chapter from Psalms. Make them hot as hell, and so willing to show it.

Her knees sunk onto the bed and crawled her way up to straddle him. "I'm gonna be late for work if you aren't quick."

By the time he gave his assent, she had already removed her Tee shirt and 38 DDD bra.

JUST BEFORE DAISY left, Coop had to remind her to remove his cuffs. Then, while he waited for the water to warm up again, he sat in his boxers at the nook, chowing down on granola and whole milk. He checked between the metal blinds in the window and watched a couple of early Costco employees arrive. That also meant it was time for him to leave.

His cell phone chirped.

"Coop here." He recognized the number belonging to his Chief Petty Officer Timmons.

"Mornin' Coop. Say, mind if we have a word?"

"Sure. When do you need me in by?"

"How soon can you get here?"

Something was up, and it wasn't good. "Can you tell me a little about it?" Coop asked.

"No, mister. I gotta do this eyeball to eyeball."

Coop hesitated a bit before answering. Timmons hadn't said it involved anyone else, so this wasn't a Team thing. Had someone complained about him parking the Babemobile at the beach? Some jerkoff dogooder Ranger exerting himself on the community they loved to bust for littering and public drinking? *Only because the girls would rather hang out with me than some overweight guy with a green gabardine scout leader uniform and a chronic case of sunburn.*

"I can be there in a half hour, unless there's a jam-up on the highway."

"See you then, son."

Son? When his Chief called him son, it usually meant he was in trouble. Coop felt dark fingers dig into his spine at the back of his neck. Something wasn't right.

He called Fredo. "Timmons calling a Team meeting this morning?" he asked his Mexican SEAL friend.

"Shit if I know. What'd you do last night, Coop?"

Cooper fingered the vase of fresh flowers in front of him, and shrugged, like Fredo could see it.

Fredo whispered into the phone, "You better pray she's over 18."

"Not to worry, Fredo. I'm heading over there now. You want to meet me afterwards for some PT?"

"Sure, you go have your meeting with Timmons, get your strength back up, cowboy, and I'll kick your ass in a few." Fredo hung up.

He skipped the shower, anxious to find out what Timmons wanted. He doubted his Chief would notice Daisy's smell or the trace of cherry lube gel instead of his usual Irish Spring. If he ran into his Team leader, Kyle Lansdowne, he'd be ordered to get wet and sandy. Old married man Kyle, with a new baby, was a real hard-ass these days. But a damn good SEAL, and the best Team leader a guy could have.

He considered taking his scooter, but decided to

drive the Babemobile instead.

He climbed over the bench seat at the nook, inserting his extra-long legs under the wheel of the beast and started her up. Coop had turned the beast into a regular fortress, installing a secret weapons compartment, a sophisticated GPS unit, a satellite tracking system with infrared, and a sound system worthy of a rock star. The entire blackened roof surface of the motor home was a solar collector. He'd rather spend his money on toys than housing, so he spent half of his paycheck on special parts and upgrades for gadgets he was constantly tinkering with. The rest he dutifully saved. Something his dad had taught him growing up on the farm in Nebraska.

Never too early to plan for a rainy day, his dad had always told him.

He opted for the *Gone Country* satellite channel, donned his sunglasses and departed for the check-in.

Coop rounded the corner to the Special Warfare base at Coronado, stopped at the guard shack and addressed the flunky on duty. A new one. Navy Regular. Clean cut. Cooper was thinking he might luck out and get on base without a wisecrack since the guy was new, but had no such luck.

"Well if it isn't the stud of Coronado and his limp dick pleasure palace."

Coop studied the new man's nametag, *Dorian Hamburg*. He and his Team guys could have fun with that name. And the look on the man's face told him he had a hair trigger. That was always fun. So the other regulars had told him about Coop's motor home. No problem. If the guy wanted to spar, Coop would spar with him, and make him pay for it.

"Nice to see the ladies've told you about it. That's why they won't lick your sorry ass." Coop watched his words punch Dorian in the face and make him redden. But the man was quick on his feet, unlike some of the other Navy regulars.

"I hear the health department wants to do a study of all the interesting cultures growing in that bat mobile, especially on the ceiling…"

"Nice try, asshole, or is it Dorian? If I were you, I'd go by the name asshole. Dorian sounds queer."

"You ought to know…" Dorian squinted at Coop's upside down nametag hanging at a slight angle. "Calvin."

Sticks and stones don't bust my balls…

"Well *Dorian,* you can call me Special Operator Cooper. But for your information, the only other Calvin I ever met was a real big black dude, and he *definitely* wasn't gay." Coop handed over his military ID.

"When are you gonna fix that rag on your head? Don't they pay you boys enough for a hairpiece or some plugs?"

"Lost all my hair going down. If the girl likes it, she kinda tugs. Hurts sometimes, get my drift?"

"Um hum." The sentry handed Coop back his card. "You be careful how you park, hear? And straighten that god-damned nametag."

The rumble of the engine left a thick cloud of black smoke in its wake. Happened every time Coop plastered his foot against the floorboard.

Timmons's office was all metal and no frills, except for the bright lime-green ceramic frog holding a surfboard that SEAL Team 3 bought him. It stood two and a half perilous feet tall, perched on top of a metal bookshelf. This was the replacement to the statue Timmons had destroyed on a rather ill-tempered day last year.

Timmons had bouts of anger, more frequently now, especially about procedural things. Coop knew the enlisted man was not longing for the forced retirement. It meant more time at home with a wife who publicly made fun of him. The Navy was his life, always had been. But that wasn't going to stop them from retiring him anyway.

"Chief?" Coop called out as he stooped under the doorframe to avoid hitting his head.

"Sit down, son," Timmons said, pointing to one of two metal folding chairs in front of his paper-strewn desk.

The cold chair matched the eerie chill that tingled up his spine every time his Chief Officer used the term *son*. He licked his lips and waited while Timmons looked like he was gathering strength. Whatever it was, it wasn't anything good.

"I'm afraid I've got some bad news. We've just been contacted by the authorities in Nebraska." He looked up at Coop with his watery light blue eyes. Coop held his breath.

"I'm not sure if you've heard it in the news, but there's been a tornado in Pender and parts nearby, and I'm sorry to say that your family and the farm are gone, son."

Cooper had been trained to deal with the death of a Team guy. He'd held them sometimes as the life force exited their bodies, rocking them slowly or telling them little jokes to ease their way home. But his real home, his roots in Nebraska, those always remained.

Gone? All of them? Gone? He never figured this could ever happen. *I'm completely alone?*

His body tensed as he came to terms with the reality of what was just spoken. One by one, every nerve ending began to shout, until the rage inside, the scream *Hell, no!* consumed all his energy. He dug his fingernails into his thighs and, without realizing it, had drawn blood through the green canvas of his cargo pants.

Timmons got up, which prompted Coop to stand as well, although he was weaving. If Timmons hugged him, he'd deck the guy and end his career for sure. But Timmons stood a healthy two feet away, which was close enough to smell the angst of the older man who nervously flexed and unflexed his fingers at his side. "I'm so sorry, son."

There's that goddamned word again. Coop took a deep breath and then felt the tears flood his eyes. *I'm no one's son any longer.* Mercifully, he couldn't see his Chief's expression. Coop's fists tightened, he stepped to the side and belted the frog statue, which crashed up against the side of the wall and shattered. Although his Team had recently replaced it for well over two hundred dollars, the green, glassy fragments exploded and fell in a satisfying tinkle all over the floor, the windowsill and Timmons's desk.

TIMMONS LOOKED OVER the mess in silence, nodding his head. He apparently thought the frog had suffered a good, honorable death, after all. Team 3 would have it replaced as soon as the donations came in. Next time maybe he should find a way to bolt it to the wall. But that could be dangerous.

For the wall.

CHAPTER 2

I T WAS A dusty day as the silver plane nosed down through billowy clouds on its way to kiss the ruined earth. A united gasp went up from passengers as they saw the raw, brown, smoking soil that would normally be covered in patchwork patterns of an industrious agricultural people. But what was missing was the green. Coop clenched his jaw, grinding ice, and rocked to the loud metallic music of selection number seven on the in-flight radio. He held his breath.

Looks like a flooded and bombed-out valley in Afghanistan.

He wasn't used to seeing Nebraska look like a wasteland. Wastelands got you killed or killed your friends. They never healed. Nobody loved them.

He stared down at the remains, and, as incredible as it was, he still loved *this* place.

He'd never felt alone before. Completely alone. He'd missed so much, being away on deployments, but he had always had home to come back to. Even as he clowned around on Coronado Island, home was always here, in Nebraska. It had always been a constant. He just couldn't deal with it being gone for good.

All of them. How could this have happened?

The stewardess walked up the aisle quickly, scanning the packed plane for seatbelt violators. Her expression was grim, and Coop would have enjoyed a little flirtation on any other day.

But the miracle of good times seemed a distant memory. Even the babies on the plane were quiet, as if suspecting their cries would be inappropriate. People with window seats looked straight ahead, not outside at the devastation. There were those in the middle and aisle seats who wanted to see, and took turns jockeying for the right position, without offending. Coop could hear sniffles and someone softly sobbing. A toddler asker her mother what *THAT* was. THAT was a huge gash in the earth that had taken his whole family and many others.

A few minutes later came a message. "Ladies and gentlemen, we have begun our final approach to Omaha International Airport. Please remain in your seats with your seat belts fastened. We anticipate a bumpy landing, due to the storm." The sweet lilting voice was not reassuring. Coop could feel the pull of thoughts sending them deeper, faster. As if everyone on the plane wanted to end their lives together.

The landing was hard, shaking everyone, but the passengers accepted it. An overhead bin burst open from the impact, dumping its contents on the balding, elderly man seated below. Underwear and tee shirts cascaded, followed by someone's hand-knit afghan and a cap. Several passengers helped unbury the gentleman, who managed to laugh and shake his head, unharmed but embarrassed.

The plane turned sharply and then revved up engines to taxi down another lane. A large Red Cross vehicle and several military transports idled nearby, swarming with an anthill of people loading packages and white plastic cargo containers marked with the familiar red emblem. Coop knew what a cargo staging area looked like. Helped that it was in the good old U.S. of A. and not some sand cave where you waited with a dying man and prayed to God the chopper would come in time.

But never in Nebraska. The land where it was green and cool. Where churches were kept clean and kids still walked home from elementary school by themselves.

Not that his mom didn't worry. All during Cooper's boyhood, Mrs. Cooper would be at the back kitchen door holding back his dog, Bay. When Coop came home from school and started down the little rise that was the only "mountain" in the county, a whole one hundred feet tall, she would let Bay run out to meet him. That dog tried to break his timed runs every day. And every school day Coop would brace himself as the brown mutt leapt into the air to nearly tackle him in a belly-to-belly thing that could only be called a hug. He felt the arms and hands that dog never had, just in the way he crashed into him. Even the last time he was home and Bay was going on twelve. He still looked out the kitchen door, waiting for the little boy who was now a man and came less often.

Bay's gone too. They're all together now.

It looked like rain outside until Coop realized his eyes were filled with tears.

The plane had been emptied.

He grabbed his duffel, put on his canvas jacket with the SEAL Team 3 logo in black stitched onto the breast pocket.

The captain was just exiting the cockpit.

"Mornin', son."

That word again. Everyone's calling me son.

Coop nodded in the captain's direction and briskly walked by before he could be snagged in an unwanted conversation.

Music in the terminal was ridiculously loud and cheerful. Couldn't they turn the goddamned thing down? Have a little respect for the dead?

Coop hunched his shoulders and sighed. He knew

life went on. He just didn't like to be reminded of it.

THE FUNERALS COULDN'T be held in the church he was baptized in, because it was missing, as well as any evidence a family of Coopers ever existed on the face of the Nebraska earth. His grandpa would roll over in his grave, if they ever found his body, at being attended at a Unitarian church. The family had been Baptist since their folk came from Denmark to freely practice their religion, and try their hand at farming. They were three generations of Danish-American farmers who had lived in Nebraska for nearly a century. But now, it was like they had never existed.

Loraie Swensen was the church secretary in charge of making the arrangements. Coop listened to the order of service and approved everything except the last hymn.

"Well, we always play *Will The Circle Be Unbroken* at our funerals," she said.

"Look, Mrs. Swensen. You can play anything you like when your family passes. Mine is going to be sent home with *Rock of Ages*, and that's that."

He didn't look back at her because he knew she sported an un-Christian-like expression he didn't need to see. Not in his home county, in the land of milk and honey.

PASTOR JEPSEN DRONED on and on over the collection of five adult-sized coffins, and one casket half the size of the others. Coop counted them several times during the service to keep from falling asleep. There was Mama, Dad, Grandpa Iverson, who was Mom's dad, Coop's sister Gayle, her husband Butch, and their little daughter Camilla, aged three. The last time he'd seen her she was sporting butterfly wings—part of her Halloween costume.

All of the boxes were empty, as far as he knew. Of course he never asked. Sheriff Lanning had been efficient, ogling Coop's tattoos and itching to hear war stories Coop wasn't going to give him. But he said, matter-of-factly, it was a blessing nothing could be found. Saved Coop from the identification process.

When Coop speared him with his blue eyes, Sheriff Lanning shrugged. "God, Coop. I don't know what to say here."

Try saying they're coming back.

But of course, the gentleman was a fine lawman, even if he wasn't a believer. And these past few days were probably totally shitty. And going to get shittier.

AT THE GRAVESITE, Cora Newsome, sitting in the middle of the crowd, laid a plant on him with her big blue eyes he could feel, just like in high school. She would always be a looker. Married right after graduation to the guy who knocked her up and then the man did the only decent thing he'd done in his life—left her for someone else. Cora still had her figure. The lively white-blond five-year-old daughter in black Mary Janes and deep velvet blue dress looked like a handful, all right. The little one reminded him of his niece he was burying today. He tried to avert his eyes each time Cora leaned over to hush her daughter to silence.

Cooper got a good view down Cora's ample chest—something he used to dream about at night all during high school. He'd lay in bed thinking about what those pillows of flesh felt like in his callused hands as he listened to the crickets outside. She caught him looking, and smiled. During the freaking funeral!

You're one sorry son of a gun.

He tried to stem the tide of erotic pictures starring Cora and how she could perform unspeakable acts of passion. She could love all his anger right off, as easy as washing a car. She used to stand in front of him with those tits she'd unload into his hands after football games, and he'd practically come before he could get properly naked. But that was then. This is now—*and-what-the-hell-am-I-doing*?

Now he was at the funeral for his dead family. And then he was going to get the hell out of this town and go dodge enemy fire. Or jump HALO at midnight.

For fun.

After the service, he accepted Cora's kind invitation to have a little dinner, along with the unspoken promise of a tasty dessert of the flesh. The little one said her goodnights in a pair of pink-footed pajamas—even planted a kiss on his cheek. Cora beamed and told him with bedroom eyes she'd be right back.

What the hell am I doing here? He didn't come here to get laid, but he needed it anyway. Cora was a sure thing, but not an easy out. It wasn't about cheating on Daisy. The real problem was it might get complicated when he tried to leave. Though his body wanted some soft flesh to help him forget, his mind told him to wait.

Cora came back from putting her daughter to bed. "You want another beer, Cooper?" she said in a husky voice.

"No. I've had enough. This was real nice, Cora. I appreciate it."

She swung around, surprised, as he stood up. "You don't have to go just yet." She walked toward him, then leaned her large chest against his and rubbed him from side to side. "I thought we were going to get caught up." She put her arms up around his neck and stood on tiptoes. Just the way she used to do.

"Much as I'd love to, honey, I just can't." He extricated her arms but then bent down and kissed her on the lips.

It was clearly a mistake.

She melted into him. And damn, it had been years since he'd met someone who could kiss as good as Cora, so he talked himself into a few minutes of fooling around until his hand found her panties under her skirt and she had encircled his cock with her left hand. Everything moved at lightning speed and within seconds he found himself pressing against her body with most of his clothes still on. She'd tried to unzip him, her hands in his pants, making him ache for her. But he just couldn't, for some reason.

His last vision of her was as she lay across her over-stuffed living room couch, unfulfilled lust in her eyes, the Disney movie her daughter had been watching earlier playing in the background.

He said his good byes, retreating to a cheap motel just off the freeway. Tomorrow he'd fly out of here, and who knew when he'd return, if ever. He decided he'd try to get one last look at the area the farm had been on his way to the airport.

Next morning he wondered why he didn't feel anything as he drove down the two-lane highway towards Pender. Maybe he was dead. Maybe he had a date with death. Maybe a stray bullet would get him. Or a rocket-propelled grenade. He just hoped it would be quick, now that there was little to live for. Only bad thing was the verbal thrashing he'd get from his dad when he got to Heaven.

Tell mom I'm coming home soon, dad. Don't let Bay get fat.

When he got to where the homestead had been, he got out and trudged unseeing over the muddy ground, barely noticing the thick black ooze of that fertile soil he'd plowed for more than a dozen years, ever since he could reach the shift levers on the big tractor. He could almost smell the fresh cinnamon buns his mother made in the mornings. And the fresh coffee. They'd be out there from sunup, and when they came in for breakfast, it was the best meal of the day for him.

Several summers ago his dad had built a summer kitchen for his mom for her canning. She had put away so many fruits and vegetables in their cool barn, she could have fed half the state with her award-winning preserves and canned fruits. His dad never could afford big combines, since they paid cash for everything. The family didn't trust those big machines with state-of-the-art computers and satellite link to digitally add soil conditioner and seed. Mr. Cooper strictly relied on mother nature, good luck and the good Lord, in that order, to provide what they needed. Their farm equipment cost less than a tenth of what other farmers used. Coop knew how to fix everything. And the family hadn't been in debt, since his dad didn't believe in credit. He shook his head.

If you can't pay cash, you don't deserve to own it, his

dad had always said.

But this, this was something they had never planned for, talked about. This was something he'd seen overseas in those hellholes. Not here. Not to him. Not to his family.

He wiped a tear from his eye and walked up the little hill that used to overlook the farm. The ground was steaming as sunlight poured silently down all around him. The row of birch trees beside the back porch of the farmhouse was gone. Limbs and pieces of wood siding lay scattered, sometimes stuck into the ground at odd angles. The birds did not sing.

He thought he could hear Bay barking, just like when he came home from school. He knew his mind was playing a trick on him. The incessant barking got louder, and echoed, unlike any vision he'd had before. He turned his back on the farm's location. Off in the distance a brown dog was trying to run, but was limping with a lame front leg.

"Bay?" He wasn't sure at first it could be, but then he found himself running to the disheveled animal. The mutt squealed in pain as he hugged his friend— pain from the wound on his front paw, mirroring Cooper's own pain at the loss of his family.

He examined the dog quickly and confirmed that, yes, God had granted him this tiny miracle after all.

CHAPTER 3

LIBBY BROWNLEE TURNED down the tree-lined street of her old neighborhood, past endless Spanish-style mansions protected by red tiled roofs and manicured front lawns worthy of any world class PGA course. It had been three months, and she needed to be back home. This time, she needed to see her parents—especially her dad. It had bothered her when he'd sounded somewhat distracted on the phone when she called him yesterday, informing them of the visit. Was there something wrong?

How stupid.

Although she was twenty-four, she was still trying please him, as she had her whole life. Her mother never interfered with this strong father-daughter bond, so Libby enjoyed almost unlimited access to him. They shared an open and frank relationship.

Am I running to them or running away from Santa Clara? It didn't matter, she decided. She just needed to be home.

But Libby also knew lately there were dark, private places where Dr. Brownlee chased the shadows of his past—a past involving the death of his twin brother, Will, who never came home from Grenada.

Libby's older brother was married to a woman the entire family had a hard time getting along with. They had children, but rarely came to visit. Though she and her father were inseparable as she was growing up, she and her brother had never been close. Their relationship was complicated, she thought. Libby enjoyed being single and not in any hurry to take the plunge, she wasn't interested in jumping right into a career or family, like her father and brother had. She wanted to live a little—outside of the Petri dish of academia.

Her dad was gardening near the front steps of their peach-colored estate. A row of palm trees grew alongside the curved driveway. She parked her Classic white 1966 Mercedes convertible out at the curb in front.

Two things she was sure about. For starters, she wouldn't tell them about her situation with Dr. Gerhardt. That just wasn't something she wanted to burden her parents with. She was handling it by removing herself from the situation, for now. The second thing was that she needed to tell them about her decision to drop out of school for a semester. She'd tell them she needed time off to travel, get out from under the grind of her studies, so she could go back and resume her Master's in Psychology. She was a little uneasy about that part, and knew her father would be concerned.

He frowned as he stood up and adjusted his back, like a day laborer, rather than like the most respected psychiatrist in San Diego. Tall and thin, he was tanned, his silver and black hair tied neatly in a short ponytail at the back of his neck. With his stunning good looks, he was often mistaken for an actor.

"Bad actor is more like it," he would say in response to the comment. Behind her soft-spoken hero of a dad, Libby knew there was a man of steel, with an ego rarely seen in public.

"Hey, Dad." Libby rushed to his side. Dr. Brownlee barely had time to dust his dirty hands before his daughter was in his arms. The reassuring scent of him set her mind at ease, and she found herself tearing up as he held her. She gave him a peck on the cheek, which tasted salty. He released her quickly, and stiffened.

"You're an hour early," he said with a frown. Libby thought he looked a little pale.

"So I'll just go down to the harbor and have a cappuccino and wait, would that be more acceptable?"

He winced and nodded. "Very perceptive of you. Sorry. I've got a lot on my mind." He placed an arm over her shoulder.

"I noticed." She pointed to the hose that was flooding the border chrysanthemums he had just planted. The overflow had already floated one plant halfway down the lawn.

Dr. Brownlee was quick to shut off the brass hose faucet. He picked up his gloves, which he usually wore but hadn't today, and motioned for her to follow him to the house.

"Let me get my things." Libby headed toward the car and, over her shoulder, saw her father retreat into the ornate Spanish metal and glass door without waiting to take her bag.

Something's definitely wrong. But thank God I'm home.

Inside the two-story bright foyer of the home where she had grown up, she felt safe from the rest of the crazy world. Coming back was always a good thing. Wherever else she lived, this was always home.

"Sweetheart," her mother said, arms outstretched. Even in her difficult undergraduate years, it had been soothing to be bathed in her mother's embrace. She'd missed them both.

Her mom was wearing yoga pants and a halter top. It was she who picked up Libby's bag and began the long climb up the wrought-iron spiral staircase as Dr. Brownlee wandered distractedly out through the kitchen to the pool area in the backyard.

Libby decided to pose the question, even though she knew she'd never get an honest answer. "So what's up with Dad? He all right?"

"Sure, sweetie. But you know your dad. He's been working long hours. I *made* him take a couple of days off."

"I've never heard of such a thing in this household. A couple of days off? Now I know something's wrong."

"Silly." Her mother laughed as she pinched Libby's nose. "None of us is getting any younger. Your father has a big birthday this year."

"So he's not perfect? I thought he was immortal."

"No. He's just a man, not like those alpha vampire hunks in those books you read."

"Education, Mom. All part of my education."

"Well, I'd rather you read about it than…"

"Too much information, Mom."

The two women entered Libby's old bedroom, and she was thrilled at the sight of Noodles, her cat, curled up in the center of her white canopy bed.

"He's there every day. Likes to take his afternoon naps there. Won't sleep anywhere else," her mother said.

"Noodles, I've missed you," Libby said.

The big cat stretched and then rolled over on his back, looking at Libby upside down. She rubbed his huge belly. The cat feigned a defensive attack on her hand.

"You're the only cat I've met who gets fat on Chinese food," She laughed.

"He'd eat it every day, if we could afford it," her mother said. "You picked out the perfect name for him."

Libby turned to Noodles. "You live one of your past lives in an emperor's palace in China?" Libby's dad had found the kitten abandoned behind a Chinese restaurant, and Libby had nursed him to health one summer between semesters at Santa Clara.

"I think he sleeps here, just waiting for you to come home for good," her mother said.

"Wish I could take him. If I had my own house—"

"He's no bother. We don't mind," Mrs. Brownlee said.

"Probably a lot safer here than with all the traffic in San Jose." Libby's insides clenched as she realized she also didn't feel safe there anymore.

Libby started to unpack, hanging up a dress and cardigan sweater. When she flipped back the top of the suitcase, her eyes glanced over her favorite toy as a child: an almost hairless brown Cocker Spaniel stuffed dog with big chocolate-colored eyes. It had a talking chord to a voice box long since silenced.

"So you've been keeping a watchful eye on my

room, Morgan, hmmm?" She grabbed the toy and held it to her chest. Her mom smiled back at her, stepped closer and sifted her fingers through Libby's hair.

"Nice to have you back home, even if it's for a little while. A week is it?"

"Um hum."

"Everything okay, Libby?" her mother asked.

Uh oh, I'm on my mother's radar. She straightened her spine. "I'm fine, Mom. Just needed a little mom and dad face time." She smiled back at her mother, hoping that would end the inquiry.

"Won't this interfere with school?" her mom continued to probe.

Yes. That's why I'm here.

Libby tossed the dog on the bed next to Noodles, who peered at the stuffed animal with disdain. "Nope." She gave her mom a cheery smile, hoping to send her away. It worked.

"Come down when you're finished. Dinner will be in an hour or so." Her mom disappeared to the hallway.

"Thanks, Mom." Libby called out after her.

She walked to her window, lifted the ivory sheers and looked down at the perfectly manicured brick walkway that was artfully framed by two colorful patches of flowers. A couple of cars and a landscaping van were parked at the curb down the street.

She turned back to her room. Everything was in its place here. Flowers bloomed. People hugged each other, cared about each other. It was the perfect kind of normal that she needed, and was looking forward to its healing balm.

Libby flopped herself on her bed, snuggling next to Noodles and the stuffed dog like she'd been doing for years, reveling in the memory of her innocent adolescence, carefully preserved in this room-shrine by her parents. But those idealistic days were gone forever. Could she just step back into this room and set back the clock?

She looked up at the canopy top made of ruffled dotted Swiss. As a child, she used to look at all this beautiful white each night before she fell asleep, visualizing a wedding dress made of the same frilly fabric. After she left for college, she'd insisted she was too old for the canopy bed, yet, her mother never removed it.

Right now, she was glad it remained, even if it was homage to a past that no longer existed. Instead of a wedding dress, her thoughts suddenly turned dark and she saw the twisted face of a man she had trusted.

Those images from school haunted her.

She had been helping her advisor teach a freshman introduction to social psychology. It all began when she was grading papers one late afternoon. He had locked the door behind him. The cubbyhole office they shared had suddenly seemed oppressively small. The lustful look in his eyes frightened her.

Why didn't I recognize the signs earlier?

Libby had been so trusting, thinking his smiles and encouragement, the lunches and dinners they shared, sprang from a deep respect for her and her abilities. She'd idolized the man, who had published papers and received a string of awards. She ignored thoughts of anything inappropriate, and loved his intellect, feeling fortunate to be the recipient of his mentorship.

There had been rumors, but she tossed them aside. One of her best friends mentioned that Dr. Gerhardt "lights up whenever you come into class." Perhaps things would have been different if she hadn't been so stubborn and listened.

The professor, who was her father's age, clearly had intentions of the sexual sort.

"Libby, you know I admire you," he said as he approached. She backed up into her desk, spilling a half cup of cold coffee onto the papers.

At first she thought she'd overreacted, made a mistake. "Dr. Gerhardt, I'm sorry, but what are you doing?"

He tried to encircle her waist as he attempted to pull her to his chest. "We would be so good together, Libby. Can't you tell? It would be a beautiful thing," he whispered, his voice low and raspy. The familiar aftershave he wore was now hideously pungent. His lips and his breath too intimate and too close to her face. His trimmed beard lightly brushed against her cheek; his hungry eyes fixated on her mouth.

"No. Stop this." She scooted to the side and away from his arms.

He didn't halt his advance. "Come on, Libby. You know you want it. We already spend so much time together. You know how much I want to make love to you, sweetheart. Don't you want it too? I know you do. Please, let me show you." He was on her again.

She tried to open the door, but couldn't remember how to open the lock. That was all the time he needed. He grabbed her again, and with his powerful arms pressed her into him. He planted a kiss that started on her mouth, but wound up in the side of her head as she turned and wiggled, clutching for freedom.

"I've had other students. My wife understands. It's just sex, beautiful sex."

"No. I'm not…" Her face heated and tears welled up. All her dreams and aspirations began to evaporate inside her. She was getting angry. Angry at herself. Angry at being so damned gullible.

She was also angry she'd never taken that self-defense class she'd procrastinated about. The professor was a tall man, physically very fit and easily twice her weight.

Her only tool was the determination not to be raped. She didn't care if he flunked her for refusing his advances. She didn't care how hard she had to fight or if she got physically beaten. She wasn't going to have sex with him.

"I said *no!*" The strength of her own voice gave her courage. His hands were roaming all over her body, igniting a fury she didn't know she possessed. His palm found one of her breasts underneath her bra, while his other hand snaked under her skirt and slipped along her backside. His hungry breath smelled of stale coffee.

He was too close for her to raise a knee to his groin. She could feel he was enjoying the struggle, and gaining in confidence. His hand slipped under her panties forcing her to make a decision. She found the opportunity and focused on it. She gripped his middle finger, bending it back with all the strength she could muster. He started to yell, attempting to retract his hand, but Libby held it firm, continuing to squeeze the finger against the top of his hand until she heard a satisfying crack as the joint shattered. He screamed like a wild animal.

"Goddammit, sonofabitch," he yelled, retreating to the corner to look at his finger pointing up in a peculiar and unnatural angle. "You little cunt. I never wanted to hurt you." He glared at her. "You'll be sorry. You'll pay." He came at her, and this time he grabbed her neck.

She missed kneeing his groin, so she kicked him in the shin. Then she turned to struggle again with the door lock, but couldn't make it budge. He was cursing her name, ripping at her blouse, pulling her back into his chest.

She'd been turning the lever the wrong way. She reversed direction and heard the click of freedom as she one-handedly opened the door a crack, only to have it slammed shut when Dr. Gerhardt's body crashed into it. She found his disjointed finger again, yanked and twisted it with everything she had. He screamed and went down on one knee in pain.

For a brief second he left her alone. It was all the time she needed.

She grabbed her purse, swung the door open, glad to smell the cool, fresh air of the hallway. Her heart pounding in her chest, adrenaline pulsing throughout her body, she passed several students as she power walked down the hall in a hurried daze, tears streaming down her face. Then she began to run, and ran all the way to her car. When she locked herself inside, she rested her head on the steering wheel and sobbed. She felt hot tears hit her chest and top of her bra. Looking down, she noticed for the first time her blouse was completely unbuttoned.

She felt ashamed. Dirty.

Libby went home that afternoon and took a long hot shower, ridding herself from the stink of his scent. She placed a phone call to the Psychology Department chair, asking for office time.

That night she had slept little, tossing and waking up seeing Gerhardt's face in her nightmares. Twice she checked the locked doors and windows of her apartment. She didn't answer her phone.

The next day she reported her mentor to the Chairman. The welcoming look on his face soured at her accusations. "You've been one of our bright, promising stars, Libby. I'm so sorry to hear this," he'd said. But she could tell he was more worried about the reputation of the University, and his department in particular.

"I'm going to withdraw from all my classes," she said. The semester was only two weeks from ending. "I'm earning A's in most of them. You can verify with my professors. I won't go any further if I'm allowed to receive whatever grades I've earned, rather than the drop-F."

"Agreed." He didn't even flinch. This had happened before, she could see.

"And I want him fired." She aimed a steely look right at him. He cowered.

"Libby, in a perfect world…"

"Don't give me that perfect world horseshit. I've been living there my whole life. I almost got raped, Dr. Halvorsen."

"He's got a problem. I think he's in therapy. But he's a gifted professor."

"No, sir. He's a sexual predator."

Dr. Halvorsen winced. "Not exactly. Consenting adults and all that. You are what, twenty-five or -six?"

"Twenty-four. He preys on his students. I've heard the rumors before. I just didn't pay any attention to them. And there was nothing consensual about it."

"Well, he didn't hurt you, and that's what's important here. I'm so very sorry, honest." He stood. The meeting was clearly over. Libby noticed the man wasn't going to offer a hug, under the circumstances. It was a smart choice.

Just before she left the office, she turned and leveled one last glare at a man who had allowed this to happen under his very nose. "If you don't fire him, I'm going to the police and will file a report. I'll let you explain to them what you told me."

FOR THE FIRST time in her life she didn't have a plan. Was she running away, or running toward an unscripted future?

The real world wasn't anything like she'd thought. She'd awakened from the dream of a perfect life. She needed safety from the cruelty she now knew lurked in the shadows, ready to consume her.

I need to go home.

CHAPTER 4

COOPER DROVE THE Babemobile, onto base without uttering a word. Bay was safely kenneled, as he had been during the flight home. His incessant barking was background music to Coop. He'd take the dog to the vet today, and start working on someone to look after him while he was overseas.

Daisy would have been the obvious choice, but not now. He was reluctant to face the attractive tattoo artist, even though she was easy about asking what was on his mind. Something had shifted. The sobering reality of being utterly alone was hard to get used to. Sorrow hung like a black cape over his shoulders. He wished he could just go to sleep and not wake up.

But then, who would feed Bay? Had the mutt saved him from himself?

The guard at the shack wasn't Dorian, or any of the other regulars. The kid looked like he was all of seventeen, and Coop didn't have the heart to mess with him.

"Thank you for your service, Mister," the boy said as he handed back Cooper's military I.D.

What the hell is happening?

Coop decided the boy needed to be messed with after all. "Got me wrong, kid. I just clean the toilets." He pointed to his tan cargo pants and light blue tee shirt.

"Yeah. You're the cleanup crew all right." The boy sported a half smile on his very fuzzy and not yet shaven upper lip. He had a pimple under his splotchy nose, right in the middle of that soft flesh, dug in like a gem. It probably hurt like hell.

But his teeth were good. Perfectly straight. That meant someone who'd raised him loved him enough to send him to the orthodontist. If Coop had needed braces, and he never did, his mom would have gotten a part-time job to pay for it.

Sun was pouring in through the dirty windshield as Coop turned to the young man and did what he never did. He checked out the plastic nametag and read *Leonard.* "You surf, Leo?"

"Um, it's Leonard, sir. And no, sir, I do not surf."

"Wanna learn?"

"Abso-fuckin-lootly!"

Bay barked as if understanding the profanity. The kid smiled and tiptoed up to peer in Coop's window at the dog. Bay appeared to smile behind the wire door of the kennel.

"Can you be here by six tomorrow morning?" Co-op asked.

"Sure."

"All right then, Lenny. We'll get wet and sandy and ride us some waves. Maybe check out the girls."

"You mean that, sir?"

Cooper raised his sunglasses to rest on the top of his head, and just looked at the boy.

"Don't ever ask me that again, son."

Damn. That was an unkind thing to call the kid.

"Sorry. I'll be here before six, sir."

Coop readjusted his glasses and put the machine in drive. He hit the pedal, spewing out smoke and a backfire, signaling he was done talking.

Okay, so maybe I'm gonna pull out of this after all.

He parked, untangled his long legs from the cab of the beast, and unlocked the kennel. Bay limped out, wagging his tail so hard he nearly toppled. Cooper took him outside on a leash so he could relieve himself before Coop checked in with Chief Petty Officer Timmons.

Once Bay was safely re-kenneled, Coop exited his home on wheels, locking it. There was an edge to his gait. He was rushing to get this meeting with Timmons over with. The sooner he could get back to duty the better. Maybe some time in the next decade he'd unearth the feelings haunting him from the empty coffins he'd watched being buried just two days ago.

He was grateful he didn't run into anyone he knew on his way to the Chief's office. Timmons' scratched metal desk was piled with papers, indicating things were normal with the Team handler. Only thing that was different was the lack of a big green frog holding a red surfboard in his webbed fingers. Coop had looked into the eyes of that frog dozens of times as he talked to Timmons over the three years he'd been with Kyle's platoon.

Not today, though.

"I'm not happy to see you, Coop." Timmons was in a sour mood. He was drinking a glass of milk, which meant his gut was hurting him.

"I didn't miss you much either, Chief."

"You shouldn't be back here. What the fuck were you thinking? I gotta have men who are whole."

"I'm good." Maybe he should have worn his cammies.

"Like hell you are."

"I said I'm good."

Timmons stood up with his hairy arms attempting to cross his growing belly. Then he dropped them. "And I say you are full of shit, sailor."

Cooper knew he shouldn't argue. But he couldn't help himself. "When I said I'm good, sir—"

"No fuckin' way you're good. You've not complet-ed your leave. You can't tell me you're going to go out there in the theater after you've just buried your family. Hell, Coop, you'll get yourself and your whole Team killed with that kind of lapse in judgment."

"I need to go—"

"Oh, I get it. You wanna take out your frustrations on the enemy. Get us all in trouble, right, just so you can process all the bullshit you're carrying around? That your plan? Those dudes in Afghanistan are bad motherfuckers, but they sure as hell didn't send the tornado that killed your family, son."

"I'm *not* your son." Cooper's fingers curled into fists. He clenched his jaw and squinted at his liaison.

"Thank God for that." Timmons kicked the metal garbage can under his desk. If the frog had survived Coop's direct attack five days ago, it would have been the target.

"Sit." Timmons pointed to a metal folding chair that was ridiculously small for the giant SEAL.

Timmons rummaged through a file drawer and pulled out a manila folder. He sat back down on his chair that made a sound like a cat squealing in heat and opened up the file. He removed a white piece of paper and began to read aloud.

"Special Operator William Brownlee. He was a medic. Died in 1983, Grenada."

Coop recognized the name as the one that was engraved on the KA-BAR knife he was given the day he received his Trident. A fallen SEAL. That knife was entrusted to Cooper's care. Every SEAL carried the memory of a fallen comrade in arms.

"You *do* remember that name, s—" he stopped himself before saying it.

"Yes, sir, I do."

"I understand his brother's family lives right here in San Diego."

Cooper stared back into the Timmons' glassy, bloodshot eyes. He didn't want to hear the words the man was going to dish out.

"Guy's a psychiatrist. Works with nut cases."

Cooper glared back at him.

"Not sayin' anything, just a point of fact, sailor." Timmons removed a piece of lint from the front of his shirt, and then looked back at Cooper with those sad eyes of his. "They've lost their SEAL. You've lost your family. I'd say that's a match made in Heaven, Coop."

"You're kidding."

"Do I look like I'm kidding?"

No. He didn't look like he was kidding at all.

AN EXTREMELY TALL shadow fell through the ornate glass and metal front doors of the Brownlee house. At first, Libby was frightened.

Get a grip.

The melodic doorbell chime had been imported all the way from an abandoned abbey in the South of France. Whoever he was, Libby Brownlee thought, he'd not be able to get through the doorway without ducking, or smacking himself in the forehead.

"Yes?" She didn't remove the brass chain connecting the door to the doorframe. It couldn't really stop anyone, especially someone of his size, she realized too late.

What she saw scared her, but in a way she didn't recognize, couldn't identify. He was a handsome, very, very tall and fair-haired young man about her age. His piercing blue eyes didn't stray from hers as he coolly nodded his head, and took inventory of her character without peeling his steady gaze from hers.

She felt undressed, yet powerless to cover up. But she didn't look away.

"Ma'am, I'm looking for the Brownlee family." He said this as he ducked his head and leaned forward. She observed he was trying to make himself smaller. The effort made him look huge.

"This *is* the Brownlee residence." Her response was worthy of a domestic. No need to let him know she was a relative.

"My name is Special Operator Calvin Cooper. I'm..."

"I know what a Special Operator is."

He smiled but continued, "—currently serving in the Navy. I've been asked to reach out to the family of Special Operator William Brownlee."

"Uncle Will." She bit her tongue. Too late to take it back. "My father's twin brother. I never met him. He's been dead for many years, since before I was born." Libby looked at the ground, but was soon distracted by the size of the young man's canvas slip-ons. The light brown hair on his ankles and lower legs, punctuated by light purple scars, blazed in the afternoon sun.

A surfer.

"Yes, ma'am. That's the reason I'm here."

"It's a little late for a color guard. He get awarded a medal posthumously or something?"

The sailor stepped back and put his eyelids at half-mast after a flash of anger. He appeared way calmer than she knew he really was. The control was impressive. No matter how hard she looked, the anger did not surface again. He licked his lips and began to speak, softer this time.

"Look. I don't want to be here any more than you want me, so let's just get this over with, so I can tell my Chief I tried to reach out and you guys slammed the door in my face, okay?"

Maybe she was being stupid, but somehow she trusted him. This wasn't the wrinkle she'd expected.

"Fine." She removed the chain, opened the door and the muscled giant walked into her home with quiet, fluid strides. He smelled like he'd just figured out how to wear aftershave. Something told her he didn't do it very often.

He scanned the large two-story living room with its carved wood ceiling done in Spanish florets. His eyes lit on the three-foot tall bouquet of fresh flowers her mother put on the coffee table every day—bounty from her extensive flower garden. Libby didn't expect to see him smile. Behind the table, a bright red velvet couch was covered with lime and fuchsia-colored silk flowered pillows. No one ever sat there, Libby mused. If they did, they'd be buried in the pillows, and hidden from view by the bouquet.

She was embarrassed by the brightness of the colors. "My mother takes pride in her flower garden." She finally said. Why had he been staring at the blooms?

He tore his eyes off the display, and, without saying a word, continued to scan the archway that led to the kitchen, then back around to the walls of the foyer and a view of the grand metal staircase leading upstairs to the bedrooms.

His silence made her nervous. She crossed her arms over her chest and waited for him to say something.

"This is about a hundred times the size of my place." He regarded her with a crooked smile she couldn't read. "Kinda like living in a church, although not like any church I ever attended."

Our house looks like a church?

"I assume you live on base?" she asked.

"No ma'am. I have a motor home I keep parked at the Silverdale Beach."

"Wow." *A homeless Navy SEAL?*

"Exactly. Got the whole ocean as my back yard."

"Sounds—different."

"It's all I need."

"Okay. Well, what's this about? Your visit, I mean."

"I'm here to pay my respects to his family. Will Brownlee's family. Was there anyone else special in his life? Like, was he married, or did he have a girl?"

Libby blinked twice. They had never discussed whether Uncle Will had had a sweetheart. "We *are* his family. I just never knew him." She realized she was being short. "My grandparents are both gone, and my father was his only brother, so perhaps he would know. My dad worshiped him." Libby started tracing the grout line of the marble floor with her toe. "Look, I'm going to need some answers here. You have to kind of spell it out for me. We don't speak military in this house."

"I can tell."

"What's that supposed to mean?"

"You don't speak military, and I didn't bring an

interpreter."

"I think you should speak to my father."

"That would be good."

"Except he isn't here. Maybe another time?"

She caught him eyeing the front of her cotton shirt, like he could see right through without unbuttoning it. With an involuntary jerk, he was focused on her eyes again. It was very odd that she didn't feel afraid of him, like she had every other man lately. Her heartbeat elevated and her breathing became shallow.

"When will he be here?" His voice sent a tingle down her spine.

"He gets home about four-thirty. But I wouldn't waste your time unless you can tell me what you want." She started for the door and he followed behind her. At the front, she stopped, and turned around. "I'm waiting." She tapped her foot to an invisible drummer.

The giant nodded, but faced his own shoes as he responded to her command, "I've been asked to do a little research on S.O. Brownlee. It's an order."

"And why would the Navy want to contact my family? What purpose would it serve?"

"It's just what we do. I was given his name when I got my Trident. I'm supposed to know about him. I'm a SEAL as well."

"After all these years? Why now? Why not let the dead remain dead? Why bother my father?" Libby's annoyance began to flare as she felt the need to protect her father.

The sailor shrugged, looked up at the ceiling, adjusting his stance. With a sigh, he turned his gaze back on Libby. She felt herself melt under the press of his intense study.

Cooper took a deep breath, and continued, "Because, I've just lost mine."

CHAPTER 5

COOPER HADN'T BEEN so summarily dusted off since he'd asked Her Highness Homecoming Queen Sherry Baxter to go with him to the prom. She'd laughed in his face, and his buddies on the basketball team wouldn't stop taunting him either. He'd spend most of his senior year trying to forget the incident.

It felt like that now. No family, no home. He was walking around like a stranger in his own clothes. Ordered to meet with people who could care less about him or the military. In less than six hours since returning from Nebraska, everything had changed.

He was faced with the stone-cold eyes of the Doc's daughter, eyes the old Coop would normally have been only too happy to warm up. She was strong, and he usually enjoyed the challenge of being with a woman with a backbone. He wanted to introduce her to the intense fire that lived inside him until she showed him her soft side. He knew she had a soft side. He could feel it already.

But he wasn't going to play that game today.

This afternoon he didn't have the patience for it. And he wanted at least another day and night to numb out. An evening of being anything but civil. In the morning, he'd teach the kid how to surf. And then he'd go face that family tomorrow evening for the meet-and-greet. If there ever was a time he should get thoroughly fucked-up-stinking-pissing-in-your-pants-drunk, it was tonight. For a few moments he thought he even missed the killing fields of Afghanistan. Or the focus he had when he worked up for a new deployment. Not this. Not this morass of feelings he just didn't want to feel. Trying to do something decent, under orders, no less, and getting rejected. Rejected!

He needed to get into action, push his body to peak performance like he did just before he shipped out. Unfortunately, he'd have another three months before that cycle began again.

Too damned long.

He'd be lousy company tonight, for sure. Even for Daisy. And she deserved much more. No, despite his lousy mood, he should find Fredo and Kyle. Maybe he was too dangerous to be alone.

Starting to think about cleaning my Sig. He knew it was a damned mistake to handle a weapon. He was ready to explode.

When he returned to the motor home he let Bay out. They ran down the beach together as Bay tried to keep up. Coop sprinted until his breathing hitched and the pain inside stopped. But, once he got his breath back, the hollow burn in the pit of his stomach came roaring back.

Coop returned to his Babemobile and jumped in the shower. He slipped on a pair of pajama bottoms when he heard a soft knock at the door.

It was Daisy. He could see she was looking for the good time he was normally only too willing to provide, and he decided he'd carefully let her down. She must have noticed something was up when he didn't immediately take her into his arms. They sat a distance apart on his couch, facing the door.

She gave a tussle to Bay's wayward hair that tufted at the top of his head, something the dog was only too willing to receive.

"Your dog needs a bath," she said, smiling.

He hadn't noticed, but damn, she was right. Bay stunk up the whole motor home. Even the flowers he bought every week, stuck in a vase bracketed to the wall, didn't cover up the dog smell that pushed everything else aside. Bay sat on the floor between them, attention focused on the ground, appearing grateful for Daisy's attention.

"Yeah, he was traumatized at first. Ran from a tornado, then plopped on a plane and now living at the beach. Never seen the ocean before."

Bay looked up at Coop with admiration, leaning against the SEAL's leg.

Coop couldn't look at Daisy, but saw out of the corner of his eye that she had moved to within inches of him. He could feel the heat from her sweet-smelling chest close to his bicep as he leaned forward and began to pet Bay.

"You okay, Coop?"

He nodded but still didn't look at her.

"You sure?" She laced fingers through the hair along his temple, then dropped to the back of his neck and gave him a one-handed massage. "So sorry about your family, hon."

Coop removed her fingers from behind his head, placing them back in her lap. He patted them onto her thighs, and then withdrew his hand. He felt like a complete dumb shit. Being close to anyone female was painful.

"Sorry. Guess I'm not very good company tonight."

"I understand. No worries, Coop."

She waited. She'd hung around SEALs long enough to know that if they didn't want to talk, there would be no talking. Then she broke the silence, and sighed. "Well, another time, then. You take care, Coop, hear?"

Are you fucking nuts?

"Thanks. Daisy…" He tried to look at her face, but couldn't. "I'm going to call things off for a bit. Got some stuff to sort out, if you don't mind."

"Take all the time you need." Her voice was brittle, delivered on an icy tray of indifference, masking her hurt. He found himself nodding to her backside as she stepped down and quickly exited the home. He watched every beautiful curve of the derriere he loved to run fingers over in bed. And he felt terrible.

Cooper's carefree world had changed. He hadn't gone into detail about his trip back to Nebraska, and perhaps he should have. Instead, he'd resisted her advances, let her know his attention was elsewhere. He guessed Daisy was wounded and holding back tears.

This had never happened before. Shut down by a woman who he *wasn't* banging, and *he* shut down the one he *was*.

Coop grabbed a mineral water and headed down the beach towards the surf. Moonlight danced on black waves in the water.

Dr. Brownlee's daughter hadn't even told him her name, but he couldn't get her face out of his mind. Was he going back tomorrow at six to see the good doctor, or his daughter?

Fuck.

Maybe he should have taken Daisy up on her generous offer. But no, he had to agree to show up at the good doctor's home with an open wound the size of San Diego. Now that wound just got bigger.

He sat just out of reach of the surf, keeping all visible activity from the beach behind him. He needed the lack of distraction, the white noise of the pounding surf. After a few minutes, he didn't even want to go out to find his Team buddies and commiserate. Usually, there wasn't a day that went by when he didn't share a meal with at least one or two of his buddies on SEAL Team 3. Even if he'd just drive by and watch some of them eat ice cream on the Strand or sit out and sip cappuccino and watch the lovelies on parade, every day he checked in. Saw someone. Even if it was to give them the finger from his scooter.

What the fuck is happening to me?

Back at the motor home, Cooper made some dinner for the two of them, tried to watch a little TV, read a book, even thought about putting some decals on his new remote controlled toy he had to have. The experimental drone he bought off a crazy inventor in Silicon Valley a week ago had been the only thing he thought about in the days before the tornado. Except, of course, for Daisy. But nothing pleased him now. Nothing.

His phone rang.

"Hey, Fredo." Cooper could hear the background noise at Gunny's.

"You back in town, man?"

"Yup."

"You okay? We was worried. Everything get settled?"

Coop thought about the empty coffins, the near-sex with Cora and his lack of interest in anything. "Everything's perfect."

Fredo chuckled. "You're full of shit, Coop."

"I just need some down time. Needed to think."

"Think about what?" Fredo barked back at him.

Cooper felt his anger begin to boil. "Shit, Fredo. I just fuckin' buried my parents. Can't you give me a break?"

There was a long pause. "Well, sometimes thinking's a bad thing. Gotta work it out. We'll come for you."

"Not tonight, Fredo. I already got in a run."

"You got plans? Gotta date?"

"No."

"Well then, we'll see you in twenty." Fredo hung up.

Tonight I really don't want to do this. But he knew it was for his own good.

COOP HEARD FREDO'S battered pickup arrive in the gravel parking lot. He kenneled Bay and locked up.

SO Armando Guzman's cologne hit Coop enough to make his eyes water. "Shit, Armani, you're gonna cause Fredo here to pass out and we'll all be killed."

"I been trying to tell him," Fredo shot back. He began to pull out of the parking lot, grinding gears in the old beater as he did so. "You make me wheeze and send me to the hospital and I'm suing your ass for cruel and unusual punishment."

Armando grinned his dangerous Latin Lover smile that worked so well on all the girls, "Only if we were married, sweetheart." He winked at Fredo who got steamed.

"In your dreams, you Puerto Rican prick."

"Well, you're definitely not in *my* dreams, Fredo."

Armando was the dresser of SEAL Team 3 and his LPO's best friend. With his movie star good looks, he was the one all the ladies fell for. Runs along the beach were almost red carpet events the way the girls chased him. Although he looked like the biggest player in Coronado, Coop knew Armando was devoted to his mother and sister, and was extremely picky about his dates, unlike some of the other Team guys who were less discriminating. Coop also knew Fredo envied him.

Armando turned to face Cooper. "When did you get in?"

"Yesterday."

"How was it?" Armando asked.

Cooper glared at him.

The handsome SEAL nodded. "You have to go

back soon?"

"I got a shitload of paperwork for the insurance claims. Makes the Navy look like Kindergarten compared to the forms I gotta fill out." Coop wasn't looking forward to any of it. "Not going back until after our next workup and deployment."

"Timmons clear you for workup?" Fredo asked as he looked at Cooper in his rear view mirror.

"Sent me on that goddamned mission. What a waste."

"But you better do it or he'll mess with *your* paperwork," Armando said as he winked.

"Roger that." It was true. Cooper had no choice but to complete the job Timmons had given him, not that he liked it at all. Even with the doctor's delicious daughter.

"So, what do you feel like tonight, Coop?" Armando asked.

"Stop!" Fredo barked. "Don't fuckin' ask him that. He'll pick tofu and steamed vegetables, broccoli and Brussels sprouts, all that green shit. Pee-ew!"

Cooper had to laugh. Their side trip to Silicon Valley via Monterey had taken them through just-harvested fields of cabbage and broccoli, and the pungent odor made Fredo carsick. Anything green, except lettuce, guacamole and cilantro was off Fredo's food plan.

"You need to eat more steak, man," Armando volunteered.

"Yeah?"

"Cooper's gonna live to be 100," Fredo said, his nose wrinkled and his unibrow bunched at the center of his face looking like a huge asterisk.

"What's the point of being 100 if you can't fuck?" Armando always equated everything to sex.

THE TRIO STUFFED themselves at a local steakhouse, Cooper begging off the trip to *Ta-Ta's*, the local strip club. He was grateful for the company, but it was wearing thin and he really needed to get to bed if he was going to keep his promise to young Leonard to go surfing at the crack of dawn tomorrow morning. They dropped him off at his motor home and he said his goodbyes.

His sheets still had the faint scent of cherries and it was too distracting. At this rate, he'd not be able to sleep. He got up and changed them, stuffing the dirty ones in his closet. He would do his laundry at Fredo's when the closet got full.

Coop didn't mean to hurt Daisy, but he could see, if he continued to give her the brush-off, he was going to be painfully removed from her Blackberry, just like the tattoos she removed from his buddies' arms and chests when they got divorced or tried to cover up an everlasting memento from a night of partying. As he slipped on his jeans and a shirt, he realized that when he was nervous or tense, Daisy knew how to love it out of him. But no, like an idiot, he'd sent her home.

No woman deserved that kind of treatment. He wasn't good enough for even the casual relationship with Daisy. He was all used up. That's why he wanted to stay single forever. He'd gotten real good at telling himself it was the only way to do what he needed to do and stay sane. There was no comfort in relationships—either casual or otherwise. Not with the things he'd seen over in the war zone. Where human life was cheap and accidents happened to good men and women every day. The randomness of the danger required he be on alert 24/7.

He'd been with buddies who'd gotten the "Dear John" letters—the women who'd divorced their brave men after running up huge credit card debt while their guy was out getting his head nearly blown off. No, best to stay free of the cobwebs of a serious relationship. Keep a clear head. Best to avoid heartache, complications, and distractions. He wondered if he ever could be ready for that type of closeness.

That's why this is such a shit-freaking bad idea. He didn't need this family. Rich people who couldn't care less how the other half lived, and died. Were these the people he was fighting for? Nothing was wrong with the family he buried. They deserved to live. What the fuck was Timmons thinking? The Brownlees didn't want anything to do with him, if he guessed right. No more than he wanted to have anything to do with them.

"We don't speak military." That's a fine legacy for a young man who was probably scared out of his mind and who paid the ultimate price, he thought.

Died for all of them. Even the ones who couldn't be bothered. He studied his face in the mirror. He looked the same, but he clearly was not anything like the man he'd been a week ago. The whole fuckin' world had shifted.

But an order was an order. *Just get 'er done.* And he did owe it to the Fallen to do his job. That much was clear. He hoped he didn't have too much *incoming* when he went back tomorrow afternoon. Wasn't invited for dinner. Hell, he probably couldn't eat anyway. And who'd want to be social with a psychiatrist?

What the hell do you say to a man who analyzes people for a living? An excellent living, from the looks of it.

Well, Sir, I sometimes get night sweats, and some awful nightmares when I get back from tour. I like to hole up with a woman the first twenty-four hours when I get home. There are girls only too happy to do this for our community.

Yeah, analyze my dick, why don't you? But leave my head alone.

CHAPTER 6

THE NEXT MORNING, Libby woke up to the bright sunshine of San Diego. She lay in bed, lazily watching the patterns on the ceiling. She heard her father leave for work, heard her mother leave for a tennis date with her girlfriends.

Libby stayed busy all morning, cleaning her room, sorting through things she'd left behind when she went off to school. She condensed all her keepsakes into one box. The rest went out to the trash. She looked at Noodles, her tabby cat, curled up next to Morgan on her bed. Some day her favorite teenage toy would have to go, too. But she wasn't ready yet to do that to the faithful companion who had listened to all her preteen secrets about the boys she liked and hoped to kiss some day. And besides, Morgan kept Noodles company while she was away, in a strange dog and cat thing.

It felt good to say goodbye to part of her past. Get rid of things that no longer meant anything to her, get rid of her prepubescent idea that life and love were meant to be a fairy tale. Time to grow up, accept the challenge she'd been handed, and get on with life. The interchange with Dr. Gerhardt had only cemented her resolve that she needed to recover from the myopic view of life that came from being a trusting, wide-eyed student too long. It had warped her vision. She hoped getting away from it all, coming back home, would give her that chance to regroup.

Soon she realized she was doing whatever she could do to keep her mind off the tall, muscular sailor with the fluid gait who had waltzed onto their porch and awakened something in her soul. Last thing she wanted was to see a guy who wanted to get in her pants. Men were all alike, she thought. Focused on one thing only.

Maybe this sailor is one of the good guys. It was hard to tell. God knew, she couldn't trust herself to make that judgment any longer. Not yet.

Everything that's good for you is bad for you sometimes, her father had told her one day. She ruminated those words round and round in her head until they made her dizzy.

She had friends who were married, and she shuddered at the thought. She wasn't ready to get caught up in the childbearing and soccer practices some of her friends had opted for. They looked happy enough, but she knew herself well enough to know it wasn't on her radar. Not even close.

Libby put three large boxes destined for Goodwill in the garage outside the kitchen door. She made some tea and watched her father's new gardener work silently on his knees by the walkway that ran from the garage to the house. He lifted his gaze up to her, and then lowered his baseball cap to completely cover his face and eyes. He stabbed the black soil in the grassy mound at the edges of her mother's zinnia patch, exposing plastic PVC tubing.

Still in her pajamas, Libby brought her tea upstairs and flopped back on the bed. She began reading one of her favorite romance novels. The hours ticked by. She finished the book just as the sun was beginning to lower toward the horizon. She heard her mother return home and deposit groceries for dinner on the kitchen counter, so Libby made a dash to the shower.

She thought about the hero in the novel. Though the author had described him as dark-haired, Libby saw the face of that SEAL bending down to kiss her, just like she'd imagined the Brazilian painter would do in her novel. She put on a black pair of lacy underwear, which made no sense at all. She slipped on her jeans and an oversized deep pink cotton shirt she felt comfortable in. She walked through a spritz of her favorite perfume.

Libby heard a sound outside, and looked through

her bedroom window as Cooper's muscular frame detached itself from—*a scooter?* The shiny red thing looked like it belonged to a tanned San Diego coed. The SEAL's black slacks hugged muscular thighs and a tight, swimmer's butt. He leaned back and cracked his back. She could see a trace of treasure trail peek just above his fly as the white shirt inched up just enough.

Lord, has it been that long?

When she dropped her hairbrush on the hardwood floor, he looked up into her open window and spotted her staring back at him.

So much for looking disinterested. She'd been chastising herself all afternoon. Her heart was racing in anticipation of being in the same room with this guy. She wasn't sure whether it was attraction or the sense of danger hovering like a cloud above him, which was strangely exciting. It defied logic. And she liked it.

Her mother had opened the front door with a loud squeak, her elegantly mannered voice welcoming and fresh. Libby couldn't make out the words, but the SEAL grabbed his helmet and climbed the porch steps slowly, smiling. She held her breath as he disappeared from view. Into her home.

There was a light tap on her bedroom doorframe. Dr. Brownlee poked his head in.

"Brownie, you think I can just send him away?"

"Oh, Dad. Didn't know you were home already."

"Just got here. You up for this?"

"He's here to see you. This isn't my show. He wants to tell you something."

"Yea? Well I want to tell him something too—"

Libby was surprised at the acid tone in her Dad's voice. "Dad, everything all right? This is just some sailor with a message from the Navy of some sort. Not a big deal, really." She saw his frown and gave him a gentle peck on the cheek, stepping back.

"They send someone who's just lost his family, so I can't tell him what I really feel about this whole war and the military machine that runs it. Smart, aren't they?"

"That what you're upset about? The war?" She wanted to bring up Uncle Will's name but something told her to be cautious. She was getting more and more nervous as she noticed the changes in her normally casual and confident father.

"I just don't like it. Not now," he said.

Why not now? "*They* aren't doing anything. Besides, you always told me to watch out for *they* and *them*." She placed a hand on his shoulder. "Let's go downstairs and face this sailor together."

Dr. Brownlee sighed, then stepped ahead as Libby followed him down the sweeping curved staircase to the lobby below. Cooper was in the kitchen, nursing a glass of ice water.

"Hello, son. Austin Brownlee." He extended his hand to the SEAL.

"Calvin Cooper." He said as he shot a quick glance at Libby. She felt her heart race.

Dr. Brownlee seemed to wince as the SEAL's large hand enveloped his. Libby sensed the civility of the evening had just passed. She braced herself.

After her dad extricated his paw from the sailor's grip, Cooper nodded to Libby. She felt her cheeks flush. Out of the corner of her eye she saw a frown wash over her father's face.

"I'm Libby." She did not extend her hand.

"Libby," the SEAL said and tipped his head.

"We do serve alcohol in this house. What can I get you?" her father asked.

Coop held up his glass, tinkling the ice cubes. "I'm good."

The silence was awkward. Did he have a past drinking problem? Growing up, Libby's family discussions often centered on addictive cycles.

"Probably wise in your line of work." Her dad dismissed Cooper's comment and stepped up to the wet bar off the kitchen. Libby felt concern when she watched him pour himself half a tumbler of amber liquid and down it in one gulp. Although she knew her father had been dreading this little party tonight, she didn't think it had anything to do with his drinking.

And he was dosing, self-medicating. Something was very wrong with the famed psychiatrist.

"Please," her mother interjected, gesturing to the front of the house. "Let's go sit in the living room, shall we?"

Libby watched as both men inhaled sharply, and in tandem, while they moved into the expansive room. She knew this was not a meeting either one of them wanted.

Why did he come?

Dr. Brownlee went to the mantle over the fireplace and retrieved the picture of Uncle Will, an exact younger copy of her father's face. The smiling young man was wearing a sailor uniform. When Libby was little, her father had told her what every bar and stripe and medal meant. She focused on the SEAL Trident that was prominently displayed at the top. It was especially painful today to look into the eyes of her father after she'd gazed at the baby-faced picture of young Uncle Will, who died more than twenty-five years ago.

"This is Will." Her father deposited the gold-framed photograph into the large hands of the SEAL. Then her dad turned and filled his glass with ice as he prepared himself another drink, leaving the young man to ponder the face of the fallen soldier.

That's your third, Dad. Damn it, what's wrong?

Cooper was breathing hard, and Libby knew he was working to keep strong emotions in check. He held the frame carefully, almost delicately. Then his expression changed into a faint smile of recognition, like he was staring into the face of a young, innocent child. Slowly, the SEAL rose, and, using both hands, he carefully placed the picture back on the mantle. Then he adjusted its position, perfectly centered on the painted mantelpiece. He stared at it a long time before he turned, looked directly into Libby's eyes, and then diverted his gaze down.

Dr. Brownlee cleared his throat, his refreshed drink in one hand, and seated himself on the sofa next to his wife. Libby sat to their right. Brownlee took his wife's hand and spoke to their entwined fingers.

"So, you want to tell us what this is all about, son?"

Cooper stiffened, raised his chin like his shirt was too tight at the neck. He gave a shrug of his massive shoulders and started a difficult speech Libby suspected had been rehearsed several times.

"We are given a KA-BAR knife when we get our Tridents, upon graduation from BUD/S. Each one is engraved with the name of a fallen SEAL, someone who was a specialist in our chosen discipline. I'm a medic. I believe Will—your brother—was a medic as well."

"Yes. He wanted to be a doctor."

Cooper nodded. "I have thought about that myself." He slipped his hands into his pockets, cleared his throat and shrugged. "I've been asked to find out about the family of this fallen hero."

"Son, excuse me if I differ. He died in a helicopter crash. At base."

Libby felt her spine straighten, her hands turned to ice water.

"Which he wouldn't have been on if he hadn't been a SEAL going on a mission." Cooper gave her father a stern look. Mrs. Brownlee turned to her husband, alarm written on her face. Dr. Brownlee nodded and continued to look at his wife's hand tucked inside his own.

"Austin," Mrs. Brownlee whispered. She softly placed her palm at his heart. Libby could see her mother's radar go into high alert.

"Look," Dr. Brownlee started. "Oh, hell." He disentangled his hand and stood up. "You will forgive me if I don't have the stomach for some long sad tale of loss, ten Hail Marys and a couple of God Bless Americas. My brother died for nothing. *Nothing!*"

Cooper crossed the room and stood a few feet from doctor. "Well, maybe he died for me and not for you. I, for one, am grateful, sir. What you do with your grief is your deal. Maybe he died so you could get rich and play around in your garden, and drink too much. I don't care what the hell you do with your life. I will honor him like he deserves."

"Well, son—" Her father didn't get very far.

Coop stiffened and pointed at the doctor. "Don't you fucking call me son. A better man than you called me that. And his body is spread all over the Nebraska farmland he loved."

Cooper strode over to his jacket and helmet. He turned and added to Dr. Brownlee's back. "You know something? I never saw him in a suit. Never. Even when my sister—" Cooper's voice broke. "Fuck," he said to his helmet. Without looking up, he mumbled, "Excuse me, ma'am." He stomped across the room, and into the lobby toward the front door.

Mrs. Brownlee was up and tried to block his way.

"So sorry, Ma'am. I can see this was one huge mistake. Pardon me for ruining your evening."

Without as much so a slight glance towards Libby, Cooper was out the door. She could hear him mutter a string of choice words until her mother closed the door behind him. Libby jumped when she heard the growl of the small scooter engine. For some reason, it made her giggle.

"You think that was funny, Brownie?" said her father, who glared at her. She felt suddenly afraid.

"Austin, I think you've done enough for one evening. Your manners. Where did they go?" Libby's mom injected.

Dr. Brownlee emptied his drink, closing his eyes like he was savoring his last. "My manners? Right now I think they're buried with Will. How dare he come waltzing in here, dredging up old wounds? The Navy took Will. What right do they have to ask me to dig up my memories to benefit some bullshit code of honor?"

When Libby looked up, she noticed her father's face was lined with tears. She had never seen him cry.

She excused herself. Listening to the heated discussion between her parents, she climbed the staircase to her room and closed the door behind her. Her father's drinking was weighing heavily on her mind. His sudden hatred of the Navy surprised her, too. She'd not heard this much about it until tonight, and she wondered why.

Dad's got something going on. She'd felt it the moment she called to tell them she'd be visiting for a few days. She saw it in his face when she first drove up. Something was distracting him, preoccupying him. The one man she needed to lean on, and all of a sudden he wasn't available.

It also wasn't like him not to be respectful and cordial, and here he'd practically tossed the young sailor out of his house. That wasn't the father she knew and loved. She shivered at the thought of the dark man who had replaced her usually warm and kindhearted father.

She thought about Cooper. It wasn't right he had been sent away thinking they were freaks. The guy was following orders, he'd said. She knew the SEALs were honorable men, and, even if it was to honor the memory of Uncle Will, her dad should not have treated him this way.

To distract herself, she picked up one of her books, and put on her iPad headphones to drown out the sounds of the argument brewing downstairs. She soon fell asleep.

Libby woke up later, noticing the sky had turned dark. The house was mercifully quiet. She got her keys and slipped downstairs to her car. *'Never let the sun set on a disagreement,'* her dad had always said. Well, it was past sunset, but maybe she could fix this just a little bit. Then she'd sort out the rest of it later. Maybe it was time to stop running and start facing the truth.

CHAPTER 7

*F*UCK ME. *W*HAT *was I thinking?*

   Cooper rounded the turn and almost clipped a vintage Datsun convertible driven by a blonde in a sun visor.

   Fucking hate this part of town. Rich people are use-less. Clueless.

   He looked upon row after row of professionally landscaped front yards, lawns looking like they were trimmed with scissors, blooming plants framing arched windows in courtyards behind stucco-fenced walls. Just about every home had some variety of bisque-colored tiled roofs. Lots of BMWs, Mercedes, Jags and even Bentleys.

   Don't belong here. Never did. Don't want to come back. Ever.

   Cooper decided he'd just tell Timmons the family had refused all contact. It was partially true, after all. The ladies would have gone along with his visit, but Dr.

Brownlee, no, he would forever be on the wrong side of anything to do with the Navy, and the SEALs in particular.

That man doesn't deserve the sacrifice his brother made. Whatever this man's beef with the Navy, it was his own shit to wear. And why? He was the fuckin' asshole who got to live in the big house with the pretty wife and...and...

The thought and resulting lack of focus caused him to swerve over the centerline. He got a honk from a green four-door landscaping truck towing a trailer and blaring Mariachi music.

Adrenaline and his well-trained reflexes kept him from hitting the vehicle. He let out the power and his scooter lurched safely back to his proper lane. The impact with the old truck would surely take away all his pain, he thought. It would be damn quick, but it would hurt like a son of a gun.

Looks like Gunny's old truck. Gunnery Sergeant Joseph Hoskins, who owned the rusty old gym Team guys frequented for their PT duty, had bought an old truck from the Forestry Service last year at auction. The thing was as stubborn as Gunny, and just as temperamental. Fredo had one, too. Maybe if his death wish didn't subside, he should get one as well. Might be safer. After all, he was more comfortable under the carriage of an old truck or tractor than meeting a pampered know-it-all psychiatrist and his…

Get a grip, Coop. You're no whiny mama's boy.

A flood of revulsion came over him, tightening his stomach and sending stinging moisture to his eyes.

Don't be a fuckin' crybaby.

He worked to reduce his stress level by lowering his heartbeat. He took deep breaths as he accelerated and wound down out of the neighborhood of perfect homes.

He became more comfortable in traffic along the Strand, heading back to Coronado. Home. Home to the Babemobile he'd left at the beach.

He lowered the rear ramp of the motor home and stowed his scooter, closing the electric conveyor door behind him. Bay was barking incessantly. Coop let him out on the beach and watched as the dog raised his leg over a shrub in the parking lot. In seconds, the big brown pooch ran enthusiastically back and forth in the sand, and then to Coop's side, begging to play.

But Coop wasn't in the mood. He took the dog inside, gave him some kibble and fresh water. He stripped off his shoes, dress slacks and button-down white shirt. Still shiny from disuse, the shoes hurt his feet. He threw everything into the corner with a satisfying *thwat*. Light was just beginning to dim outside. He donned his swim shorts, told Bay to stay put and promised he'd be back in a bit, locked the motor home, and ran across the warm sand. He dove into the surf, thankful to be back in the water, where he felt safe. Where the world was right.

Cooper swam parallel to the shore, back and forth in one-mile lengths, like he had done hundreds of times before. He preferred the ocean here, rather than the inlet near base, which was full of debris, oil and gasoline residue. The cold water soothed his soul.

Like a bee sting, he couldn't shrug off the lack of respect Brownlee had for his fallen brother. It was so wrong on so many levels. At least he had a family.

Big house. Doesn't even understand how easily it all could be taken away. He thought about his mom patching his shirts with leftover pieces of shirting from discarded clothing. She even used to tie his shoelaces together to make whole ones, which got him in trouble with the kids at school. One time she'd asked his dad if the soap they got in a motel cost them extra, since she'd brought her own. They'd worked so hard for every penny they had, but everything they had was theirs. They owned it completely, outright.

And now it was gone forever. As if it had never existed.

The sun was sinking on the horizon. Coop sat for a few minutes to enjoy the view, letting salt water drip down his skin. The warm sand felt good as he buried his toes in it. It was going to be a clear night tonight.

The stars would be out there in droves, like tourists in Heaven.

The last crescent of bright salmon-colored sun melted into the watery horizon. It was a routine Coop liked to do every day he could: watch the sun die. In the remaining afterglow, he walked silently up the beach toward his silver home.

Coop heard banging car doors and saw Fredo, Kyle, Armando and a new guy running towards him.

"You are to get wet and sandy, sailor," Kyle barked. His LPO looked serious as a heart attack but Fredo and Armando were still punching each other in the arm. The new guy, a handsome African-American who was almost Coop's height, smiled with the biggest white teeth he had ever seen. He had the air of an officer. Career man all the way.

Cooper tried to look relaxed, but he didn't really want to be around anyone tonight.

"I said, get your butt off the sand, or these mother-fuckers are gonna bury you right here," Kyle yelled back. He did a right good job imitating one of their BUD/S drill instructors.

Coop just sat in the sand and pushed some of it over his wet legs.

That was a call to action. The resulting sand fight lasted almost ten minutes. When it was all done, Cooper looked like a creature from a horror film, crusted with wet sand, Kyle had been pants'ed and was trying to pull up his cargos before tourists would get a look at his naked ass, Armando's hair was wild and full of sand, and Fredo was swearing up a storm in Spanish, having broken one of his gold chains. He was on all fours looking for it in the orange light of dusk. The new guy had stayed out of it and was sitting on the step of Cooper's motor home, looking neat and organized.

On cue, the three of them got down and joined Fredo until Kyle found the chain and returned it to Fredo's sandy palm.

"First one to the surf doesn't have to jump in," Kyle yelled out. Everyone headed for the white water. Cooper turned and saw Kyle call out to their new Team guy. "C'mon LT. That means you too."

So this guy was a new AOIC, Assistant Officer In Charge. Technically above Kyle's rank on the Teams, he would be learning all he could from the capable Team 3 LPO.

The new guy looked very by-the-book prissy. The horrified expression on his face egged the guys on. They cat-called him until he started to run. And man, the guy could run! He beat Kyle by a good ten yards, but stood just outside the surf. Like everyone else, the new guy tossed his shoes and dove in.

The five of them formed a school and swam down the water's edge just past the surf, parallel to the shore.

Coop was already winded from his earlier swim, so he let Kyle win, but normally he'd almost be able to lap them. But, God, he needed this. He needed the sand. He needed to exhaust himself playing in the water.

As they completed their swim and walked back up the beach, Kyle turned to Coop, and his stomach clenched. He knew the questions would start in now. He just wanted to crash in bed, but no, his Team leader had other plans. "You okay, Coop? I expected a call from you."

"Talked to you yesterday, Landmine." Just like all the rest of the guys, Kyle Lansdowne's name was morphed into anything that resembled his former pronunciation, Lannie, Landing Gear, Landmine, being the favored. Calling him Lannie would earn you a punch in the arm, if you were lucky.

"You know what the hell I mean."

"I was visiting that family Timmons asked me to go see."

"Uh huh," Kyle answered, taking deep gulps of air. "I don't hear from you and I worry. You wouldn't want me to worry, now, would you, Coop?"

"Nothing to worry about," Coop hoped his words would give Kyle a warning to let it go. He didn't want to talk about anything right now.

"Well, normally, Armando's the one I would be worrying about."

"Me?" Armando asked, feigning innocence. "I always find my way back home."

"Now, Daisy was making some serious moves on Tootsie Roll over here," Kyle said pointing his thumb to the new guy. "And I knew she wouldn't do that unless you said it was cool, and all."

"She doesn't owe me anything—"

All three of Coop's buddies began to whistle.

"Now I'm really worried," said Kyle. "So you haven't been fucked since you came back from Nebraska, I take it?"

Coop hesitated before answering, which earned him more whistles and cat calls. "Almost, but no." Coop smirked as he recalled the look on Cora's face when he'd left her. None of the guys would ever believe he'd actually walked away. He wanted that to remain a secret, too.

"That's just not natural, Coop. See, what did I tell you about all that tofu and shit." Fredo leaned into him and, with a whisper finished his thought, "Makes you soft, man."

Everyone laughed, including Cooper. Even Jones was shaking his head.

"Nothing wrong with my dick," Cooper said.

"I don't want to know what you're thinking about. An old married man like me can't have such ideas. I might get a heart attack."

They stopped outside Cooper's door.

"I'm ordering you to the Scupper tonight, 'kay?" Kyle said.

Fredo stepped forward, "Yeah, Coop. You gonna let us shower at your place first?"

"Fuck no." He knew the hot water wouldn't last and he'd have to fill up the propane tank afterwards.

Kyle put his arm around the Mexican SEAL. "Fredo, we're going over to your place. That way we can wash our pants, too. Besides, I've got to iron my money until it's dry."

"Oh shit, that's right," Armando swore. "My new wallet is toast." He pulled a dark shriveled piece of leather from the Velcro pocket on the front of his cargo pants.

Kyle turned to Cooper. "One hour. That's an order."

"Roger that."

COOP TOOK A longer shower than normal. He usually tried to make his propane tank last for two months, but tonight he didn't care. With the anger worked out of him, his mind went to the vixen he'd met today at the doc's house. All auburn hair and red pouty lips. He smacked his forehead with his palm while he was shaving, making a splat of the white soap on his mirror.

"Holy shit," he said to his Santa Claus image. *She was the babe at the Aquarium.* Just a week ago, which now seemed like last century, he and Fredo had taken a trip to Silicon Valley to buy his new drone from that dork inventor. They'd taken a detour to the Monterey Bay Aquarium, where he'd seen her, and then again when they stopped to do some laps in the bay before heading back to San Diego.

His little brain was doing pushups and had turned on the rock music in his head, getting ready to par-tay. Coop remembered falling asleep in the cheap motel, thinking about what the top of her head would look like while she gave him a blow job. Well, to be honest with himself, he fantasized about what it would feel like, too.

He picked up the slacks and the white shirt, now wrinkled. He only owned one good outfit so he carefully pressed them against the bed with his hands, and then hung them up on the same hangar. His closet was nearly bare. Except for the gun cases and duty bags stuffed into the end of the small space. Who needed clothes when you had enough equipment and weapons to start a small war?

Maybe he could crawl out of the cave he'd fallen into. Maybe there could be life at the end of the dark tunnel. Maybe he could make up some excuse to see her again.

God, I hope so.

THE SCUPPER WAS slow tonight, since it wasn't a weekend. Above the bar were pictures of fallen SEALs, the dates and locations of their demise. When he was first on the Teams, he didn't like to look at them. He was surprised when, like most the other Team guys who hung out there, he got so that he liked looking at them, paying his respects. God willing, if he should have to pay that ultimate sacrifice, there would be some young newbie Team guy staring up at his picture, toasting him with a beer, or, as in his case, a mineral water.

Coop's eyes stung. Maybe there was too much cigarette smoke tonight. He winced and looked over the sparse crowd. No sign of Kyle and the others yet, so he ordered his regular mineral water with lots of ice and lime and leaned against the bar. A big screen TV was tuned to a basketball game he had no interest in watching.

He fished a couple sugar packets from the counter, along with a small handful of toothpicks, and stuck them in his shirt pocket. He fiddled with the drips of condensation easing their way down his tall glass.

He used to get plastered here on a regular basis when he was on SEAL Team 5. He'd just come back with his BUD/S swim buddy from a refresher course at

Bragg on amputations in the field. He remembered it was bothering him a little more than it should have. His buddy had gotten a Dear John letter from his girlfriend in Florida, so they were celebrating their "freedom." Truth was, his friend was pretty torn up about it. But they were laughing at all the stupid things they'd told girls they'd dated. The Frog Hogs, girls that liked SEALs any way they could get them. Coop knew Gary was on the lookout for a lovely to take his mind off his pain. Tonight the pickings were slim.

"You have the softest skin," Coop had said in falsetto.

"I love rubbing your ass," Gary had one-upped him.

"I'm a one-girl guy," Coop continued. They both laughed, even though Coop knew it was true.

Several others from Team 5 came in. After getting almost too drunk to walk, someone got the harebrained idea to go for a swim.

Zeke had gone for some Chinese take-out and some brews, but the rest of them headed to the beach. They horsed around until the food and drink showed up, and then they ate their fill. Everyone decided to shed their clothes and go in the water stark naked. Cooper had forgotten to take off the wristwatch his dad had given him, so came out of the water to put it in his shorts. He laughed watching his Team buds splashing in the surf and acting like ten-year-olds.

After that, everything went to hell. Gary was in the water too long. He'd had a reaction to shellfish in the food and wound up in a full-blown cardiac arrest. And there wasn't a damned thing any of them could do about it, although God knows they tried.

Dumb shit must have known he'd get a reaction to the seafood. He couldn't believe it was anything but a horrible, pathetic accident, exacerbated by the alcohol.

Coop found himself in a cave of depression. He almost went to a shrink about. Didn't want it on his record, so he held off. He just couldn't look at the guys he'd spent Gary's last night on the beach with again without getting torn up inside. He asked for a reassignment and it was granted ten days later. And he never took a drink again.

Rest in Peace, Gary. He finished off his mineral water and started chewing ice, which meant he was nervous as hell.

I need to go home. He needed a good rest. His muscles were going to be sore with two PTs today, and all the roughhousing they'd done at the beach.

Kyle and the new guy entered the bar.

"Sorry we're late. Good to see you here, Coop." Kyle slapped him on the back and took a stool next to him. The new guy sat on the other side.

"Fredo get a date?"

"He's over at Mia's with Armani."

"Good for him." Fredo had a major crush on Armando's wild child little sister. Coop looked at the new guy. "We haven't been introduced properly. I'm Calvin Cooper," he said when he extended his hand over the bar, in front of Kyle.

"Malcolm Jones." The guy was handsome as hell. Big, strong hands.

"You're that guy," Kyle said.

"What guy?" asked Malcolm.

"'I'm your father, Luke.' That guy."

Jones grinned.

"Malcolm here is giving us a tryout. Graduated top of his class at the Academy." Kyle's eyes sparkled in the light of the television over the bar.

Cooper whistled. "Gimme your arm then, Darth Vader." Coop said to Jones.

"Come on?" the handsome Lieutenant asked.

"Your arm. I gotta see if you got the mark." Cooper was going to rub it in.

Jones rolled his eyes and presented his bare left forearm. Cooper guffawed. "That's what I thought. A virgin."

This upset Jones, who gave an angry scowl. "What the fuck you sayin'? I'm no virgin."

Kyle helped, "You don't have the tats. Everyone on our team gets the frog prints from here to here." He pointed from his wrist to the inside of his elbow.

Cooper added, "Except in your case, they're gonna have to do it twice so it will show up."

"I got tats," Jones spat out with a frown.

"Yeah? Where?" Kyle asked.

Jones pulled down the polo shirt collar to reveal an anchor tat on his bicep.

Cooper and Kyle burst out laughing. Jones quickly covered up. Kyle added, "Nobody in the Navy Special Forces gets anchors. That's for fleet scum. Didn't they teach you that at the Academy?"

Jones focused back on his beer and there was a long pause.

"Where you from, Malcolm?" Coop asked. He could tell they'd maybe rubbed the guy too hard about the tats.

"Mississippi. Folks still live there," Jones said without making eye contact.

Cooper took in air quickly. His hands trembled. His old instinct of reaching for a beer came back and he took on some ice cubes, starting to crunch them down loudly.

"Sorry, Coop. Heard about your people. Real sorry for your loss, man." Jones was trying to be a good guy, but Coop was too pained to look back at him.

The three of them were quiet, not looking at each other.

"Well, aren't we a pathetic sack of bones? Kinda reminds us of the old Team guys trying to relive their glory days." Kyle said, leaning first toward Cooper and then Malcolm.

"Yeah," Coop whispered. "Look, man, I'm dog tired. Beat as all hell. I had a good swim before you guys showed up. Even went surfing early this morning. And I'm afraid I'm terrible company."

Jones was staring into his beer. Coop knew he felt bad about bringing his family up, but the guy was just being nice.

"I can trust you to go home?" Kyle asked.

"I'm okay. Sorry I wasted your evening, Landmine."

"Oh, hell, don't be. Christy has designs on my body."

Coop laughed and knew it was probably completely true.

"I shouldn't be here, but just wanted to make sure you were taken care of, Coop." He paused and then asked, "Daisy coming over?"

That got Jones's attention. "Not anymore. Understand she has her sights on some chocolate," Coop answered and nodded to Jones.

He'd never thought he'd be able to see a black man blush, but Jones sure as hell did.

"First you let her work on your arm, get you those

nice little frog prints," Kyle said as he whispered to Jones just loud enough so Cooper could hear. "She has the best hands. Let her pick out another tattoo for you and let her place it, too. She loves that. Then you let her work on your dick."

Cooper almost spit out his soda.

"I'm not really into that stuff," Jones replied.

Cooper and Kyle stared at the man.

"I'm not gay or anything. Hey, guys—I just kinda like to get to know a girl a little better, that's all."

Both Coop and Kyle commented in unison, "Why?"

They all laughed. Coop knew they could trash talk all they wanted to about women, but most Team guys respected them more than they would ever admit in public.

Coop said his goodbyes, thanked his LPO again for trying to babysit him. With Kyle's new little one at home, this was a sacrifice, he knew. His Team leader rarely hung out at the SEAL bars anymore.

Coop headed back to the Babemobile. He locked up the scooter and then walked down the beach to sit by the surf.

He was grateful for Kyle, who cared about him as much as anyone could. Going outside the Teams, especially to a family who obviously didn't want anything to do with the military, was a mistake, and he intended to tell Timmons so at the next opportunity. Everything he needed to get right in the head was in front of him, or behind him in his home on wheels. And his comfy bed would help.

He figured he'd work on the drone tomorrow, maybe shop for an infrared or thermal camera to mount on the UAV. He had a '40's pinup decal of Lana Turner he was going to mark his new toy with.

He turned and headed back home.

A small figure stood outside the metal door, knocking. Bay was having a fit inside. At first Coop thought it was Daisy, back after having an uncharacteristic change of heart. But no, it was someone with auburn hair. Long auburn hair. Long legs. The shape of her ass as she stood on tiptoe while she knocked looked vaguely familiar.

He'd been trained to move without a sound, and he did so, until he got to within a foot of the woman. He smelled lavender, and vanilla. She wore a pinky ring on her right hand that glinted in the moonlight.

"Can I help you?" his voice was husky.

She immediately turned, eyes wide and fearful. She slammed her body up against the shell of his silver beast, trying to distance herself from him.

Libby Brownlee.

"Oh. My. God. You scared me to death."

"Not quite. You look quite alive to me." The anger

he felt toward Libby and her family evaporated. "Why are you here?"

"I—I just came because—I—felt bad—I wanted to—to—apologize for my father. You don't understand. He is a very fine man. He just—"

"He just blames the Navy for the loss of his brother." Bay was barking. "I've got to let him out or he'll shred the insides of my home."

"No problem."

She stepped aside and he unlocked the door, letting the dog, who had not been kenneled, practically topple Libby. Coop reprimanded him, but Libby was laughing.

"Who's this?" she asked between giggles.

"This is Bay. I brought him back from…from my home. He's just getting used to things out here."

"Ah. Well, Bay," she said as she knelt and rubbed Bay's ears, putting her nose close to the dog's, "how do you like our ocean and our great weather, huh?"

"C'mon, Bay. If you're gonna just socialize, you've got to go back inside."

The dog ran off a few yards down the parking lot, sniffed the ground around several cars parked in the darkening early evening. When the he returned, Coop put him in the trailer and locked it.

"So, you were talking about your father being a good guy and all—"

"Well, yes. But what I meant to say is that he is a fine, caring person—"

"Save it. Not interested in excuses. He send you?"

"Of course not. I just thought it was wrong. Wrong how he treated you. That's all. I guess this was a mistake…"

Libby turned to go and Coop grabbed her arm. "Sorry." He dropped his grip. "Stay for a bit. Then you can go."

The two stood close enough that he could feel the heat from her body. She was a lethal, complicated, combination of spirit and emotion. Cooper liked girls who were easier to figure out. Though it wasn't wise, he found himself *making nice.*

"I'd invite you in, but that wouldn't be appropriate. Besides, the housekeeper has the day off. And Bay has had his way with the decorating and all." His little smile was returned. Her eyes softened. Even in the dim light he could see her full lips, painted a deep pink, pucker as she formed her careful words.

"No problem." She searched his face. He wanted to step to her, see if she would shrink if he slipped his hand up under her cotton top. But he held firm.

"You cold?" he asked.

She nodded.

"Let me go get a blanket. We'll sit outside and finish our talk, okay?"

"Fine."

That word again. Why do women like to use it all the time?

Coop unlocked the door and in two strides grabbed the throw on his dinette couch without turning on the lights. He bid the dog stay curled on the dog bed inside the kennel. He didn't want Libby to see the interior of his soul. After all, this wasn't a date.

He walked down the beach toward the surf and she followed slightly behind. He placed the blanket around her shoulders, feeling the smooth texture of her neck and upper arm as he did so. She grabbed the blanket together at her chest and sat down in tandem with him.

She was looking out to sea, the last remnants of the now-purple sky turning grey. A few stars began to come out. She leaned back and scanned the blue twilight ceiling.

"I love how you can see the stars here. Not like where I live," she said.

"You don't live in San Diego?"

"No. I'm in San Jose. I was going to the University of Santa Clara."

"Was?"

"I'm taking a semester off."

Coop didn't know what to say. He hadn't gotten his college degree yet, though he had started. "Time off can be a good thing," he said but didn't mean it.

"I'm getting my Master's in psychology. I've been going to school non-stop for seventeen years. I don't know, I just needed a break. Probably a stupid idea, but the thought of plunging into another year of studies frightened me for some reason."

"So you'll live at home, then?"

"No. I can't think there."

Coop was going to let her tell him. He didn't want to ask, but he was dying to know.

Better stop this or you'll get your dick in a ringer. Last thing he wanted to do was report back to Timmons that he'd not made contact with the brother, but fucked his daughter.

Shit. Cooper, you're a fuckin' asshole.

"I think best here. Everything seems right with the world when I'm in the water, or at the beach. Especially just after sunset." Cooper chastised himself for being such a fucking romantic.

What the hell are you doing?

Libby turned her face to his. He watched as her pretty eyes fluttered over his features, ending with his mouth. Unless he had totally gone off his rocker, the lady was feeling something for him. Although excited, he wasn't sure he should be.

"I'm sorry about your family," she whispered over the sounds of the waves in the distance.

This unexpected painful reminder that he was a

damaged soul bothered him. He understood why she'd said it. Why do women always want to heal guys? He'd seen his share of relationship train wrecks in the SEAL community. He wasn't sure he believed it was possible to do it successfully. But if he did, she might—

Damn. Stop this right now.

Cooper tore himself from her eyes and sifted sand between his bent knees. She was barely touching his thigh with her own. He hadn't noticed that before. The warm glow tingled up his leg, sending his junk into alert status.

"My father had no right to treat you that way. I want to apologize for his behavior. That isn't who we are. We've never met—" Libby stopped, her voice wavering. This was hard for her.

Her eyes searched his. It was so simple and happened so fast. He leaned in and placed his lips over hers to stop her from talking. He was going to back away, but she moved forward and increased the pressure. His tongue slipped along her lower lip until she parted them and he was in.

He touched her cheeks with the back of both hands, and then sent his fingers into her hair at the back of her head, pulling her into him. She did not resist, but melted into his chest. He kissed her neck and heard her moan. Her smell, her breath, the taste of her lips put him in a trance. He wanted her. It was so wrong, but he wanted her more than he'd wanted a woman in years.

Her hands smoothed over his shoulders and down his chest. Her fingers moved further and rubbed over his erection tenting the front of his cargo pants. She stroked him, barely touching his sensitive part through the fabric.

You want this? You want to do me right here?

Coop was surprised. He didn't want to ask if she knew what she was doing. Hell, he didn't know what he was doing. Before he could think further, she had moved a thigh over his legs and was straddling him. She reached for his cock, coaxing it outside, and moved her fingers up and down, squeezing him.

"I don't have anything," he whispered.

"I'm on the pill," she whispered back and kissed him.

"But what about—"

"Shhh."

Well okay, then. Then he remembered he might have something in his shorts. "Wait," he said as he reached down and thank God he had a shriveled foil packet in the lower pocket that had probably been through a couple of washings. But it was better than nothing.

She grabbed the packet from him.

Coop lay back, slipping a hand under her and felt

her press into his palm. He unbuttoned her pants and peeled them off her hips as she raised her body. He pulled the blanket up over her bikini-clad butt as she sheathed him with fingers that sent his erection into outer space. His fingers massaged the cleft between her cheeks. Under the blanket he diverted her panties to the side and placed his throbbing cock there. She inhaled, raised her torso up and then came down on him to the hilt.

Like magic their two bodies moved in the moon-light. He couldn't get enough. He stroked her wet insides, moving against lips that hugged him. He raised her body up and down on his shaft as she moaned her pleasure.

She leaned forward and covered his mouth with kisses. The woman was beyond hot. He arched his cock up and into her while she pressed her breasts against his chest. She raised her shirt, slipped her bra up over her mounds and pressed the delicious flesh against his pecs.

He needed the feel of her skin. He needed to see all of her. He needed to kiss all of her. He was not going to let her go until morning.

LIBBY COULDN'T BELIEVE what they'd just done. On a public beach, in front of God-knew-anyone-who-happened-to-walk-by. Would she have noticed? Would he?

Where the heck is your pride, your common sense? You don't even know this guy.

She'd never done this before, and recognized the risky behavior as a warning. But, in spite of her training, now she wanted more. He'd come into her, thrilling her insides with danger. She'd been sure she wouldn't let a man touch her for months after her near-rape at the University. And now she came begging for it. Literally hanging all over him.

What were you thinking? She counted the months; no, it had been a couple of years since she'd had any kind of sexual relationship. She had friends, but casual sex wasn't part of her DNA. Somehow, she felt he might feel the same way.

Not smart. He could be an axe murderer for all you know. A little voice in her chest told her *no.*

They walked to the water's edge without saying a word. She was trying to answer her own question:

What is this?

She was always careful. She didn't just jump on some guy's bones on the beach—someone she didn't know, so why now? Had she needed sex so much she couldn't help herself?

No, it wasn't that. She'd always told herself she was good at reading people, but this was clearly over the line. Yet, she'd uncovered something there in his eyes she'd never seen before. There was pain, for sure. Loneliness, matching the hole she felt in her own chest, something that resonated.

But there was something else—an honor, a devotion to duty. Everything she had studied indicated she was drawn to him like a moth to the flame. This unwise attraction could prove dangerous. He was unlike any man she'd ever met, ever kissed, ever…

All her questions conveniently slipped away when he took her hand in his. She was still wrapped in the blanket. He was naked. He cocked his head and searched behind them, scanning the beach. Libby didn't want to look.

"Swim with me. Do you swim?" he said.

"Now?"

"Yes. Swim with me." He kissed her again.

Her resolve melted. Before she knew it she'd slipped off her top, her bra and panties, leaving them in a pile on top of the blanket. In the moonlight their bodies touched. She felt the hard abs press into her stomach, his groin splitting apart her legs. She grabbed his ass and squeezed his cheeks as she pressed herself into his chest.

He picked her up. She looked over his shoulder and didn't see anyone on the beach, but would she be able to tell? Did it matter?

Like a sea creature taking his prey out to a watery

kingdom, he waded waist-high into the white foamy surf and then let her body slide down the length of his until she was in the water. The initial shock of the cold surf made her jump, but he held her, and warmed her as he pressed her to his chest. With steam coming off his flesh he made his body into a raft and pulled her up on top of him. She held on to his neck as his powerful arms pulled them out beyond the swirling surf.

Her shuddering subsided as she got used to the chilly water.

It was quiet except for the lapping sound of the un-broken swells. The distant pounding of the ocean against the sand accentuated her heartbeat. They were treading water together, legs and arms entangled and then parted. He touched her all over. She rolled over on her back next to him and they floated, looking up at the stars.

Never done this before. Never felt the ocean as my bed. Never floated with a lover and gazed at the stars. She could feel the ocean breathe.

What was happening?

They lolled in the water for several minutes. He swam a few strokes away from her and then came back for a kiss. Each kiss seemed to get longer and longer, until at last they were entwined again. She mounted him again as his powerful arms kept them both afloat. Weightless, she tried to move up and down on him, but settled for just being filled with his girth. She could see his teeth gleaming in the moonlight.

"You are a fish," she whispered. He grinned and moved his hands over her buttocks.

"But I'm so glad I have hands," he said as he caressed her, "and legs."

She started when Coop pressed a thumb against her anus. He didn't force himself to penetrate, but waited for her. She looked into his eyes. Could she trust him? Hitching her breath, she didn't pull away from him.

Cooper lifted her body up, and then pulled her down on him again, his hands gripping her upper thighs and hips. He looked into her eyes as he pressed her to his groin.

After several wonderful moments, Cooper spoke into her ear. She was still impaled on his cock, loving the feel of him inside her.

"I need traction," he hissed.

"Yes," she returned.

They swam to shore, retrieved their clothes and the blanket, and ran to the trailer. He had to fish through his pants to find the key. She leaned her naked body against his bare ass while he worked the lock. At last the door opened, with a guttural moan, and she was brought inside his man-cave. Bay seemed resigned to catching up on his sleep and paid little attention to either of them. She saw an odd bouquet of flowers mounted on a wall bracket next to a small gas stove/microwave combo unit. Lines of blue Kerr jars decorated the wall in a wooden hand-made rack. They were filled with packets of sugar, salt and pepper, and matchbook covers from local businesses. She thought it odd this huge guy lived in such a tiny space and collected sugar packets and matches. But she felt safe here, for some reason.

"We need to get rid of the wet and sandy," he said with cool efficiency. He led her to a tiny bathroom with a fiberglass shower stall rigged with a spray wand. The skylight was opened and she could see the dusting of stars through the portal as he turned on the warm water and began to soap down her body. His silky fingers smoothed over her flesh and made her crave more.

He kneeled as he soaped her sex, and then covered her body with the warm jet from the spray wand. The water continued to sluice down her chest, legs and arms. He spread her knees apart slowly, and licked between her lips. The sandpaper of his tongue rubbed over her nub. His warm breath stimulated every cell. As he inserted his tongue she leaned into him and gave him everything she had.

"God. That feels wonderful."

"Yes."

Cooper's stiff cock stood ready. He was still kneeling in front of Libby, but reached over with his long arms and found a foil packet in his medicine chest over the sink. His shoulders were hard as she smoothed soap over his neck and upper back, feeling the rippling muscles moving under her fingertips. After he covered himself, he worked fingers into her opening as his tongue laved her. She began to shudder.

He rose, gently turned her around and bent her over, pressing her into the fiberglass wall of the small shower. He placed himself at her sex from behind. His powerful hands held her hips in place, as he plunged in. She spread her legs to the side to accept him deeper. He pumped her from behind for several minutes until the water began to get cold. She loved the feel of the plastic wall smashing her breasts as his muscled torso and powerful hips urgently commanded her.

Libby turned off the faucet and pushed herself back onto Cooper, who sat on the tiny shower ledge behind her. It was barely big enough for one butt cheek. His massive hands were all over her breasts, squeezing, tweaking the nipples with his fingertips.

At last, a climax gripped her body. She pressed back to get as much of him as she could. She panted into the damp shower wall, screamed as he rammed inside her. His spasms were hard, as he stood, pressing her into the smooth fiberglass enclosure again. He bit her neck without breaking the skin as he finished filling her.

She was sated, for now, but the raw need of him had scared her, even as it made her feel wonderful. She knew, as they dried each other off without saying a word, that perhaps she had finally found a man she would not be able to get enough of.

There was a threshold she'd just walked through as a new fear emerged. She preferred this new fantasy to the reality of what was smart.

And that scared her even more.

CHAPTER 8

D R. BROWNLEE SORTED through the previous day's mail in the shower of morning sunlight coming through their kitchen window. The coffee was strong this morning because he made it that way. Libby hadn't come home last night and he was stewing about it. He heard the familiar footsteps of his wife coming down the stairs.

"You're up early," Carla Brownlee said. She grabbed a mug from the cupboard, pouring herself a cup of the dark brew.

"Um." Dr. Brownlee was engrossed in his sorting, trying to concentrate, hoping there weren't another one of those disturbing letters. He didn't want his wife to find it, if there was. Phone bill and gas bill to the right, a magazine to the left. Two catalogues in the front for his wife to grab. A couple of handwritten letters from someone unknown, both with hand-drawn smiley faces where the return address should be.

Oh fuck, another two.

"You have trouble sleeping last night?" she asked him.

"Not really," he lied, as he slipped the letters inside the psychology trade magazine. Truth was, he had hardly slept at all. He couldn't stop thinking about the SEAL who'd visited his home, daring to accuse him of drinking too much and being disrespectful of his dead brother. He'd been up most of the night ruminating over the young man's words.

"Maybe he didn't die for you."

Dr. Brownlee looked up. His wife was waiting for an answer he didn't want to give.

"You thinking about the SEAL or Libby?" So she had checked Libby's bedroom, too, and found the bed unused.

"Both of them," he replied. "I think she's at Gen's house."

"That's what she said." Carla turned her back to him and walked over to the French doors leading to her bright flower garden. The hiss of sprinklers was the sound he'd heard all night. He hoped her flower garden had survived the deluge.

"I'll call him later on today," he said as he neatly stacked the mail.

"Who?" His wife turned back to face him.

"The new guy. The gardener. Obviously he isn't as

experienced as he said he was."

"Oh." She shrugged.

"God, Carla. You don't think I would call that fuckin' sailor, do you?"

"And why wouldn't that be a good idea? Austin, your manners were horrible. And I've never seen you drink so much in front of a perfect stranger before. If I'd done it, you would say something to me about it." She sauntered over to him, letting her fuzzy yellow robe untie, exposing the fact that she had on a very sheer nightie he'd not noticed before. "You know you've been distracted," she said as she drew his hand up to her breast, and then maneuvered it down between her legs.

He sucked in air so quickly he almost started to cough. His libido was back.

Thank God I won't have to use the little blue pills today.

Maybe fear and worry were good for his sex drive. Not likely, though.

AUSTIN BROWNLEE CAME downstairs, preparing for a swim after a very enjoyable romp with his wife. He was even more in love with her body now than the first time she'd given herself to him twenty-five years ago in that cheap hotel in Coronado. He'd just grabbed the first room he could find that evening, they were so hot for each other.

But their sex life had changed in the last few years. Some of the passion subsided as his practice grew. He not only had a string of huge successes, he also had some gargantuan failures. It was some of the failures he couldn't get out of his mind, especially the patients he'd lost to suicide. He'd often replayed their sessions, wondering what he could have done here and there, to perhaps save them from the ultimate choice of ending themselves. He'd only had a handful. But that handful was tormenting him to the point that he entertained suicidal thoughts himself. It had begun as a fleeting thought, but now stuck with him day and night like a thick oil sludge. His dark side bubbling up and contaminating his decent life. God knew, he recognized all the signs.

And now these letters started coming. He'd read them after his swim. Almost sounded like one of Dr. Dolan's patients that he'd asked Brownlee to take over. He wasn't interested in immersing himself in someone else's failures. He had enough of his own.

He halfway thought maybe he ought to get help himself. Maybe it was a mid-life crisis thing. He'd been so happy. Their son was married and had a successful career. Libby was happy at Santa Clara, and going to follow in his footsteps. He was hoping some day to have her be part of his office, if that's what she wanted to do with her life.

Out of the corner of his eye he noticed glass glinting in the morning sunlight. He'd left a tumbler on the mantle next to Will's picture. He hesitated as he got close to that picture, as if it was his own face staring back at him in that uniform, sporting the smug smile. The thought of how Will died made him sick to his stomach. His eyes stung.

He placed his forehead against the mantle, closed his eyes and prayed. "Please. Give me peace." A friend had recommended AA, but he felt he was too high-profile to try it.

Not yet.

He looked at the photo again. Will had not changed. God, he wished he could talk to his twin. His best friend.

All throughout their growing up, Will had excelled at sports. Although they played on the same teams, Will had all the playing time. He was the one who made the huge plays that counted, the MVP. But while Will had the athletic edge, Austin's grades were just a little bit better. He was usually ranked one, two or three in all his classes, and while Will did well, he wasn't outstanding.

They looked alike, which was fun, because the girls they dated never could tell the difference. They acted alike. Austin didn't mind getting the congrats as he walked down the hall, congrats intended for his brother. They halfway thought maybe they could continue their friendship and healthy competition by attending the same schools and remaining roommates in college. They'd talked about it many times.

He remembered the day they got the first of the letters. Both of them had applied to Stanford, UCLA and Berkeley. In a twist of fate the responses came within a week of each other. Austin got three acceptances, including a combination financial aid/scholarship package from Stanford. Will got three rejections.

The next week, Will enlisted in the Navy, and before Austin's classes started in the fall, was off to basic training in Michigan.

Could I have helped him with the grades? He felt guilty, but Will said he was having the time of his life jumping out of planes and helicopters and doing shit Austin was afraid to even think about. Will also wanted to be a doctor, and the Navy was going to see to it he could. But after Will's death Austin had survivor's guilt. It almost derailed his scholarship at Stanford until he realized his brother would be furious with him for squandering an opportunity he'd been given.

Thank God Carla had come along just at the right time. He'd met her the summer between his junior and senior year, when she'd come out to visit a friend living in San Diego. And it had been the right thing, too. After they'd fallen in love, he'd focused on his studies, his new girl, and, then later on his family and his practice. And he'd tried not to look back.

But now old wounds were being re-opened. Brownlee didn't like God's sense of humor, nor the knife stuck in his gut. Especially now.

Fucking KA-BAR with Will's name on it. He could just imagine what that sucker looked like. He could see it in the SEAL's grip.

Enough! With a sigh, Brownlee tied the string on his swimming shorts and walked through the kitchen barefoot, across the covered patio to the pool area. The sprinklers shut off. A fluffy yellow towel was draped on the chaise. He grabbed it as he made his way across the paver tiles to the pool's edge.

He was looking at a spot of red on the towel when he saw a dark shadow in the bottom of the pool. A small animal.

Libby's cat.

THE POLICE WERE respectful to the good doctor who had helped them profile some dangerous nut jobs. Brownlee knew they hadn't taken the situation very seriously when he'd called them. But when he told them who he was and how he had helped Detective Clark Riverton, who was a legend in the San Diego PD, profiling some pretty notorious killers, they agreed to come right over. Riverton was out of town until tomorrow. Brownlee intended to tell him about the letter he'd tossed and the two waiting for him in the magazine. It upset him that he'd tossed the first letter into the fireplace; it had been an unprofessional and uncharacteristic lapse in judgment.

Even if it was a child or an adolescent—anyone who caused the death of an animal, especially a pet that would come up to strangers, trusted humans, and liked to rub against everyone's legs at the drop of a hat as Noodles had done—a person who would destroy a pet like that would grow up to be very violent, if they weren't already. It was a pattern of criminal behavior every student learned about in Psych 101.

He'd seen a number of his patients after they'd been incarcerated for doing such things, or worse. It devastated their families. It was as if everyone in the family was placed behind bars.

Even though the detective said it wasn't, Brownlee thought this was personal. He just wasn't sure whether it was against Libby, or him. He would call her; make sure she was somewhere safe. Or...*Oh. My. God.*

"Yessir?" Detective Bamer looked up from his notes.

"Libby. My daughter Libby." Brownlee was short of breath from the quick run across the lawn. "This is

Libby's cat. She didn't come home last night."

The detective was going to call something into his shoulder radio when Brownlee heard his daughter's screams coming from inside the house. With a mixture of relief and sadness, he saw her run toward the edge of the pool, where the small, dark body of the wet feline lay on a yellow plastic sheet. It was guarded by a member of San Diego's finest, one who was way too short for his girth.

"Noodles!" she screamed. It broke his heart. She ran past him, sank to her knees and wailed over the dead animal. "No. No."

Brownlee was filled with panic and stood watching his daughter unravel, unable to move. She was hysterical. He wasn't sure what to do.

Carla ran past the doctor on her way to her daughter's side, giving him The Look.

"Carla," Brownlee whispered as he caught Carla's arm and pulled her back to his side. "Where's she been?"

"She's been with *Him*."

"Shit," he whispered. It got the attention of the investigating detective.

"Now is not the time, Austin. Would you just shut up for once?"

She was good at showing him non-verbally something he could never say to any of his patients: "*Are you out of your mind?"*

AN HOUR LATER, all the police and rescue workers left the Brownlee back yard. A report had been made. Libby had gone upstairs with Carla. He heard the two women talking in whispers, an occasional sob punctuating the echoes.

Like the whispers in my own head. Perhaps he was losing it, after all. He knew many of his patients heard these whispers, commanding them to do things. Unspeakable things. Could one of them have killed Libby's cat?

After verifying it was after three o'clock—his personal rule governing when he could have his first drink before dinner—he poured himself what he knew would be the beginning of several drinks of the day. Dinner would take care of the first buzz. The second buzz would put him into a comatose sleep, until he woke up sweating at about three in the morning, unable to sleep again. He knew he needed help. As a doctor, he recognized it. As a patient, he was powerless over the grip of the fear immobilizing him.

With his drink in one hand, he sat back down at the table and continued his mail perusal. There were those two smiley-faced letters. He took a sip of courage, inhaled and slit open the first one with a steak knife. He pulled the letter from the envelope. Did he really want to know what it said?

Hell yes. Denial again. He wasn't afraid of anything. Not yet.

Placing his hands in sandwich baggies so he wouldn't taint the evidence, he slipped the letter out from the envelope. A single piece of paper. Perfumed. Something familiar about it. On pink stationery. The letters were cut out of magazines and formed the message:

Y-O-U W-I-L-L P-A-Y

The other message was just as brief:

G-E-T R-E-A-D-Y F-O-R H-E-L-L.

He'd thought perhaps someone had found out he'd donated to the Women's Free Health Clinic. Perhaps they got a copy of all their benefactors and sent out hate mail. But this was definitely more personal. Seeing his daughter's cat at the bottom of the pool, and hearing her anguished screams did feel like Hell itself.

He gulped down the rest of his drink and stared at the letters.

Why? For a mistake I made? He couldn't think of anyone with this level of anger that was not institutionalized. He scanned his files, mentally. Could not find any animal abusers he was treating, or treatments that had gone wrong. Except for the ones he couldn't stop from taking their own lives. Those haunted him daily.

He slipped the notes back inside their envelopes, and tucked the two envelopes inside the bills and took them to his study. Opening up a file drawer, he slipped the bills and the notes in the To Be Paid file and re-locked the drawer.

The little headache that had niggled around the back of his head now came on strong, pounding his skull at the temples. He'd go see his friend on the force and show him the letters. Tonight he needed to be with his women.

Carla closed the door to Libby's room behind her as he rounded the top of the stairs.

He took her in his arms and held her while she wept silently. His big hand rubbed through her hair, finding the top of her spine, where he massaged her neck while he held her.

"Who is doing this, Austin? Do you know?"

"I have no idea."

"Why?"

"Someone deeply disturbed." He sighed. "I'll go see Clark at the precinct. Maybe he will give me something to look for."

She drew back to stare into his eyes. "Look for? You think you know this person somehow? One of your patients?"

He didn't want to answer that question, but he could see she'd figured it out. Twenty-five years of marriage made it easy for her to spot his fear, to intuit what he feared. He'd learned long ago it was useless to hide his feelings from her. She read him like a book. The way he wished he could read his patients.

"Maybe," he whispered. "But no one that I'm aware of." He held her face between his palms. "Carla, no one, understand? I wouldn't be treating someone like this without precautions."

She nodded.

He felt like a heel, but he didn't want to tell her about the letters. Maybe the cat caper would satisfy the pervert. Or, maybe there was evidence on the letters the police could use to catch the guy. Either way, he didn't want Carla alarmed. He would tell her to take precautions tonight, after they'd had a family meal, and after his head cleared. In the meantime, he'd set up a meeting for tomorrow with his friend in the San Diego Police Department. He'd also be rehearsing that speech to Carla several times.

It was going to be nearly impossible to get Carla out of the house, but he knew it was time to face the reality of their situation. He had to make her understand, without showing her the letters.

If that was possible.

CHAPTER 9

T HE NEXT DAY, Dr. Brownlee knew Detective Clark Riverton was not happy about his call, and had probably spent the morning cleaning up his office in preparation for their meeting. It was Sunday, after all, and Brownlee had insisted they meet at the detective's office, not the Brownlee home. That made it more official. And meant he didn't yet have to tell his wife and daughter about the letters.

The surface of Riverton's dented metal desk was hardly ever exposed, not like today. The detective's man-cave was a perpetual cleanup in process, one never completed. The desk's soft plastic top was perfect for pressing hard when filling out quadruplicate forms for the Department. Over the years he'd seen the man grip his medium point blue pens and press so hard, as if to savor making indentations in the soft grey surface beneath. After coming back from an interview or profile meeting, Brownlee would watch the detective rummage for a patch of desk surface, and fill out those reports. It was totally unnecessary in this day and age of computers, which of course could be altered with a keystroke.

The good old days.

He was struck by how heavy Clark had gotten. He'd gained as much weight as Brownlee had lost. Riverton stood and extended his hand.

"Austin. Good to see you. We're overdue." He pointed to a chair and Dr. Brownlee sat down as the metal groaned beneath him. He suspected these chairs were uncomfortable for a reason. Riverton wasn't the chit-chat type of cop.

"Thanks, Clark. Sorry to bother you on a Sunday," Brownlee said while rearranging his legs. It did no good. He decided to get right to it. "I've got something going on."

"Okay. Saw the report about your daughter's cat. Not good. Not good at all."

"Agreed. That's why I'm here."

A series of rings distracted Riverton. He wrinkled his forehead as he searched the outside nearly deserted room. Several lines ringing continued. He swore.

"Just a minute, Austin. I gotta get someone on these damned phones. Been crazy over here all morning."

He yelled at one of the female staff. "Helen, the

phones!"

She delivered him a murderous look while she slowly ambled toward a headset. A pair of detectives were drinking coffee in another office and came out to give her a hand.

"Thanks, guys."

Riverton closed the door behind him, adjusted his wrinkled tie, and deposited his frame in the cracked leather swivel chair. He gave full attention to his friend. "Sorry."

Brownlee looked at his lap, pulling out a plastic baggie containing two envelopes. He handed them across the desk. "You'll want to look at these. I got them yesterday."

The detective slipped on a pair of gloves and opened the sealed freezer bag. Side by side, he laid each letter over the envelopes they came in, and looked back and forth between them.

"Jeez, Austin."

Brownlee began, "I got the first one on Wednesday of last week, but tossed it. These two came yesterday morning. I opened them after we found the cat."

"They came after the cat was killed?"

"No. They were already at my house when I found the cat." Brownlee took a smaller baggie out of his inside jacket pocket. "And then I got this one first thing this morning. It didn't come in the mail, of course. It was left in my box sometime last night or this morning."

Clark opened the offered bag and laid the contents on top. There was a photocopy of a picture. A man's muscular fist was around the neck of a grey and white tabby cat. The cat's body was limp. A tattoo of a three-toed frog tracks extended from the man's wrist to the inside of his elbow.

"I've seen this tat before," Riverton said.

"Where?" Dr. Brownlee asked.

Riverton fired a look that drilled all the way to Brownlee's soul. "On my dead brother-in-law."

Brownlee didn't know what to say.

"He was in the Navy. Special Forces. In Afghanistan, about four years ago."

"I'm sorry."

Riverton looked back at the picture in his hands.

"That was—is—Noodles, Libby's cat," Brownlee said.

Riverton slowly shook his head. "He's one sick bastard."

Brownlee knew by the expression on Riverton's face this wasn't going to have a happy ending. "I gotta ask you, Austin. Why the hell did you wait until you had a dead cat and three letters to show me?"

His shrugged. *Denial? Yeah, probably.* He felt tired, defeated. "No reason, Clark. Just thought it would blow over."

"And the last time one of these fuckers just rode off into the sunset without killing someone human, was when, exactly?"

Did Riverton think he was an idiot? His right eye twitched.

"Austin, look, I know you are one helluva psychiatrist, but you know as well as I do, this is a police matter now. Besides which, you're too damn close to work this case or try to do things on your own. You don't mess around with these types. Ever. You understand?"

"Yes. So, where do we start?"

"*We* don't start anywhere. You're out."

"That's not possible. This involves my family."

"These situations always involve someone's family. Hell, I don't have to tell you that. Someone's family knows about this guy, and has overlooked the symptoms. Gave him the benefit of the doubt and now he's out causing all kind of havoc for innocent people."

Innocent people? What if I'm guilty?

"So, I'm supposed to sit on my hands?" he said. He was getting irritated.

"You won't like this answer. I'm going to need a profile of all your patients."

Brownlee shook his head and held up his palms. "Can't do that."

"Yes you can, if it will save a life."

"I think the guy is targeting *me*, and isn't a danger to the public."

"That's horseshit and you know it, Austin." Riverton held up the picture of the cat. "He's already a danger to the public. See what I mean about being too close?"

He knew Clark was right. Just didn't want to think about it more than he had to.

"You got a monitoring system on the house? Cameras?" Clark queried.

"Wouldn't have helped the cat any."

"Fuck's sake, Austin. I'm not thinking about the goddamned cat!"

"I'll look into it," Brownlee said, adjusting his collar and rolling his shoulder.

"You better treat this seriously, Austin. And watch everything going on around you, even if you think it doesn't matter."

"Okay, point taken. But, I don't think it's someone I'm treating. Clark, you have to give me some credit. I'd spot this guy a mile away."

Riverton leaned back in his chair. "I understand. I might even agree with you. But we just can't take any chances. I think you seriously should consider moving out of your house. Take a vacation. You need to get away from here and let us do the job we get paid to do."

He'd never get Carla out of the house. There had to be some other way. He didn't want to let this letter-writing cretin feel like he'd won. If he could spare telling Carla about those letters, he would.

Not a chance. Have to tell her now. Tell her tonight.

"Clark, we're not going anywhere. We stand and fight," he said at last.

"This isn't a war, Austin."

"Oh, no?"

"Look—you recognize the signs—this guy wants to get caught. He'll keep doing this until he does. He can't help himself."

"My only concern is for my wife and daughter."

"Exactly. Glad you're thinking straight. I'm worried about the whole lot of you, even if you're not. *They've* got to leave. If you won't go, then please, Austin, make sure *they* do."

DRIVING HOME, DR. Brownlee didn't know how to tell his wife he agreed with his detective friend. He'd have to dynamite her from the property. It would be easier to transplant their twenty-five year old fruit orchard and her flowerbeds than get her to leave. But he had to try.

Or, he could hire a private security firm to watch the house. He knew Carla would hate feeling like she was in prison. So would he. Maybe get some cameras and monitors added to his alarm system. Yeah, that might work. And if it didn't?

He had to discuss it with her before Riverton's team came over tomorrow to interview the three of them.

If she had to move, he wasn't sure how he'd protect her unless they stayed together. It wouldn't work to have her move and him stay behind to help catch the guy, so that option was out. Libby would be back in grad school, living with her roommate off campus, but probably rarely alone. She would be safe enough. Brownlee doubted she was the target, anyway.

He didn't like either option. He didn't like not being in control, not that he didn't trust the police and his friend of twenty-plus years. He just knew he was likely to notice things they would miss. If he was not there, how would those instincts be able to help?

As he approached his house, he saw a red scooter parked up by the rollup door at the end of the driveway, making it impossible for him to enter his own garage. Anger welled up. That damned SEAL had already inserted himself in his family, no doubt using his charm on his wife and daughter.

Briskly striding over the patterned concrete stones leading from the garage, he made it to his front porch just as the antique metal and glass door opened and out stepped the SEAL, towering over him.

Sneaky bastard, visiting with my wife and daughter while I'm away.

"Excuse me, sir. I'm afraid I left the scooter in your way." The Navy man averted his eyes.

"Damned right, son." Brownlee watched the SEAL fist both hands, leaving them at his sides. "Our guests usually park in the street, where it doesn't interfere with our needs. You *do* understand that don't you, son?" Cooper stepped as close to him as he could without touching. "I take offense being called your son. *Sir.* Besides, I'm not here to visit you. I came to see Libby."

"Well isn't that just what a father wants to hear?" Dr. Brownlee stared up at the towering giant and tried to grin. He was counting on the element of control being on Cooper's side.

He wasn't disappointed.

"I'm going to move my fucking bike." Cooper finally said, breaking eye contact as he stepped around him. The SEAL walked the scooter across the Brownlee's lawn and parked it at the edge a flowerbed, kickstand firmly on concrete, but *not touching* the street.

You Navy asshole. Somewhere deep inside Brownlee knew that his brother Will, if he were angry, would have done the same.

"You think *I'm* tough?" Brownlee started, "You'd

better hope that thing doesn't fall into my wife's flowers. You'll get a piece of her mind you won't forget. She tends those flowers like her life depends on it."

"Yeah?" Coop said as his gangly frame ambled up the pathway like a huge dancer, on his way toward the front door. He put his hands on his hips and forced a grin. "I guess I'd play with flowers all day long if I was married to the likes of you."

"You fucking asshole. I think…"

"Austin!" The sound of Carla's voice punctured the air. Libby stood just behind her mother on the porch landing. Both the women were looking at *him,* not the giant who wore that stupid victory grin.

Then Carla leveled her gaze at Cooper. "Both of you ought to be ashamed. Acting like a couple of grade school kids on the playground. Grow up." She left the porch and Libby ran outside and into the arms of the SEAL. No mistaking the signs of a budding relationship between the two, Brownlee noted. It made him sick to his stomach.

Cooper was whispering in his daughter's ear, and, as much as Brownlee wanted to hear the words, he also didn't. It hurt that the sailor was being the one to console his daughter who had spent most of last night in tears over the loss of her cat. Tears Brownlee couldn't stop for her.

Brownlee retreated to his car, started it up,

punched the door clicker, and parked inside. He sat for a moment in the silence and the darkness of his garage. How had his world gone so completely off-kilter? When did it change? Then he did the unthinkable. He had that thought he counseled people all day about. But he couldn't help it.

Why me?

He vowed it was time stop being a victim and to start taking control.

CHAPTER 10

LIBBY NOTED THE grim expressions on the faces of both Cooper and her father as they entered the house. Coop's eyes softened as he gave her a slight nod, not to worry. She was so glad he'd called and that he had been available to come over. She blushed when she thought about their night of sex. The blush must have shown, because her father's expression had gone dark, and it frightened her. He was angry. She knew he was the loose cannon in the room.

Her mother arrived from the kitchen with a glass of ice water and offered it to Dr. Brownlee, who winced, but took it anyway. Cooper had his arm around Libby, rubbing her shoulder gently. It calmed her. She felt the delicious ripple down her spine as her body responded to his touch.

God, I need him.

"I've asked Cooper to stay for dinner tonight, Austin," Mrs. Brownlee said.

"Great. Just great," her father answered, without looking at the SEAL. "I'm going upstairs to change. Don't let me interfere with your little party. Be down in a couple of minutes."

"What in the blazes is the matter with you?" Carla asked. "You don't need to change, Austin." Her forehead wrinkled.

"It's *me*," Cooper inserted. "Thanks for the invite Mrs. Brownlee, but I'm going."

Libby grabbed his hand but he didn't react.

"You just got here," she said.

Before anyone else could speak, Mrs. Brownlee blurted, "Cooper, I want you to stay."

Libby braced herself for a huge altercation. She thought Coop and her mom might have words. Her mother turned on her husband and added, "I'm not going to do this again, Austin. We will all talk and have dinner like *civilized* people."

Libby wondered what that meant in real terms. She squeezed Coop's hand again, and this time was rewarded with his tightened grip. Then he threaded their fingers together, and she felt the familiar dull ache for him in the pit of her stomach.

"I'm going to get my *civilized* clothes on now, and then I'll be down." Her dad stomped up the curved stairway and disappeared at the landing on top. Her mom excused herself and followed him up in a huff.

Cooper turned to face her. "I should just leave. Your dad hates my guts," He whispered.

"No, he doesn't. I don't know what's going on with him. He's stressed."

"Doing a pretty good job stressing out your mother, too. Really isn't fair. Besides, you're the one who lost your cat. You'd think he could be a little more—I don't know." He followed her to the kitchen. Sounds of arguing filled the air, coming from upstairs. They were having one of their legendary fights, although it had been years since Libby had heard the kind of vitriol that had erupted this week.

"Sorry you have to hear this, Coop."

"The police have any leads on what happened?" he asked.

"They only came over because my dad is an official friend of the Department. I'm not convinced they think there is anything to it. Maybe there is no boogey man. It could have been an accident," she said.

"Cats don't swim, Libby."

"Exactly. So maybe he fell in."

"You ever see or hear of a cat falling into a pool? I don't like it at all," he said as he shook his head.

She couldn't help it. The tears started to come. The image of the fluffy cat who had warmed her bed every night she was home from college, who played with her in the back yard as a kitten, saddened her. She would never see him again. How could someone want to destroy this gentle creature?

Cooper pulled her close, holding her tight to his chest. "I'm sorry. I'm so sorry," he said as he laced his fingers through her hair. "I wish I'd been here yesterday for you."

"Cooper," she said to his shirt pocket, "they are doing everything they can. Dad went down there this morning and talked to his detective friend. Don't worry."

"Can't help it. I do that for a living. I'm trained to react to threats, to protect the innocent."

True. But in the state the world was in, the loss of one little cat hardly seemed significant. She worked to buck up her courage.

"Come on, let's go outside." Libby said. She could still hear the heated discussion her parents were having upstairs. She wanted to get away from the discord.

Libby stepped backwards, pulling both his hands. She studied the tall man walking towards her with a lopsided grin. For a few precious seconds she got the impression he'd follow her anywhere. All too quickly his composure returned and he dropped his hands, but put an arm around her waist and drew her to him.

"I'm not very comfortable hanging out where I'm not wanted."

"You're wanted."

He squeezed her close to him. "Your parents. I'm talking about your parents."

"He'll get over it. Besides, I thought being where you're unwanted is what you did for a living?"

"That's my job. This is social."

"Thank God! Although it would be a pleasant fantasy if I needed protection, and you were assigned that detail," she said as she leaned sideways into his chest. They kept walking.

"Hmmm. That would be interesting…"

She loved the smell of him, his muscles moving against her side, the movement of his long legs at her hip, the way his voice rumbled in his chest when he said anything at all. In his presence she felt safe. Her biggest fear was that she would lose him in the end. She tried not to hope for too much, but couldn't help feeling she belonged right next to him. For now, that was going to have to suffice.

She knew this new relationship wasn't old enough to contain the bad parts. There were always bad parts. Her father's lack of acceptance of Cooper was only a tiny portion of that. But damn, the good parts were really good. Unbelievable.

"How would you protect me, if it was your job?"

He raised one eyebrow. "Why I think I'd have to search you for weapons first." His voice was getting husky.

"How would you search me?"

"I'd take you somewhere, like over here." He pointed to the storage building at the end of a crushed granite path. The old wooden structure was part potting shed, part greenhouse storage, and held a new riding lawnmower, and various gardening tools. He pulled her into the cool darkness. "I'd have to pat you down," he said as he rubbed her behind, then pulled her against his groin. He moved his palms to her chest and squeezed, then traced a finger up her neck, under her jaw and around to her hairline. Pulling her head towards him, he commanded a kiss from her.

Libby was lost in a swirl of scent and passion that left her dizzy. She drew both her arms up over his shoulders and crossed them behind his head. She pressed her breasts against him and felt the delicious erection tenting his pants as he rubbed against her belly.

"Wouldn't you have to remove all my clothes to be sure?" she whispered.

"Absolutely. A close examination would be in order. Can't be too careful."

"No. It could be dangerous if you didn't search me completely naked," she whispered to him between kisses.

"Very."

"But you'd be thorough. So I won't have to worry?"

He smiled. "You won't ever have to worry about me not being thorough."

She leaned back to get a good look at his eyes. In her heart the only worry she had was that this wouldn't last, that he would leave her. He watched her without a smile, letting her have his full attention, waiting for her to make the first move.

"I need to touch you, need your hands on me," she said.

He looked around the shed for a place to take her. An old bench sat in the corner, covered by a tattered oilcloth tablecloth. It was tucked away from the shed's opening. They walked over the hardened dirt floor and then he removed the old oilcloth and sat on the bench, his knees pointed out to the sides. Standing in front of him, she started to unbutton his cotton shirt, sliding her fingers up underneath his tee shirt, feeling the smooth ripples of his chest. Her fingers hungrily touched him, felt the indentation down the middle of his warm torso and then traveled below to his beltline.

Coop's hands found her panties beneath her skirt and looped a forefinger around the satin waistband, slipping them down her thighs. She stepped out of them and then climbed up onto his lap. The wooden bench was hard against her knees, so she balanced on his thighs to take the pressure off. His fingers found and massaged her opening. Lingering there, while making circles around her nub. His touch sent waves of pleasure up her spine as he slowly stroked her, and then penetrated her deeply with two fingers.

"I need you inside me," she said to the top of his head as he buried his face in the space between her breasts. His fingers deftly worked her clit and slid against her insides. In one smooth motion he'd removed her bra with one hand. Her nipples ached to be tasted. He laved one, and then the other. Their eyes met. She saw the desire burning inside him.

He needs this as much as I do.

He stood her up, leaving her sex feeling vacant. After removing his shirt and pants and laying them over the back of the bench, he searched his pocket, found the foil condom packet. Libby helped him cover himself as they kissed. It made her hot that he was prepared.

Then he picked her up and lay her down on top of the clothing, peeling her skirt up as she spread her legs for him. He smiled and then mounted and covered her with his naked body, positioning himself for entry. Looking down, he slowly thrust upward and deep, scanning her whole face as he filled her.

She needed him, pulled his buttocks closer as she felt her body melt under his kisses. Everything around her faded. She was consumed with the heat between them, the wonderful feel of his body claiming hers. No hesitation. She gave everything she had back to him.

He quickened his motions, kissing her neck, then watching her face as he plunged in and then withdrew in long strokes. Her body tingled in delight with each stroke. The more he pumped, the more she needed him.

"Cooper, Cooper…" He cut her off with a kiss, his tongue burrowing deep as he buried his cock to the hilt inside her. He groaned in her ear as he pushed himself deep.

A cell phone rang in the distance. She felt his body tense. In an instant he drew her to sitting position, slipped his pants on and put his finger to his lips for her to be quiet. Barefoot and bare-chested he walked in the direction of the phone ring. It came from a backpack hanging on a wooden peg by the door opening. When the ringtone stopped, he began searching the shed, darting a look around outside, without zeroing in on anything in particular.

Libby waited on the bench after retrieving her clothes, her body craving the man she saw before her, in spite of the fear that someone may have found them. A part of her didn't care what audience they had. But…

Who?

Cooper returned. "I don't see anyone. Whose backpack is that?"

"Have no idea." Then she remembered the landscaper her father had hired to repair the sprinkler system. "The gardener. But I haven't seen him today."

"I think we should leave."

"You want to check out the backpack?"

"No. I don't want to touch it." He was working on relaxing himself, and her. "Come on, let's go back to the house."

She was sorry the mood had been broken. Fully clothed, they left the shed to enter the late afternoon golden glow of the sunset. They held hands, stopping to look at her mother's flower garden, listening to the sounds of the crushed granite pathway as they walked along it on the way back to the kitchen.

The back door was ajar. Inside, the house was quiet. They heard sounds of a dust blower outside. She pointed toward it and mouthed, "The gardener." She listened, but couldn't hear her parents arguing any longer.

Her mom appeared at the doorway to the kitchen, her eyes red from crying. "Austin has gone to his office. He said he was going to eat later."

"Mrs. Brownlee, that's okay. Don't worry about it," Cooper said evenly.

"I'm so sorry, Cooper. My husband is very confused right now. He is not himself," she answered.

Libby stepped forward and engulfed her mother in an embrace. "It's okay, Mom. No worries." The two women hugged each other, gently swaying. At last her mother broke away.

"Come, let's have a quick bite," her mother said as she wiped the tears from her face with the back of her hand. She dove into her cooking duties, removed salad fixings and a cooked chicken breast from the refrigerator. "I made some French onion soup this morning," she said as she removed a purple-lidded cast iron pot and placed it on the stove.

COOPER AND LIBBY waited until after dinner, making small talk, but the awkwardness and huge chasm created by Dr. Brownlee's leaving could not be overcome. Her mother set up a china plate and silverware at the dinette table for her husband in case he returned. Everyone took turns staring at that place setting during conversations, but Cooper avoided eye contact. Libby felt the strain too, watching how hard her mother was trying to stay upbeat. She wondered, for the first time in her adult life, if her parents were perhaps going through some marital problems she had somehow missed.

And Cooper was definitely in some internal pain. Libby could only guess the cause.

When the trio heard the sounds of the doctor's car entering the garage, Coop said his goodbyes quickly. Libby knew he didn't want any further communication with her father. Not tonight.

Maybe never.

He was in a hurry to leave.

"I'd like to go with you," she whispered at the front door. Coop looked over her shoulder first, and then searched her eyes.

"Not tonight. Think you need to be home with your parents."

She bristled. "Cooper, I want—"

"Shhh, baby. You know how much I want to be with you, but this isn't the time. This isn't right."

"But can't we go somewhere and talk about it, first?"

He still hadn't smiled back at her. "Somehow we don't seem to do a lot of talking when we're together." He softened as he looked at her lips. "It isn't just your dad. This is all wrong. The timing's wrong."

"Didn't seem to have any trouble with your timing in the shed." She was starting to boil inside. He was going to leave. She should let him leave, but she was pissed she'd given him so much and now was getting nothing from him in return.

"Don't do this, Libby." Then he adjusted his tone, "Some other time, but not now." He leaned forward and gave her a peck on her cheek. He drew her to him and whispered, "Libby, I…"

Libby pulled away. "That all you're going to say,

after what we've done?"

"Libby quiet. I don't want to discuss it. Please."

She couldn't help but watch his mouth as he spoke, remembering the electric tingle those lips made as he'd kissed her body. It was so unfair. She wanted to be angry but just couldn't do it.

"When are you coming back, then?"

"I'm not sure."

"Love 'em and leave 'em, that the way of it, sailor?"

"Libby, don't do this. It isn't right that I'm here. I should have thought about it before." She could see he was preoccupied as he heard the door to the kitchen swing open. "Gotta go."

The shock of what he'd just said began to make her knees turn to rubber. He embraced her again, kissed the top of her head, and then he was gone.

Libby pressed her forehead against the doorframe and felt like she'd been stabbed right through the heart. What if he never came back?

Of course he'll be back.

She stopped being brave and let the tears fall. Now her whole world was scrambled without a lifeline in sight.

CHAPTER 11

L IBBY'S HEART FELT like lead as she heard the sputter of Cooper's scooter fade down the tree-lined street. Her soul was bleeding from the inside out. She wondered if she would ever see the SEAL again.

And then the horrible thought hit her. Was this just an elaborate way to get into her pants? Could this man be trusted?

She thought about how quickly he'd had his way with her. This had never happened before. Here she was, having sex with a virtual stranger. For all she knew, he wasn't a SEAL at all, but a wannabe. She'd heard they were out there. But then she wondered how he would know about her uncle Will.

Was she substituting the loss of her mentor's care for something else? Reminding herself that she was the world's worst when it came to reading people correctly, she decided to err on the side of caution. After all, she'd decided to study psychology partly to learn about her own hang-ups. It was easier studying others than studying herself. Her father told her a lot of psychiatrists went into the field for the very same reasons.

Perhaps it's a good thing if he never comes back.

But, damn, the sex with Cooper had been scorching hot and filled a need she had never known existed.

Some things that are good for you are also bad for you.

Was Cooper one of those things? Was she being wise? Did she really want to know?

Her father appeared in the doorway. His eyes fell. His expression was grim and without a trace of warmth. Wrinkles on his upper lip puckered as he thought hesitated to speak. She hadn't noticed those little lines before. He sighed. "Brownie, we've got to talk. The three of us," he said.

"I agree," she replied, but what she really wanted was to run upstairs and fall into bed for a good cry.

Her dad put his arm around her shoulder. It felt odd, more like he was propping himself up against her than the other way around. They retreated into the kitchen.

Her mother dished up leftover lasagna and green salad as Dr. Brownlee sat in the breakfast nook, nodded at her mom's happy chatter and allowed the two women to wait on him. He sat with his right hand gripping the fork and his left clutching the knife, waiting for them to stop their fussing. He looked like he expected her mother to tie a napkin around his neck, as if he was a child of four.

"You need anything else?" Her mom was asking him about needing a drink. Libby saw that yes, he did want one, but he shook his head, *no*, instead.

"We need to talk. Sit down, you two." He pointed to two vacant dinette chairs with his fork. It seemed to take all the effort he had to get the two women to the table so he could eat.

Libby had gotten a soda from the refrigerator and joined her parents at the table.

"Now, about today and this sailor—" Dr. Brownlee began.

"That subject is off limits, Dad," Libby interrupted.

"Would you just *listen* to me at least?" Her dad set down his fork and sighed.

Her mother's worried gaze didn't ease Libby's fears. It was going to come off too harsh, so Libby adjusted the volume on her voice, and respectfully answered, "I'm listening, but I'm not a child." She was worried it sounded petulant.

"Libby, honey," her mother started, "No one is doubting your judgment."

"Exactly," Dr. Brownlee said. "With all this—this mess about the cat—well, Clark thinks we should consider some options. Most likely you'll be safe at school, but—"

"I'm not going back to Santa Clara," Libby interrupted.

"Excuse me?" her mother's forehead was creased and the little lines around her eyes sprang to life with her squint. "And what the hell options are you talking about, Austin?"

Dr. Brownlee looked back down at his dinner, scowling, but said nothing.

Libby continued, "I'm taking a semester off, maybe a whole year off. I'm not registered." She'd wanted to give them a more thorough explanation, but she was finding the right words difficult to come by.

Her father planted his forehead into his palm, with his elbow on the table. "Why for God's sake now, Libby?"

"You think I could have known about all this—" Libby waved her arm in the direction of the backyard and the turquoise pool where Noodles had been found.

"Of course not, honey," her mother softened. "It's just that the timing is—well, it couldn't be worse. And no, how could you have known?"

"I don't want to go into it," Libby continued. "You don't need to hear the sordid details with everything else that's going on around here. Let's just say I needed a break. It's a story for another time, perhaps." Libby could see it was still difficult for her mother to grasp.

"This have to do with the young SEAL?" she asked timidly, with a forced smile.

"No. I made this decision before I came home. Before I met him."

Dr. Brownlee's sour expression was difficult for Libby to stomach. He glanced up at his wife and then stared down at the rest of his dinner, pondering the pile of cheese and red tomato sauce like it was something from a horror film. Finally he pushed aside the plate.

Libby continued, softly at first to ease them into the idea. "I withdrew from the University a week ago," she confessed.

"I need a drink." Her dad got up and poured himself a tumbler and stared out the kitchen window at something. Libby could see and hear the sprinklers going off in the distance.

"Damn it all," he whispered as he adjusted his hips to lean against the countertop, swirling the ice cubes in the stubby crystal glass.

"You either get someone else to fix it or stop complaining," her mother answered. "Austin, can we just stay on point here? To hell with the landscaping."

That brought a smile to Dr. Brownlee's lips. He raised his glass to her. "That's my girl. Telling it like it is." He looked at Libby. "Your mother is so wicked lovely when she's focused. She could have commanded a battleship."

Her mom sat with her arms crossed, staring at her lap, shaking her head. Immune to his considerable charm.

He finished his drink in one long gulp, put the glass in the sink, and rinsed it off. Leaning against the counter, he spoke again. "Clark thinks we should move out of the house for a while. He isn't sure it's safe here."

Libby's mom bristled, her eyes widened in horror as she stood up. "What? I'm not moving out of this house! What do you mean by 'safe,' Austin? Why wouldn't it be safe?" Her hands were on her hips.

Dr. Brownlee peered across the kitchen island at her mother and displayed that affectionate smile that usually melted any female standing nearby. But it didn't work today, Libby could see. He motioned for Carla to sit back down, which she did in a huff.

Dr. Brownlee rolled his neck and then looked at Libby. "Maybe someone is targeting me. Could be after me for something. I'm thinking it's a whacko upset about the Clinic at Lavender House. Someone's got hold of the donor list—something like that. Anyhow, I think Clark agrees."

"But it was *my* cat," Libby interjected. Carla put her head in her hands, elbows leaning on the table.

The restraint in her father's voice sounded like a kettledrum. "How would anyone know that? Not like someone else lives here with us. You're—well you *were* away at college," he said. "The cat lives here."

Libby stared at her soda. She was definitely not away at college. She was here. Right here. As a matter of fact, she was at the beach, in the water, wrapped in the arms of...

"Good lord, Austin," her mother began, bringing Libby back. "So Clark thinks this is more serious. Something more than just the cat?" She hardened her gaze, glaring up at her husband like she was going to spring on him. "What are you not telling us?"

"Look, I think Clark is just trying to make sure we are paying attention."

"Attention?" Both Libby and her mother responded.

Brownlee hesitated, looking at the corners of the kitchen ceiling as though searching for a Heavenly ally. "He has to say that. He has to consider the worst-case scenario. Just wants us to be careful, be prepared."

Libby could see her mom wasn't buying the sell job her father was trying to promote. Carla crossed her arms, and tried again, "I still get the feeling you're hiding something from me, Austin." Libby heard the waver of her mother's voice, like a hand was placed around her throat.

She was right, of course. Something was seriously wrong. Her father's attempts to make light of it only intensified the eerie feeling in the room. There must have been something he wasn't telling her and her mother. He was obviously worried—distracted, really—beyond what he was saying. Something wasn't adding up. She looked between her parents for answers and found none.

"Nothing," Dr. Brownlee said with finality. "He's just being careful."

"But, where would we go?" her mother asked. Her voice had a brittle tinge to it.

"We have lots of choices. We could stay with Neil and Marsha," her father said.

"I'm not going to ask my son to put us up when they're expecting again and they've already got two other little ones under foot. That's not fair to them. Besides, Libby can't stay there too."

"I'll be fine. I'll find another place," Libby chimed in.

"I say we all stick together," her father said. "If we can't stay at Neil's, we can rent a place, find a vacation rental."

Some vacation that'll be. Take a vacation when we're all scared to death?

"I'm going to have a security specialist come over tomorrow. Friend of Clark's. In the meantime, we start using the alarm system every time we leave the house. Maybe we can borrow Neil's dog for a few days."

Libby knew something was seriously out of whack. No one in their family liked Neil's Pit Bull, who had a fondness for bare ankles and wasn't entirely housebroken.

"Austin, why all this... this precaution?" Libby's mom asked again, ignoring the dog comment.

Libby knew her mother's radar was functioning just fine. She had come to the same conclusion as Libby.

But her dad begged off an explanation. "Listen, Carla. Better to be safe than sorry. They've got investigations to do. They can't just drop everything and work on this cat incident." He looked over at Libby who shrugged back at him. She had cried herself dry. "Sorry, Libby, but they have rapes and murders to deal with. I think this is someone who wants to be cruel, just scare me for some reason. I know I'm the target."

Libby knew her parents would be up until all hours of the night discussing their plans.

And she needed Cooper now more than ever. In her own house, under the protection of her mother and father, who had always made her feel safe, she was suddenly afraid. Something dark was looming on the horizon.

After she went to bed, she thought she heard the mailbox open around midnight. When she went to her bedroom window, she saw red tail lights winking between the dark trees and shrubs of the street, disappearing around the turn.

There wasn't any sign of anyone lingering around. Moonlight made the cool metal glow with an eerie blue-grey hue.

The flag was down.

She checked the flashing red alarm light in the hallway anyway before turning into bed. She felt a chill wash over her body, and wished she could talk to Cooper. He would have something reassuring to say about all of this.

She needed him for more than the hot sex she didn't get enough of this afternoon. She needed his experience rooting out bad guys under pressure. Home no longer was the safe haven she'd been running to.

CHAPTER 12

PART OF HIM wanted to spend the night with Libby again. He couldn't get their lovemaking out of his mind. How her body responded to his, how he felt like part of his hard shell was cracking, softening to her touch. And he was filled with the growing need to protect her, like she belonged to him already.

But that was a stupid thought for a guy in his position. He couldn't offer any chance of a long-term relationship. All he could do was become a wedge between a father and his daughter. And for what?

He knew relationships were detrimental to his occupation. He needed his focus. The Navy was his life now, even more so since the loss of his family. He suddenly wanted to go back to work in the worst way. He didn't need to be reminded of what he no longer had.

But he knew Timmons wouldn't allow it.

How would he spend the next few days without

her? Even surfing, lying around on the beach, or working out at Gunny's, weren't appealing. Everything had shifted.

In the old days, he'd have gotten a new tattoo. The pain of the scabbing flesh would be a reminder of how mortal he was. He'd get hard watching Daisy and her huge tits, leaning over him, brushing against him, teasing him, and smiling without looking at his eyes. She had known he lusted after her long before they became intimate. Now, that was out of the question.

No, meeting Libby, being inside her, kissing her neck, her full lips, hearing her moan and feeling her shudder beneath him had ruined it for him with anyone else. Much as he tried to tell himself otherwise, he was tethered to Libby just as if he'd been hogtied physically.

He'd have to keep things in balance, though. He needed to slow things down, give himself time to think. He knew better than to go jumping into a long-term relationship, even though he realized he was powerless to stop himself. He'd never had that problem before. He'd always looked at his buddies, who'd gotten snagged by a cute little thing that came waltzing into their lives, and turned their man-caves into honeymoon suites. Was that what could happen to him?

He knew if he wasn't careful, he was about to experience a terminal case of...of... *What the fuck am I feeling?*

He couldn't deal with this any longer. He was certain his sorrow over the loss of his parents had drawn him right into the middle of Libby's life, and that was just not fair to her. He had nothing he could offer her. His tank was on empty. And he could see in her eyes that she expected—she deserved—so much more. He decided he'd just not call her back. He should have exercised better judgment before he'd taken advantage of her. Oh yeah, he'd taken advantage of her all right. He'd been an animal. Couldn't get enough.

And the reason he felt so bad was because, while he'd gotten what he wanted, he knew he couldn't give her what she wanted—needed. No fuckin' way he could do that.

Time to get numb. He decided to call his Team 3 LPO. Kyle picked up on the first ring. "Coop. How's your love life? Fredo thinks he got stood up Friday night."

Cooper knew Kyle's comment was intended to be a joke, but had misfired. "Yeah? Well, you'd have been proud of me Lanny. I got 'er done."

"That's mighty fine, my boy. Just what the doctor ordered. And did it help?"

"Nope. Think I'll get shit-faced tonight. You be my DD?"

"I'll be your mule, but you sure? Thought you gave

it up. You got some years invested in being sober."

"I changed my mind."

"Maybe you better rethink that one, Coop. Not tryin' to be your nursemaid…"

"Then shut the hell up, Lanny. Get off my fuckin' case."

"Oh, no you don't, SO. Remember, you called me. You're really starting to piss me off."

"I want to get shitfaced and then fucked. Royally fucked."

"I got you. I can't help you do either, but I can grab a cup of coffee with you."

"Fine." Everything was not fine. It sucked. Big time.

"Let me get permission and I'll call you back."

A few minutes later Kyle affirmed, with his new baby screaming in the background, that he was free to help slide Cooper into the delirium of an alcoholic stupor, if he insisted, and would respectfully deliver him back to his motor home at the end, even if he had to carry him.

THE SCUPPER WAS within walking distance of the beach. Cooper was on his third beer, Bay asleep at his feet, by the time Kyle arrived, and Coop didn't have an ounce of regret. Behind his LPO, Fredo swaggered in, wearing a ridiculously bright Hawaiian print shirt over jeans which barely covered his flip-flopped feet.

The Mexican Hawaiian.

Coop was happy to see his buddies. Been a while since Fredo tried another one of his legendary takedowns. Maybe he'd challenge him this evening. Most of the time Fredo, who was a foot shorter, won, but Cooper was of a mood to play hard tonight.

Fredo nodded and they touched knuckles. He whistled when he saw the beer. "You look terrible, Calvin," he said, "and you smell like dog, man."

Coop wondered if the waitress he'd tipped to allow Bay to stay with him, as a SEAL service dog, got a whiff of him before she said yes. Bay was too old, and way too fat to be considered a service dog. Maybe she'd thought Bay was a companion dog for a mental returning vet. But Molly had accepted his word.

Figures. He knew sure as hell he could pass for a mental.

Fredo was going on and on about the dog smell. This tickled him, a little. "Frodo," he said, referring to his buddy's nickname—one that the SEAL hated being called—"meet Bay. Bay, say hello to Frodo."

The dog popped his head up at the sound of his name, looked up at Fredo, and then examined Kyle, before laying his head over his paws with a big sigh.

"Frodo here's been in some movies, Bay. Be respectful and don't lift your leg on him, okay?"

The dog looked at the Mexican SEAL, who was

scowling like he'd been punched.

"You're in a nasty mood, Coop. What happened, Daisy get your penis all infected?"

Cooper was immediately on his feet. Kyle kicked him behind the knees to make him sit. "Enough. You're being stupid now. Both of you." He glared between the two best friends. "Shake on it," Kyle commanded. There would be full compliance with this direct order, but they didn't have to like it.

Fredo said something in Spanish and submitted his paw for the grip of his friend with hands twice the size of his.

Cooper found some of his humor filtering through the fog of his psyche. "Daisy only did one guy's penis, and it wasn't mine." He got the effect he was going for. Kyle winced and Fredo swore.

Bay yawned so wide it looked like his jaw was going to be unhinged. Coop noticed the dog's breath smelled like rotting cabbage. His two Teammates were wrinkling their noses.

"Come on, guys. Haven't had him groomed. He's only been in the ocean a few times. Haven't had time for a bath."

"No, dog lover, you're too damned cheap," Fredo said.

"What's the point? He's gonna get dirty again." Through the beer fog, Coop thought it was a plausible argument.

Fredo's eyes got wide with fire. "What's the point? You, the guy who dusts his floors with his toothbrush. Mr. don't-get-the-sand-in-my-duty-bag-kind-of-guy? The guy who reuses baby wipes—oh, yes, I've found those little brown used wipes at the bottom of your medical kit."

"Hate to waste the sanitizer."

"You're the guy who counts the dryer sheets. Don't tell me it isn't about money. And now this poor dog is suffering, you asshole!" Fredo looked genuinely worked up.

Cooper shrugged and turned back to his beer. Fredo grabbed the glass from him and finished it off. In a lowered volume, Fredo continued, "They got cute little chiquitas that take them and bathe them, paint their nails, too. Dude, you gotta give that dog some love, man. Your pimpmobile must smell like dog hair, man."

Cooper looked down at his empty glass and smiled. His bed smelled like Libby. He wasn't sure he would want to wash his sheets for weeks.

"Oh, God in Heaven," Fredo chuckled as their beers arrived. "I know that look. You been scoring for the last three days since you been back. I knew it! I told Gunny your pecker was going to fall off."

"Not quite."

"She lose her touch? Or is it someone new?"

"Come on, Fredo," Kyle interrupted. Cooper was starting to blush.

"Fuck me! It *is* someone new. You got yourself one of those Junior College chiquitas?" Fredo's eyes were sparkling.

"There's more to life than—" Cooper started to protest.

"Since when?" both Kyle and Fredo said in unison.

Kyle gave Fredo a look, and Coop knew that was going to be the end of the disrespectful banter. His leader was going to make sure Coop was right in the head. He'd start probing now. It didn't take long for the series of questions to begin.

"So, while you're able to talk, you never told us how it was back there. You have to go back anytime soon?" Kyle asked.

Coop filled his lungs and let the air out with a rush. He ordered more beers for all of them. "Buried them last Wednesday. Paid for coffins, but we never could find anything."

No one said a word. Kyle's eyes bored into him.

"You going to sell the land? Timmons told me nothing was left of the ranch and all."

"Nope. Keeping the dirt. They got disaster aid coming. I could have the farmhouse rebuilt, if I wanted to. It's gonna take four or five months to get it settled, but my folks actually left me some serious money." Coop felt guilty coming into so much money when he didn't need it, especially since it had been obtained through the death of his family. He had a sheaf of paperwork an inch thick at his trailer. He'd get to it when he good and felt like it.

"Where'd you find the dog...what's...?" Fredo asked.

"Bay."

Bay perked his ears but didn't raise his head.

"Sorry, didn't mean to dis your dog, man. You musta known he'd spend the last of his days at the ocean, Coop."

Kyle looked at Fredo with a question.

"He named him Bay. As in San Diego Bay?" Fredo said to Kyle, who was sporting a puzzled look.

Recognition crossed Kyle's face.

"Funny," Coop mumbled and took another swig.

"So, where did you find him?" Kyle asked.

"Near the farm, like he used to wait for me when I was a kid. He injured his right front paw, a cut of some kind. But he musta run like the wind and outrun the tornado." The group fell silent. Coop was more comfortable talking about Bay than talking about himself to his Team leader.

"I found him after the funeral. Thought I was hearing things when I went back to see the farm and heard him bark."

It was a grim reminder of odd things he'd seen—they'd all seen—overseas. A litter of puppies they'd saved when their mother got blown to bits. Babies crawling in the dust, being rescued by a soldier. Sharing water with a child only to find him murdered the next day. Things he didn't want to remember much. Things no one should have to try to forget.

The steady wheel turning, the circle of life and death came with them on every deployment. That and the randomness of the sorting process: who was going to live and who would die today.

Kyle squinted at Coop's comment and nodded, staring down the bubbles in his own barely touched beer. "Grief does funny things to a man."

"I'm right as rain." Coop defended his state of mind.

"Yeah, Timmons told me you'd say that," Kyle said without looking up. "And I agree with him. You're full of shit."

The comment smarted, but Cooper wouldn't let them see it. He had too much respect for his Team leader, who had saved his life on more than one occasion.

"I feel like ice cream. You want one? I'll buy," Fredo barked. Coop knew one of Kyle's favorite haunts was the Dunkin' Dandy frozen yogurt shop. Kyle couldn't resist the chocolate dipped soft swirls with sprinkles on top.

"What the hell. I promised Christy I was going to lay off the sugar, but if you promise not to tell her, I'm game."

The trio sauntered outside and down the sidewalk, Bay on his leash. The dog stopped at every parked car, sniffing and peeing more than Coop thought his bladder would hold. In between, he stopped for a pat from each passer-by.

"Dude, at this rate, we'll get there by tomorrow at noon, Coop. Can you tell him to stop being so social? Starting to act like a politician." Fredo was smiling, but Coop knew he was in a hurry for his ice cream.

"He's just getting used to things. He barks when I leave him behind."

"That dog's gonna be hoarse and then dead when you deploy. You gotta find someone to take care of him. I hear Daisy—"

Cooper cut him off. "No. I'll find someone else. She doesn't want a dog to take care of. She has a hard enough time taking care of all of us," Cooper said.

Fredo turned, shaking his head, pushing through the glass door of the yogurt shop.

Coop declined Kyle's invitation to enter, saying he was keeping an eye on Bay. After both his buddies were out of sight, he realized these two had saved him from a lonely night of drinking at the Scupper, getting into trouble on two fronts: alcohol and female. Neither of these two troubles would be a comfort to him in the long run.

Tonight, he'd chosen well. He was grateful. For the first time in the past week, he started to feel like he would make it, after all. Maybe there could be a normal life ahead of him. Although it had been something he appreciated before, he realized he had taken it a bit for granted.

You always miss stuff after it's gone.

And then he began to think about Libby. She'd called him. Maybe he could trust himself to call her back.

He'd sleep on it tonight. Wake up with a hangover tomorrow and then call her. Maybe tomorrow. Maybe the next day.

CHAPTER 13

CARLA PADDED OUT to the mailbox in her flip-flops. It was nearly nine o'clock Monday morning, and the mailman had just made his rounds.

Mrs. Brownlee was wearing the expensive silk robe her husband had brought back from Japan years ago. The smooth fabric caressed her bare skin underneath. She loved the feel of the sash as it cinched her waistline.

She and Austin had been experiencing an on-again-off-again married couple affair, between bouts of Austin's foul moods. On a warm sunny morning, as most days in San Diego were, she was grateful for the rise and fall of their shared emotions. Passion was strong in their family—all sorts of passions.

He'd taken off for an early appointment at the office. But not before he said he was sorry for several things yesterday, stopping short of apologizing for his tone with the SEAL. He finally admitted that perhaps he was overreacting about the cat incident. She was relieved he agreed that they'd stay at their house. Today, Clark Riverton's friend was coming by to check out the security and make some recommendations for their additional safety.

She opened the mailbox flap and immediately smelled something foul and metallic, like rusty iron. A thick, burgundy, pudding-like substance coated the floor of the aluminum box. She was shocked to realize the dark liquid was blood. Envelopes had been tossed on top. She slammed the mailbox shut.

Gasping for air, she put her palm to her mouth to stop her choked scream from alarming the neighborhood. She heard Libby's bedroom window slide open from the second story behind her.

LIBBY SCRAMBLED OFF the bed, letting her paperback fall to the floor, and threw open her bedroom window. It had sounded like her mother had been attacked. But then she saw her mom hunched over in her bathrobe, hands on her knees, like she had just thrown up. Her mom let out a low, gravelly groan.

Dashing out of her room and taking the stairs two and three at a time, Libby raced to the front of the house and down the brick pathway that bisected the flower gardens. She grabbed her mother in her arms, pulling the older woman back into the house. Then she locked the substantial front door safely behind them.

Carla proceeded to the kitchen, dragging Libby along with her. She looked so determined Libby knew there wasn't any way she could shake her mother's focus. In a raspy and strained voice, her mom leaned over the countertop, and pointed to the faucet, and mumbled, "Water."

Libby produced a glass from over the prep counter, filling it with cool water from the refrigerator dispenser. After several gulps, Carla stood up and took in a sudden gasp of air, then sighed.

"You okay? Mom, what happened?" Libby's voice sounded small and wavering, like when she was a child.

"I am now." Libby watched her mom raise the water to her lips. Her hands were shaking so hard Libby thought perhaps she'd drop and shatter the glass.

"Here," Libby said, her arm around her mother, leading her over to a kitchen stool. "Sit down and just catch your breath a bit." She gave her mom a hug, and swallowed hard. "Tell me what happened out there."

"No," Carla waived her off. "We've got to call your father first. He needs to get the police over here." Carla's voice was almost a whisper.

"Why?" Libby asked.

"The cat...it has something to do with the cat."

Panic spread through Libby's chest. Her eyes filled with tears. "What? Did you see the man...?"

"No. I didn't see anyone. Call your father. Get the

police."

"If you promise to stay put, I'll go call him. But *tell* me first."

"Blood.   Covered....in...blood...blood...every-where..."

Libby was haunted by images of Noodles and the violence that was done to him.

That was just two days ago!

"Mom, the door's locked. We're safe in here, okay? Don't move. I'll be right back."

Carla was staring off through the kitchen windows vacantly.

Libby went to her father's study so her mom wouldn't hear the scolding she was going to give him.

Isolated incident.

I'm the target, not you.

Just some nut who didn't like cats.

She was frustrated to get her dad's answering service.

"This is his daughter. It's urgent. This is an *emergency*."

"Is anyone hurt?" the nasally voice of the dispatcher asked. "If it's an emergency, you should call 911."

"I KNOW WHAT THE HELL TO DO! FIND HIM! Send. Him. Home. Immediately."

When Libby returned to the kitchen to pick up the police detective's card, her mother wasn't there. Panic seized her as she searched the large great room, then out to the dining room.

"Mom?" Her voice echoed, and tumbled onto the marble foyer.

Then she heard traffic. The front door was open! Libby dashed to the porch and watched her mother with steely determination walking back out to the mailbox. A truck was driving by the front of the house, slowly. Birds stopped chirping. Libby felt like she was in a time warp, or vacuum. Her lungs sought air as she tried to catch up to her mother. Her running felt like in slow motion.

"Don't touch a thing, mom. Please. Stop!" Libby shouted, but Carla didn't flinch or slow her speed. She pulled down the flap of the mailbox again. It made a metallic high-pitched groan. Blood pudding dripped.

Libby stopped her mother's arm from plunging deep inside the metal container. Dark burgundy ooze was dripping onto the petunias below.

"We need to get back in the house. Let the police deal with this, Mom."

But her mom wasn't having any of it. She retracted her arm, holding a fist full of bloody mail. She clutched several envelopes to her chest, getting the red sludge on her beautiful silk robe. With straightened spine, her mother turned and headed back toward the front door. On any other day, she'd have stopped to admire and touch her flowers. Today, her grim expression made her look older. Rigid and cold.

She's scared out of her gourd.

Inside the house, her mother deposited the bloody envelopes onto the kitchen island and walked up the stairs to her bedroom, completely ignoring her daughter, who stood at the bottom of the stairs watching.

Libby was stunned. She eyed the envelopes covered in crimson goo. One of them did not have a stamp on it. That was the one she wanted to open first.

Getting a set of rubber gloves from under the sink and a sharp knife, she opened the top of the envelope, carefully took out the letter inside, and spread it on the marble countertop.

The letters had been cut from magazines and pasted in a sick collage on pink stationery she recognized, revealing the single message which sent a shiver through Libby's body:

A-N E-Y-E F-O-R A-N E-Y-E.

The pink stationery was from Libby's own desk drawer. It had been a gift from her father.

This sicko has been in my bedroom!

AUSTIN BROWNLEE ARRIVED the same time Detective Clark Riverton did. Libby directed her dad upstairs. Riverton eyed her, nervously hitched his pants up by the waist and sighed.

"You got any ideas who could have done this? See anyone?" he asked.

Libby shook her head. No.

Riverton poked the letter with the end of his pen. "You use these to open it?" He pointed to her crumpled pile of rubber gloves.

Libby nodded. Yes.

"You see anyone outside last night or this morning?" he asked.

"Nope. But around midnight I thought I heard the mouth of the mailbox open. Thought maybe my Dad put something in there."

"Your Dad put something in?" Riverton was frowning, alert with concern.

"No. Didn't see him. Just heard the flap squeak. It was too dark to see who it was."

"What made you think it was your dad?" Riverton wanted to know.

"Who else would put something in there or take something out late at night?" She looked down at her feet, and took a deep breath.

Riverton studied her for a minute, then asked, "Everything all right at home?"

Libby shot him a glare to show him he'd better watch his line of questioning. Riverton didn't budge. He stood impassive, continuing to silently observe. He was good at his job.

"My father's been a basket case lately. Under a great deal of stress. I'm guessing he knows a lot more about all of this than he's letting on. And I'm guessing you do, too."

It was Riverton's time to nod.

"Well, detective? What's next?" Libby was drilling for a direct answer this time.

"That's hard to say. But I'm going to be very straight with you. You guys are all in danger. This whole business is escalating. The guy is picking a fight."

"So you're telling me someone's out to get my family?"

"Don't know. I think the guy is a crazy."

"We don't use that word in his house," Dr. Brownlee said over Libby's shoulder.

"Fuck's sake, Austin." Riverton leaned toward Libby and whispered, "Pardon me, Libby." He continued to Dr. Brownlee, "When are you going to join the human race, doctor?"

Dr. Brownlee turned to Libby. "Go upstairs and be with your mother. She's getting dressed."

"Dad, I'm not moving until you tell me what's going on."

"I don't know what's going on."

"Like hell you don't. Are there more of these letters?" Libby could see from the guilty look in her father's eyes the answer was yes.

"When were you going to tell us about this? And you had the nerve to send that SEAL away…"

"SEAL?" Riverton suddenly wanted to know.

"This guy came to the house a couple of days ago…"

"Four days ago, Dad," Libby corrected.

"Four days ago. Saying he wanted to meet the family of Will Brownlee. My brother. Who…" Brownlee couldn't finish the sentence and briskly walked to the wet bar pantry and poured himself a drink.

Riverton nodded at Libby, getting a note tablet from his chest pocket and began to write. "You think he's involved, somehow?" he asked while looking down at his notes.

"No." Libby answered, annoyance rumbling beneath the surface of her words.

"How's that?" Riverton probed.

"Because she *thinks* she's in love with him," her father shouted across the kitchen. "She's fucking him."

They were words Libby never thought she'd hear coming from her father. Even in anger, he'd always maintained control. She was seeing another side of him, a shadow cast over the shoulders of the man she'd loved her whole life.

"How dare you! Can't you hold yourself up without

a drink? Can't you quit the self-absorption and think about the rest of us in this household?" Libby spewed. The venom of her words heightened her anger toward him. She was spinning out of control, ready to launch into another verbal attack.

Her cheeks flushed with anger at hearing the words spoken in public *she thinks she's in love with him* when she hadn't said the same words to herself.

"Wait, wait a minute, you two," Riverton interrupted. "Stop all this. I need to ask some questions here."

Silence. Fire was in the air, but it was mute.

Riverton began again, cautiously. "Who is this SEAL? I need you both to settle down and give me his name."

"Cooper," Libby said, glaring at her dad, who was twirling his drink over several ice cubes, frowning, deep in thought. He was avoiding eye contact.

"Cooper what?"

"I don't remember," Libby said. "We call him Cooper, Coop for short. He told me, but I'm…too freaked out to remember." Libby was filled with embarrassment. She'd had sex with this man several times, and didn't even remember his first name.

What have I done?

Riverton was about to ask another question when Libby's cell phone went off. She didn't recognize the number.

CHAPTER 14

"**C**OOP." LIBBY WORKED not to sound too needy, but her knees were shaking. She bit her lip.

"Libby, I'm sorry about last night. Maybe—"

"Ah, I'm in the middle of—"

"Sure. I can call back later."

"No." Was that a plea? She looked to the faces of her father and Detective Riverton, who stopped their conspiratorial whispering to watch her.

"Libby, what's wrong?" he asked.

"Can you come over? The police are here."

Riverton put his finger to his lips and her dad frowned.

"What's happened?" Cooper asked.

"Just—I can't go into it on the phone. Can you get over here?"

"I'll be there in fifteen minutes. Is someone hurt? Did someone hurt you?"

"No, I'm fine. Everyone's fine." It was a lie and a

gross misstatement, but it hopefully gave Cooper enough of an excuse to come to the house. Besides, the blood in the mailbox didn't belong to—

Oh my god!

She turned to her dad. "What about Neil and Marsha and the girls? Should we be alerting them, too?" Libby looked between the two men, forgetting Cooper was on the phone.

"I'm coming over right now," Cooper said and hung up.

Dr. Brownlee winced as he searched the detective's face. Riverton scowled and answered her curtly, "I'll contact them later. I don't want to get anyone else involved unless I have to. We simply don't know enough and all I'd do is scare them, perhaps unnecessarily. I've barely started to study the letters—"

"Letters? As in plural, *letters*?" Libby interrupted.

The two men gave her a blank stare.

"How many letters?" she shrieked.

Riverton said, "Three."

Dr. Brownlee said, "Four."

"Four," Riverton corrected himself. "One your father threw away. I've got three to study, plus this one."

"You didn't think it was important to let us know we were getting letters?" Libby insisted. "Letters like this?" Libby thought her dad looked small and older as she pinned him with her angry stare. "This is my stationery, Dad. This came from my bedroom here at the house."

Her dad gasped.

"Libby, you're sure?" Riverton wanted to know.

"Absolutely."

Her mother made her entrance, hair still wet. She stood beside Libby and crossed her arms. Carla leveled her gaze at Libby's father. She was not smiling.

"I want the truth. All of it, Austin," she said.

"Ma'am," Riverton began, "we're talking about the other letters I have down at the station. We're studying them."

"Letters? What letters?" Carla looked at the display on her kitchen countertop, and walked over to it. After reading the note, she looked up to her husband's face a second time.

"You lied to me," she said.

Brownlee leaned back against a countertop and stared at the ceiling, appearing to be searching for words. "I had no idea it would come to this, Carla. I brought them into Clark on Sunday when we met. We were starting to investigate…"

"Investigate?" Carla spat. "You kept us in the dark on purpose, Austin. *On purpose*! We're the bait while you investigate?" She nodded to Detective Riverton. "This your idea?"

"No ma'am. We're just doing our job. Look, if you

don't mind, before he gets here, I'd like some information on this Navy SEAL fellow your daughter's been seeing."

Carla laced her fingers through her wet scalp, swizzling her hair haphazardly. "You don't really think he had anything to do with this, do you?" she asked the room. Libby couldn't understand why no one had a quick response.

Dr. Brownlee made the point in his gentle negotiator voice, "All of these letters arrived after the SEAL did, Carla. Detective Riverton *has* to investigate him."

"If we can figure out a motive, we have a much better shot at getting the guy," Riverton offered.

"Hasn't this cretin who's writing these letters told you what he wants?" Carla added. "It says, *An Eye For An Eye*. That's pretty clear to me."

"But we aren't sure if it's directed at me, or…Libby." Dr. Brownlee hesitated.

Libby felt another wave of confusion and fear wash over her.

Could this have something to do with Dr. Gerhardt? Perhaps her reporting him to the Department Chair made him snap.

Is this retaliation because he lost his job? How could they think it was Cooper?

Her stomach did cartwheels. She found it impossible he could be the one responsible for all of these events. It had to be coincidence. Just had to be.

COOPER PARKED THE scooter in the driveway, blocking the garage door. He knew he might catch hell for it, but wanted the bike closer to the house. Besides, the unmarked and marked police cars took up the majority of the parking on the street.

His splitting headache hadn't subsided, even though he'd taken something for it. His hangover this morning had been an unwelcome event. It had been three years since he'd taken a drop. Those beers last night came as quick and smooth as in the old days. Back then, they would have been the prelude to oblivion. Yes, his Higher Power was definitely on his side this morning, not screaming in his ear, just giving him a good headache and plunging him right into some drama with Libby and her family.

Libby was out the front door before he could ring the bell. She smelled wonderful. The distance he had tried to create between them suddenly shrank. He had to work not to take her in his arms.

He was grateful to be sober enough to deal with whatever was going on today. He was grateful for the way Libby seemed to be happy to see him, perhaps needed him.

He looked into her terrified eyes, pushing unruly hair from her face. "Tell me."

Pools of tears started forming as she whispered, "Someone is sending letters—horrible letters. And there's blood in the mailbox."

Cooper turned to look at the innocuous metal object, with its mouth shut, dripping onto the flowers below. Vampire mailbox.

Weird. Twisted. Someone very sick.

He recalled Libby's tale about the cat. How angry he felt as she was telling him. Bad guys were one thing. He could deal with those, no problem. But he was not trained to deal with a sick, twisted individual, a crazy person who hurt animals. He knew about zealots, evil men who knew only death and destruction. It was easy to send them back to *the source* as they called it. But someone with his own private war against a family, against Libby? He felt ill prepared. But he damn well had to try, even if it wasn't wise.

Dr. Brownlee was at the opened front doorway. "Cooper. The detectives here need to ask you a few questions, if you don't mind."

"No, sir. I don't mind. Someone going to tell me what's going on?" Instinct made him take Libby's hand as he followed the doctor into the house. He smelled coffee. Carla called to him from the kitchen and, yes, he certainly did want a steaming cup. Black.

He was led to the living room, where he took a seat next to Libby. She clutched his fingers between her own, their hands buried in the couch cushions between them. Her public show of affection made him a little uncomfortable. He sipped from his coffee with the other hand, resting the mug on his right knee. A non-uniformed policeman started first.

"I'm Detective Clark Riverton, San Diego PD." He showed a badge Cooper couldn't possibly read.

"I'm SO Calvin Cooper." He observed Riverton making notes in a small spiral book the size of his vest pocket.

"SO as in Special Operator?"

Cooper nodded, taking another sip.

"Spelled just like how it sounds?"

"Yes, sir."

"So, I have to ask you if you know anything about this incident with Libby's cat, and the letter."

"Just what I've been told."

"And what have you been told, son?"

Cooper heard that name again and flinched, but held himself in check.

"Libby just told me there were *some* letters, not just one, and something about blood in the mailbox." He rubbed Libby's upper arm and shoulders. She was so stiff, and he couldn't get her to soften. It was a natural reaction, and it felt damned good to try to bring comfort.

"You have anything to do with these events?" Riverton asked pointedly.

"No, sir." He began to see something forming. He was becoming a suspect. "You don't think I—"

"We're just here to investigate all angles. Tell me again how you came upon the Brownlee's doorstep."

"I was ordered to go meet the family of a fallen SEAL. Dr. Brownlee's brother, William. I carry a KA-BAR knife with his name engraved on it."

"You have this knife on you?"

"No. I keep it at home."

"And where is that?"

Cooper cleared his throat and eased himself away from Libby. "I live in a motor home at the beach."

"Which beach?"

"Mission, mostly, but it varies."

Riverton tilted his head and looked at him askance. Cooper knew he was being summed up and wasn't sure what the verdict was.

"There's no public parking at Mission Beach."

"I have a private arrangement with the guy who lives there. Used to own the park."

"You got a permit for that?"

Coop just stared back at him. No, he didn't have any permits. And he wasn't going to get any, either.

"Would you mind if I search your place?" Riverton asked.

He balked at the intrusion into his private life of

guns, destruction and surveillance—his job in real life. But this was a civilian matter, and he was charged with cooperating with all local authorities, even if he didn't trust any of them.

"You may. I'll have to tell my liaison."

"Um hum." Riverton was staring at his notes. "Okay, then. How did you find the Brownlee's address?"

"Like I said, from my Chief. He gave it to me."

"I've never heard of a Team Guy—Dr. Brownlee has told me you are a SEAL, right?"

"Yes, sir."

"Never heard of a SEAL doing this."

"Well, you wouldn't, sir. We don't do this as a routine. But we study the past and have respect for the fallen. We have compassion for their families—even ones that don't want or need it." Coop looked into the dark eyes of Libby's father.

Like he'd been slapped, Dr. Brownlee stood up straight and went to the kitchen, returning with a cup of coffee.

"So, why you? Why were you sent?"

Coop didn't want to tell them. He inhaled deeply and then sighed. This was going to be tough. "Because, sir, all my kin back in Nebraska were killed recently in a tornado. My liaison thought it would give me something else to focus on." He shot Dr. Brownlee a glare,

"Not that it has helped much."

He needed all this complication like a hole in his head. Coop began to doubt the wisdom of being here at the Brownlee home. But the sweet-smelling lady at his side squeezed his hand, and then he remembered.

Yeah, I'm all in. God help me.

COOPER THOUGHT ABOUT the questioning—really, a low-level interrogation—while he drove Libby to the Babemobile. Here he'd decided he really shouldn't see her any longer, and the first thing he did was come running over when she called, and now he was taking her to his place in her car.

Cooper had witnessed some skilled CIA techniques first-hand when he did the Tactical Surveillance Course in Virginia before his last deployment. Riverton was rough around the edges, but he managed to get a boatload of information out of Cooper. All things the cops could follow up on. One wrong answer and Coop would be in the spotlight, if he wasn't already.

He tried not to worry about it as he silently piloted the little car. Libby let him think, which was a good thing right now. He had no secrets, just didn't like revealing his private side. Or thinking he was a lab experiment, no matter how much it aided the locals. They were wasting time with every second they considered Cooper a suspect, and that irritated him. Not catching the perp could cause harm to Libby or her family.

He could recognize certain signs of battle stress, what it does to a man. This guy who left the letters and killed Libby's cat, whoever the hell he was, had made close friends with Dr. Death. Almost like the cretin didn't have anything left to lose.

Driving up and over the Coronado Bridge, he remembered back to the day he got his first tattoo. The artist at Daisy's shop gleefully palmed his flesh, like Coop was a virgin canvas. Well, he had been. The owner sent Daisy over to shave Cooper's leg before the old fart could begin. And that was a real nice treat. Coop knew next time he'd ask for her. She had the softest hands and biggest tits...

He glanced over at Libby and she smiled back at him. He felt like a heel. But he could see in her eyes she trusted him. Thing was, did he trust himself? Was he taking her home to protect her or for the fantastic sex?

The crusty old guy with rough hands had talked to Coop that day while drawing the Celtic ring around his baby-skin-smooth right calf. His hands were gnarly, but steady as a seaman's.

He didn't know the guy's first name. Everyone called him Gladwell. He wouldn't stop talking while he needled his way under Coop's skin. It hurt like a son of a bitch.

"When do you go over? Or can you say?" Gladwell had asked him that afternoon.

"Four to six months."

"Know where?"

Coop laughed inside as he recalled his answer. "Somewhere you wouldn't go on a vacation."

"Bring me back some ears and we'll roast them and eat 'em."

"Excuse me?" Cooper wasn't sure he'd heard right.

Gladwell put his fingers over his own ears, folding and wiggling them while he gave Coop the brown grin. Gladwell's teeth were coated in chewing tobacco tar.

Cooper thought he was going to lose it right there all over the guy. He swore and hoped to God the man was kidding.

The artist whistled. "So you're gonna get familiar with Dr. Death?"

When Coop looked up at him, he smiled again, showing off his brown grin. Gladwell continued, "He's a sly one. Taken some of my best buds," he said, as he bore into Cooper's skin especially painfully.

Coop often thought back to the timing of that particular afternoon. The next day Gladwell had wrapped his Harley around a tree and had his own private party with Dr. Death.

May he rest in peace.

The old Marine had left the shop to Daisy, which

was the subject of conversation all over the community. A few months later he found out Gladwell was
actually Daisy's father, but never told her until she read
it in the will. Gunny told him not to grieve over the
Marine. "He had some pretty fucking big demons,"
Gunny had said. Cooper left it at that.

*Everyone has a private war going on somewhere
within them.* His team leader had told him that one
time while they were waiting on a rooftop, doing
advance surveillance for a high-level meeting of locals.
The waiting was the hardest part, always. Just like now.
Waiting for something else to happen. Although he
didn't know about this kind of domestic bad guy, one
thing was always for sure. You either took care of
things or they got worse. Much worse. The foreboding
was so strong it almost eclipsed his headache.

He couldn't do anything for the family he'd lost
back home, but he wanted to help Libby. He just wasn't
supposed to get involved in local law enforcement, and
it was eating a hole in him.

"You hungry?" he turned and asked her as she
snuggled against him in the front seat.

"Starved."

He knew she meant something else, and his groin
lurched. He still knew it was wrong to continue with
Libby, but he just couldn't help himself. A part of him
wanted to help just because that was who he was. But

he also knew his little brain was making plans and was alert and ready to party, despite his splitting headache.

No, he just couldn't walk away while everything was so unresolved.

All during lunch he'd had an especially hard time eating his chowder with her foot inserted in his crotch, hidden under their table as she sat across from him.

"You're not hungry now?" he asked her, and then loved the look on her face as she told him what she was hungry for. He knew it, of course, but liked to be reminded of it every fucking minute.

She took an ice cube and rubbed it over her bottom lip. He wanted to chew that lip. The cube slipped between her breasts and her mouth made the perfect "O", her eyes wide and dancing. He thought about reaching across the table and snaking his forefinger into her shirt to retrieve it, without worrying who saw.

Whoa, boy.

Libby was the hottest thing he'd seen in a long time. Naughty and nice all wrapped up in a perfect package for him. Such a ridiculous and dangerous combination. He could spend the afternoon playing with her body, as long as he had a bucket of ice cubes and a big box of condoms.

When they were together, he didn't miss his family as much. Bay accepted her well, but didn't like that he had to continue to stay outside the door. When they returned from lunch, he gave Bay a bone he'd gotten from the cook, another ex-Team guy. The dog went to work on it right away.

"Welcome again to my humble abode, Miss," he'd said as he picked her up by the waist and placed her inside the trailer. He closed and locked the metal door behind him. Libby was already removing his shirt.

They peeled their clothes off and left them on the ground where they fell. He watched the soft cheeks of her rear as she skipped down the hallway to his bed.

"I love the view from here," he said to her backside.

Libby looked over her shoulder and broke into a devilish giggle. Then her eyes lowered to the size of his erection. "Me, too."

He came up behind her before she could make it to the bed. He pulled her back against his chest as he massaged her breasts and pinched her nipples, sending a little squeal and shiver his way. Her smooth skin caused his dick to engorge so that he wondered if he'd be able to make it deep inside her before he exploded.

She arched back, kissing his neck. His hand slipped down over her mound and pressed between her legs. She dipped herself, bending her knees, arching her back as he inserted his forefinger inside her, and listened to the delicious ripple of her ragged breath. He carefully slipped his thumb over her nub and she jerked with pleasure.

"Need this," she said.

Hell, he needed it too. He bent her over the bed and slowly spread her knees to expose her peach, ripe and wet with her own arousal.

He remembered the condoms he'd recently bought. They were stuck in a brown drugstore bag in the saddlebags at the back of the scooter.

Damn.

"Honey, I don't have anything. Do you?" he asked her.

She righted herself and ran to her jeans, extricating a foil packet from her pocket. She handed it up to him while she caressed his hardness. Cooper groaned with the pleasure her hands gave him.

She assumed the position on all fours on his bed, looking at him over the smooth mounds of flesh at her rear. With her tight little ass in the air, he sheathed himself in a ribbed condom, and then positioned his member between her supple lips, edging them aside as he penetrated just his crown. Then he plunged in all the way to the hilt.

Libby gasped, forcing herself against Cooper's upper thighs. He leaned over her, pressing his chest against her back, nibbling on the soft skin under her right ear. She grabbed the back of his neck as she pushed her butt into his groin, pulling him deeper inside.

The gentle rhythm became more urgent as he pumped her. He'd been dreaming about this ever since yesterday, when they'd been interrupted in the garden shed. He watched sweat glisten on her back and shoulders, and the sweet, fleshy cheeks of her ass that drove his thighs crazy.

Her orgasm surprised him. She stopped touching him so that the only point of contact was his cock inside her. Deep inside her. Her muscles clamped as she squeezed her own breasts and threw her head back, sending her auburn hair onto her back. He entangled his fingers in her locks, pulling back her head gently. He grabbed her shoulder with the other hand, bracing himself against her and exploded. He released every drop he had.

They collapsed on the bed together. She was trying to keep him inside. They lay spooned and breathing heavily. She brought his hands to her breasts. She rubbed his fingers, his forearms, and the top of his thigh. He snuggled into her rear, burying his nose in the mass of hair at the nape of her neck, and kissed her there.

He raised his head up and whispered in her ear, "Libby, you're incredible."

She wanted him to say something else, he could tell. But she said, "Thank you," and rubbed her sinfully smooth little butt against his groin. He'd be hard in another hour. He knew it. He liked the way the golden late afternoon sunlight played on the red and blonde strands of her auburn hair.

His family had gone Heaven ten days ago. Cooper knew he was there, too.

CHAPTER 15

LIBBY WOKE UP in Coop's motor home hearing the gentle roll of the waves in the distance. She could feel the SEAL was in a deep sleep. She remained nestled in his warm embrace; her body spooned in front of him, her back resting against his chest. Air whistled through his teeth. She turned to look at him over her shoulder. His deep rose-colored lips were smooth and just waiting to be kissed. She squirmed to roll over and face him and his arms tightened around her waist at first, then his hands lowered to the cheeks of her ass as he allowed her to turn in the bed. The sheets were musty, pulling up from Cooper's corner, exposing the mattress underneath.

He pressed her to him, his large hands on the back side of her waist, pulling her toward him. She felt his hardness as she played with the hair around his ears and kissed him. Several kisses later, he adroitly encased himself in a condom, moved on top of her, on his hands and knees, making entry into her swollen sex. The pain of his thrust inside her was delicious. She needed his hard strength, the feel of his passion. She loved how urgent he was. He dove deeper. Her insides began to explode.

"Need this," she said.

"Yes," he whispered as he bit the lobe of her right ear. His tongue followed up the tiny tug as if he'd caused pain. It wasn't pain. She wanted to be consumed by him. Powerful hips pressed into her as she accepted him deeper, as she clamped down on him in a long, rolling orgasm.

She'd been moaning, her head thrashing from side to side as he slid out, then rammed in again pushing her higher, bringing her along the long ragged trail of her need. Her body reacted in quivering jolts as she dug her fingers into his buttocks and pulled him inside deeper still. She felt him lurch and then relax in rhythmic spasms as he filled her.

Their lovemaking was always intense, but each time she was on the brink of something else. She was changing. Her world was changing as her body felt more alive. She was filled with possibility and hope. He was becoming one glorious addiction.

Afterwards, his forehead rested on top of hers as they gazed silently into each other's eyes. Their breathing began to slow. She assessed the lines of his face, noticing a tiny thin scar on his chin. She touched it with her forefinger and followed it up with a long, healing kiss, luxuriating in a soft moan coming from deep inside his chest.

A door had opened to her soul. Wide and gaping, it longed for this tall muscular SEAL to step inside. She couldn't get enough of him, and hoped to God he felt the same way.

Can you love me back, Cooper?

She knew it was love. More than hunger for the sexual liaison, it was a required element deeply implanted in her body. Removing it could be fatal.

I am not afraid when I am with you.

Except she was afraid to ever have to live without him. That was the only fear that remained. Would she have to endure that?

Please love me back, Cooper.

He smiled as if he'd heard her inner thoughts, gently massaged her lips with his own. "Libby, Libby, Libby. What am I going to do with you, hum?"

He arched back and looked at her face again, and gave her the crooked smile that snagged her heart every time. She could see he'd been a shy boy growing up. He was shy with her now. Big, powerful Cooper, was shy at heart.

"Anything you like, sir," she said in a whisper. Her smile was returned and then punctuated by another gentle nuzzling kiss.

He laid his head against her chest and she splayed her fingers through his hair.

She could spend the rest of the afternoon and evening here, in his bed, in his arms.

They heard Bay scratch at the door and whine.

"Bay wants his breakfast," Coop said, watching her face.

She nodded, but wasn't going to let the SEAL go. The dog's timing was pretty good. He'd waited for their lovemaking to subside before telling his master he was hungry. But Libby wasn't ready to give Cooper up just yet.

Coop kissed the insides of her forearms as he peeled himself from their embrace.

He rose up, after giving her a respectful, quick kiss on the lips. He slipped on his shorts. "I've got to get him his food. What about you? You hungry?"

"Always," she said while she put her hands under her head and let the sheet expose her full torso. Libby watched as her SEAL perused her body. Now, that just made her want him all over again, just the way he looked at her that way.

When he turned, she watched his lanky frame amble to the kitchen. Cooper scooped out some kibbles and added some heated meat from the microwave, stirring it up. He passed the silver bowl out to Bay and sat down on the stoop. Libby saw just the curve of his muscled back and a few pillow-fluffed wisps of sandy hair as the SEAL murmured a few words to Bay she couldn't make out. She knew she was witnessing part of his daily routine.

She looked at the light-patterned ceiling of the home and dreamt what it would feel like to live here with Cooper. Perhaps this was the safest place for her. She was more concerned about her parents and where they should go. But she knew she'd be the safest here with her SEAL.

If he'd allow it.

She pulled the top sheet from the bed and wrapped her body in it. Walking down the hallway to his seated frame, she decided to broach the subject.

"Cooper, my parents are probably going to move out of the house."

Cooper nodded. He leaned over and patted Bay's head. The dog was getting his second meal: Cooper's affection and praise. He raised his paw onto the SEAL's knee and Cooper began to delicately unwrap the bandage, examining the red wound inside. His nimble fingers pressed and prodded the wound. Libby could see several thick stitches and a shaved area from Bay's paw halfway up his foreleg. Coop looked like he was checking for signs of swelling or heightened temperature.

"He going to be okay?" she asked.

"He's healing great, aren't you, old boy?" Cooper said as he scratched the dog's head. He had removed the bandage. He stood up, moving past Libby, to remove a roll of white gauze material and a small pair of silver surgical scissors from one of the upper cabinets. After he sat back down in the doorway, he rewrapped the wound carefully and gave Bay another pat on the head.

As Cooper stood up and arched his back, Bay jumped into the motor home.

"Okay. You can come in for a bit," Coop said as Bay came over to Libby and sniffed the sheet she was wearing. "No, Bay. Be nice," he said.

Libby rubbed her fingers through the thick hair atop the dog's head. She received a grateful brown gaze and lick in return. "You're a good boy, Bay. So glad you're getting well," she said.

But Cooper hadn't answered her. He was washing his hands in the sink.

"So, about my parents. They want me to go with them."

"Um hum," was all Cooper said as he deposited the hand towel on the towel holder and leaned against the countertop, one tanned long leg crossed over the other. "You want to do that?"

"They don't think it's safe in the house. Detective

Riverton thinks we need to move temporarily."

"Um hum."

"I don't want to stay with them. I want to stay with you." There. She'd said it.

His reaction wasn't what she'd hoped.

"Here?" he said with a shrug.

"Yes."

"Heck, I'm not here all the time. You wouldn't be safe here. No way I could make you safe."

"Then I could go with you." Libby knew it was a ridiculous request as soon as she'd uttered the words, and instantly wished she hadn't.

"Libby, this is all real nice," he said as he looked at the bed, pointing to it with an outstretched hand, "but…"

Her heart stopped beating. She'd gone too far.

He redirected himself and sat next to her. "Honey, I'm not in the position to have someone here 24/7. I do things, go to meetings. We do stuff to get ready for our next deployment. You can't go everywhere I go. You know that." He gently put his arm around her, but didn't squeeze her to his chest. "It would be easier if you let the police handle this."

"But I feel safer with you."

She felt him stiffen. He withdrew his arm and stood up. A couple of petals from the bouquet of flowers mounted to the side of the kitchen wall dropped to the countertop. It made her sad.

"I think we need to get on the same page here. Unless I'm mistaken, the police consider me sort of a suspect. Hell, someone might have followed us here, could be following me around. Maybe following you."

Libby was getting a sinking feeling she was going to get a talk about doing the right thing. Her stomach rumbled and she swallowed hard. She was thirsty.

"Could I have a drink of water?" she asked.

"Sure." Cooper poured two short glasses with cold water from a jug in the refrigerator. He handed her one just before he gulped his down with one snap of his head.

"I just don't have any confidence in the police. And my father is in some kind of La La Land or something. He's distracted. He's never lied to me before like he has been doing lately."

"He's not lying to you, Libby."

"Yes he is. He's deliberately downplaying this whole thing. He's not facing the reality of the situation."

"Well, what is the reality of the situation?" Cooper squinted, worry lines transcending his forehead.

Libby didn't have an answer for him.

"Exactly, honey," he whispered. "Who knows what's going on? You've got to stay together to make it easier on the police to do their job. Besides—" she could see he was being careful how he spoke, choosing his words slowly, "I'm not really supposed to interfere with civilian things. I'm strictly military. I probably have gotten too involved as it is."

He was looking down at the floor and Libby felt the chasm of her empty stomach. She waited for the awkward pause to get his attention, and it did. When he looked up at her, he wasn't smiling.

She didn't want to ask, but she had to. "Translate that for me, please, Cooper." Her heart felt thick. Surely he could hear its beating from across the space between them.

"It's getting complicated, Libby. I'm not into this all-inclusive thing. Surely that can't be a surprise to you."

He'd have looked hard if he wasn't so damned good-looking. She could tell he was more practiced at saying goodbye than she was. But then his training helped with that. Of course he would learn how not to let his feelings show if it compromised a mission. Man of steel.

No friendly chink in that armor for me?

She knew the answer to that was a resounding "No."

THIS WAS THE part of relationships Cooper couldn't handle. He'd gotten involved sexually, and was now looking at the woman he was going to have to hurt, and he hated himself. Part of him looked for a way out, any way to allow him to spend more time in her company. But, as much as he wanted it, signals were coming to him loud and clear like those damned red extraction flares. Part of him wanted to be rescued. The other part wanted to fall down a hole and take Libby with him.

That was no way to live. No way to treat an innocent. And he knew better, had told himself to watch out for this very thing.

You dumb son-of-a-bitch.

He needed to think. While Libby was anywhere close to him, when he could see her hot with arousal, hear her moaning—even the sound of her breath as she lay sleeping or the taste of a quick kiss—he was distracted. That part of him, the part that always figured everything out, was grossly disabled.

This had never happened before. He'd rescued a mother and child in Fallujah just before their hovel of a home was blown to bits. He got them to triage, helped the woman cover up again so he wouldn't be accused of being disrespectful. And the little boy, probably a fatherless boy, looked up at him with wide brown eyes filled with fear. He didn't want to walk away, but he was able to do it and pray to God they'd survive the hell they were living in. He'd had his family waiting for him at home in Nebraska.

But now they were gone. He hadn't time to feel the pain of their passing. Or he wasn't letting himself. And Libby's family could never be a substitute for his. Was this God's way of issuing payback? Telling him no matter how much good he was doing, he was still one sorry SOB?

Be honest, you frog asshole. You're thinking with your little brain.

Logically he knew this to be true, but there was something else going on, too. Cooper decided he just couldn't go there.

He sighed and placed an errant lock of Libby's auburn hair behind her left ear. "Libby, honey. I wanted to spend the day with you, but I think we should slow things down a bit."

He felt the instant vibration as she swung her head up to look at him and try to focus on his eyes. "What?" she asked.

He could tell she wanted the truth. He hoped he gave her enough reassurance that he meant what he said. Maybe he was telling her this to convince himself.

"I want to. I really want to honey. I didn't expect for all this to happen."

"You fucked me and didn't expect that you'd have to be nice afterwards? You don't like the strings, is that right?"

He winced, but couldn't deny it.

Her face was becoming hard. Her left eye twitched. "You're good at the screwing, Cooper, I'll grant you that. It's the being a decent guy afterwards that you are a little short on."

It hurt more because he knew it was true. All of it. And because Cooper had never in his life been called short.

CHAPTER 16

"**S**O, JUST TAKE me home." The words didn't seem to come from her. Libby was as shocked as Coop appeared to be. He stiffened and then turned back to the bedroom. She chose not to dwell too much there in that no-man's land, wondering if he really felt so dismissive, or if a part of him was tempted to stay with her, like he'd said. Either way, there were no winners in that mental tug-of-war.

She remained on the couch, shoulders slumped, distancing herself from the agony that waited at the edge of her consciousness. She fixated on how ridiculous her pink toes looked against Coop's indoor-outdoor green carpet. She wished she was on the fairway at one of her father's favorite courses instead of staring down at the plastic lawn, which looked like someone's cheap idea of paradise.

She rose slowly as he put on his jeans, and then slipped a white tee shirt over those pecs and shoulders she'd been admiring earlier this morning, when her world was purring like a kitten. When that feeling of his arms around her, his body merging with hers, made her feel glorious and absolutely immortal.

Again, she cut those thoughts off. *Not helpful.* Coop studied her. She could detect an inkling of emotion behind his eyes just before they glazed over, maintaining control over—what? Over a breakup? Was *that* what this was?

"So I guess we're done, then," she said, pushing the limits. She hated herself afterwards. Why did she say such stupid things? Why couldn't she just zip it?

"If that's what you want," he said. His half-whisper and melodic man-voice-vibration made her tingle in spite of the dull ache in her heart and the lurch in her stomach.

She stood up with the sheet still draped around her body and pulled herself together. With a deep breath, she stepped towards Cooper, felt him inhale sharply as she put her palms on his thinly covered chest.

"What I want, I can't have." She pressed her fingers against his white shirt and looked into his face. She let him see her emotions and near lack of control. Her naked soul. Her need for him. Best to show him her truth if it was to be the end of their relationship.

He didn't bend to suckle her lips, as he would have just a half hour ago. He seemed to soak in her discomfort, all of it. Was this what he was used to? Her tears spilled over and dripped silently down her cheeks, onto the white cotton sheet, but she wouldn't let go of the gaze. It took every ounce of strength she had left to will the weeping to stop.

But it did.

Her eyes fluttered down to his lips that parted, came closer, and engulfed her and for just a second all was right with the world. One glorious second. A gallows' kiss.

Testing him, she moved closer to feel his hardness against her belly until he moved back, separating them. Then he withdrew his mouth and enveloped her in his arms, hugging her tight, but safely. It wasn't a sexual hold. It was how someone would hug a child they wanted to protect.

COOPER WAS GRATEFUL at first that Libby didn't want to talk as he drove her car back to her parents' house. But soon the thickness of the dark space between them pressed against him and raised his hackles. It was always like this when he was ready to walk into harm's way. He'd learned to pick up the hotheads—people with strong emotions and the weird energy emanating from the insanity of life under extreme pressure. His training gave him the instincts to recognize when those around him were overwhelmed and would do things they normally wouldn't do.

He'd asked her if she wanted to go somewhere for breakfast, but she politely declined. Part of him was grateful for that.

As the blocks leading up to the Brownlee home passed, he began to relax. He was getting more and more confident a major scene had been averted. She was a strong girl. God, how he loved that about her. She bore her pain silently, didn't go bringing down the whole world when she was hurting. Kind of reminded him of the way he'd been brought up, and then trained as a SEAL. Okay to feel the hurt. Not okay to show it.

Except this time, something felt slightly off, as if he should be sharing something more with her. He didn't want to tell her thank you for the great sex they'd had. He couldn't apologize. He just needed to shut the fuck up. And keep his fly buttoned.

He parked her car at the curb behind a pickup truck. His scooter had been moved to the side yard, a safe distance away from the garage doors. He went around the car to open Libby's door, but she was already out and walking up the brick walkway, past the now infamous mailbox. She walked tall. He could tell from her gait she was holding her breath.

At the front door, she abruptly turned and extended her hand.

"Thank you for the good time. Good luck on your

next deployment."

He avoided the obviously ridiculous handshake and had to look down. She was way too brave for him right now. It wouldn't be proper to show her anything of his soft side.

Tilting his head to look to the house next door, he began, "I'm not really the one you want, Libby." She didn't say anything, so he got the courage to scan her face, and stepped to put his arms around her waist. "But if I was—"

Just then the front door opened. Carla Brownlee came outside to join the two of them on the porch. Cooper dropped his arms immediately, took a step back and cleared his throat.

"Oh. I thought I heard something. Forgive me for intruding," Carla said with a shy smile. As an afterthought, she added, "Glad you're home safe and sound. Your father's been worried and…"

"Please, Mom," Libby began. Cooper could tell she was annoyed with her mother. "I just need a minute. I'll be right in."

"Cooper, you kids want something to eat? I still have breakfast out," Carla Brownlee asked.

"No, ma'am. But thanks. I've got to go." Food was the last thing on his mind.

Carla retreated inside the house and closed the heavy glass and metal door behind her. Just then,

Cooper realized that her mother had seen his embrace with Libby and had still chosen to interrupt.

No matter. We're done, anyway. He was sad, but getting used to the feeling. He knew a couple of guys who could help him forget his woes. An action plan was forming.

Then he remembered the cat, the letters and the possible danger Libby and her family were in. Well, he could do something about that. It was wise he extract himself from her life, but he needed to let her know she could still count on him, in an emergency.

"You're going to want to cooperate with the police fully," he said. "They know how to handle creeps like this. My hope is that he'll either be stupid and get himself caught, or tire of the caper and go prey on someone else. But do everything they tell you to do, okay?"

Libby nodded her head like she was seven and he'd just told her how to feed a cat.

"Give me your cell," he said.

At first, Libby furrowed her eyebrows, cocking her head to the side. While he remained quiet, she began the task of rummaging through her considerably filled bag until she produced her phone from the bottom. She presented it to him with a huff. Her gentle scent filled his nostrils and he started to get hard.

He began to punch numbers into her contacts file.

"This is my cell, but it won't look like this number when I call you because it's scrambled in the routing."

"Okay." She was looking down as his fingers worked.

"Call me if something happens. I can be here usually in less than a half hour. Don't go anywhere without your cell, okay? That way, you're always tracked."

"Tracked? You actually think I'm in danger of being kidnapped?"

"Of course not," he said, but felt his stomach clench. "I just want you to be careful."

"I see," she said with steely coldness. "Protection, using my head, being prepared, like I so haven't been doing the last two days."

It hurt, but anger flared up inside him at her reaction to his genuine concern for her safety. He was only trying to help and here she threw it in his face.

Women!

"Be safe, Libby," he whispered.

"Of course I'll be safe. I have my cell phone to protect me." She held the phone up in his face, and then entered the front door, slamming it behind her.

Cooper cracked his neck and rotated his right shoulder. He turned, and walked across the pathway in front of the triple garage doors, and drove off on his red scooter.

A HALF HOUR later, Cooper was devouring a large crab omelet at the Scupper. He saw the familiar stubby shadow of Fredo at the doorway, walking into the ever-dark restaurant bar. Fredo sniffed the air right in front of his table.

"I don't smell dog," he said.

"Fuck you, Fredo. Bay's at home. He figured he wasn't exactly welcome here."

"Oh, he's okay. It's his dog hair and salt water-smelling pelt that isn't," Fredo said with a wince. He hailed the waitress for some coffee, and sat down across from Cooper.

"So, you want to hit Gunny's after breakfast, or you get enough exercise this morning?" Fredo looked up at Coop under his bushy eyebrows. Creases on his forehead made him resemble a Shar Pei.

Cooper knew he deserved the ribbing. He'd neglected his best friend and constant companion. They commonly introduced themselves as twins. It never ceased to draw laughter from the fairer sex since there was more than a foot difference in their heights. Cooper resembled a Viking king and Fredo a Mayan priest.

"Sounds good to me. You eat?"

"You'll be happy to know I did. Armani's mom made some fresh salsa and I doused everything in it."

"I'll bet." Cooper finished the last bite of breakfast

and took a long sip of water. After grabbing several packets of sugar, stuffing them into his back pocket, he rose and brought his ticket over to the cash register. Fredo followed behind.

"Let's take the truck. You can get your scooter later. Or, do you want to scratch it up putting it in the back?"

"I'm leaving it right here. Safer than Gunny's."

Cooper opened the rusted green door to Fredo's beater and climbed inside. He found the floor of the truck after brushing aside a few fast food wrappers with his canvas slip-ons. He flicked the hula girl stuck to Fredo's dash and she performed for him.

The smoking truck made it down the quiet street, backfiring just before they turned right. After a short drive over the bridge to the Strand at Coronado, they drove a few more blocks until they crossed railroad tracks in an industrial area. *Gunny's Gym* it said on the plate glass window. Below the lettering was a Popeye-like character holding a barbell, sporting an anchor tattoo on his forearm.

They pushed open Gunny's glass front door, tinkling the little bell that hung at the top of the doorframe. Gunny was reading the paper, but the TV was blaring a newstalk program. Two older well-built men were spotting each other with free weights. Cooper recognized them as retired SEALs from Team 5.

"Gents," he said to them. He got a nod for his effort.

"Well, if it isn't lover boy," Gunny blurted out loud enough for the silver SEALs to hear. Cooper sighed and prepared himself for another ribbing. It was always this way. Everyone in the whole community knew he'd just lost his entire family. Knew he'd spent some time with a sweet young thing after he got back. Knew that Timmons had ordered him to stand down for a few days, and knew that the only thing he probably wanted to do was go back on deployment to forget about both situations.

They also probably knew that it could cost him his life if he didn't pay close attention when he returned overseas. There was no way in hell he would make it without the community around him, but he could be counted on to get himself right in the head so he wouldn't be anyone's liability.

Cooper was just going to do what everyone expected of him: do some PT, physical training, get some rest, keep his damn mouth shut, and deal with it.

Gunny threw white towels at both of them. It was going to be a hot day, and the retired Marine was wearing a logo tee shirt with the sleeves generously cut out of it. As he bent over to wipe down a couple of benches and some of the rusty iron equipment, Coop could see the edges of Gunny's tattoo inked right over the man's sternum. He knew it read, "Already Gave," which was a comment intended to address the sorry son-of-a-bitch who might try to harvest Gunny's lungs in the event of his demise.

Cooper searched the rack of free weights while he wondered about Gunny's health. It was widely held among those in the community that Gunny was just too ornery to succumb to his cancer. He was one tough Marine. One lung had been cut out a couple of years ago, and the other one was working overtime on half speed. Didn't help that Gunny still occasionally smoked, in spite of the cancer.

Gunny didn't have fancy equipment at the gym. Nothing digital, except for a scale. He'd been forced to get the new one because guys kept tinkering with the old manual one to cheat. The floor was covered with heavy black mats that smelled of plastic and sweat. That made it easy to throw down the barbells when a man was finished. That was one of the unwritten rules everyone followed here. Placing the barbells carefully back on their rack instead of throwing them to bounce on the mats made a newcomer stand out like a lamb in a stampede.

Kyle and Armando arrived, laughing about something so hard, they bumped into the side of the doorway. Armando swore as he rubbed his right shoulder, which had taken the brunt of the contact.

Both of them stopped short when they saw Cooper.

"I'll be damned," Armando said. "Didn't think I'd see you for another couple of days at least. What happened?" The Puerto Rican SEAL grinned, as his hands gripped his hips. Armando was shirtless, except for his dog tags.

Fredo offered an answer. "You know he's got that dog. Small place. Ew!"

Even Gunny laughed at that one.

Cooper knew he wasn't required to answer, but it was important he show he wasn't overly sensitive. He knew Kyle was still assessing his mental state.

"She has to eat and shop some time." He shrugged, figuring it might be believable. No sense drawing attention to their breakup.

"She's gotta get rid of the fleas, first," Fredo quipped. Cooper pushed him off the bench and the short SEAL fell backward on his rear.

Kyle came over and drew an arm over Cooper's shoulders, which was difficult because of the difference in their sizes. "Good to see you here, sailor," he said. "Armani here's looking for houses for Mia this afternoon. I think he might need your opinion on all the gadgets."

"Just what I wanted to do this afternoon," Cooper returned. And why not? It was good to pretend things were back to normal. A year and a half ago, Armando's sister, Mia, had been kidnapped and had just barely been able to bring a baby to term throughout the ordeal. The Team had rescued her and Armando, who had been abducted to ensnare their Team leader, Kyle, in a gun-smuggling ring. Afterwards, they'd done their 4-month workup and then deployed. Now everyone was getting on with their lives.

Cooper glanced up at the TV monitor. In the center of the screen was a picture of the Brownlee home with the red banner below that read *Breaking News*.

CHAPTER 17

COOPER, KYLE, ARMANDO, Fredo and Gunny rode over to Libby's house in Fredo's four-door salvage beater. Cooper discovered he'd been rocking back and forth as he stared out the passenger side window.

Looking for what?

He wondered about so many things. The Team gave him a silent, wide berth as he thought about Libby and what they were going to face.

No. He just couldn't bring himself to think anything serious or permanent had happened to her. *What if she's—?*

When they arrived, he noticed Kyle giving him the long look. Cooper had jumped out the door before their truck stopped rolling. Kyle, right behind him, slammed the rattling door of the old beater. Fredo and everyone else exited the other side.

Cooper was on his way to mounting the front steps two at a time to meet the yellow crime scene tape when

Kyle grabbed his arm. "We wait for the Team, Coop," Kyle reminded him.

Of course. This isn't a single soldier mission or a suicide mission.

Fredo's stance was rigid and wide as he whistled appreciation for the size of the Brownlee house. Blocking the street ahead of them was a large fire truck with two more parked just beyond.

"Her dad a rock star or some shit?" Fredo asked him.

"Doctor. Her dad's a psychiatrist."

The group stopped for a second and looked at Cooper like he was an idiot.

I am an idiot.

Fredo spoke the words Coop knew were coming. "Look, man. Something wrong with a man who would get snuggly with the daughter of a shrink who lives in **this** house. She's got to be all fucked up, man."

Coop reacted, but his LPO was quick to grab him from behind, keeping his arms pinned to his sides.

"Not helpful, Fredo. Your timing sucks big time." Kyle shouted to his sharpshooter. He was struggling to keep Cooper restrained. He leaned into Coop's ear and whispered, "You be careful, Coop. You know Fredo's just jealous of your success." Then his Chief laid a kiss on that same ear, which made Coop explode out of his restraints and whirl around to face his Team leader.

"Fuck you. Fuck you all," Coop said as he sneered at their laughter. He usually didn't mind the chuckles at his expense. But he didn't like Libby being laughed at. Not today, when he wasn't sure how she was doing and how he felt about it.

Well, he knew how he felt about it. He was scared he was too late. *She's not the fucked up one. I am.* How the hell had he gotten so involved in such a tangled mess?

Coop rolled his neck and swung his arms around in the air to loosen his shoulder sockets. He felt Armando give him a big slap on the back, which started their forward momentum again.

"Don't mind him, Coop. Fredo's an asshole, and Kyle's right. He's fuckin' jealous. Besides which, Mia turned him down again."

"Now who's the asshole?" Fredo shouted. Coop could see the embarrassment on his best friend's face. The little Mexican SEAL was not very successful with the ladies. He acted like a teenager around Mia, Armando's sister. Making matters worse, Mia kept forgetting Fredo's name, calling him Frodo, which didn't help the height-challenged Team guy.

"Alright, everybody chill," came the command from their leader, Kyle. "We gotta focus on what's going on. Then we'll get the hell outa here. Just remember yourselves. We don't really belong here."

They came up to an African American uniformed policeman who stood just in front of the brick pathway to front door. On guard. The beefy guy gave Cooper a glare like he was the leader of a terrorist cell. Cooper saw he had unsnapped his holstered gun and was ready. His eyes softened when the officer got a look at Kyle, who stepped up to him and gripped his hand backwards and gave him a brief hug.

"Hey there, Lannie. You know these folks?" he asked.

"My medic does. There's a girl inside he's sweet on. She okay?"

Cooper winced but listened carefully.

The policeman grinned. "More than okay, I'd say." He nodded in Cooper's direction, "She's fine."

Cooper wasn't liking the small talk. He was anxious to see her for himself. But he was relieved, just the same.

There wasn't any smoke anywhere. "Please, can we go in?" Coop asked the dark officer.

With black gloves, the San Diego policeman nodded, adding, "Don't touch anything, and if anyone throws you out, I wasn't the one to let you in, okay? Say you snuck in behind me."

"Got it," Kyle said. "We're known for being invisible anyway."

The guard chuckled. The SEAL group made their

way up the brick walkway to the front door like one crab-like creature. They walked in silence, carrying their chests tall, swinging their arms casually. Coop knew that on the inside they were ready for anything.

Maybe something to do with Libby's mother, or Dr. Brownlee? Whatever it was, it had to be bad enough to draw out three huge engine crews.

The front door was ajar, so Kyle let Coop step into the entryway. The acrid smell of burning upholstery and woodwork hit his nose and made him cough. He lead their little SEAL delegation and caught Carla's attention as she was coming out of the kitchen. Her face was white, her eyes wide, and for a moment, Cooper thought perhaps something terrible had happened to Dr. Brownlee. The news hadn't said anything about someone being harmed. But Cooper knew that a fire, if it was that, was no accident.

"Oh Cooper," she said as she ran over and gave him a hug. Then she adjusted her hair and stepped back, embarrassed.

"Ma'am. These are friends of mine. This is my Senior, Kyle Lansdowne. There's Armando, Fredo and this here's Gunny." Everyone took turns shaking Mrs. Brownlee's hand. She was speechless.

"I'm surprised they let you in," she said.

"Did two tours with your guard out front, Ma'am," Kyle offered. "He lost part of an arm in Afghanistan."

Cooper understood completely. He turned to Mrs. Brownlee. "Can you tell us what happened?" he asked.

Carla looked around to see who else might be listening and then started, "Someone set Austin's office on fire. There's not much structural damage, but it's a mess. Fire's out, I think." She waved her hand in front of her face to swish remnants of smoke from her eyes.

"Anyone hurt?" He meant that to mean Libby.

"No, we're all fine. Who would do such a thing, Cooper?"

"Not sure, ma'am. No offense, but I'm not the shrink here," he answered.

She narrowed her eyes and leaned towards him. "Libby's out by the pool." She waited, looking into all the faces of Cooper's Team. "You boys come on in, but stay away from the investigators. Coop, I think she'd want to see you, privately, of course."

Of course he wanted to. But would she be happy to see him? He knew she'd be terrified. Suddenly he needed to get to her.

The guys sauntered through the entryway to the foyer, doing a double-take at the tall ceilings and intricate metal staircase leading to the second floor, as Cooper pushed by them on his way toward the kitchen and rear yard. He heard the squawk of police and fire radios.

Fredo ran to catch up to him. He didn't need a

nursemaid or a witness to whatever he was going to say to her, but a part of him was grateful Fredo had his back. As they passed by Dr. Brownlee's office, three large yellow-clad firemen had their arms filled with boxes of smoldering papers, which they dropped on cue and began spreading out on the floor. A dark black streak went up the side of one wall of the study, originating from the opened window to the backyard. Dr. Brownlee was absent-mindedly wandering around the room, looking at various piles of manila folders and paperwork, generally making himself a nuisance to the firemen.

Detective Riverton appeared out of nowhere, his little notebook and pen out and ready.

"Surprised to see you here," he said. "Wow, you brought reinforcements too," he said as he noted Kyle and the rest of the Team. "You just happened to stop by today?" He drilled Cooper a look that almost hurt.

"We saw it on the TV, sir. I recognized the house. Thought we could help."

"Oh good," the detective said with emphasis. "Well, as far as I know, this wouldn't require the SEALs. Not exactly an international incident. Not that it isn't a big deal to Dr. Brownlee, here."

Cooper saw Riverton wasn't as casual as he was making it seem.

Kyle was usually the first to speak to an authority

figure, so he inserted his body between Riverton and his man. "We understand, just wanted to be of help, if we could." Coop knew his LPO was trying to deflect Riverton's attention.

Riverton was relentless, pushing Kyle aside with the back of his hand. In another place, at another time, that would be a call to action. Cooper could feel the men tense up behind him. Kyle stepped back and allowed Riverton to question Cooper at close range.

Coop raised his forearms up in the air in mock surrender. "Just wanted to be sure Libby and her parents were okay. If you say they are, we'll be going," he said, but Riverton was staring at the tats on his forearm underside.

"Let me take a look at that, son." He grabbed Cooper's hand mid air and twisted his wrist so he could view the frog print tattoo extending all the way to Coop's right elbow. He hailed the police photographer to take a picture. Cooper didn't refuse permission.

Kyle stood right next to him. "You want to take a picture of mine, too, detective?" He held out his arm with the identical tattoo.

Fredo and Armando extended their arms as well. Riverton was surrounded by frog prints. He gave a wincing glance to Gunny who grinned.

"Mine's in my shirt," the ex-Marine said as he started to pull at his collar.

"No. Wait. That won't be necessary." Riverton's face flushed in anger. Cooper was grateful he had lucked out and the rest of the Team had his back. Another lesson in not getting himself too far out on his own. Stick with the Team. Best be on the inside of the pack. On the outside is where all the predators pick off the strays.

Riverton sighed, slumping his shoulders. He looked like he'd been yanked early out of bed and it was getting to him. His coat was wrinkled and the remnants of a tie was hanging out of his sport jacket pocket. His white shirt was also wrinkled and stained with coffee.

"The young lady is out back, son."

That word again. Not. Your. Son.

"C'mon, Coop. My sinuses is giving me fits. I need some air," Fredo said as he pulled Cooper's arm and forced his buddy to take a couple of steps back and away from Riverton's attention.

Fredo's vise-like grip on Coop's upper arm hurt like hell. But it kept his forward momentum, even though he wanted to turn and watch his LPO talk to Riverton. He knew he could trust Kyle to vouch for him. But he was dying to get some information before he had to see *her*.

And then he did just that. He almost ran right into her without noticing Fredo had released his arm. And there it was all over again, that chemistry. Where his forearm had brushed up against her chest and pressed into her delicate flesh, he felt the electric current that perked the hair all over his body to full attention. Not to mention the unit in his shorts.

She stepped back and put a hand to her chest. Her jaw was tight. Her eyebrows were drawn in an upward angle, pointing to the little lines in her forehead. Her hair was mussed, just like he liked it. She was scared to death and she was still the most beautiful thing he had seen, ever. He knew if he took her in his arms, he'd smell that familiar scent of arousal that would drive him to the beach and long midnight swims. She was going to be hard to get out of his system. And this was a crime scene.

You are such a fucking asshole.

Her eyes were long as she languished unkissed and unhugged, not more than eight inches in front of him. The painful space might as well have been a football field. Libby looked at Fredo, who was staring back at her with what appeared to be shock.

"This is my friend, Fredo. He's on my Team."

She didn't say anything, but nodded a quick acknowledgement and returned to search Coop's face.

"What happened?" he asked her finally. His hands were searching for a back pocket to dive into, but he'd worn the kakis with pockets everywhere but on his butt. Half afraid they'd reach out and grab her, he tilted his hip and perched them there at his waist. He felt ridiculous.

Carla broke the spell. "You guys go on out onto the patio. Leave these men to do their work. Don't need to get in anybody's way." She pushed Coop at the small of his back with both her palms until he had no choice but to step forward and into Libby.

Libby collapsed in his arms for a brief second, and then stiffly righted herself. She would have fallen on the floor if he hadn't caught her. He wanted to take her in his arms and tell her everything was going to be okay, that he had changed his mind, that he would protect her.

But he just couldn't. What she needed most was to be with her own family. He had no right to take her away from them. He had nothing to offer. They'd discussed this before.

They'd even shaken hands on it.

Fuck!

CHAPTER 18

LIBBY WANTED TO run to Coop, to collapse in his arms, but that was just substituting one problem with another. She was so scared of the escalating situation that she was about to do something she promised herself she wouldn't do. She was certain her fear was what was driving her to his arms. Well, that and the great sex, of course. No denying that chemistry they shared.

But the sex wasn't a relationship, and wouldn't be the reason for their relationship. She'd studied this in college, couples who got together at a particularly low point in their lives, and later, when they healed, when they grew up, they couldn't keep it together. They grew apart.

No. She wanted a relationship with someone when she was healed. When she was whole. Besides, she needed to get her life back on track. This delicious detour was just that, a detour. Although his kisses were scorchingly hot, his moves made her bones turn to rubber, she knew better than to think a relationship based on sex alone would last. And she didn't want to entertain anything unless it had a future in it.

It was time to deal with real life. This sailor was a rolling stone who needed to be exactly that to function in his dangerous world. She had been a privileged princess living in a conch-colored house and been given all the luxuries a girl could want, including the dusty rose wallpaper and white canopy bed. Her parents had paid for a great college education. She could graduate and start a practice without owing a dime to anyone.

She needed to prove to herself that she could make it on her own. She was done running into the arms of the men in her life.

The breakup would hurt for a while. But she jutted her chin toward Cooper's face—that face she'd kissed and loved watching as he'd nibbled his way down her bare front.

Can I do this? She decided that somehow, the answer to that was yes.

"Cooper," she said as she backed up far enough away from him so she couldn't feel his heat. "Thank you for coming, but, as you can see, it's like an anthill here. While my parents and I are grateful, I don't think we need the SEALs getting involved in this."

Cooper's eyes glazed over. There was a twitch in his right upper lip. He looked like he'd been slapped. Fredo was staring at her.

It was a matter of logistics, she told herself. She was a logical person. Had a career path, had everything figured out, until that damned Dr. Gerhardt and his wayward libido sent her packing and home to San Diego. And now Cooper, with his cadre of friends just like him. Being honorable. Being just the kind of guy she didn't want to be reminded she wanted. The kind of guy she wanted to run home to.

Except she couldn't, wouldn't let herself. She knew she wasn't ready. Looking back at him, she was determined to show she was unaffected. She willed ice water into her veins, and raised her head atop a very straight neck. She got as tall as she could, inhaled quickly, and then exhaled slowly as she drew the courage to look at him again and this time show him her conviction.

Sometimes things that are good for you are also bad for you.

Damn!

It didn't help. The stubble of his beard began to glisten in the sunlight. She focused on the crease at the right side of his mouth and, when he swallowed, she watched his Adam's apple dip and rise from the top of his tee shirt. She had kissed that spot and knew the musky man scent of him there, felt those sharp bristles of early beard against her lips. The attraction pulled her almost to a swoon, and she struggled not to give in. Logically, she knew this was wrong, all wrong. But her body told her it was so very right.

Maybe it's the fear. Maybe she just needed the security hanging around him gave her. Maybe it wasn't attraction as much as need for protection. Of course, he would play the hero, be concerned. But she had to be strong and give him the out he needed, they both needed. She would have to act like she didn't need him, want him so much. Maybe then she'd start to believe it. Some day.

It sure as hell wasn't today. But she'd do the best she could.

Cooper stood before her in stunned silence. She guessed he hadn't anticipated this. Just like at their first meeting, she'd showed him the distance between them. A clarity was coming to his eyes and he nodded slightly.

"So, I just don't think there is anything you and your boys can do. Thanks, though."

Cooper jerked to attention. "All right. Good," he said. He scratched the back of his neck, his left hand snagged in his belt loop. "We don't want to interfere." He looked over at his Mexican buddy who was still fixated, staring back at her. Coop smacked him on the shoulder and Fredo came to. "Looks like we can go," he told his buddy.

It broke Libby's heart to hear the words. But he was right, of course.

Libby looked out to the garden shed and saw the gardener being interviewed by one of the police. The man was standing in his uniform: blue jeans and long-sleeved khaki brown shirt. He was holding a pair of pruning shears with a curved nub end.

Cooper nodded in her direction, "Well, if there is anything, you have my number. Give me a call."

"Yes, I've got my trusty cell phone," she said, drawing on the ice water in her veins. "I'll be okay. You don't need to worry, Cooper."

"Libby, be careful," he whispered. "I mean it. We have a saying in the Teams, 'Not everyone who appears to be your enemy is, and not everyone who helps you is your friend.' Don't trust anyone but the police."

She wanted to brush off the words. It would have been smart to keep her mouth shut. But she wasn't feeling especially smart. She was getting angry.

"Well, I guess I can draw comfort from those parting words of wisdom. Thank you for the gift of your advice. And for your cell phone number, Coop." She dug her phone from her pocket, holding it up.

How dare he stand there so handsome, so commanding, so concerned? What right did he have to come marching into her life, demonstrating his six-foot-something-of-a-hero-stuff, when she'd made a fool of herself? Giving her Team advice like she didn't have a brain, or was one of the Team guys? She didn't own chainmail undies or stainless steel bras. She was flesh and blood and she was in scared to death. And somehow it was all up to her to figure it out.

The duct tape and steel cables were failing her right now. Her heart was crumbling.

"Libby..." he started to respond. His eyes had softened, but Fredo was pulling his arm and dragging him off the patio back into the kitchen.

"Come on, bro," Fredo said to everyone within earshot. He was intent on getting Cooper out of the kill zone just as if a hello was waiting for them for an extraction.

Libby followed, not taking her eyes off Cooper's massive back as he moved with long fluid steps toward the front door. She wasn't going to make this easy at all. She half way wanted to give his gorgeous butt a push with her pink toes accented with daisy flip fops.

The team gathered in single file and left her house just as quietly as they had entered. Libby slammed the glass and steel door behind them and turned around before she changed her mind and went flying into his arms. She stood face to face with her mother, who was standing in the foyer with her hands on her hips.

"Just what the hell was that, Libby?" her mother

asked.

"Nothing." *God, help me. Can I do this?*

Her mother raised one eyebrow, shifting her gaze to the closed front door as if she'd see the team saunter back in.

Libby shrugged her shoulders. "Too much going on. It was a mistake that they came over. They realize that now."

"I think they wanted to help," her mother said.

"Really? I'm not sure I'd call it help. I just think they have to get involved in everything. They can't stay out of the fray. Occupational hazard. Egos the size of California, I'd say. Meddling. Just like Coop coming to this house in the first place. They can't leave us alone. We don't need their help. Or their memories."

Libby brushed passed her mother, who still stood with her hands on her hips. She ran up the metal staircase to her room. Once inside, she threw herself on the bed and grabbed Morgan. The stuffed dog smelled like her cat, Noodles. Libby burst into tears and sobbed herself to sleep.

COOPER DIDN'T SAY anything as they maneuvered around the police cars and groups of onlookers on their way down the street. His heart was pounding in his chest, sending vibrations all the way to his toes. He thought the tips of his ears were on fire. Back in the truck, he stared blindly out the dirty window as he sat in the second seat. He felt like he'd been punched in the stomach. He knew the guys would give him a little space, but then they'd be all over him. Kyle would be the one to indicate when that would be. It was up to Coop to make the adjustment, and he was going to put all his effort into doing that. He didn't want them thinking he was anything but whole.

Kyle's phone rang. He was sitting next to Coop on the second seat.

"Hey there, Christy."

Coop could hear his wife's voice on the other end of the line. He'd forgotten they were supposed to see some houses today for Armando and Mia.

"Sorry, honey, but we got caught up in something. We're on our way."

Got caught up with something. Not exactly the right way to put it. Coop felt a friendly thump on his shoulder from Gunny, who was stretched out on the third seat behind him.

"Where to, Senior?" Fredo asked from the driver's seat.

Kyle hung up the phone and gave directions to Fredo. Armando leaned back over the front seat and shot Coop a wink, which pissed him off. But Coop knew it wouldn't be a good idea to react until he knew for sure what he was feeling, or could bury it. For the second time in the last twenty-four hours he wished he still drank.

Where'd that thought come from? Although they pissed him off, he was grateful to be with his buds, the guys who would lay down their lives for him. And Gunny, well Gunny had nothing better to do.

Coop turned around and looked at the old Marine. "How you feeling these days, Gunny?"

"No, I did not quit smoking," Gunny answered. "Don't you guys ever fucking stop?"

"Thought we were gonna get another look at that chest tattoo again, Gunny," Armando shouted back to him over the roar of the old beater. "That detective seemed kinda sweet on you."

Everyone laughed, at Gunny's expense. That was always the way it was. In an instant, the somberness of the moment was broken and Cooper began to loosen up. His need for alcohol vanished.

They drove down a tree-lined street of mostly small, single story homes with well-kept yards. They pulled up behind Kyle's Tahoe, which was parked in front of a small yellow home with white trim and red tile roof. Kyle's wife, Christy, got out of the truck, holding Brandon, their six-month-old son. Christy was jangling some keys as she turned the drooling baby over to his dad.

Kyle was totally focused on his son, making faces

and imitating his baby talk, like they were two old men engaged in a meaningful conversation. It touched Coop how this man, so devoted to his wife and young son, was the same guy who could shoot enemy combatants while running in between women and children in the killing streets over in that hellhole. Kyle never made a mistake, and had covered Coop many times while he tried to give first aid to one of their own fallen, or to an innocent who had gotten caught in the crossfire. His LPO had so much to live for, yet the nature of their job was such that he could very well lose his life trying to help someone who wanted to kill him.

Not everyone you see is your enemy. Not every friend can be trusted.

But he could trust Kyle. Coop said a little private prayer that Kyle would always be rewarded with a long and fruitful life, to be able to watch little Brandon grow up.

Team jobs are for single guys. He couldn't see how a married man could do it. The baby reached for him and gave Coop a gummy smile. Coop let the youngster grab his little finger and squeeze.

That's right, little man, I'm gonna protect your daddy, just like he's protected me.

Christy was opening the front door, talking to Armando in her cute, saleswoman banter, tapping across the floor in her high heels. Cooper saw that Kyle, gingerly holding the baby, was following behind her, watching every movement. He looked like it turned him on for some strange reason.

"You like going to open houses, LT?" Coop asked.

"Yeah," Kyle said and Coop knew, no matter what, no matter how many times he asked, that was the only answer he was going to get.

Armando was interested in the recently remodeled kitchen, whistling as he ran his fingers down the new granite countertops. Gunny had checked out the master bedroom and bath down the hall. "Shit, guys, look at this love tub," he shouted out. "Armani, you sure you want to buy this for Mia? With her taste in—"

"Shut the fuck up," Fredo pounced on Gunny. "Don't disrespect his sister, you asshole."

Armando rolled his eyes and let the two of them work it out, obviously annoyed. Kyle was sharing a private look with his wife and was completely oblivious to anything else, even the baby, who had spit up and sent a buttermilk-like substance down the back of his shirt.

Coop paced back and forth. The house didn't do anything for him, just like Libby's huge house. He liked the size of his mobile home. He knew where everything was, and it was within arm's length almost any time. This forced him not to collect too much stuff. His mom was the keeper of the mementos, which were all gone now. Buried in the rich, dark earth he'd loved. He wished that perhaps he had more than a couple pictures of his family. But it never occurred to him before.

Gone forever.

CHAPTER 19

L IBBY'S DAD CLOSED the front door behind their insurance adjuster. That left them alone with Detective Riverton. All the other police and fire crews were gone. A pungent burnt smell permeated the house. Even with the opened windows and fans, provided by the adjuster's emergency crew, the house smelled unbearably toxic.

The family waited while Austin Brownlee slowly walked across the living room to sit beside his wife on the couch. Riverton sat on a cranberry overstuffed chair, identical to the one Libby sat on, with a coffee table between them. She was holding her breath, until she realized it. No matter how much she scolded herself, she couldn't escape the fact that she was afraid, and she was very much alone.

It was a scene right out of a horror movie, Libby thought. Black streaks of smoke covering one wall in the foyer giving off a thick acrid smell. Water and large quilted moving blankets to sop it up were strewn all over the entryway. And her parents sat on the couch, hand in hand, behind a fresh bouquet of ridiculously bright and cheery flowers from her mother's garden. Nothing was as it had been just a week ago. Libby's life had literally gone to hell.

She remembered the words Coop had given her, to trust the police. So, with great effort, she tried to follow those instructions and forced out of her head and heart everything else.

"Okay, folks. This is what we got," Riverton began.

"Whatever is going on, it has escalated to the point that I think we need to have a serious discussion about moving all of you out of this house." He scanned the faces of his audience, and continued, "I'd be lying if I told you I could protect you here. This creep isn't going to go away, and, although I'd love to tell you we have good leads, I'm just going to give it to you straight. We don't."

"But you haven't finished your investigation, right?" her mother asked.

"Carla, we haven't even started. Things are moving so damned fast. Tomorrow the fire investigator will be back over. His job is to make a determination as to the cause, after all the dust has settled. Your insurance is going to need that, too."

"Of course," Dr. Brownlee said. His face was pale,

even with the suntan. His lips were dark pink, meeting in a flat line without a hint of a smile or frown. Libby thought he looked like he was in shock.

"Hopefully, he'll be finding some clues, but right now, there just isn't anything that points anywhere. We know the fire was started with some liquid, probably gasoline, and we think it was poured in the room from the window. We've taken the gas can down to the lab, but there are so many prints on it, I doubt anything unusual will come up."

Carla looked at her husband, and then back at Riverton. "Who is under suspicion at this point?"

"Well, we've got the gardener, of course."

"Oh, he's not a threat to anyone," Dr. Brownlee said. "He's a grateful relative of a patient of mine. I've profiled him, and he's clean. References checked out. He needs the money, and I don't think he'd mess up his situation here."

"Still, Austin, we have to treat everyone as a suspect. You understand," Riverton replied.

"Indeed I do."

Libby couldn't hold back her curiosity, and her fear. "And Cooper? He a suspect too?"

Riverton turned towards her and his mouth fell into a scowl. He squinted at Libby as if sunlight were hurting his eyes. "Yes, I'm sorry to say. We have a photograph that matches the tats on his arm."

"They all have them. I saw it myself," Carla blurted out.

"I'm fully aware of that, and it complicates things a bit, but it doesn't get him off the hook. Everything that's happened has occurred since Coop first showed up at your door." Riverton looked back over at Libby, eyes rheumy and tired. "I'm afraid I'm going to have to ask you not to associate with him any longer. Until he's ruled out."

Libby's stomach knotted up and overflowed with bile. She stood before she realized what she'd done. "That's not a problem. We've already come to that conclusion. I doubt he'll be back," she said. Her hands were flailing wildly at her sides. She wanted to run. Run away from all this.

"What could this boy have against Austin?" Carla asked. "And why would he and his friends come over today? Wouldn't he stay away? He seemed like he genuinely wanted to help."

Some people who look like the enemy are not. Not everyone who helps is a friend.

Is that how it was done? Was Coop trying to get to her dad by using her? As much as she might find that the solution to her confusion, it didn't ring true. She just couldn't think Cooper would have anything to do with this.

"Who knows? I'm going to talk to his Chief and see

if there is anything in his past, anything at all, that may have some bearing on all of this."

"Well, he did just lose his entire family in a tornado last month," Carla said.

"That's convenient. But it's also easy to check out." Riverton stood up and walked to the window, watching the gardener drive off. "I'm going to want to see what you have on that man, Austin. One of our investigators didn't like him."

"My office is a mess, Clark. It will take me awhile to find his application and the profile I gave him."

"You gave him a personality profile?" It was Carla's turn to stand. "I can't believe you gave him a test to be our gardener." She crossed the room and then turned and came back. "Did you get a profile on the pool man too? The house cleaners?"

The pause was pregnant and said it all. Libby knew the answer was yes.

Riverton chuckled and shook his head. His hands were in his pockets, his notebook tucked back into the vest pocket of his coffee-stained shirt. "Your insurance will probably pay for your relocation, although you will have to check your policy. But I'd get working on that right away. Don't spend tonight here. We'll send a patrol around several times during the evening, for an extra set of eyes. You can lock up everything but the library. Put some plywood over the broken window, and I think that should secure it. But you have to leave, and I think you should do it right away, before anyone gets any other strange ideas."

"What do we tell everyone?" Carla asked.

"Just say it was an accident. And look for people who are too interested. Like that team that just 'stopped by' today," he said using his fingers as quote marks. "You call me if anything is out of the ordinary. Austin, you keep your normal schedule tomorrow, today, if you can."

Riverton handed each of them a couple of business cards, noting his cell number on the front.

"So what happens next?" her dad asked.

Riverton smiled. "We catch the guy."

The three family members stared back at Riverton in shock. Carla was the one who asked how he was so sure.

"Well, these types never give up until they are caught. You see, they really want to be caught. You know this, Austin."

"Hmmm." Her dad said, nodding.

"My job is to catch him before he does something really bad. To kill a cat or set fire to a house is one thing. Means he's seriously disturbed. Means he won't give up until he hurts that someone he's after. At this point, Austin, I think it's you, but it could be Libby— even you, Carla. I want you all to look over all your communications with people over the past few weeks, see if anything sticks out. Anyone made any enemies lately?"

All three of them shook their heads.

And then Libby thought about Dr. Gerhardt.

CHAPTER 20

LIBBY COMBED HER memory, looking for anything that pointed to her former advisor. Although she didn't trust the man, she also couldn't see him as being responsible for the attack on her cat and, even worse, the fire in her father's office. As far as she knew, he had never met her father.

She thought about the late night suppers she and her mentor had together at Santa Clara. They'd shared a bottle of wine frequently at Vesuvio's, his favorite Italian restaurant. One or two glasses was more than enough to get her feeling tipsy, but she never went beyond that limit. In hindsight, he'd started behaving beyond her comfort zone.

She'd always said no. No to the more wine, that is. She found it hard to say no to his company, especially if it was going to help her with a good recommendation when she got out of graduate school. He never asked for sexual favors, although there were rumors of

him with other students. Was he involved with someone else at the time and didn't want to double-cheat on
his wife?

Every villain is the hero of his own journey.

He'd had lots of opportunity to slip a little something in her water or wine glass during those dinners.
He could have tried to take advantage of her on those
nights when she was feeling a little vulnerable. But, she
had trusted him. No, he wasn't high on her radar for
being the guy who was stalking her family. Maybe a
lousy husband, but not a killer.

She had enjoyed seeing his face light up when she
would tell him about her conversations with some of
the undergrad students, and their shared projects. He
seemed to really care about their discoveries. She
performed some independent research for him in the
dream lab and helped get willing subjects for him.
Libby remembered that very first day, when he opened
up his Psych 101 class with the following statement:

*"This class comes with a three-hour lab requirement,
where you will do all manner of fun things, like clean
out rat cages and learn how to shave the hair off small
furry animals without killing them or hurting yourselves. You will be asked to volunteer for experiments,
and your answer will be 'yes' or you will fail my classes.
Understood? If you stay with a major in psychology, as
an upper classman, you will graduate to higher forms of*

animals: Freshman Psych majors. Hopefully, no shaving will be required by the time you get to that point."

She remembered how the class had cracked up, and she knew immediately she wanted him for her advisor. How could someone with such a healthy sense of humor have such a dark side? But Coop had said to be careful. She hadn't expected the dramatic change in Dr. Gerhardt's behavior, either. Was he a much better liar than she'd previously thought? Could something have happened to him during the semester, something she hadn't noticed? Some major, life-changing event?

Though disgusted and disillusioned with Dr. Gerhardt and his morals, there just wasn't anything about him that seemed any darker. And she was really looking. Hard.

I am so naïve. Who can I trust?

Libby decided she would have to talk to Detective Riverton about her advisor. If they were thinking Coop could be a suspect, certainly the doctor should be looked at as well.

Libby was writing in her journal when she heard a soft knock on her door.

"Come in, Mom," she said.

"Hi, sweetie. I was just wondering how soon before you'd be ready to go. We're going to spend the night at the Hotel Del Coronado. Your dad has booked a suite there."

Libby had always wanted to stay at the Hotel Del, but under much better circumstances. Spending the next few days in a suite with her parents wasn't anywhere close to that fantasy.

Her mother must have noticed her scrunched-up nose. "Libby, your dad's trying very hard. I know it's not what you want. Just for a few days. He wants you close. He wants to make sure you are safe."

"He can't watch me 24/7." Libby noticed how a sharp pain in her chest erupted at the reminder of what Coop had told her just yesterday. She was using that same argument on her mother.

"I know. But Libby, darling…" Carla came over and sat down on the edge of Libby's flowered bedspread. "Let him try. You know how he likes to be protective. It's his job."

"Did it ever occur to you that I don't need protection?" Libby sat up and took in her mother's handsome face. "I've got to find my own way. Am I supposed to stay with you two until this guy is caught? What happens if it takes years? Then what do we all do? Do we just put our lives on hold?"

"Well, we'll figure something out." Carla looked down at her hands, folded in her lap. "I was hoping your SEAL friend would help you out a little."

Libby stood up with hands on her hips. "Mother, for Chrissakes, that's over with. It was foolish of me."

Carla went back to examining her hands, looking down, and flipping her wedding ring around her finger. "Can you tell me what happened?"

"No, mother. It's none of your business."

"But you don't think he could possibly be the, the, the—"

"Cat killer? No. Absolutely not. Not a chance in hell of that."

"Well, I don't want to pry—"

"Then don't. Just let me have my privacy. I have other friends I can stay with."

"Well there's Neil and Marsha's.

"You've *got* to be kidding." Libby was barely able to stand her sister-in-law.

"Well, humor me, then. Just for tonight. You'll come with us to the Coronado. We'll make a plan—your plan. But tonight, let's be together as a family, okay?"

Libby didn't answer.

"So come on, get yourself packed up and let's get out of this house. My headache gets worse every minute I stay here."

Libby knew her mother was way more stressed than she let on. Poor woman was walking that difficult divide between two people she cared the most about in her life: her husband, and her daughter. And Libby wasn't making it very easy on her.

Carla Brownlee left the room after Libby promised to be ready in five minutes.

She began throwing clothes into a suitcase she'd just unpacked a few days ago. Yes. She'd go to the Hotel Del with her parents and try not to think about being a blushing bride of some strong hunky guy who would make love to her all night long just like—

Stop this! You've got to wake up. Get real.

She hoped, when it all was over, she could find herself ready for a happily ever after. She wasn't there yet, though. She knew the right, the smart thing was to focus on her future—getting her degree and finding a good job to support herself. Focus on her studies and leave all this blackness and pain behind her, even if she had to use duct tape on her resolve to hold all the pieces together today. And for the first time in a long time, though there was little hope, she didn't feel like running away. It was time to stand and face the fact that she didn't need anybody, and she could take care of herself.

COOPER PLAYED WITH pencils on a vacant sales associate's desk at the Patterson Realty office while Christy Lansdowne worked with Armando and Kyle in the conference room, leaving him alone with Fredo. Gunny had taken off to oversee the close-up of his gym. The Mexican SEAL was swinging his short torso around on a wheeled office chair, testing and adjusting the height and angle of the back until the thing flipped over on top of him when he landed on the floor.

Coop gave a hand to his best friend, who was sputtering a string of curses in Spanish. The back of the chair had become dislodged from the frame and parts had scattered all over the floor. As if on cue, both Team guys kneeled and began collecting items scattered around before them. Without saying a word, they located the screws, levers and other parts and began to put the chair back together again. They guessed at the height and back tilt and set about adjusting the finished project accordingly. Once it was completed and judged to be sturdy, Fredo rolled the chair gently into the desk cubby, and let out a satisfied sigh when the armrests made it safely under the wooden surface without scraping.

Cooper watched Fredo look around the office for something else to do, something to fix. He knew it was hell on his friend to wait. It was hell on him as well. Overseas, that was the worst part: waiting. Waiting for some action. Hard for civilians to understand, but it was way better than waiting to die. Boredom killed people. Lack of concentration could get a Team guy in real trouble. Better to be in action. Doing anything. Thank God for video games.

Coop used to tinker with a gadget he brought with

him on his last tour. It was a plastic arm piece, a toy remote control device, except it didn't control anything, just squawked and flashed lights, running on four AAA batteries. A kid's toy.

Coop added some switches and some simulated detonator buttons and made the thing look entirely lethal, although harmless. No one ever let on that the thing was a complete fake, something they were grateful for later.

One time, when they were on an emergency snatch and grab mission, he'd forgotten to take the device off his arm. There was some limited exchange of fire, and a mob of Tangos was gathering at the end of a dusty street, menacing and angry. Coop held up his arm with the toy device, and did a mock aim into the crowd, turning on the red laser light. All they saw next were asses and elbows. The team had to struggle to maintain straight faces and not to laugh their butts off. But the toy had probably saved their lives.

Coop mused that perhaps he could make a few more of them while he waited for their next workup. He'd stop by the toy store later this afternoon. If not, there were some upscale kid's stores around the island that might carry something that looked halfway real. That would be a good start, he thought. He had boxes of spare parts and deadly-looking wire switches back at the motor home. Shoot, if he ever got tired of being a

SEAL he could work on a Sci-Fi set in Hollywood.

GOTTA GET MY mind off things. His insides ached and his pants felt tight. No question about his need. And no question who was the only person on the planet who could fill that need.

He thought about getting another tattoo. He remembered the feel of Daisy's delicate fingers on his sensitive flesh, and how hard she used to work on him. She'd bite her pouty lower lip as she was concentrating, her boobs brushing against him, depending on the placement of the new tattoo, until it would drive him crazy.

But hooking up with Daisy wasn't fair to her and probably wouldn't work anyway. Besides, Daisy deserved much better.

So Kyle had gotten himself a wife and now had little Brandon, who was slobbering all over the sliding glass door in the conference room, trying to stand up. Brandon spotted Coop, and the toddler's eyes lit up.

"Time to babysit, or we'll be here until nightfall," Coop said to Fredo as he walked towards the glass door. Brandon fell back on his well-diapered butt and started to play patty cake with excitement. The little one knew all the Team members and was comfortable playing with any of them.

Coop slid open the door and the three at the table

looked up. "I'm going to take Brandon for a bit, you mind?" he asked.

Christy smiled and nodded. "I have a little bottle in his diaper bag here. Coop, he might need a change."

Coop instinctively held the toddler at arm's length just in case the baby's wetness became his problem. Brandon squealed and wiggled, his chubby legs busy with bicycle kicks.

Armando threw his head back and laughed. "A million dollars' worth of taxpayer's money spent on your training, and you're going to play nanny, Cooper."

"Yes, and he cooks, too," Kyle added.

"And I can still kick your asses any time you two decide is right, and you know it," Coop retorted. He tucked Brandon into the crook in his arm, leaned over to pick up the blue diaper bag covered in dinosaur print, swung the heavy bag over his other shoulder and exited the war zone. "Sorry Brandon," he said to the baby. "I'm going to have to watch my language pretty soon or you'll start swearing like a sailor, and that won't work at preschool."

Brandon was still trying to wiggle out of his arm. This was going to be fun. Trying to change a diaper on a toddler who wanted to slime the entire office.

He found a receiving blanket and spread it on one of the unoccupied desks, and lay Brandon on top of it.

The baby tried to flip over, but Cooper held him firm. "Stop it. We're gonna see if you have…" A large gob of yellowish poo was exposed just as soon as Cooper released one side of the diaper tape.

"Holy shit," Fredo said as he came over. "What's she feeding him?"

Annoyed, Cooper swore at Fredo, and, with one large hand on the baby's bare chest turned to his Team buddy and said, "Guess."

"Cereal? Bananas. That looks like bananas, all yellow and shit," Fredo answered.

"You are an idiot, Fredo. Didn't your mama or your sisters talk about this sort of thing while you were growing up? Ever date a gal with a little one before? Yeah, you have. Don't you know anything about babies? He only eats one thing. He gets what you dream about every night, Fredo. Breast milk."

CHAPTER 21

LIBBY AND HER parents situated themselves in, of all things, the Honeymoon Suite. She wondered why the suite had a second bedroom. Perhaps it was for hesitant brides who weren't sure they wanted to consummate their wedding night? It could have been amusing if it wasn't such a damned sad joke. But it did give her a separate room with a private entrance that locked securely.

The rose-colored suite was a bit much, but featured a great view of the Pacific Ocean. The beautiful Coronado beach stretched in both directions, with only a smattering of adults, children and dogs playing in the surf. Seagulls were standing guard on the balcony next door like tiny lifeguards.

A huge spray of Fire and Ice roses stood in a crystal vase on a glass and chrome coffee table, next to a chilled bottle of champagne and a platter of cheeses and crackers. The modern kitchen was fully stocked with drinks and some covered entrees they had ordered ahead of time. Antiques dotted all the rooms, along with framed sepia posters of movies that had been made at the Del over the years. A mahogany sideboard, stocked with books Libby recognized as romance novels stood against one wall. In more normal times, this could be a place where she could have hibernated in for months, if money was no object.

She entered her room and dumped the meager contents of her bag on her queen bed, and then hung up her travel case on the towel rack in her white marble bathroom. She was used to the vibrant colors of her parent's Spanish-style home, with its bright, intricately colored tiled trim and red pavers. Just as well, she thought. The clean white lines of the bathroom felt soothing. The evening called for a soak in the tub and then to bed early, maybe with one of the books from the living room. She wondered if she'd have the place to herself, since her father would normally go down to the bar for a nightcap before falling asleep in front of the TV.

She scanned the bookshelf and picked out a thick book with a naked man's torso on the front cover, by an author she recognized. Reclined on the couch, she nibbled on crackers and cheese, since her parents were occupied behind their closed bedroom door.

Glad someone has a little romance in their life.

LIBBY WOKE UP with a start, dropping her book to the floor. The living room was dark except for a light coming under her parent's door. She didn't want to disturb them, but she was restless. The pink-orange glow of the sunset was long gone and all that remained was a faint blush at the horizon. A couple of bonfires in fire pits were spaced at intervals along the beach right in front of the hotel.

To her left, bright lights from several military vehicles shone down on teams of men in single file formation. They looked like ants. She'd watched the BUD/S trainees before. She wasn't sure it would be smart, but she felt drawn. She left a note for her parents and made it through the creaky hallways of the old hotel, brushing past ghosts of romances past and present. At last she was out on the beach, with the sounds of the surf muting every other noise. The early evening was clear and gorgeous. Warm sand seeping between her toes made her feel oddly at peace.

The moist sea air caressed her face. One of the things she loved about living in San Diego was that the temperature rarely varied more than about ten degrees. She wore her sleeveless white ruffled blouse and a light tan pair of cargo pants, along with her favorite pair of daisy flip-flops.

She heard the barked orders from one of the BUD/S instructors, assigned to pour pain and fear all over the young recruits. One crew of eight was struggling to get a rubber boat up over a seawall of sharp boulders. Out of the blackness of the ocean another crew emerged, laying down their oars and picking up their boat to attempt the same task. From her research, Libby knew they'd do the same thing over and over again until they worked as one crab-like unit with one mind, one purpose. The men would be switched. They'd be paired up in all sorts of ways. Weakest with the strongest. Weakest against the strongest. There would be the Smurf crew, and the giants. All while doing timed tasks where what you were doing was as important what your neighbor was doing. Elimination runs put pressure on everyone, and no one wanted to be on the boat that got eliminated.

She'd done a paper in high school on the SEALs, and brought several items to class that had belonged to her uncle Will. She'd read about the training. She missed never knowing her dad's only brother and best friend.

Her father had acted ambivalent about her paper and had refused to let her take the medals and the folded flag her dad got when her grandparents passed on. But her mother secreted the mementos, placing them in Tupperware containers, disguised in paper towels. Libby had gotten an A+ on the paper, and cemented what was already a very solid A in the class.

She found she had more of a taste for history than she had imagined, and considered a minor in it at Santa Clara. But she rationalized her interest was because she never knew much about her uncle Will, as if there was some big dark secret there her parents, especially her father, would never let her in on.

Gradually, her studies in psychology took over, and she became as disinterested in the military as her father was.

Until now.

Yes. No doubt about it. Her world had been rocked. And she needed to get over it very quickly. Maybe it was time to start thinking about either returning to Santa Clara or applying to some other graduate program. A friend of hers loved the University of Hawaii, and she made a mental note to check online for their Masters programs.

She took a seat in the sand and watched from behind orange plastic netted barriers as the teams of men worked their muscles, worked their attitudes, and made all the necessary adjustments. She wondered what it would take to become someone like that. To think with a quick mind of a killer, but to love with the intensity she knew Cooper had. That capacity for loyalty, honor, courage, no matter what the cost. Nothing in her life until now had even come close to the adversity he'd seen.

Her childhood had been so different from Cooper's. He was a hard-working son of a farmer. Libby had grown up in a beautiful house, with two successful parents who provided her with everything monetarily a child could ever want. And yet, as she looked at the faces of the young recruits, she realized something had been missing.

Cooper lived a simple life. How could she ever have considered staying with him in his tiny motor home that was half bed? Well, the bed part, and the shower was okay—actually it was fantastic—but the rest of it, no. Water hooked up by green garden hose to some guy's house next door, and power from a long yellow extension cord. It was set up for a single guy with simple needs. There was no room in Cooper's life for her. And she knew her needs were far from simple.

But something else was there that she'd always wanted. Some singleness of focus, of deep determination—a calling. Did she have that kind of calling to be a psychologist or family counselor? She knew she could help people. Was it enough?

Could she do this? Could she face her fears? Could she heal herself and go on, determined to prove to everyone, but mostly herself, that she was self-reliant, strong and capable of handling anything life would throw at her?

And do it without a man?

One of the wet and sandy boys from the surf tipped his helmet, painted with his name and class number on it, and gave her a big toothy grin. He was a handsome guy, and she pictured him in his dress whites, his cap under his left arm. She could see him bowing before her at a dance. The two-story doors of the arched ballroom were opened to the sea breeze, golden sheers bellowing inward while the two of them danced the night away. Just the two of them. She'd feel the white gabardine, rub her fingers over the medals on his chest, smell the light lemon aftershave and mint toothpaste as he'd bring his face close to hers, and…

It was Cooper's face that kissed her in the ballroom. Cooper's arms around her waist, lifting her up and against him, pressing her to him, and then setting her down and twirling her around like she was made of tissue paper. His smoldering gaze would never leave her as she turned this way, and then that, feeling her lips and cheeks flush red, smiling at the knowledge that he was thinking about doing all manner of things to her when he could peel off her dress. When they would be alone and naked.

The young recruit got yelled at by someone and he shrugged and joined the line of men jogging to sit atop an overturned boat.

SHE MADE HER way back to the hotel lobby, dawdling

along the promenade of little shops. She entered one that contained an array of stuffed animals, mostly whales and seals. Eco toys about the oceans and climate change done in bright colors for little hands and minds to wrap around were interspersed with coloring books. There were mechanical frogs and windup helicopters that buzzed and tweeted with flashing red lights overhead.

One drone replica swooped down and almost hit her in the head, and she turned to give a good dose of her mood to the operator, and stood face to face with Cooper. His eyebrows rose as he gently put down the white remote control device and stuck his hands in his pockets, raising his shoulders.

"You checking up on me?" she asked. Suddenly her stomach was boiling and her heart started pounding.

"No, not at all. I came to look at the toys," he said, looking down at the ground.

"Sure." She turned and began to walk out of the store. The urge to leave and go up to her room was overwhelming. She needed to get out of the tiny store.

"Libby wait. Honest. I wasn't checking up on you. I didn't even know you were here."

She turned sideways and spoke into the doorframe. "It doesn't matter. Nothing matters anymore." Her words fell like lead weights. She hoped her attempt at lying worked just a little. She waited for him to say something, deciding not to run again. After all, she had every right to be here, too.

"This must be hard for you," he said softly.

As in it isn't hard for you? God damn it.

"Not really. I'm hoping this creep will be caught and then I can get on with the rest of my life. You gotta admit, I picked a hell of a time to drop out of school." She felt better about those words, and so looked up at him with what she hoped was a smart smile, hoping not to reveal anything.

It wasn't any use. He could see it, all the way to her soul. She was sure he could see her worry, her hurt, and her confusion. In that moment she wanted to run to him, collapse in his arms. Have him whisk her away to an island somewhere where they could dance in the breeze at sunset and make love all night long. Another world. Another life.

But not my life.

He cut the distance between them in three long strides and stood before her, slowly bringing his arms to her shoulders and rubbing down all the way to her elbows. It was a tender touch that set her skin on fire, filled her belly with need.

Two fingers lifted her chin as he spoke to her. "You know that if I could, I would be there, watching out for you."

She was disappointed he didn't bend to kiss her.

Was that really what she wanted, though? Was he giving her what she needed or wanted? He *cared* about her. Wasn't that enough?

Libby felt her emotions swell so she stepped back, and out of reach of his gentle fingers. "So you've told me. Yes. I understand, I think." It was all she could say. Confusion was making her dizzy. The pain in her chest was increasing.

"I wish we'd taken it more slowly," he said.

"Really? Because you sure seemed to be enjoying yourself," she said through clenched teeth.

There was that little smile at the corner of his upper lip, and the crease that formed there.

Damn. Would you quit with the being in control? A part of her hated him for it.

But then she stood up straight. She was going to demonstrate the reign she had over her own emotions. She took a long pause before speaking up.

"What if we call a truce and concentrate on what works and forget the rest?" she asked.

His puzzled expression showed her he was interested, but wasn't sure.

"What if we just stick to the mind-numbing sex?" She saw him frown. "Oh, come on, Coop, you know that part of 'us' is great."

A father and teenage daughter looked up from a rack of tee shirts and then exited the store. Libby realized perhaps the conversation wasn't entirely appropriate for this location.

Cooper grabbed her arm and pulled her outside. The warm evening air was sweet with the smells of the ocean. He drew her into an alcove beyond the protruding storefront window, where it was dark. Hope began to kindle inside her and she could feel her cheeks begin to flush. Her arousal was delicious. She softened her gaze and turned on the sultry voice she'd practiced so many times in the mirror to herself when she was a teenager. She needed all the ammunition she could get her hands on right now. And she needed to hold it all together. She wasn't going to be the one to actually make the move. She wasn't going to throw herself at him.

His eyes turned from smoldering to pure liquid fire as he took in a deep breath and let it out slowly. He was examining her all over, her hair, her mouth, the V down the front of her white ruffled blouse, let his eyes wander down to her pink toes and then back up again slowly.

"Just a little harmless sex. That's all, Coop," she said as she twisted herself from side to side, looking down, feigning innocence.

She felt the shift in his body. Without looking up, she could see that first his hands bunched up in fists, then one hand went up, probably combing through his hair, which he usually ended with a neck squeeze. Whatever he'd done, it set his other hand into a fist again. He changed his stance. A quick peek had reassured her that he had a huge erection. She knew that was going to be a problem for him, because she suspected that brain was bigger and stronger than the one in his skull.

But she waited for him. She wasn't going to do anything but talk, and wiggle a bit, twirl her hair between her fingers, look out to the lights glittering on the water. Her hormones were raging and her pheromones had to be hitting him right across the face, sending instructions to a certain body part that was screaming right about now. But she wouldn't fall at his feet. She couldn't do that.

"Just sex," he said as his voice broke on the second word.

"That's right. Uncomplicated. No strings. As much sex as either of us wants. And then we'll go our separate ways."

He stepped to her and she could feel the heat from his trembling body. He was less than an inch away from her flesh. "What if I don't want just sex. What if I want more?" His husky voice pulled at her heartstrings. She wanted to shout for joy at the possibility. But she had to be smarter about it.

"Then you'll miss me, Cooper, because I'm not

agreeing to that. I'm not ready for that."

She let him put his arm around her waist and felt his trembling hesitancy. She watched him do it, watched him pull her to him so slowly she thought she would faint. She felt the tendons in his forearm under the frog tats tense, and pull her, as his hand made its way down her backside to approach her rear in an all too familiar way. With very little pressure, his hand guided her lower belly into his groin and she received confirmation of his need for her. Huge confirmation.

Smiling, she raised her arms to his neck, tracing the outline of his mouth. She still avoided his eyes. She let him come to her, bend to her, cover her lips with his. She let him slip his tongue into her mouth and find hers. She couldn't help the little moan she gave him, which earned another squeeze of his hand, sending her closer, rubbing her against him.

She was glad the room upstairs had a separate entrance.

CHAPTER 22

I T DIDN'T TAKE them long to make it back through the narrow hallways, brushing past tourists, sports teams and retirees in walkers and wheelchairs, past the espresso stand, the valet parking desk and the house-keeping station to the large green, dented doors of the staff elevator. Protected by bumpers of cotton-stuffed canvas, Cooper and Libby were finally alone. It was not a logical place to make love, but their urgency for each other was so great it almost happened anyway.

Cooper had hitched up her top, and peeled her pants down nearly to her knees, his hands roaming over Libby's smooth, satiny backside. He would have hesitated, but there wasn't anything from her that indicated she wanted to wait even one minute before getting him to mount her.

But then the doors opened. He was standing there in his shorts, with his lady wrapped around his groin, his tee shirt hanging off one shoulder as she pressed herself against him, showing breasts bursting out from the top of her white lace bra. And a trio of Mexican housekeepers, each holding a red Hoover vacuum cleaner in one hand and a feather duster in the other, dressed in grey uniforms complete with white frilly aprons stared back at them.

There was more than a language problem going on here. One lady, the eldest, covered her eyes and cowered. Cooper turned back to face Libby and he almost came on the spot. Clearly she was ready to let him fuck her right there in front of everyone, but he just couldn't do that. The woman had absolutely no control, and it made his package turn to granite.

He lowered her to standing position, picked up his pants, and, taking her hand, led them out and down the hall, even though he had no idea what floor they were on or which direction would lead to her room.

Libby was giggling as they heard the doors to the elevator close.

"You're going to be the death of me yet, Miss Libby Brownlee."

"Counting on it."

"Where the hell are we?"

Libby looked at the room numbers at a corner before they turned. "Looks like seventh floor. I'm on ten."

He stopped in front of the regular elevator and slipped on his cargo pants. She reached the button to push the up arrow and he stopped her.

"You sure about this?"

"Does it matter?" she asked as she avoided looking him in the eyes, instead backing up against the wall and pushing the button with her hand behind her back. "Come here," she said as she crooked her index finger. Of course he obeyed. He couldn't help himself.

A family of four stood at the back of the elevator, the children being barely grade school age. Cooper waved to indicate they'd catch the next elevator. Before the doors closed they heard the little girl giggle and be reprimanded by her mother.

"I say we go for it, next one, no matter what," Libby said.

He'd had no idea she could be so demanding. She could have commanded a whole platoon if the stakes were high enough. No doubt about it.

As luck would have it, just as he was praying for an empty car, a very full one showed up, stuffed with partygoers in their dinner finest, on their way to the Penthouse. Libby was first to squeeze her way in, dragging Cooper behind her. The crowd parted for them like the Red Sea. Even Cooper had to admit this was becoming almost a religious experience.

He batted down her hand as it tried to sneak beneath the waistband of his pants, something that wasn't lost on the deathly quiet crowd. It was kind of hard to concentrate, as all his effort went into keeping Libby from literally getting him naked in front of complete strangers.

He couldn't look at any of them in the eye as the doors opened to their floor, and he bolted out and down the hallway to the left at Libby's direction. Several doors later, Libby stopped and dug through her purse for the key, inserted it, and stepped inside to a small air-conditioned space that about froze his nuts off.

In the middle of the room stood her father, Dr. Austin Brownlee.

CHAPTER 23

"**O**H!" LIBBY BLURTED out as she backed up a step, right into Cooper's tented shorts. Coop could not believe his bad luck. Just when he was about to have possibly the best sex of his miserable life, *her father* had to be standing two feet away from where he undoubtedly knew they were going to do the down and dirty.

Fuck me.

Cooper shook his head and adjusted the contents of his shorts. There was a seriously agitated beast inside that didn't get the memo about the aborted mission.

"You think this is all a big joke, you two?" Dr. Brownlee looked back and forth between the two of them. Coop didn't know what expression Libby had, but his own smile was from pure nervousness.

What do you say to the father of the girl you're going to do?

They both talked over each other. Libby was trying

to say something like, "I'm sorry you had to see this," and Coop was saying, "No, it isn't funny at all." But neither one finished their sentence. Nothing he would say or do seemed appropriate, under the circumstances.

Dr. Brownlee's hair was uncharacteristically mussed. He was wearing silk pajamas and holding a suspicious tumbler of brown liquid in his left hand. That's when Coop realized Libby's fruit hadn't fallen far from the old tree. Her father had been having sex with his wife earlier. He could almost smell it on the man.

Libby held her hands out to the sides. "What? You didn't know that I have my own life to live, Dad? You think putting me in the Honeymoon Suite with you two meant I have to ask permission to have a little fun?"

"He's a suspect, Libby. What the hell is wrong with you?" Brownlee spat out.

That pissed Cooper off big time.

"Excuse me, sir. I'm not the fucking guy who's doing these things to your family, and you damned well know it," Coop was going to walk up to Brownlee, even in his current state of undress, but Libby finally put her arms around his waist, and he calmed down. Her touch was like an aphrodisiac. His heart rate stayed elevated, but his urge to fight got tucked away.

"I'm in love with him, Dad. I've loved him since the day he showed up at our front door."

Coop was uneasy at first, not sure how he liked hearing the words spoken to someone else before he'd heard them himself. After a quick gut check, he found he rather liked the idea, even though it was a huge surprise. So much for the mind-numbing sex and just sex bit. But before he could say anything, Carla again rescued him from saying something stupid, by appearing at the bedroom doorframe.

She looked over his bare chest, and he found himself standing a little taller, clutching Libby a little tighter.

"Have you two had dinner?" she asked in her best hostess fashion. Cooper could see she was shaking. Brownlee whipped around as if to say something to her in anger, but stopped himself. Carla ignored him and waited for an answer.

Libby sighed. She looked up and asked Cooper for some direction. All he could do was imagine the little mewling sounds she made as she came in his arms. He saw her naked flesh beneath the kisses he was going to strategically place all over her body. Whether it was in five minutes, or five hours, he'd stay beside her until they could be alone.

Whatever you want, Libby.

"I apologize for my state of undress. If you'll give

me a moment, perhaps, if Libby wants to—"

"I have some things in the fridge, and we can always order something from room service." Carla was focused on his face, and not his bare chest. "We'll leave you two to….get dressed…Come on, Austin. Let's give them a few minutes privacy."

Dr. Brownlee was led from the room in shock. As soon as the door closed, Coop had to push Libby away, holding her at arm's length.

"Not sure I can do this, Libby. I'm sorry."

"Not your fault." She wrapped her arms around his bare back, resting the side of her head against his chest. "I want you to spend the night here."

He hesitated, but wanted to say something.

What?

"Coop," she leaned back and those pouty pink lips, accented by the mock worry lines forming between her eyebrows finished the sentence and sent him into orbit, "I want you to make love to me all night long. I need this more than anything I've ever needed in my whole life."

"Not here, Libby. That wouldn't be right."

"Then we'll get our own room."

"I—I don't have—"

"Shhh. I got a credit card. You okay with that?"

"Well, honey, I'd rather pay for our room myself."

And yes, he was all in. He just hoped dinner didn't

last too long.

And that there was another room available that didn't cost a half month's pay.

CHAPTER 24

I T WAS PAINFUL to sit and watch Cooper across the table from her, sitting next to her mother. Libby guessed he usually had that giddy-making impact on women that her mother was exhibiting. It made her father frown.

The first time she crossed her legs she felt Cooper's calf rub up against her. While looking at her mother and asking for salt to be passed, she felt him nudge her foot up until it almost hit the underside of the table. Then they had a regular back and forth, touching and rubbing that was making her hot and wet.

Her parents didn't appear to notice. Her father said next to nothing. He was extremely focused on his food, despite her mother's attempts to draw him out.

"I was surprised to see you here, Cooper. After today…"

"Mother, we ran into each other at the toy store downstairs."

"The toy store?" her father asked. "What were you doing there?"

"Remember, I wrote you a note? I went down to the beach. I was bored. I was on my way back to the room when I almost got hit in the head with a helicopter."

"A remote controlled toy. I had the remote," Cooper added helpfully.

Libby could tell her mother was dying to know how they happened to get back together when it had been obvious earlier that the they were no longer going to be seeing each other. But she was wise enough not to ask.

Thank God for small favors.

"So, how long are all of you staying here at the Del?" Coop asked.

"Well, Cooper, that's a very good question. My daughter wasn't very happy about being here, at least not until you showed up," her father answered. "I will have to go to work every day. I'm guessing Carla and Libby will be here a week. Unless something changes."

"They any closer to catching someone for this?" Cooper asked him.

Libby's father glanced ostentatiously at his gold Rolex. "Let's see, in the 4 hours since we've seen each other? No." He cocked his head and pursed his lips before addressing Cooper again. "Any suggestions? I'm all ears."

Cooper played with a couple of leftover peas on his place, using the tines of his fork. "As a matter of fact, I was going to make a recommendation."

"Oh?" Her father took another pull on his amber liquid and appeared to weave in his chair slightly. It was her mother's turn to frown. Libby could tell he was getting nasty again, the alcohol making him loose his inhibitions.

Cooper was watching her father drink as if he wanted one too. Dr. Brownlee pointed to his tumbler and Cooper shook his head.

"Why is it you don't drink, Coop?"

Libby and her mother exchanged panicked glances.

It put Cooper in a pensive mood. He leaned back into his chair, his hands folded in his lap and regarded Dr. Brownlee. Libby knew his words would be weighed and measured, but it didn't stop the panic from spreading all over her body. They'd been itching for a fight since day one. Maybe tonight would be the night. It wouldn't do either of them any good.

"There's a story that goes along with it." Cooper said, nodding toward Dr. Brownlee's nearly empty glass.

Her father shrugged his shoulders. "Enlighten me."

"Not tonight, sir."

No one said anything for several minutes as they finished their meals.

Her mother began to clear the table.

Her father got up, holding his empty glass tumbler, and then hesitated, setting his glass in the sink.

Libby heard her mom turn on the charm as she spoke to her husband. "Austin, I'd like to go downstairs and have a little dessert and an espresso. How about we leave these two alone?"

"You'll stay put, young lady?" her father commanded. "No more wandering along the beach by yourself, okay?"

Libby looked at Coop with raised eyebrows, silently asking for his okay to stay there rather than get a different room. He nodded his acceptance. She grinned. "No worries, Dad. Besides, I'll have Coop here with me. We aren't going anywhere."

When she looked over at him she discovered for the first time that a Navy SEAL could blush.

CHAPTER 25

COOP WAS STANDING next to the sliding glass door, surveying the beach bonfires and the white surf beyond. Under the light of a nearly full moon the water was a deep Navy blue. The splashing sea foam looked like lace trim on a woman's skirt.

Libby came up behind him, and he could feel the contour of her body fit sweetly against him. Her warm arms encircled him as she ran her palms up over his tee shirt clad chest and lay her head against his shoulder blades. Then she freed the white cotton shirt from the waistband of his khakis, slid her palms up against his spine and began kissing his bare skin one vertebrae at a time. It had been over an hour since the hurried-almost-sex in the service elevator. Now that he was thinking more clearly, he wondered if this was such a good idea, but it felt so damned good.

Her nimble fingers slid down and around to the front of his pants, finding him. She slowly caressed and gently squeezed his package, while her tongue made little darting motions as her lips and warm cheeks softly brushed against his flesh.

He'd never been with a woman who was so horny for him. But then, he'd never really given anyone time to get serious. No one but Daisy, who had a reputation for sleeping around the Teams, when in fact, she was extremely choosy. Later, he learned Daisy only had one love partner at a time. He still felt bad about discarding her for Libby, but the buxom tattoo artist to the SEALs must have known it wasn't going anywhere serious. Daisy appeared okay with the goodbyes, and never seemed to have expected much. In that respect, he was just like her.

But now things with Libby were getting complicated again. He was getting drawn into the Brownlee family, even though he knew Libby's dad still didn't trust him. And even so, he couldn't just walk away from the family of a Fallen, leave them alone to deal with this whacko. It was like leaving someone behind, and you just don't do that to the Teams or their families, past or present. Once someone was a SEAL, their family was always part of their community. Whether or not they wanted to be wasn't even part of the equation.

Libby was slipping off his shirt when he turned and saw the need and want in her eyes. There was no strategy, no logic here, though he searched for an excuse, but couldn't find a reason not to partake of what she was offering. Time for what she called mind-numbing sex. And he knew the deeper he got, the harder it was going to be to get out.

Maybe I don't want out.

"This is crazy, Libby. What if your parents come back?"

"I think we have enough time. But if you don't want to—"

He grabbed her and gave her a deep penetrating kiss. She rested her hands on his bare shoulders as he unbuttoned her white blouse, peeling it away and then looking at the lace bra that dared to hide those perfect breasts from him. He slid down her straps, unfastened the clasp in the front as she threaded her fingers through his hair.

The sight of her rosy nipples, knotted and puckered for him, shot straight to his groin. He cupped her and ran his thumb over one side as he kissed it. His other hand was undoing the button on her kakis. She was compliant, letting him explore her belly and the warm softness under her panties with his fingers.

Libby leaned over, kissing the top of his head. He kissed her in the center of her chest, then nuzzled first one and then the other nipple, biting down slightly with his teeth until he heard her moan with satisfaction.

The zipper on her pants was easy, and he discovered her panties were wet as he slipped them down and off her ankles. He slid his fingers over her nude mound, to the little nub holding guard at the entrance to her sex. He parted her knees with his other hand and she used him to steady herself, giving him full access to whatever he wanted.

Yes.

His lazy forefinger traced circles around her clit as he pressed it, squeezed it between his thumb and finger. He turned the angle of his palm and sent his thumb very slowly down lower, to her entrance.

And then he stopped before penetration. He rimmed her wet opening slowly once, twice and a third time.

She pushed herself towards him, trying to impale herself on his stubborn digit. He continued to massage her there, and let her wet goodness cover his fingers, one at a time, as he inserted them in and then out until every one had had a taste of her warm sex. She was gripping the tops of his shoulders, leaving marks he'd see tomorrow.

He kissed her belly button, inhaling her scent below. He streaked a line down to that little bump, and then sucked hard.

She nearly collapsed over him.

Come for me, Libby.

He could feel her legs shaking as her control was slipping. He wanted to make it last. He wanted her to flower and grow and come long and hard. It was all about giving her the pleasure she deserved.

"Come for me, Libby," he whispered as he licked his way down into her opening and tasted the sweet cream she gave him.

"Cooper. Oh. My. God. Cooper."

"Yes. Come for me, sweetheart. Let me taste it."

She let out a series of deep groans as she shattered. He wouldn't pull out but kept the steady in and out with his tongue and one or two fingers. With each deep penetration she arched her back with renewed vigor. She jolted backwards as he held her and would not let her go.

"More, Libby. I want all of you," he whispered.

At last she collapsed to her knees after losing her balance. She held his head between her palms and kissed him, her full breasts pressed against his chest. Her tongue reached for his, her lips tasting her own juices. She threw a knee over his thigh and rode him, rubbed him with her wetness, and pressed into him, messaging her need for him to claim her.

Cooper's erection was pounding into her belly. She tilted her pelvis up, adjusted her other leg and raised her sex on top to mount him. On his knees, he held her off the ground as she straddled him and let her slowly fall down around his shaft, squeezing his bulging cock until it was pulsing deep inside her. He raised her up and then back down on him as they both groaned. He was buried inside her to the hilt, and, God, he never wanted to leave.

She whimpered as he pushed deeper still. She arched away, and he supported her carefully as she leaned back onto the carpeting. He moved himself forward, adjusted his knees to her sides and thrust up, covering her body with his. He laced her fingers with his, palms to palms, and held her arms out at her sides as he gently rode her, driving up and deep, feeling the glorious ebb and flow of their chests pressing and releasing. Her knees raised and locked over his shoulders and he let the rhythm of her breathing guide his long even penetrations at first. But he picked up speed and pumped her. Her breasts were shivering with the force of their mating. Her long beautiful neck strained back as she shouted her passion to the ceiling with her eyes shut.

Come for me, Libby. Give me everything. I want it all.

Her body convulsed and reveled in the orgasm that overtook her finally. Just as he wanted her to, she lost herself in a long rolling spasm as she continued to writhe beneath him. He struggled to hold her hands at her sides, needing her there. Right there. He rode her hard and pushed her orgasm further. Then he released her palms and penetrated deep. He felt her clutch his back, his buttocks as she ground into him, accepted him, all of him, as deep as he could get there.

"Cooper. Please. Cooper." She was begging him to fill her, and his cock began to release. Her mouth made a soft smile as he pulsed inside her, exploding and pumping her full of his seed.

"Yes," she whispered.

He gave her more.

"Yes."

He looked down into her face and knew he would do anything for her. He was filled with joy at the beauty of her body, at how she moved her head from side to side, closed and then opened her eyes, and how she smiled at him. He loved the feel of her thighs as they slid off his shoulders to cling to his hips, the smooth sweetness of her bottom as his hands roamed and explored her flesh.

He collapsed on top of her and they lay together until their breathing was no longer ragged.

CHAPTER 26

LIBBY LAY ON the soft peach rug in the middle of the bridal suite living room at the Hotel Del Coronado. Although she didn't have a ring and a date, it was definitely a honeymoon glow that tingled all over her body. The man who snored against her chest and whose legs still pinned her down, whose hands encircled her wrists and wouldn't let her move—this man owned every part of her body and soul.

She should have felt tied down, restricted, and with any of her other lovers she would have been moving their limp body off her so she could breathe. Not so with Cooper. Her shortness of breath because his massive chest pressed against hers was welcomed.

Her parents would be returning soon, so Libby knew she'd have to get them to the bedroom. She let her fingers lace down his muscular back and she felt his body jerk, then shudder.

He rose up on one elbow, but still kept her pinned

beneath his thighs. "Hi," he said as he brushed hair from her forehead, and then kissed her there, and again just under her ear, and then under her jaw line. At last he claimed her lips. His kiss was soft but not long.

They stared at each other. Libby wished she could guess what he was thinking but decided he was thinking about her. She smiled back at him, grateful to be the object of his desire. "Hi, yourself."

"Your folks will be coming back soon," he said.

"Yes, that's why I woke you up. My parents—really it is my father—are tolerant up to a point. You're growing on him."

"Oh, good." Cooper rolled his eyes. "Like a wart, right?"

"No, I think he likes you. You are quite a bit alike, truth be told."

He bent down and kissed her again. "I love the truth you tell me when you are coming in my arms."

Libby felt her cheeks blush. She could feel he was starting to get aroused again.

"But," he said as he continued to kiss her neck and down to the top of her shoulder, "I can certainly understand how he would feel finding his naked daughter on the floor wrapped in the arms of a very naked sailor."

"Quite right."

"Besides, I have to go let Bay out, get him his dinner."

"Can I come, please?" She held his head between her palms for emphasis. "Please." She rose up and kissed his neck, wrapping her thigh around and over his. "I'll make it worth your while. I promise."

"Hmmm." Cooper moved against her, his full arousal searching for her opening again.

"Say yes first," she said as she moved away from him slightly.

"Okay," Coop said as he sucked her right nipple, and then ended it with a tender kiss.

"Okay what?"

"Okay you can come."

"Oh, I intend to. I want to come again in your bed. Can you do that for me?"

"I can make you come right here."

"Okay," she said, mocking him, moving away from him until he held her down again.

"Okay what?" he imitated her.

"Okay now—if you make me come again later."

Cooper groaned as he edged between her thighs and slid into her. She was deliciously sore but her body accepted his girth. With long smooth strokes he rode her, stopping randomly several times to kiss her chest and neck. His hands were cupped under her rear cheeks as he raised her for fuller penetration.

She loved looking up at him when he closed his

eyes as he thrust deep. Then she slipped her leg in front of her and he fucked her from the side and behind. He was kissing the side of her face as his fingers felt her nub and he squeezed. She exploded, clamping down on his cock, giving him everything. His ragged breathing in her ear sent her over the edge. The familiar little internal spasms elicited a groan from him as he pushed harder, and began to fill her all over again. He squeezed her breast as they shook in unison.

THEY LEFT A note for Libby's parents, and the next thing she knew they were motoring down the strand to the beach where Cooper's motor home was parked. The red scooter seemed so tiny under his massive frame, so Libby held herself against his back, enjoying the warm wind breezing past his cheeks and over his shoulders. She put her nose in the base of his neck and inhaled his wonderful man scent infused with the dryer sheets he used on his white tee shirt. It thrilled her that he would want his clothes to smell nice.

She laid the side of her head between his shoulder blades and heard a rumble in his chest in response. He took one hand from the handlebars and let his fingers mate with hers. Then he returned to his focus on the road.

Everything was so right when she was with him. She wasn't afraid of anything. She felt protected, cherished. Libby knew it was probably all her fantasy, but she overruled her common sense and decided to surrender completely, to steep her whole being in the incredible experience of loving Coop.

They pulled up to Coop's home, which now seemed so small. As she got closer to the front door she heard Bay barking inside.

Coop unlocked the door, after removing a small round object from the underside of the long door handle. He slipped it in his pocket before she could get a good look at it.

"Okay, Dude. You can go out for a run. Just hold it a few seconds longer. Sorry."

The door exploded open and Bay leapt in the air, ran as fast as he could in circles, and then started to come back towards Cooper. He got distracted by a large boulder on the edge of the parking lot, and raised his leg. It seemed to take ten minutes.

"Just in time, I think," Coop whispered as he watched his dog pee endlessly.

"What would happen if you were gone too long?" Libby asked.

"Dunno. I've never done that. I think five or six hours is the most." Bay came bounding over towards them, but, instead of coming to Cooper first, he made a leap toward Libby. It almost toppled her.

Libby worked to stand her ground and turned to

the side, preparing to give Bay a good knee to the belly. Bay stopped himself mid-air and sat in front of her, looking like he expected a treat for his restraint.

"Good boy," she said as she leaned over and rubbed his ears and put her nose right up to his. Bay snuck in a lick that extended from her chin to her forehead.

Cooper was looking at her with a crooked grin, matching his crooked stance, hands on his hips. If she could only have a picture of that look that melted her.

"You're quite good with dogs," he said, grinning.

"Thank you," she returned and stepped to within arm's reach. "Thank you for letting me…come."

It was Cooper's turn to blush. He examined his shoes and then raised his blue eyes to hers. Little creases at the sides ran all the way to his temples. His sparkling expression made her wet instantly.

"Oh, I have plans for you, all right, Miss Libby." His voice was husky and she could barely hear over the roar of the ocean. But she heard it perfectly well. Even without the words, her body picked up on his intent.

The pause was broken by Bay, who wedged his way between them, making sure his meal needs were not ignored.

Cooper laughed, swung the door open, and bowed. "Your carriage, mum," he said to Libby. Before she could step up and inside, Bay cut her off and was in the trailer and on the only couch.

"We'll train him. Now, missy, will you please get your butt inside to I can feed Bay and get you properly nekkid?"

He hoisted her up and through the door, slamming it behind him.

"Since Bay's on the couch, you can sit there," he pointed to the bed and wiggled his eyebrows up and down.

"Of course. My favorite spot." Libby knew his gaze followed her down the hallway because when she turned, he was grinning again. She leaned back slightly and balanced her upper torso on her palms, crossing her legs carefully. Cooper watched every movement. "Bay's getting jealous, Coop. Don't forget his dinner." She felt perfectly wicked as she unbuttoned her shirt. "Seems like it's getting awfully hot in here. I've had this shirt more off than on today, it seems."

Cooper emptied some kibbles into Bay's dish, darting sideways glances at Libby as she squeezed the breasts still encased in her white lace bra.

"My nipples hurt. This bra is so tight," she said as she slipped her fingers under the satin trim at the top of her garment. Cooper held Bay's dish midair for a second with one hand while his other hand adjusted his pants.

"You'd better feed Bay."

"Yeah" he said as he turned and opened the door. Bay waited for his command and then jumped off the couch in an instant and out the door. Libby heard the metal dish hit the sandy parking lot surface and then saw Coop's frame darken the doorway, then take up the whole hallway as the door slammed behind him. His long arms hung on an air conditioning unit suspended from the ceiling. He tilted his head to the side, pressed his forehead into his arm and crossed his legs at the ankles and stood, watching her.

"What, Cooper?" she asked as she continued to rub the tops of her breasts with one finger.

"That this here is one hell of a thing to come home to."

For just a second it took her breath away. *Did I hear this right?* Then Cooper cleared his throat, looked to the side and rubbed his palms through his hair without making further eye contact.

He turned and showed her his backside as he took in a big breath and exhaled, staring out the kitchen window to the darkened beach beyond. She knew he couldn't see anything out there. But he was looking for *something.*

Her heart broke. She could tell he was struggling. She got up off the bed and wrapped her arms around him from behind. "Cooper, hey, don't worry. I'm a big girl."

At first he stiffened, but then slowly he turned and they were chest to chest. She reached out and drew a finger over his lips. He encircled her waist and drew her against another one of his legendary erections, unafraid to show her.

She needed to show him her strong side. "This is just this. No more. Don't worry. No strings, no…"

He had lowered his mouth and was nibbling on her neck, right under her ear. "Yes?" His voice was husky again. His breathing was deep and hard. She was suddenly glad she had shampooed her hair this morning, had dabbed a little more of the perfume from Capri between her breasts before they left the Hotel Del.

"Just this," she finished. She couldn't risk spooking him with talk of love. She knew it was love. Did he?

She took a step back from him and released her bra to the floor. She slid down her pants and stood in her panties.

He looked over her mouth, down her neck, between her breasts and lower, until he ended at her toes, then drew his attention back up just as slowly. He wasn't going to say anything, so she brought her palms out to the sides.

"Just this."

Suddenly, he was right there, holding her, kissing her hard, his tongue claiming her mouth and down her throat. He held her so tight to him she willed herself to melt. No one had ever squeezed her so hard, loved her with so much passion, and needed her so much.

If only…

It wasn't smart to think about the *if only's*. And besides, she was sort of distracted by the feel of his flesh against hers. He had removed all his clothes so quickly she hadn't even realized he'd done it. Libby felt his cock root around her lower belly and up and down the crease between her closed legs.

He picked her up, walking her back to the bed.

"What about Bay?" she asked.

He set her down, pried open her knees and leaning over, inserted a finger inside. "Don't go anywhere," he said. "Stay just the way you are right now. Don't move a muscle."

"Or what?" she asked, her eyes half closed. Her voice was raspy. She loved the things his fingers were doing.

"I'll have to punish you."

"Promise?" She looked down at his hand, two of his fingers gone from view.

"Um hum," he said as he bent over and kissed her again, tracing her lips with his tongue. "I could do things…"

"Promise?"

Bay let out a yelp and Cooper pressed his forehead against hers, and sighed. "Be right back."

"Meet you in the shower, in about two big ones, sailor," Libby replied.

CHAPTER 27

COOPER FIRST LAY the dog comforter down over the couch and then let Bay inside, with a command to stay. He heard the water start to run in the shower and felt his cock lurch.

Close one.

He'd almost said something like, "I wish I could come home to this picture every night," or some such shit. Something he would have regretted as sure as he was a fucking US Navy SEAL. And what right did he have to go say or do something like that? He couldn't offer her anything except some endless nights of fucks and blowjobs. He'd never had to say dumb crap like that with any of his other girlfriends to get into their pants.

Except it wasn't Libby's pants he really wanted. Well, yes, he did want to fuck her six ways to sunrise, to be perfectly honest, but he wanted her to *want* to be there. In that split second, he fantasized that Libby felt she *belonged* to him.

It was dangerous territory. Why couldn't he just fuck her so hard she wouldn't be able to walk, and would have to go home and rest? Wouldn't that be safer for them both? She wanted it, after all. Give it to her, and then walk away. Get out now. Satisfy the shit out of her and then get out of Dodge.

You are a dog. You are a fuckin' dumb-as-cum-type-of-scum.

He was standing at the bathroom door with an erection so large he was surprised it bounced. He was a fucking heat-seeking missile. There she was. He could see where her flesh bumped into the frosted glass shower door. This wasn't any oversized two-person shower. There was barely room for the both of them in it, if they pressed themselves close against each other, which was exactly what he had in mind. If they didn't hurry up, there'd be no hot water left. Not that it would matter.

She was properly sudsy, her hair in a clip but part of it dangled in the bubbles sliding down her back. She greeted him and he stepped inside and immediately pressed her back against the wall. Her soapy goodness spiked his libido as her legs wrapped around his hips and she was kissing him while soaping his neck and shoulders.

Why can't I get enough of you, Libby? What do you

see in me? You know I am only a simple man who cannot offer you anything. Why don't you say no? Why are you always so open and available to me?

She wanted him inside her. She was so slippery, his cock was pushing every which way and not finding home base. He didn't want to get soap in her cave, but Christ, she must have used up all his shower gel because he almost lost his footing trying to ram inside her. She threw her head back and laughed.

Fuck me. Libby, tell me to stop.

But she kept laughing. Then she looked at him, all serious, like a young virgin. As if she was doing this for the very first time. Demure. Almost afraid. Trust in those brown eyes of hers that reached down and grabbed his balls. The water was turning cold, but she didn't change her focus. She looked down to his lips and very tenderly leaned in and claimed him in her soft way, like breathing life into him.

Something deep in his chest began to ache. He spread his thumb over her cheek, over her lips, and repaid the kiss. His hand caressed her chin and raised her carefully like she was a china doll. Soft kisses. Cold water.

What is happening?

She adjusted herself on top of his cock and he didn't have to press very hard to be inside her. Completely inside her, slowly, bit by bit, while they looked at each other, watching the other feel the joy of the union.

Something was definitely happening.

She reached over and punched the water off. She levered herself up and down on him in slow, deliberate movements. He braced her, hands under her backside to help her stay right there, riding him, loving him. She closed her eyes and he knew she savored the feel of their joining. He could see it on her face. It wasn't his size, it wasn't the place or the urgency and excitement of the sex, and it was *him*. She was loving *him*, like he'd never been loved before.

He let her lead. He let her show him how she loved this. He let her be soft and supple, he let her heal him in the only way he could be healed.

He felt connected. Opened. Introduced to a new part of himself he'd never seen before.

Cooper's eyes began to ache as he realized he had never cried for his family, for all the years he would never have with them, the first kisses and dates his little niece would never have. But he was spared. Spared to have this. This was about being alive, about being a part of something else greater than just himself. Life wasn't to be wasted by being just lived.

Life was meant to enjoy, meant to be shared with someone else.

Her thumbs brushed aside the wet on his cheeks.

He'd never cried during sex, goddamit. Maybe she just thought it was part of the shower water. He hoped she didn't notice.

But no, it would be his dumb luck, she would figure it out. And did it matter that he would keep this from her, as he pulsed inside her, meeting her orgasm with his own version of the Fourth of July? Another unprotected encounter with someone he just could not keep his hands off? Someone who deserved more, but seemed to be quite happy being here with him just the way he was. Was it wrong that he enjoyed her satisfied smile afterwards as much as the moment he was exploding inside her?

No shit. Something was definitely happening. And fast.

And for the first time, he didn't want to run away.

CHAPTER 28

"**A**USTIN, I THINK we should cancel the dinner tonight," Carla said as she stepped out of the shower. Morning sunlight poured through the picture window in their bedroom. Dr. Brownlee was shaving in his shorts.

"Can't do that, Carla. Riverton says we go about our lives just like normal. I go to the office. But you stay here, or if you go back to the house, you get help, or have Lib—"

Dr. Brownlee turned and strode across the bedroom, opened up the door to the living room and stepped inside, noting the opened door to the other bedroom. Her bedroom that had not been slept in.

He stormed back into the bathroom. "She didn't come back last night."

"No, of course not. She's with him, like the letter said."

"The letter said she'd be back later," Dr. Brownlee

answered.

"The letter said she was with HIM and I think she's safer there than over here with us, if you want the truth. Austin," she dropped her towel and stood completely naked in front of him. "You are so tense."

She glided toward him with liquid grace, and lifted her hands to massage his temples. It felt good. She smelled good, too.

"How much time do you have?" she whispered as she slid her palms down to his shoulders and to his neck. She leaned into him and did what she knew he couldn't resist. She pressed those beautiful orbs of flesh against him as her mound pressed against his groin.

"Enough," he whispered back and kissed her. Her lips were hungry for him. He could still smell the fresh soap on her body. He suddenly wanted to taste all of her.

DR. AND MRS. Brownlee had invited Cooper and Libby to join them for breakfast.

Cooper hoped it wasn't too obvious to Libby when he dropped her hand just before they entered the Beach Bum restaurant down the street from the Hotel Del. They were ushered to the balcony, with a view of the ocean and beach below, protected from wind by a clear Plexiglas barrier.

He felt pretty good, although he and Libby had gotten practically no sleep. Plus, Bay had decided he needed to go out twice to explore. Coop suspected the dog wanted to make sure he wasn't being ignored.

The sleep deprivation caught up to him as he faced Libby's dad, who stood up when they approached their table. He extended his hand to her father and managed to avoid making eye contact by saying something to Carla Brownlee. He could see out of the corner of his eye that Dr. Brownlee sat back down with a scowl.

Yessir, I have fucked your daughter. Every time she wanted it and a couple of more for good measure. Cooper smiled as he looked down at his canvas slip-ons. If Libby's mom was anything like Libby, Dr. Brownlee was a very satisfied fellow this morning as well.

"Something funny, son?" Brownlee blurted out.

Cooper pulled out the chair for Libby, brushed the top of her shoulder as she sat down, then sat down next to her. His thigh rested against hers. He looked up to the good doctor and glared at him at first, then decided to give him the cat-that-ate-the-canary grin.

You can treat me anyway you like, sir, but I still fucked your daughter.

Brownlee leaned back, his back hitting the back of the wooden café chair, and took in a deep breath. Carla was searching between both their faces. Libby seemed to be distracted by the look of her exposed thigh against his.

They ordered food and then her father leaned over the table and cleared his throat. "Libby, honey, your mother and I have been invited to a dinner for the Lavender House. I'm getting an award tonight."

"Nice, dad. That's wonderful."

"It's nothing."

Carla looked at Dr. Brownlee and blinked without expression.

"They give these every year," he said. "I've always passed them over. I just couldn't duck this year. And Riverton thinks we should keep up with our normal routine, so I wasn't going to go, but now think we should. We should all go."

Cooper was glad they were following the police de-tective's orders.

Wait a minute? Go to a dinner? An awards dinner?

"Honey," Carla began, "We want to have you and Cooper here go with us tonight. As our guests."

"No, mom. I don't really want to—"

"It would mean a lot to your dad," her mother in-sisted.

Dr. Brownlee rolled his eyes and looked right at Cooper, who had been successfully avoiding him again. The doctor's eyes locked him in place and wouldn't let go.

Of course he has to know I've been fucking his

daughter. Cooper had personally kissed every square inch of her lovely body. He decided to do the right thing.

"Libby," Cooper said as he laid a palm against her back and stroked her up and down. "I think your parents are right. Probably better to show that this creep hasn't interrupted any of your normal activities as a family."

"Going to this dinner isn't anything like normal—" she said firmly. But when their eyes met he could see she softened.

"I'd like to accompany you to your father's important dinner. Please." He smiled, then watched her search her parents' faces. He squeezed the top of her shoulders and neck. "Okay, honey?"

Cooper saw Brownlee flinch, but remain controlled. He was actually enjoying making the doctor squirm. But, like it or not, it was still the right thing to do to go to the dinner.

"Well, seems like I'm outnumbered. I'll have to get some things from the house," Libby said.

"I don't think that's wise, Libby."

"I can take her, sir, if she has to get some things. I don't mind."

"Thank you, Cooper," Dr. Brownlee said. "Glad we got that settled. Now there is something else I need to discuss."

Cooper had no idea what was coming up next.

"Last night, you said you had some recommendations about making our home safer. I understand you have spent some time with our boys in Quantico and have some special training on surveillance."

"Yes, sir, I have."

"I could hire someone to help us out here, but I don't know where to start. Thought maybe you could help me find someone. Someone good."

"Just what did you have in mind?"

Brownlee scratched the back of his head, taking a quick glance at Carla before continuing. Coop could see he was extremely nervous.

"I don't have to tell you I think this guy isn't going to give up. Everything he's done has had some connection to our house: Libby's cat, our swimming pool, my office, the letters in the mailbox."

"Okay, I'll grant you that."

"I think he'll be back."

Carla dropped her fork on her plate as everyone at the table jumped.

"Austin, I thought you said—"

"Now, please, hear me out. I've had some time to think about it. He'd be dumb to do anything here," he waved at the Hotel in the background and the crowds of tourists milling about on the beach. "He thinks he has free access to the house. He doesn't know what we are planning to do, but I'll bet he's noted we're away for a few days."

"You're not thinking of moving back into that house, are you, Austin? You can't be thinking that?" Carla had thrown her napkin on her half-finished omelet.

"No. Not yet. I was thinking Cooper could wire it up, help us monitor it. Then we could move back in and—"

"No. You didn't discuss this with me."

"Carla, the police have no leads. It's the only way to help catch this guy."

"Using us as bait?" she said. Her words fell like boulders all around them.

Cooper could only describe Carla's look to her husband as murderous. No one said a further word. Cooper appraised Brownlee and saw for the first time the man was not a coward. A coward runs away, and Cooper could see Brownlee wouldn't do that. He was an idiot to think he could catch the guy without the police, of course. He was an idiot to think he could pick the guy out from a group of strangers, or that a personality profile would yield any secrets if someone was adept at conning the system.

But Brownlee was no coward.

Libby searched his face, placing her hand over his arm. All three of them were looking at him.

"I'll need equipment. Take me a couple of days to put it together," he said.

"Anything you need, we'll pay for."

"We'll pay you for your time, too." Carla said.

"Not allowed, ma'am. Thanks, but that's not something I can do."

"Cooper, I think it might be a good idea if you moved into the house." Brownlee looked at Libby. "Alone, of course."

Cooper thought it was funny. He wondered what Bay would think of living in such a huge place. And then he realized that might be a problem. "Dr. Brownlee, I do have a dog, and he would have to come with me."

"He's a really nice dog. Very well behaved," Libby offered.

"I'll bet." Brownlee scrunched up his mouth and then shrugged it off. "Cooper, the dog can stay too."

Brownlee extended his hand and the two men shook.

"Now, if you will excuse me, I am almost late for my first appointment, and we have a dinner to prepare for tonight." He stood. "Carla, buy some new things. I don't want you going back to the house just yet, okay?"

"That's not necessary, Austin. I have everything I need here. Besides, Cooper can take me," she protested.

Brownlee shook his head. "I can never figure out

women. You give them the opportunity to do what they love to do, and they come up with reasons why they shouldn't." He leaned down, held her chin tenderly in his fingers and planted a kiss there. Carla's cheeks flushed and Cooper knew he was right. She was a hot one, all right.

And she was keeping Brownlee sane through all of this.

CHAPTER 29

C OOPER HAD TO get back to his Team and let them
know what he was up to. He left Libby and her
mother to go shopping in downtown San Diego while
he rode his scooter over to Fredo's apartment.

He knocked twice on the front door and didn't wait
for an answer before he tried to open it. It was locked.

"Fredo?" he knocked louder. The SEAL's truck was
in the parking lot, so he knew the Team guy was home.

Fredo appeared at the doorway in his shorts and a
sleeveless tank top. The security chain was still affixed
so the door was only open a few inches.

"You picked a helluva time to come showing up at
my door," Fredo whispered.

"Why, you getting a nooner? I thought you dated—"

The door slammed, then Fredo walked outside and
closed the metal door behind him. A pair of shiny
silver handcuffs dangled from one wrist. "Asshole, I'm
paying by the hour, get my drift?"

Cooper shook his head with renewed respect for his buddy. He had been wondering lately, with Fredo's luck with women, how he was handling his needs, not that it made any real difference.

"So what the fuck's so important you couldn't just leave me a message?" Fredo asked.

A string of high pitched Spanish shot through the door, something to do with a frog and a whip. Cooper had never taken the time to learn proper Spanish to communicate with his best friend, except swear words and slang. They understood each other just fine.

"I gotta go, man. Sorry I couldn't offer you better hospitality, or are you here to do your laundry again?"

"No. Sorry. Hey, Fredo. I need to borrow your truck for a day or two."

"You're leaving the red demon with me?"

"Yes I am."

"Boy this must be serious. What you up to?"

"I gotta help Libby's parents with some surveillance, and I need something big enough to transport my stuff. You okay with this?"

"I'm not washing your scooter, and I can't be responsible for any scratches—"

"Just don't wreck it, okay, Fredo?"

"Holy shit, this is serious. Don't start any wars without me, com-pren-day?"

"No worries. No improvised explosive devices, although, come to think of it, that might be a pretty good idea."

"Just a minute, I'll go get my keys."

Fredo disappeared behind the door. Cooper heard him laugh and heard a woman's voice squeal. When the door opened, a woman's soft-looking hand with long, deep-red fingernails slipped out, holding Fredo's keys in its palm.

Cooper took the keys, replacing them with his scooter keys and the hand retracted, followed by a slam of the door.

Cooper tossed the keys into the air several times as he whistled and walked down the stairs to the parking lot. He started the salvage vehicle up and, after he put it into reverse, it backfired before sputtering out of the parking lot in a cloud of smoke.

LIBBY SWUNG THE motel room door open, eyeing all six-foot-four inches of Cooper standing in the hallway. She inhaled his lemony aftershave. Just the sight of Coop's square jaw and clear blue eyes made her swoon. It had been only a few hours since they'd last been together, and now just being so close made it hard to think straight. Images of muscles of steel lurking beneath his dark blue suit made her weak at the knees. He'd never worn anything but cargo pants or jeans with tee shirts.

Or nothing at all. She blushed.

Libby wobbled on her new three-inch heels, and then took a step back. It didn't help. Her heart was rattling around like a runaway freight train inside her ribcage. The force of its thumping threatened to knock her onto her rear.

"You look pretty amazing," he whispered.

Libby was so glad they had found this deep blue satin gown with the plunging neckline. She wore pearls.

Coop did what he always did. He coolly reached forward and placed his long fingers and palm against the small of her back, and held her so she wouldn't fall.

Then he smiled that crooked half smile that exposed the one dimple on his left cheek.

"You're beautiful," he said.

Kiss me. Shut up and kiss me. Her well-developed common sense dribbled to the floor. "I'd forgotten how handsome you were. And wow, look at you in that suit." What was it she *wanted* to say?

Cooper released her without drawing her toward him. He raised his right hand and brushed her right cheekbone with the backs of his fingers, his warm thumb smoothing over her lips. "I could never forget you," he whispered.

It was all the invitation she needed. She pressed herself against his torso, flipping her arms up, holding hands with herself behind his neck. "I hope you never have to."

Cooper frowned just before she bridged the gap between them, planting a kiss onto lips that she coaxed open. He softened, melded into the heat of her body, and brought both arms around the back of her waist. He drew her against his prominent arousal.

"Ahem." Libby heard her father's throat clearing a few feet behind. When she turned, he was staring at the two of them without expression. Cooper quickly dropped his arms to his sides. But his long thigh was pressed against hers. The electricity between them gave her courage. She wound an arm around the back of Coop's jacket. Her palm pressed against his shoulders, rubbing. She heard him gasp with a little intake of air.

She was going to die until she could get this man naked and kissing every square inch of her again.

Carla Brownlee bustled to the entryway. She was dressed in a form-fitting black low-cut sheath and silver wrap they'd chosen together this afternoon. Her silver eye shadow shimmered in tandem with her new multiple-karat diamond teardrop earrings that Libby's father had given her. Libby realized that on anyone else the huge earrings would look like too much cheap bling. On her mother, they matched her personality perfectly.

The four of them went downstairs, through the

lobby, and out to the valet parking attendant who waited beside the Brownlees' S600 black Mercedes sedan. Libby and Cooper took the rear seat, and Dr. Brownlee drove towards the ballroom gala. Libby flipped on the heated seats in the rear and watched as Cooper realized what she'd done. She pressed the toggle for gentle rolling seat vibration. It drew a chuckle from the big SEAL.

"How many quarters do you have to use to get it to do this?" he said with a grin.

Libby leaned over, planted a soft kiss on his lips. "Oh, it'll cost you."

Cooper squeezed her hand and adjusted himself on the groaning leather seat.

Libby noticed her father staring her down in the rear view mirror with a scowl. "Just try to concentrate on the crowd, Coop. I know my daughter is distractingly beautiful, but you wouldn't be here with us tonight if I didn't need those well-trained eyes and ears."

"And instincts," Carla added. She smiled at her husband. Libby noted the beautiful profile of the strongest woman she'd ever known. Her parents were a match for each other, in every way.

Dr. Brownlee nodded in deference to his wife and returned her a polite smile.

"Sir," Coop began, "You can rest assured, I will be

on high alert. I think this is the perfect cover. You just need to be yourself. Let the perp come to you. If he's here, I've got you covered." Coop was all business.

Libby's father winced, one eye reduced to a small slit as he cocked his head. "I doubt he'll be there. Too many people around. These types usually do their creepy things at night, in secret, when they can plan with their little devious minds."

"So he'll hide in plain sight, then," Coop answered.

"Perhaps. But I think not."

"The guy who wants to kill you usually tries to make hard eye contact with you first, sir. Just remember that."

"Jesus, Coop. I *have* eye contact with most the people I talk to. I'd say this guy will be shifty. He won't look at me."

"I disagree. He's going to want to see your fear. He lives for it. If he just wanted to kill you, he'd do it and get it over with. Move on. He wants to terrorize you first."

Carla began to unravel in the front seat. Her earrings began to flutter wildly. Cooper leaned over and patted her shoulder. "Sorry, ma'am."

This made Dr. Brownlee quiet and pensive. They rode the rest of the way to the dinner in silence.

Cooper sat back, slightly leaning against Libby in the rear seat. He was watching his thumb rubbing over the tops of Libby's knuckles. Libby couldn't tear her eyes away from the sight of their fingers entwined. With each gentle massage, she felt her anxiety and tension dissipate. She wished she and Cooper were heading off to a candlelit private dinner, not a banquet with a hundred other couples.

When they arrived, Cooper was out and around the car the second Dr. Brownlee stopped. He first opened Carla's door and helped her out. Carla was blushing as she thanked him and then waited for her husband.

Coop opened Libby's door next and extended his palm inside, holding onto her firmly and drawing her close. He tucked her at his side while he closed the car door and brought them beside her mom.

Dr. Brownlee stopped at a registration table and picked up a plastic name badge with several ribbons attached to the bottom side. He clipped Carla's name-tag to the neckline of her dress, gave her a peck on the cheek and handed Coop and Libby their plastic badges.

Inside the banquet hall a band was playing at one end of the long room. Round tables were arranged along the edge of a small dance floor in front of a dais with one long table holding court over all. They were shown to their seats at the head table, Dr. Brownlee being placed at the center near a podium. Her father waved to a few people in the lower audience whom he recognized. Cooper looked over several couples dancing, and led Libby to join them.

The tempo was fast, but Libby and Coop danced slowly. She noticed he didn't seem to follow any rhythm. True to her ballroom lessons, she followed his lead and enjoyed the thrill of his hard torso pressed against her body. She wondered what it would feel like to dance with him in his full dress whites. In his arms, she felt like she could almost fly. He maneuvered her around the floor with no effort at all. His movements were panther-like, smooth and fluid. As they turned he surveyed the room, always able to maintain a partial view of Dr. and Mrs. Brownlee and anyone who came up to them.

Libby watched her mom and dad up on the dais. They seemed to be having a serious conversation, with her mom doing most of the talking. Her dad was nodding his head, while looking down at the crowd below, giving an occasional wave.

Libby recognized several faces in the crowd. People were munching on stuffed mushrooms and canapés presented on silver trays. Most drank wine. Within a few minutes Libby watched her father make his way, stopping at several tables and shaking hands along the way, to the bar to get his first drink. She was apprehensive what this would bode for the evening.

"Libby, you need to help me a little," Cooper whispered, not taking his eyes off Dr. Brownlee's trajectory.

"Sure. What do you want me to do?"

"Just tell me if something's out of whack. Something that doesn't make sense, okay?"

"You were trained for this?"

"Yes. Six months on an intelligence deployment. They taught me to mind read."

Libby looked up at him and saw Coop grinning. She'd completely fallen for his little joke and loved him for it.

"Not quite, but it's profiling. Israelis do it much better than we do," he added. They continued to dance, although the music had stopped. A slow tune began.

"You mean I'm supposed to look for socks that don't match or if someone is packing something bulky around their middle?" she wondered.

"Very funny. I'd say look for someone who is way too interested in your dad, or your mom." He suddenly stopped. No smile. He looked directly into her face. "Or you."

Did he see the little jolt of panic she felt inside?

Probably. Though he didn't say it, she realized he considered her more of a target than her dad.

"Nothing's going to happen to you or your family, Libby. You can trust me on that."

Libby wanted the answer to a question that had been bothering her.

"Cooper, are you carrying a gun?"

"I'm going to pretend you didn't ask that question. What do you think?"

"I'm guessing you are."

"It's only in case of an emergency."

Libby was looking down at her shoes when Cooper grabbed one of her hands and led her over towards Dr. Brownlee at the bar. Two men in tuxedos were in a heated conversation. She recognized them as colleagues of her father's. Cooper was interested and nudged her to within earshot.

"You can't just take them out of the home without knowing where they'll go. Foster care isn't always the answer," one man scoffed.

"I don't have time to interview all the potential homes. That's not my job," the other answered.

"Maybe His Highness could donate some of his considerable salary to bankroll another part-time position. It's the least he could do. He's getting all the awards and plaques. That way he could *earn* them."

Libby saw the other man's eyes grow wide as her father positioned himself behind the man who just spoke.

"I gather I didn't have your vote, then, Charlie." Dr. Brownlee said to the back of the man's head. Charlie jumped, turned and mustered a brittle smile.

"Austin, it wasn't what you think," he gushed.

"Just tell me, Charlie. Is it the plaque you object to,

or my *considerable* salary?" Libby could see Charlie was trying to think of something to say. "A salary that most doctors right out of college would turn down. Or, are you thinking of my *private* practice?" Her father frowned, and then continued, "And how the hell do you know how much money I make working for the Foundation?"

Brownlee appeared to leave the pause long and awkward on purpose. Then he gathered himself, and poured out the charm in a smooth voice thick as honey. "We have to trust the system. Way from perfect, but it's all we have. You're right, for once. We do need more caseworkers, not admin or doctors. You can ask our contributors. Everyone's spread thin these days with all the budget cuts."

Brownlee tossed back his drink and turned to the bar for another while his two colleagues fidgeted. "Not so much ice this time," Brownlee whispered to the bartender as a co-conspirator.

Libby noticed the bartender roll his eyes, dropping two cubes into a fresh glass and filling it with Dr. Brownlee's choice of Scotch.

"Sir." He held the drink out, with military bearing. Brownlee grabbed it without saying a word and turn back to his guests.

Libby saw her dad finally notice her and raise his glass in salute. After taking a long sip, he addressed his friends. "Gus and Charlie, I want to introduce you to my daughter, Libby."

The two men looked like they wanted to be anywhere but at Brownlee's side, being introduced to his daughter. Libby had a hard time taking her eyes off the drink in her father's hand. It was nearly gone already.

She leaned in, "Dad—"

"Libby," her dad interrupted, "Dr. Statler and Dr. Shane." He pointed to them one at a time. "I went to school with Charlie at Stanford."

"Nice to meet you." She shook their hands. "This is my friend, Calvin Cooper."

"Austin, you can be glad she takes after Carla," Dr. Shane said. Everyone laughed.

"Pleasure, Libby," Dr. Statler said as he bowed and left with Dr. Shane to go find their seats.

"We should sit down too, Dad," Libby said as she locked elbows and pulled him toward the stage. She could hear Cooper's footsteps following closely behind.

Half the room had seated themselves and were being served. As they stepped up on the dais, Carla was talking to a white-jacketed server who was pouring white wine. He bent over her with lavish gestures and laid her white cloth napkin across her lap, but his fingers lingered. Carla giggled. She was blushing.

"Are you through?" Dr. Brownlee boomed, addressing the waiter. It caused a momentary pause in the conversations below. Libby's father sat down, bumping the short black-vested server, and apologized a little too loudly.

Dr. Brownlee leaned forward toward Coop, who was already seated next to Libby, at the doctor's left. "Probably not the type of dinner you're used to, son."

Libby could feel Cooper flinch. She squeezed his hand, which had buried itself close to her thigh on her padded chair.

"You're right." Coop leveled a sharp glare at Dr. Brownlee. "Had to borrow the shoes, sir, and they hurt like hell." He dropped his eyes to Libby's lips and she could feel him soften.

Brownlee shrugged and dove into his Waldorf salad.

Cooper ate everything put before him, including the basket of bread after everyone else passed on it. He struck up a conversation with an older gentleman on his left Libby recognized as Dr. Fredrick Dolan, a former partner of her father's. She presumed that perhaps Dr. Dolan was going to introduce her father and present his award.

Libby's dad whispered to her, "Brownie, tell that sailor of yours he'd better be careful or he'll get a bill in the morning."

"I'm sure Cooper can take good care of himself," she answered.

"How many psychiatrists do you think he's used to talking to?"

Libby looked at Cooper's thick neck and shoulders, the back of his head and chuckled in response, "I'm going to guess none."

"I rest my case, then," her dad said.

The dishes were cleared. Coffee was brought out, along with thin slices of chocolate torte. The lights dimmed and the crowd settled back into their seats for the presentation honoring her father. The gentle tinkling of silverware and coffee cups was a comforting background to the low rumble of polite conversation.

Dr. Dolan stood up, walked past Libby and lightly traced his fingers over her shoulders, which made her jump. Then he slapped her dad on the back as he made his way to the podium. A water glass and spoon was in his left hand. He pinged the glass and the sound was repeated throughout the room until all were focused on the stage.

"Welcome to the annual Lavender House Jewel of the Bay awards banquet." The crowd was still. A photographer's flash blinded everyone at the head table momentarily.

"We've prepared a short slide show presentation, a little departure from our usual menu of boring speeches. And Austin," he leaned toward Dr. Brownlee as he tilted his head and winked, "if you don't like the pictures, you'll have to take it up with your wife."

The room erupted in titters.

Carla looked at Dr. Brownlee, smiled and shrugged.

Libby could hear her dad ask, "What the hell did you do?"

Libby felt Cooper's rigid attention. He had dropped her hand and had his left hand swinging free at his other side. He jerked as a white screen was lowered behind them. Just before it stopped unrolling, she saw him dip his head and search behind it before the back of the stage was obscured. Recorded music filled the room, at first blaring, then adjusted down. She recognized some of her father's favorites: Credence Clearwater and the Grateful Dead.

The entire head table turned to watch the screen behind them. Pictures flashed of a handsome young dark-haired man with the distinctive jawline and lanky frame she knew so well. Her mother looked just as beautiful as she was now, in a peasant blouse with hand embroidery, her shiny brown hair reaching all the way to her waist. There was a picture of her dad with Libby as a toddler, while he smoked a pipe in his study. Libby bounced on his knee and waved at the picture taker, presumably her mother. There were pictures of Libby and her brother, Neil, at the beach with their parents. In every photo, Austin was either smoking a pipe or had his nose in a book. His face seldom bore a smile, as if the picture-taking were somehow painful for him.

There was a yellowed photo of her father and Dr. Dolan in front of a bungalow with a sign out front *Psychotherapy Associates.* She remembered playing as a preschooler on the wooden floor of that older post-war building, and recalled the white and black octagon-tiled bathroom. Libby remembered the bathroom windows had wavy glass with thin wires embedded in them.

Dr. Dolan leaned forward and spoke to her father. "Should never have sold that place. We'd have made a fortune, Austin."

Her dad was staring off into a dark corner, biting his lip absent-mindedly.

One picture took Libby's breath away. It was of the six of them. Libby's father and mother with a teenage Libby and Neil. Next to them stood a childless couple, Dr. Dolan and his wife. They were childless because their daughter had committed suicide the summer before. Jennifer had been in Libby's class and the two girls had been friends. A year later, Mrs. Dolan herself had a heart attack and died. It was an odd addition to the happy biography of the man they were honoring tonight. Jennifer had been one of Dr. Brownlee's patients.

"What's wrong, Libby?" Coop whispered in her ear.

"I'll tell you later," she murmured. She noticed her

dad was looking at his lap.

Several more pictures followed, including one of the costumes her parents had worn to a Halloween party at the Lavender house. Dr. Brownlee was dressed as a very pregnant woman and her mother was dressed as the physician in a white lab coat. Making the picture more humorous was the fact that Dr. Brownlee was drinking a pink cocktail and looked like he'd had several already.

"Where did you get these?" he asked Carla loudly enough for the whole table to hear him.

"That wasn't one I gave him," she said and looked back up to the picture behind them.

The last frame appeared as the music ended. Dr. Brownlee and Dr. Dolan were cutting a light purple ribbon tied around the front door of their little non-profit clinic, with the distinctive purple sign affixed to the top of the building. The logo was filled with painted flowers blooming on green lacy vines. A small group of pregnant teenage girls was sitting to the right on freshly painted wooden steps.

Libby curled her finger and Cooper lent his ear. "After his daughter's death, he wanted to do something for the young unmarried women of San Diego County. My dad helped him acquire this building and get the clinic started. Dad got the investors together."

Coop nodded in understanding.

"Ladies and gentlemen. Three years ago, when we opened, I was given this award," Dr. Dolan began. "I suggested Austin receive it, but he turned it down. *Turned it down!*" Dolan leaned back on his heels as the white screen rose with a faint mechanical buzzing noise. The lights had been turned up on the raised platform, but the gallery was still dark.

Dr. Dolan spoke again. "He took his name off the nomination list two more times, ladies and gentlemen. *Always* selfless. *Always* thinking about the other guy, aren't you, Austin?"

Libby noticed how her dad squirmed and was breathing hard. He was bouncing his right knee until Carla laid her hand on it to stop the motion.

The floodlights gave Dr. Dolan a ghastly pale coloring. Libby noticed how his skin had aged, red veins and lines scarring his fleshy jowls. Sweat dripped from his jaw line onto his white shirt. Under vacant dark eyes were caverns of pain. He had a twitch she had never noticed before.

"He's one in a million, ladies and gentlemen. The last of the really good men. So without further ado, I give you Lavender House's 2012 Jewel of the Bay, Dr. Austin Mercer Brownlee."

The crowd erupted in applause. Libby could see flashes from the dark gallery and glitter of jewelry here and there. Dark bodies were silhouetted against the lighting in the lobby of the hotel beyond. The table votive candles did little to help her see the faces of the audience.

Cooper was at full attention. She could smell sweat soaking into his blue suit. He had beads of perspiration on his upper lip. His breathing was full and raspy.

As Dr. Brownlee stood to address the group shrouded in darkness, Libby saw the deep crease on her father's forehead, punctuated by raised eyebrows. He didn't look like a man happy to receive an honor.

He looked like prey.

CHAPTER 30

DETECTIVE CLARK RIVERTON watched the crowd from a corner in the ballroom, back in the shadows. These people always made him nervous. Movers and shakers and people who could end his career with a phone call, and nothing the union could do would save him because they were in bed with them, too.

He'd watched Libby dance with the guy she was definitely involved with. It didn't take a detective's eye to see the comfortable way in which their bodies glided across the dance floor. She was a gushing young bride, if he wasn't mistaken. He'd have to talk to them again about cavorting with someone who was a suspect. He thought he'd made himself pretty clear earlier.

Hormones.

He'd seen girls fall for these sailors before. His sister had been one of them. Thought she'd snagged a SEAL, but in the end he'd been killed in Afghanistan. She was left with a broken heart and a little girl she had to raise on her own.

The SEAL married her in spite of the fact that they didn't love each other, but at least the guy tried to be a good dad. Give him credit for trying to do the right thing. Clark knew his sister made the young man's life hell. The guy asked Riverton to be his best man, but he declined. He always felt a little bad about that.

Riverton's legs were tired, but he didn't want to go expose himself sitting out in the open at one of the tables, and he didn't want to hang out with the wait staff or dirty dishes. He grabbed an unused chair and kept to the shadows.

The women were lovely. If he were a younger man, he'd be interested. He had convenience girlfriends to take care of his needs. He didn't do long term relationships. Saw too many ones that proved destructive. Besides, he knew a lot of the people here were not nearly as happy as they made out to be.

Demons. Everyone has demons.

His sister's kid was a sweet girl, a little shy. But then, living with his sister wouldn't be the easiest. And now his sister was obsessed with doing all kinds of new husband interviews. Riverton knew she was entertaining men at her house overnight, and there was something just wrong about that. Her attempts to find a replacement daddy for his niece were bound to be hard on the little girl. Wasn't a good thing for a seven-year-old to witness. Besides, his niece was the one who had loved her daddy more than anyone else. Of course the kid would be shy. She probably still missed her dad.

He thought about the tats his brother-in-law had, just like the ones Coop and his buddies had. Maybe they'd served with him.

Now he knew many of the SEALs got the same tats. So that meant the perp hounding the Brownlee family was a SEAL. More than likely ex-SEAL, since it didn't make sense otherwise. It definitely was someone who had a big beef with someone.

It was way too personal.

Brownlee? His daughter? Based on what the guy had done so far, it didn't make sense that his beef was with the Navy.

A group of very large women decked out in sequined dresses that made them look like drag queens sauntered by him on their way out to the lobby. One of them dropped him a look.

Sheesh. This store's been closed for a long time, sweetheart.

They were beginning the ceremony and the house lights were turned down. A colleague of Dr. Brownlee's was speaking, his face bright red and his veins protruding at the sides of his neck. Riverton could see them from where he sat at the back of the room. The guy was stuffed into his suit and shirt like he was poured into it.

Riverton went over and snagged a bottle of Coke from the hosted bar, flashing his badge. He popped open the top and guzzled half of it down. His throat was on fire.

He replaced the plastic top and watched the program, wondering what his life would have been like if he'd made different choices. What if his sister didn't drink so much? He hoped she'd find someone good and be quick about it. Her downward spiral was not pretty to watch.

It was a shame, really, his brother-in-law checking out like that, just when Riverton was beginning to let down his guard and get to know the kid.

No, nothing was as it seemed. Heroes weren't invincible. They did stupid things just like the rest of us, he thought. It was all in the fixing their mistakes that made more of a difference, like his brother-in-law. Dr. Brownlee had let some pretty colossal killers off with his reasoned approach to their treatment and incarceration. The doc liked to play God and thought he could tell a good guy from a bad guy. That's what most these psychiatrists thought. Still, Brownlee did help out more than half the time, and Riverton was grateful for his expertise. Sometimes that was the only break he had in solving some of these gruesome cases.

Brownlee was good for the community too. And Carla had really helped out when his sister was making plans to bury her husband. Thank God for his military pension the little one would get until she was of age. All the health care they needed. Free college. That part had been a good deal. Even in death he was a good provider.

Except his little niece didn't have a daddy, and his sister was a tramp. He vowed to spend more time with the girl, try to help out if he could. He owed the SEAL that, at least.

That kid he'd watched tonight on the dance floor with Libby sure was a big guy. Riverton had been miffed to see they didn't take his advice and remove themselves from a known suspect, but then, did he expect Brownlee could stop his daughter? No more than Riverton could stop his sister. There was something there that he trusted, in spite of his police training. Well, maybe it was part of his police training.

Coop was intimidating. But he looked like a good kid in the wrong place at the wrong time. He didn't look hard like some of the guys who stayed in too long. He was just a dumb young sailor having the time of his life blowing shit up and putting his body in dangerous spots. Letting the ladies rub off all the rough parts.

What a life.

Cooper's liaison, Chief Petty Officer Timmons, had vouched for him earlier today, and also verified the story about the sailor's family. Riverton had to ask if he thought Cooper was okay in the head. Could he handle it, that sort of thing?

"*Most of that crazy shit we drill out of them before they get through Hell Week,*" Timmons had told him. "*We aren't looking for the proud and the few. We're looking for those that will not think about how they feel, they'll just jump off a three story building and not question it.*"

Had his brother-in-law had some of that and he just missed seeing it? Maybe he was too cynical for his own damn good.

Timmons told him to go look up Detective Mayfield in the downtown precinct. Said he'd worked with the man last year when some San Diego gang members, trying to coerce their cooperation in getting guns and equipment for them, had kidnapped one of the SEALs and his sister. He said Mayfield could vouch for Cooper too.

Well, maybe I'll do that tomorrow. Riverton looked up at the screen again. Boy, there were a lot of slides. They went on and on. And the doctor who had introduced the program was in every one of them. Who's banquet was it, anyway?

He sipped on his Coke. He didn't look forward to the conversation he was going to have to have with Brownlee and his daughter. But he had to.

The bevy of bejeweled rotund ladies returned, and

they weren't graceful as they sashayed between chairs that didn't leave enough space for their large frames. They sparkled a hell of a lot, though. Was kind of funny to watch, in a sick sort of way.

Riverton felt old. He knew years ago there was no sense getting married and trying for the happily ever after. That time was long gone. Besides, he spent too much time trying to fix the rest of his family.

He could understand how Brownlee would want to proactively protect his daughter, without worrying about himself, and could very well get in the police's way. If he had a daughter, he'd do the same. But he didn't.

No use going there.

All during the slide show he looked up on the screen at a life he barely knew about. Brownlee was as much a stranger to him now as he had been twenty years ago when they had first met at the scene of a homicide. No one had a life like that, at least no one on the force. It was all destruction and decay, everywhere he looked. He'd done his time in the Army, and then police work was the only thing he felt suited for when he got home.

Some of his buddies went to college. Riverton's parents were sick most of their lives, and when it was time for college his mom was heading into her first rehab. It had used up the last of the equity in their family home. There was no money for college. And he had to get a steady job with benefits so he could help them, since his sister was still at home, in grammar school.

He finished off the Coke and left it standing next to the chair.

Night school had suited him fine. He came alive at night. The day was for people that believed in sunshine and love, true love. Happy endings.

No, if he could just get this one last creep out of everyone's hair, he'd be satisfied. That was the only happy ending he wanted. Just one more bad guy behind bars, then perhaps he'd put in for retirement. Maybe take a job in a dusty small town in the middle of nowhere. Or, get himself lost in a Mexican fishing village and just check out.

The lights came on after Brownlee took the crystal bowl back to his table. There he was, with his beautiful wife and daughter. A good man, not perfect, but a good one. Living a life Riverton could never have.

Because he was too tired to fight anymore.

CHAPTER 31

THE GUESTS WERE leaving the grand ballroom. Cooper noticed Riverton as he filed out between Carla and Libby. He gave the detective a nod but no smile. He knew part of the reason Riverton was there was to watch him interact with the Brownlee family.

Everyone trying to play psychiatrist. Get inside my head. He saw the man disappear behind a potted plant and then reappear before they made it out on the driveway at valet parking.

"Where's Austin?" Riverton asked Carla.

"Oh, he's back there talking to a friend. He'll be along. Asked us to get the car."

Riverton gave a brief nod of recognition and then spoke to Carla again, ignoring Libby and Cooper. "Might I have a word with the two of you ladies? No offense, Cooper."

Of course I take fucking offense. He wondered what Riverton was up to.

"I'll go get your father," Cooper said to Libby as he kissed the top of her head and removed his arm from around her waist.

He tried not to make eye contact with the partygoers as he made his way across the floor. Women especially were trying to catch his attention. Big time. No doubt he'd been seen up on the dais with the Brownlee family.

I'm no fuckin' rock star. The audience was dotted with young ladies who no doubt were former customers of the Lavender House. These were girls who had grown up a little too fast. He could spot them all right. They were all over his community and the SEAL bars.

Frog hogs.

He saw doctor Brownlee in a heated argument with the man who had introduced him, his former partner.

What's his name? Doctor-I'm-a-fuckin'-good-sport. Cooper didn't like the man, and suddenly he found himself more than a little concerned and protective about Libby's dad.

"Look, I'm not trying to take any of your patients. I have more than a full load," Brownlee was saying as Cooper came up beside him and waited.

The other doctor extended his hand to Cooper. "Hi there again, son. You enjoy yourself tonight?" he asked.

"It was his party. I'm just the escort," Coop answered, and then wondered why he answered it with that sexual innuendo.

It did raise the doctor's eyebrows.

Cooper shrugged his shoulders. "That came out wrong. Look, I'm a friend of Libby's. Dr. Brownlee wanted his daughter to come, so that's why I'm here." Cooper hoped that ended the discussion.

Brownlee inserted himself in the conversation with his biting sarcasm. "As opposed to something else he wanted to do tonight,"

Brownlee's colleague looked confused. Among the three of them, Cooper noticed there wasn't an ounce of friendship anywhere.

"Call me tomorrow, Dolan. We'll have coffee and hash this out. Let me see if there is someone from my schedule who might be better served working with you, okay?"

"I'm not interested in your rejects, Austin. And I don't need your pity or your sloppy seconds." Dr. Dolan was bright red. Cooper noticed something was not right about the man, who huffed off in the opposite direction.

Brownlee and Cooper sliced through the crowd that was thinning out.

"Sorry that you had to witness that, Cooper."

"What's gotten into him? You guys are partners."

"Were. Very past tense. The man's had a rough couple of years."

"You think maybe you should tell Riverton?" Coop asked, trying to be helpful.

"Oh, hell, no. He's going through a little rocky patch is all. Lost his wife two years ago. Lost his daughter about five years ago, too. A suicide. I'd just started to treat her, as a favor, of course."

"You don't think that's important?"

Brownlee stopped, pointed his index finger at Cooper's chest, and, lucky for him, did not touch Cooper. "Look, you do what you do best. Let me do what I do best. I know people, and I've known Dolan since before Libby was born, before Carla. So don't tell me what to do, who to name and not name."

"I understand," Cooper said as quietly as he could. "But even with all the training we have, you can't always tell your enemies from your friends. There are only truly a handful of people you can ever trust."

"Hmm." Brownlee turned to head out through the doors to the parking area. Cooper grabbed his arm and stopped him in what could be a dangerous physical move, if Brownlee was another SEAL.

"You do understand this guy is not right?" Cooper said.

"Which guy? Dr. Dolan or the guy trying to scare my family?"

"Both. You ask yourself, doctor, could this be the same man?"

LIBBY NOTICED COOPER was not talkative all the way back to the Hotel Del. But neither was her father. Had the two men had a fight?

She wanted to tell him about the warning Riverton had given her and her mother.

"Surprised to see him here tonight," Riverton had said. *"Thought I told you not to have further contact, until I could rule him out as a suspect."*

"It was Austin's idea," Carla had said.

Cooper kept looking out his side window, facing away from her, which shouted he wanted to be left alone with his thoughts. Her mother was suspiciously watching her father too. She held the heavy crystal bowl in her lap almost like a burden. The whole evening seemed suddenly petty and ridiculous to Libby. Keeping up appearances. Her father and Cooper in some private war. Some creep in the shadows somewhere. Even taking up occupancy in the bridal suite at the Hotel Del seemed like a bad joke. A blanket of doom descended over all of them.

When they arrived at the hotel, Cooper did his usual thing, showing deference to her mother and letting her out of the car first, then leaning in and reaching for Libby's hand. He wasn't smiling as he carefully helped her out of the car. He was careful. And solemn.

Her dad finished with the valet and caught up with

them as they walked inside to the lobby.

"Ladies," Dr. Brownlee started, "I want to have a little chat with Cooper. If you don't mind, I'll meet you upstairs in a few minutes."

Libby felt her heart lurch as Cooper nodded in agreement and wouldn't look at her.

She grabbed his hand and he looked up. "You coming up later?"

"Not sure. I've got some things to arrange. Tomorrow's going to be a very busy day."

"Come say good night before you leave, then, okay?" She saw the faint smile as he leaned in and kissed her forehead—not her lips.

The women turned and aimed for the elevator, but just before entering, Libby looked at her father and Cooper, walking down the narrow, dark corridor towards the bar, side by side. She wondered if the two men realized they were both removing their ties at the same time. Even their gait seemed to be the same. Cooper was almost five inches taller than her father, but they both were lean and handsome. Their actions were so similar, they could have been mistaken for father and son.

DR. BROWNLEE SLUMPED into an oxblood-colored booth and Cooper followed behind and sat across the little table from him. The place was dark, lit by small votives. Some jazz was playing and the bar was barely one-third full. Signed, autographed photos of movie actors lined the wall above the shiny walnut wainscoting. Several colorful movie posters, encased in Plexiglas, were displayed between them. A cocktail waitress in a black, low-cut body suit was there in an instant. She leaned into Cooper and gave him a generous view of her rack.

"Hey there, sailor. What's your pleasure?"

Cooper wondered how they always knew he was in the Navy. None of his tats showed. He didn't want to ask. Brownlee was watching him.

"I'll have mineral water, with some lime, if you don't mind," Coop said.

"Don't mind at all. And you, sir?" She gave Dr. Brownlee a practiced smile. Libby's dad cleared his throat and asked for Scotch. Neat.

Cooper noticed he didn't order a double.

Brownlee folded his hands in front of him and fiddled with the cocktail napkin. He waited until they were served before he began. Coop wasn't sure what was on his mind.

"First, you want to tell me about this?" Brownlee pointed to Cooper's mineral water while he took a sip from the glass tumbler.

"Not much to tell, really. I prefer it," Cooper lied.

"Sure you do. That's why you watch me drink so

closely."

Cooper smiled and lowered his eyes to concentrate on the little bubbles traveling up his glass. Without looking at Dr. Brownlee, he nodded. "That obvious, huh?"

"You forget what I do for a living, son."

"Would you stop calling me that?" Cooper pierced him with a stare he hoped the doctor would understand.

"You're good at changing the subject, Cooper. But I get what you're saying, and will try not to do it any more. I don't mean to annoy you. You know that, don't you?"

"Not really. I think you enjoy annoying me."

Because I'm fucking the hell out of your daughter, and loving it. And she does too.

"You've got me wrong, Coop. So, maybe I better tell you a story. It's about Will."

Cooper wasn't sure he wanted to hear it.

"He and I were the best of friends, more so than brothers, really. Very competitive in all ways. As a matter of fact, we thought if we didn't get into college, we'd both try out for the Teams too."

Cooper wondered why Libby had never told him this, and suspected it was because she never knew.

"I got accepted to Stanford with a scholarship, and Will didn't. We'd have gone together, in fact, we'd have gone to the same school, if we could. But Will got the wrong letters. I went to college, and he enlisted in the Navy."

Brownlee finished off his drink and indicated for another. "My folks were scared to death about us both going overseas and getting hurt. The war in Southeast Asia was over, but those were wonky times, men coming home not physically damaged, but mentally damaged. Just seemed like the whole world had exploded. Never knew who you could trust. Kinda like now."

Cooper knew exactly what Brownlee was saying. He'd thought about the same thing.

"Yeah, first to enter, last to withdraw," Coop whispered to his glass.

"Exactly. I wanted to be a doctor, so I did some volunteer work at the VA hospital in Palo Alto. Will did his medic training after joining the Teams. I saw all these young boys coming home—it was a shame how they were treated. The more I saw, the more I was convinced I'd be able to help." Brownlee inhaled and then pushed out his breath, leaning forward on the table, moving his drink aside. "I tried to convince Will it was too dangerous. He kept telling me it was bad luck. But I kept it up."

"No one would have been able to talk me out of it either, if it makes you feel any better. My folks just—"

Coop couldn't finish the sentence.

"Grenada. Botched operation in Grenada," Brownlee said. "What a waste."

"Which led to the intel they needed to get it right the next time. You know as well as anyone we learn from our mistakes." Coop had heard it a million times. He'd said it a million times.

"I hated him for dying. I really hated him. Can you understand that?" Brownlee said, after a long pause.

"I do. I've felt the same from time to time. Lost my roommate in BUD/S, and I've lost others, too. It's not something that ever gets easier. They lie about that."

"The lingo for it is 'survivor's guilt.' I'm here, falling in love, fulfilling all my dreams, and building a great practice. I was the lifeline for my parents until they passed. Will was always the golden boy who could do no wrong. He would always be remembered as the perfect son. And that's because he just didn't live long enough to screw up and disappoint them. He was remembered as being perfect, while I was merely human. Made no sense, though I tried to accept it. Just was his time to die."

Cooper didn't want to delve any deeper. What the hell did he know about all this psychobabble, anyway? "We all have that date, sir."

"That's a fact, Coop. And every night I come home and see his smiling face on the mantle." Brownlee's eyes teared up. "And every night, I wish it was me. I wish Will was the one living in this house, having a beautiful wife, a beautiful life. I often wish it was me they hauled all the way home to bury here in San Diego."

Brownlee was getting very morose, and Cooper suspected it had more to do with the depressive effects of the alcohol than anything else. He was starting to feel very uncomfortable. He wasn't so sure he should know all this.

"Where are we going with all this, sir?" he finally asked.

"Not sure, but I think an apology is in order."

Cooper wasn't sure he was hearing the doctor correctly.

"You don't owe me anything, sir."

"Oh, yes, I do. I'm sorry. Sorry for being an asshole. A royal asshole."

They looked at each other for a long few moments, and then finally Cooper broke the gaze.

"You wanted to know about my not drinking," Cooper began. "Well, I used to. I drank a lot."

"Um hum," Brownlee said softly.

"I was with a couple of my Team buddies. We were getting ready to ship out and we were tying one on at the beach. My friend got a 'Dear John' letter from home and, it pretty much tore him up. We got shit-faced." The vision of that night came flooding in. He hadn't thought about it for a good couple of years. He'd worked really hard to bury it. Deep.

"My friend wanted to go for a swim. He looked okay. But I knew I was in no shape to go into the water. We laughed at him, made jokes about it. He dove into the surf, and we didn't see him for a long time."

"He was a good swimmer, though? All you guys are. What happened?" Brownlee wanted to know.

"Found out later on he was allergic to shellfish, and we had it in the take-out we'd ordered. He had a reaction, drowned in his own vomit. His body came rolling in like a discarded telephone pole. We worked on him until the paramedics arrived."

"Nothing you could have done," Brownlee said. "It was his time."

"No it wasn't. I might have been able to save him. Maybe it was what he wanted, but that wasn't the point. He had to have known he was eating seafood. Or maybe not. I really don't know. I was too shit-faced to keep him out of the water. Too trusting of his survival skills, even under impaired conditions. Too fucked up to realize he'd been in too long. We didn't look out for him. We didn't have his back."

"I'm sorry, Coop. Really sorry about that." Brownlee's pained expression looked honest.

"I wasn't the hero I thought I was. Ever since, I

made a course correction and decided not another drop of alcohol. Ever."

Brownlee rimmed the tumbler with his forefinger. There was a half inch left in his second round. He pushed it aside and looked into Cooper's eyes, not even trying to hide the tears rolling down his cheeks.

"Life is pretty messed up, sometimes, isn't it, Co-op?"

"That it is, sir."

"And then someone comes along, and makes you whole again. That's what Carla did for me. I found her just in time, Coop."

Cooper wasn't going to say anything else. He was still staring at the unfinished drink. He knew it was Libby' father's way of saying he'd meet Cooper half-way. But Cooper would have to do the rest of the heavy lifting.

If they were all to survive this ordeal.

CHAPTER 32

L IBBY WAS TRYING to concentrate on a television program her mother was watching, but she found herself daydreaming, and hoping Cooper would want to spend the night. She knew he'd have to get back to take care of Bay. She'd left her dress and stockings on. So had her mother.

Both women stood when they heard the key card and then watched the door open. Dr. Brownlee looked tired, coming over to give his wife a hug. Cooper gave a boyish grin to Libby.

Thank God. All is well.

At least they appeared to be getting along, and that was a huge relief. Cooper had his shirt unbuttoned, and the back of his hair was mussed a bit, as if he'd been rubbing it. The dark blue of his suit matched his dusk-colored eyes. She could watch him forever, how he walked with that free-flowing style of a world-class athlete, slight hip movement and flat stomach muscles.

And the best of all, he was walking straight to her, eyes fixed on her mouth.

That's where they touched first. The kiss. Tender, careful, but needy. She wrapped her arms around his neck and he pulled her into him and he sighed into the side of her hair as he held her. She let him just hold her for several minutes.

And then it occurred to her. He wasn't going to be spending the night with her. He was saying goodbye. Well, she was just going to have to live with it.

Her mother had gone off to the other bedroom, but her dad stood waiting for them to break their embrace. When Cooper turned, he kept his arm around Libby, his cheek upon the top of her head like he did so often.

Libby's dad smiled. "Cooper and I have come to an understanding, I think," her dad began.

"Yes, sir," she heard Cooper say.

Dr. Brownlee walked over to the two of them and put his hand on Libby's cheek. "So good to see you happy, Brownie."

"Thanks dad." Libby placed her hand over his and held it until he dropped it to his side.

"Coop?" Her father extended his arm and the two men shook hands. He stepped back. "Well, I'm off to bed. I'm exhausted."

"Get some rest, doctor. We have a big day tomorrow," Cooper said to his back.

Libby looked up at Cooper after the bedroom door closed. "What's going on?"

"I've got a boatload of things to do tomorrow. I'm going to call it a night. Get some rest, for a change," he winked at her. "And then get my gear and get set up at your house before dark."

"Can I—"

"Libby, no. I'll call you tomorrow, okay?"

"Anything I can do to help?"

Cooper looked over at the Brownlee's closed door. "Be here for your parents, Libby. Someone also needs to call your brother and alert them, just in case."

"In case?"

"I have a hard time thinking this creep doesn't know everything about your family. Everything. Not fair to leave any family member unprotected. You understand? We might not need to, but it would be very dumb if we didn't alert them."

"What about Riverton? He doesn't want us to be around each other, until—"

"That's my problem." He kissed her forehead and then he placed his fingers under her jaw and lifted her face so he could place a kiss on her lips. "And it's even a bigger problem—" he said as his lips brushed against hers, the lemon scent of his aftershave and the late-night stubble brushing against her cheek making her dizzy, "—if you don't want me around."

She had to smile at this. "Not a chance. You'll have to pry my arms away before you can get out of this hotel room."

He drew her in again and held her. "What am I going to do with you, Libby Brownlee?"

She had some definite ideas. "Anything you like, sailor."

COOPER DID WANT to spend the night with Libby in a decent-sized bed, even if her parents were two rooms away, but it wasn't the smart thing to do. If he did his job right, they'd have lots of nights together.

But something else was changing, too. He felt protective not only of Libby, but the rest of her family as well. He realized it was something he had to do. Was born to do. He'd never gotten a chance to rescue his family in Nebraska.

It was just like AA's Big Book said, *accept the things I cannot change, the courage to change the things I can, and the wisdom to know the difference.* There were a lot of things he would change, including the death of his family and all the other good men who'd honorably served their country. But there wasn't any point dwelling on it, while there was a war going on.

Some people who look like the enemy are not. Not everyone who helps is a friend. Well, he knew some guys he could definitely count on.

Cooper called Fredo on his way to give Bay some relief. He left a message about needing the truck for another day or two. Then he called his LPO, Kyle.

"I'm going for PT at oh-eight hundred, Coop. Meet you at the Salty Dog for breakfast?"

"Sounds good to me," Cooper answered.

FREDO WALKED IN first, followed by Kyle. The new guy came with them, and Cooper wasn't sure he liked this at all. Cooper stood.

"Relax," Kyle said. Malcolm nodded in agreement.

"Diversity and all that shit," the new man said. "Nice to see you again, sailor." He extended his hand.

"I wasn't expecting anyone else, and this stuff's kind of personal," Cooper said back to Kyle. He addressed Malcolm. "No offense, but this isn't much of a career building meeting, sir."

"Roger that. Kyle here was talking about the stuff going on at your girlfriend's house. Unfortunately, I've had some experience with this sort of thing. I'd like to help catch this guy, if you don't mind. I hate bullies."

Cooper considered how to respond. His LPO was going to let him make the call whether or not to include Malcolm in their plan. Trust was always an issue with a new Team Guy. But if Kyle had felt comfortable informing the new guy of the situation with the Brownlee family, that would have to be good enough for Coop. "Okay, but this is it. I'm telling Timmons, and no one else. I don't care how much history you got with anyone else. No one else is gonna get involved, understood?"

"Perfectly," Malcolm smiled with his brilliant set of huge teeth. "Only want to help. Minute I think I'm in the way, I go."

Malcolm stood nearly as tall as Cooper. His frame was heavier, and he had shoulders like a body builder, not a Naval Academy officer, although those guys were getting bigger these days. No more empty suit look where the hat came down over the eyes. He remembered one of the officers in BUD/S was usually first or second at everything physical, from timed swims in the inlet to running with full pack and combat boots on the beach. They were turning out animals, but smart animals. Guys you could believe in, and that was important.

Stupid warriors get themselves and everyone else killed. All his training could be summed up in one phrase, *drum stupid out of your life.*

"Please, sit," Cooper motioned and then did so himself and worked on finishing his omelet.

"What are you needing, Coop? What's on your list?" Fredo asked.

Cooper gave him the list he'd prepared earlier.

Fredo read it over, nodding. "I can help you with

some of this. We got more of those little flag pins, too. Where are you going to hook up?"

"I think Brownlee's study, and then probably Libby's room, plus the master, maybe down in the kitchen. The adjuster will be done today, from what I understand, and it will be undisturbed until they settle and hire a contractor."

Everyone nodded.

"So, I'd start upstairs. Probably Libby's bedroom, the master. Focus on rooms that are most often occupied," Kyle said.

"The two guest bedrooms are never used. And they're upstairs, so I think no one would be climbing in the windows there," said Coop.

"I got a new little speaker, Coop. We can boost the signal to outside the house," said Fredo.

"We'll need about three of them. And we need motion sensor night recording devices, too," Coop said. "I've got to go gather some stuff at the warehouse I recently bought on eBay.

"No problem."

Kyle asked another question, "You're not going to do all the surveillance yourself, right? You can't do it 24/7."

"Hell, we've done it all the time. You know that."

"I don't want you taking all the risk. We'll create a schedule, take turns."

"As long as I get the lion's share of those turns. I'm going to sleep at the house. They gave me permission."

"Seriously?" Fredo asked.

"Bay, too."

"Oh man, he's gonna fuck up the motion sensors. That won't work, Cooper."

"What if you set them above waist height?" Kyle said.

Malcolm piped up. "You mean to say your dog never jumps up on stuff?"

"Coop, we're gonna have to figure something out. I say we all go over to the house and check it out first," Fredo volunteered.

"One thing Malcolm can do. We need to find out about this tat. You think Daisy did it, Coop?"

"Seems possible. Perhaps someone put something over on her?" Cooper answered. "I'd like a better look at the picture the detective has."

"What about Brownlee?" asked Fredo.

"Turned everything over to the cops. Evidence." Cooper looked out the window and had an idea. "I'm going to ask Timmons. Maybe he could get a copy, professional courtesy and all. Then I'll send Malcolm on his first assignment." He winked at the handsome officer.

"Sounds like a plan, Cooper," Malcolm said. "You get that picture and I'll go ask Daisy. I'm assuming all you guys got the tat already. I'd be the one looking to have my flesh painted."

"She'd know you were joining the Team. She's probably more than a little sore at me. It wouldn't be right if I went," answered Coop.

Fredo leaned against Malcolm and whispered, "She thought she was going to be Mrs. Cooper. I'm kinda glad she's still single so I can have her work on me again. Her partner's a little rough, you ask me."

COOPER WENT OVER to Timmons's office on base and gave him an update on what he was doing.

"Not fond of you getting the new guy entangled in this, Coop. Kyle and Fredo better keep their mouths shut, too." Timmons was in a foul mood again, like he'd been for the past year, since before their last deployment.

"Didn't want to. He kind of forced himself on me. What's his story?"

"I think you could be looking at another Joint Chiefs member in the making, Coop. Graduated first in his class, can you believe that? His liaison officer told me he didn't even read until he was in second grade."

Coop whistled. "I know some guys who still don't read. Seems like a smart squid. Built like a tank. An okay guy, too."

"More than that. Turned down a football contract to join the Teams. He's so athletic, I'll bet he could still have a career there after he's done here."

"Well let's hope the Navy gives him every bit of his below-poverty pay and hazard pay, so he doesn't get tempted," Coop tossed back to his liaison.

"Right."

Several guys on Team 3 came from professional football. They'd had a senator's son and an astronaut's son in their BUD/S class, but both washed out. He knew better than anyone that only guys who could focus on one thing at a time made it. Was hard for a guy to make the training if he had too many choices. Often the most successful SEALs were damaged goods when they arrived, or kids intent on making something of themselves.

"Well, if he turned down a life of the rich and famous to work on my Team, I guess I can give him a little respect. Thanks for telling me."

"So, how can I help you?"

"I was just trying to keep you informed." Coop was hoping Timmons didn't catch on.

Not a chance. He should have known.

"Bullshit. You could have said all that over the phone. You want something. Now you going to tell me, or are you going to make me play with my dick all afternoon until you do?"

Cooper tensed at the slight thrown his way. But he had to show Timmons his skin was thick. "I want a picture of the tats the police got."

"What tats?"

"These." Cooper rolled up his sleeve and showed Timmons.

"Shit, Cooper, the guy has a set of these? Riverton didn't tell me that."

"Well, he's a detective. That's why I'm one of his suspects. You know what the guy did, don't you?"

"Yes. Killed the daughter's cat. He said a picture was sent to the doctor. I just figured it was your dumb luck to have called on these people right about the time some psycho decided to—"

"That's why I want to study them, carefully. Might tell me who did it. You know I would recognize Daisy's work anywhere."

"Why don't you just ask her?"

Cooper had left out the part about him seeing Libby Brownlee. And he certainly wasn't going to tell him he was in a get-nekkid type of relationship with her. Even though her dad seemed to be cool with it, he didn't want to tell Timmons.

But what made Timmons such a good Team liaison was he could tell when there was a good story. In fact, he usually expected it.

As if Timmons could read Cooper's mind, he shot

up to his feet and threw a file down on the desk. The top of the manila file was folded and wrinkled where it had been crushed by Timmons's death grip. "God damn it, Coop. You guys have about as much sense as—" he whirled around and spotted the frog statue.

Oh shit. Here he goes again. Need to take up another collection.

But Cooper saw him sit down without destroying the Team 3 mascot, in a rare display of control.

"I'll get your fucking picture," Timmons said to his desktop. "Now get the hell out of my office."

CHAPTER 33

COOPER STOPPED BY the *Babemobile* and retrieved Bay, who wasn't used to riding in Fredo's truck, and he had to help the dog up and into the second seat. As planned, Cooper stopped by the Hotel Del and picked up Libby, who needed some things at the house. Carla had also given her a list of things to bring back for her and her dad.

Libby was dressed in mid-calf capris and a stretchy peach top that showed off all the parts Coop liked the best. But he preferred to not have to feel or look through stretchy cotton and lace, even though it was enticing as hell. He was hoping somehow they'd be able to get lucky over at the house, but he didn't want to push Libby into anything about which she felt uncomfortable.

"Dad told me you guys really had bonded last night in the bar," she ventured. "Must have been pretty important. Neither my mother nor I could get him to say two words about it."

Cooper made a note that this was a good sign, and he trusted the doc a little more. He preferred the story about his failed beach rescue attempt be kept secret too.

"Um hum," he said. He was smiling inside, because he could see how completely irritated Libby was that he was going to share in her father's conspiracy of silence. He loved it when she got that way. She was absolutely hot when she got frustrated.

I can take care of that, Libby, sweetheart. Give all that energy over to me where it will do some good.

His dick was hard as marble. He knew he'd better not let her know he was toying with her, or he'd not get a thing. And, boy, did he need her today. More than twenty-four hours and no sex made him an animal.

"Cooper. Are you paying attention to me?" She said as she began to raise her voice.

Oh yeah, I'm paying full attention. If he wasn't mistaken, her nipples had knotted under her little flimsy peach thingy. He could see the top of her thong underwear against the tanned flesh of her hips as it made that soft beautiful bulge over the tops of her capris.

He loved it that she wore her tee shirts small and her pants low. Every time he walked behind her he was hoping for a clothing malfunction. Anywhere.

Bay decided something was wrong, and pushed his

nose between them, drooling over the back of the seat covered in a Mexican serape.

Libby pointed to the dog. "Even he wants an answer."

"No. All he wants is food." Cooper was having difficulty keeping his eyes on the road. He didn't want to get caught sneaking a peek at her delicious midriff.

"I gotta tell you something, Coop."

His stomach clenched and he squeezed the steering wheel. *Oh no.*

"Since everyone is baring their soul, I have a secret, something I've not told my parents, Coop. And I'm going to."

"You sure?"

"Absolutely. I don't want any secrets from you. Not anymore."

Coop tried that on for a while. He wasn't sure he was going to like it, but he decided he was all in at this point. "Okay, shoot."

"At Santa Clara, my mentor, my advisor came on to me."

"No shit." Coop swallowed, waiting for the next part. He held his breath until she continued.

"He cornered me in the office and I—"

"Did that fucker rape you?"

"No. I was able to stop him." Libby was looking at her hands folded in her lap. She was chewing on her lower lip.

"How the hell'd you do that?" He felt like a dick talking to her like that, so softened his tone. "I mean, how did you manage to get away?"

Libby paused, then looked out the dirty windshield. "I broke his middle finger."

Cooper was splitting a gut inside but didn't want to show it. *Damn straight.* He knew she had it in her to fight, and she did.

"You got him good?" He allowed a small smile to form on his lips. She was beautiful. Deadly and beautiful.

She returned his gaze, and, looking at Coop's lips, answered, "Well let's put it this way. I doubt he'll have a future playing a guitar, a piano or certainly not a flute."

"Serves the bastard right." Coop encircled her shoulders with his right arm. "You are a wicked lady, Libby Brownlee."

"And there's something else," she said softly. They were stopped at a stoplight and Cooper was nervous.

Oh shit.

"I got him fired."

Cooper burst out laughing, and squeezed her shoulders into his side. "Good for you. I'm damned proud. I'll show you some moves so next time you can castrate him."

Libby laughed. God, how he loved that little care-free laugh. Bay started to whine.

"Just a little bit longer, Bay, then we'll get your food," he said.

"How could he be hungry?" she asked.

"Because he's a dog," he said as he leaned over and kissed her mouth before she could pull away. They were at another stoplight. "And so am I."

"You're hungry?" she said softly.

"Extremely. Famished. I can hardly concentrate." He kissed her again several times and got honked at from behind as the light had changed. If Libby had let him, he'd have done her right then and there, traffic be damned. She pushed him back to his side of the truck behind the steering wheel. He proceeded into the intersection right after the guy behind laid into the horn again.

She crossed her arms across her chest and tried a loud "humph," but he could tell she was faking it.

"You really mad at me? For wanting you? Or for making the guy behind me have to honk his horn?" he said, looking at her without fully turning his head. He saw her break a smile and he knew he had her. "Un-cross your arms. You're wrecking the view."

Her eyes got wide in mock outrage.

"I just need a little taste to tide me over a bit. Look, we're almost home now."

She pointed her chin to the cab ceiling, snuggled even closer to him, and slipped out of one arm of her shirt. Her left hand squeezed his package and Coop was in heaven. "What about my needs?" her voice was husky.

"Honey, I'm going to give you everything you could possibly want, and more, if you'll let me."

"Promises. Promises," she said as she massaged his length. Her delicate fingers found the button fly on his jeans and made fast work of the first two. They were cool and probing as they found him. She leaned over and put her tongue in his ear and he almost ran off the road.

Not a promise, Libby. It's a fact.

NOW THAT SHE had her fingers on his cock, her tongue exploring around his velvety earlobe just before she gave him a little nip, she knew it was going to be near impossible to live without the feel of this strong man at her side. The sex was great, but what she loved most was that he matched her newly-awakened appetite. She'd never felt this way before with any of her previous boyfriends. She didn't have to pretend with him. He knocked her socks off each time he touched her.

And she suspected that he felt the same way. She would find him just looking at her. Most of the time they made love their eyes were open to each other, as if he wanted to see how she felt. She didn't hold back. She could show him anything.

Well, anything except her true feelings. It was that glorious glow that consumed her, made it difficult to sleep next to him, made it difficult to think or feel anything else in the whole blasted world but Cooper. He was becoming her first thought in the morning, and the last thing she thought about at night. She wished she could remember the vivid dreams she was surely having, too.

They pulled up to the driveway of her parents' house, and she slipped her hand from his pants. He stilled the movement with his right hand, holding her in place. With the engine still running, he slid his palm under her shirt and into her bra and gave her left side a squeeze. He kept his foot on the brake and the clutch, but as he moved to ease himself, the engine died and lurched forward.

He sighed. "Sorry."

"I'm not," she said as she continued to rub the length of him up and down, holding her fingers in a ring. He ducked to kiss the flesh of her left breast that had been freed. He sucked on her nipple and bit her, then kissed the bite. She threw her head back and groaned.

"You want to fuck me here, in my parents' driveway, in front of all the neighbors?" She whispered.

"Hmmm," he said between kisses. "Would that turn you on?"

"Not as much as fucking you in my parents' swimming pool, where I can have you all to myself."

"That's nice. Now, why didn't I think of that?" He looked around toward the street. "Are we alone today?"

"Does it matter? You remember? You asked me that on the beach that night?"

"I have no recollection what I said, but I sure do know how it felt."

He claimed her mouth, and electricity shot down her spine to explode between her legs. Now she was hungry. "I think we are alone, yes."

Bay moaned his objection to being ignored. Libby chuckled and, with a pout, removed her hand from Cooper's pants and turned to get out of the truck.

"Bad dog," Cooper said. Libby looked over at her grinning SEAL hunk with his hair all mussed up. Bay barked. Cooper grabbed an empty gym bag from the second seat after Bay dove over the seat back and onto the driveway.

Libby slammed the door and dug in her purse for the front door keys. Bay was taking a long pee on her mother's flowers in the front yard. Cooper stood watch, searching up and down the street, his duty bag slung over one shoulder, hands in his front pockets.

"All clear?" Libby yelled out to him.

Cooper put his finger to his mouth, but nodded. Bay followed him as the three of them entered the foyer. Cooper spotted an open sliding glass door to the patio from the kitchen.

"I don't like that at all," he said to her. "Stick with me. We'd better check things out first."

Libby came up behind him and embraced him from the rear. "I have no intention of going anywhere."

They looked through the kitchen windows to the back yard and, other than the sprinklers running, nothing appeared out of place. They locked the slider and then tried all the windows downstairs. Cooper made sure the plywood covering the broken window in her dad's study was secure. The office still smelled of damp upholstery and charred paperwork, so they closed the double doors behind them as they exited.

Bay wouldn't let Cooper out of his sight. They let him run up the stairs first.

Cooper took Libby's hand and followed behind the dog. His expression was grim and she noticed he was on high alert. They climbed the steps without a sound. He kept putting his finger in front of his lips to keep her from talking so he could listen. Other than Bay's nails clicking on the plank flooring upstairs, there was no sound.

They searched her bedroom first, checking the windows overlooking the street, which had remained locked. Nothing in the room appeared out of place, from what she could see. Morgan lay alone on the silk cushions, and a stab of pain hit her as she recalled seeing Noodles curled up beside her childhood stuffed animal. Cooper dropped his bag and laid a warm hand on her shoulder, and she realized she'd been holding her breath.

Bay was surveying her parents' master bathroom. The Spanish tiled floor and colorful and intricately tiled trim design was spotless and shiny, unused since the last cleaning. Her father's closet door was ajar, and Cooper sent Bay in first before he turned on the light and went in himself. Nothing.

Nothing was out of place in the first guest bedroom, either. There was an opened window in the second guest room.

"Mom often keeps this window ajar," Libby whispered to Cooper.

Bay was totally distracted with all the new smells, but didn't appear to react to anything in particular. "I think everything's okay." He pulled Libby into his arms. "Why don't you get your parents' things first, and I'll meet you in your room, okay?"

"What about our swim?"

"We can still do that. After." He kissed her neck, and cupped her rear in his two massive palms, pulling her against his erection. He released her and, with a pat on her butt, said, "Go. Hurry. I'm hungry."

Libby filled a suitcase with underwear and clothes her mother had specified, as well as her favorite shampoo. Her father's things were more difficult to choose, so she picked two pairs of slacks and three dress shirts on hangers as well as some white tee shirts and some underwear and socks. It seemed odd to be packing for her parents, as if they were somehow missing from her life. She suddenly felt protective of them.

She wheeled the suitcase to her own room and found Cooper stretched out on her bed, her silk pillows behind his head, Morgan resting on his chest. What a sight, his long legs sticking out from under the waterfalls of white dotted Swiss that draped from the canopy on her bed—that bed where she'd spent so many nights dreaming of a life of some day. All he wore were his boxers, but Libby focused on the tent in his groin, and blushed.

Bay had positioned himself on the other side of the bed and was preparing to take a nap, oblivious to what else was going on in the room.

"Show me what you're packing. I want to approve it first," he said to her.

"You mean my underwear?" She said as she unzipped the gym bag. "I never knew SEALs liked underwear so much, but you definitely do."

"We all do. If anyone tells you different, they can't be trusted. It's part of your equipment, and we like good equipment."

"I like your equipment just fine, Cooper."

"And I love yours, Miss Libby Brownlee."

Will it always be like this? All the little things in my life that now have meaning? Seeing him in my girlie bedroom, watching me pack things, looking over my body and making me wet with anticipation?

She drew a pair of pink panties out of her drawer and held them up.

"I approve," he said.

"And these?" She held up a red satin thong and bra combination.

"Deadly. Put them in. But trust me, you won't wear them for long if I ever catch you wearing them."

"You like white?" She held up two pairs of white lace panties.

"I love white. Especially on you."

She added some shirts, after holding them up to him and receiving his nod of approval. She added two pairs of jeans and an oversized sweater and another pair of shoes. She looked at Morgan, still resting on his chest. Cooper held the stuffed dog out to her.

"Thanks." She smelled the toy and then lay him down on top of her clothes in the rolling gym bag and zipped it up. "Done."

Cooper curled his finger, asking her to come over to the bed. "Not done. Not nearly done with you." He sat up and placed his hands on her backside. "These have to go," he said as he unzipped her pants and let them fall. She was standing in another pair of white lace panties. "Nice. These I like. You can wear these again some time. I approve."

"Oh, really?"

"Absolutely," he whispered to the apex of her legs. One long finger slipped around the elastic and found her wet lips which opened to receive him. Slowly he encircled her opening as he kissed her belly button. "So nice. So lovely. I am so hungry."

He slid her panties down her thighs and leaned back on the bed and looked at her nakedness from the waist down.

"I never get tired looking at you."

Libby removed her shirt, but left her lace bra on. She wanted him to remove it. She turned around and bent over so he could take care of the clasp.

"You have the most perfect ass I've ever seen. I love that ass."

"I'm glad you approve. Now, would you release my restraints?" She said as she gazed over her shoulder at him kneeling on the bed behind her. She moved closer and soon felt his fingers on her bra clasps. And then she stood with her back turned to him, fully naked.

Coop's hands smoothed over her belly, as he kissed first one buttock, then the other. She could feel his knees barely pushing into the backs of her thighs. He pushed her shoulders a bit forward and laced his fingers between her butt cheeks until he found her opening and inserted two fingers there.

She moaned at the pure pleasure of him feeling her arousal, as she heard his breathing grow raspy. "So lovely. So…" He bowed his head as she arched her rear up, giving him full access to her sex. He slid his tongue along the lips of her labia until he breached her opening. He lapped as he stroked her with fingers, applying pressure to her clit. "Come for me, Libby," he whispered.

Libby squeezed her breasts and then dug her fingers into her own thighs as her whole world was focused on the feel of his tongue inside her, loving her, tasting her. He ministered to her patiently, slowly, letting her feel everything he was doing. Finally, she was overcome and a long series of rolling spasms began. Her knees began to buckle as she shook, wrung out from the pleasure his tongue was giving her body.

"Come." His deep murmur rumbled down her spine. He drew her back toward the bed as he moved his legs to sitting position on the edge of the bed. Sitting behind her, he separated her cheeks and placed her opening right at the head of his cock and held her there. She wrapped her ankles around his, spreading her knees as he pulled her down on his lap and then back up. The slow feel of him tunneling deep inside her, as she stretched to accept all of him, as his commanding cock demanded to be fed was driving her wild with pleasure. His knees moved up to support the backs of hers as she was impaled by the thick girth of him over and over again, each time deeper than the last.

His angle and position as it rubbed against the walls of her insides almost hurt, but it was exactly what she wanted, needed. She bounced on him, feeling the ribbing pleasure inside her. Coop's massive hands squeezed and massaged her breasts as they filled his palms, as her nipples knotted against his pinching fingertips. He pushed deep and up off the bed, supporting her with his thighs. She held her hair up on her head, the pleasure almost too much to bear. He kissed her neck and whispered into her ear, "I can't get enough of you, Libby. I can't get enough."

"Yes. I want more." And then she almost said it. "I...want more."

He came to standing position and carefully positioned her onto the bed on her stomach but stayed inside her. She drew to her knees, raising her rear up to accept him deeper and he stroked long and hard, bending over her, holding her hands pressed into the bed above her head. She was coming apart again. His thighs were slapping against hers as he increased the rhythm. She clutched the comforter as pillows bounced and fell to the floor. She reached back with one hand to feel his thighs tight against hers, to feel the mating of flesh on flesh. Everywhere he touched her she was on fire. She smelled the faint lemon of his aftershave as he breathed into the side of her head, as his sweat washed her cheek. His hip action was smooth and circular, lifting her, sending her to new heights with each stroke.

She reached under her raised torso with one hand, squeezing his balls, and he moaned. He began to jerk inside her and she exploded. Locked in a lover's death grip he held onto her, squeezing her hips, forcing himself deep inside her as he spilled.

HE HADN'T REMEMBERED falling asleep, but from the position of the sun through the window, they'd probably been at the house more than an hour. He'd wanted to get some work done, but he couldn't help himself. Libby was becoming a serious addiction for him, and not one he wanted to lose anytime soon.

He moved against her, one hand resting in that glorious space between her two lovely breasts. His lips found the nape of her neck and he began kissing her there. He was still inside her, which was something that was happening more often, the more they made love.

He'd never met anyone who loved to do all the things he wanted to do sexually. The intensity with which she loved him was something he was becoming dependent on.

What are you saying?

As his hand idly slid over the smooth goodness of her upper arm, and as he heard her muffled moans into the comforter, all he wanted to do was be inside this woman. Her pleasure was his pleasure. He'd never felt that way before. He loved watching her come, watching her reach new highs of ecstasy. And knowing he had caused this change in her thrilled him. It wasn't anything that he wanted to end. As he'd told her, he couldn't get enough. Each time he wanted more. Couldn't wait until the next time.

He'd never had a problem with stamina. But suddenly he felt as strong as a mythical beast and knew he could fuck all night long and half the next day too.

He remembered the beautiful azure pool in their backyard.

"I want you in the water."

She laughed into the comforter. "Later."

"I want you in the water," he repeated.

She moved her butt into him again and groaned. She spread her legs between his and turned over from their side position to beg him to mount her from on top. He followed her lead, but leaned over and pulled her leg over and withdrew while he turned her delicately over.

They were chest to chest. His fingers explored her wetness, and the mixed juices of their lovemaking. She gripped his shaft and worked her palm up and down. He pushed himself into her hand and reveled in the feeling of her tightening against his sensitive flesh.

She slid down the bed and he let her take him into her mouth and he gasped. She took his whole length as she sucked and rolled her tongue over the ridges and veins of his cock. She twirled the probing end of her tongue over his crown and he lurched.

"The—pool—I—must—have—you in the water. I—must—agh!" It was no use, she was locked onto him and would not let go. She sucked his balls, flicking them around her mouth with her tongue.

"Cooper," she murmured. "Come. Come for me."

God, what was happening? Just minutes after making love he was ready again with full intensity. This had never happened to him before. Her hot mouth moved back and forth. He found himself arching and driving himself in as deep as she could take him. She would not let go.

"Please," she whispered. She let the tip of her tongue press into the little ridge at his crown and that was all it took. He was surprised how much sperm he had left. When he was finished, she shimmied up the bed and placed her head into that spot just under his chin and they fell back together as he held her there until their breathing returned to normal.

"You are something else, Miss Libby." He didn't know what else to say. Well, yes, he knew what to say, but he dared not say it.

She rolled her body on top of his and he enjoyed the feel of her softness draped against his. His hands touched the delicate skin of her pert buttocks, the firm backs of her thighs. They moved up and down her spine as she purred like a kitten and dug her arms around him, under him, pressing her chest to his and listening to his heartbeat with the side of her face.

It wasn't just the sex, he thought as he looked up at the white canopy over the bed. It was that he never wanted her to go. He wouldn't be able to ever let her go.

Never.

And suddenly, it was even more important he complete this mission to get this weirdo away from—yes—from the love of his life.

He wasn't going to say it yet, but yes, Cooper knew he was finally in love.

CHAPTER 34

DETECTIVE CLARK RIVERTON was on his way over to Detective Mayfield's office, on recommendation of Cooper's liaison, Timmons. He was determined to check out Cooper's background. He knew the kid wasn't the real suspect. But the case wasn't going anywhere at the moment, and he had to be doing something. So, eliminating him as a person of interest was part of the job he could do. He wasn't focusing on what he couldn't do.

His cell phone chirped. It wasn't a number he recognized.

"Riverton."

"Detective Riverton, this is Gus Mayfield of the downtown precinct. I'm afraid something's come up, and I'm not going to be at the office."

"Sorry to hear that. Can I meet you later today?"

"Um. Well, it's kind of a personal thing. Not sure how long it's gonna take."

"I got you." Riverton was disappointed. He'd wanted to get this done today. "Look, this isn't really a big deal, Mayfield. What I've got to ask you will only take five or six minutes."

"How about over the phone?"

"No. I have a photograph I need you to identify, if you can."

Riverton heard some background noise. There were two women arguing in an adjacent room. "Sorry about that," Mayfield mumbled.

"I don't mind. Used to it," Riverton lied. "Is everything okay. You—"

"Ah hell. I'm over at—a friend's house. She's a lady friend and she's having some trouble with her daughter."

"No problem. I don't mind." Riverton paused and then added, "Please. I really need to do this today. It's kinda holding up the investigation."

Mayfield finally agreed to give Riverton the address of his friend.

THE HOUSE WAS covered with bougainvillea vines in full bloom of bright fuchsia. Large dahlias exploded four feet in the air in front of a raised concrete porch with metal handrail. Cana lilies and zinnias lined the fence dividing the house from the front yard next door. True to form, the fence was painted white on the house side, while the neighbor's side hadn't been painted in a decade.

As Riverton got out of the unmarked police car parked nose to nose with a San Diego cruiser, he glanced up and down the street. The salmon-colored bungalow with tile roof was the only house one would look at on a drive-by. The person who lived there wanted to be seen. It was a statement.

A huge man in khaki uniform, bearing a badge he knew to be San Diego PD, appeared in the shadows on the porch and waited for him to open the rickety gate and walk up through the owner's flower garden. The hulking man looked out of place, until Riverton saw his kind blue eyes and forehead lined with worry.

And then he got it. Mayfield was worried what Riverton would think of this. This woman, whomever she was, had a special connection to Mayfield, and the man was trusting Riverton could keep a secret.

"Thanks. I'm sorry about all this, but I'm going to be tied up for a few hours here."

"No problem, Mayfield." Riverton extended his hand and the two men shook. He swung an arm through the air in a broad gesture towards the fourth of July in greenery and flowers defining the front yard. "Quite a place to conduct a covert operation."

Mayfield winced and adjusted his belt, weighted down with his sidearm, flashlight and other implements of his trade that must have calc'ed out to be thirty pounds. Riverton said a little prayer of gratitude he hadn't had to spend much time doing that early in his career. He'd made detective right away and desk work suited him better.

He heard the women shouting at each other in Spanish the same time he saw Mayfield turn his head and go alert.

"I gotta go inside. You're welcome to come in, if you want," he said over his shoulder.

"Don't want to intrude, Mayfield."

"I might need the backup. Women, you know—"

"I understand."

The two men entered the house. A dish had shattered in the kitchen. A younger woman was ranting. Riverton was glad he didn't understand Spanish, except for a few swear words. The level of disrespect annoyed him.

"Mia," An older woman's voice shouted in English, "You will stop this right now. You do not mean these words."

Mayfield had breached the doorway to the kitchen and had stood slightly in front of a handsome Spanish-looking woman not more than five feet tall, with silver strands feathered through her otherwise jet-black hair. Her braids were wound back and forth on the crown of her head. She wore a white flower-smocked dress and red flip-flops. Her tiny toes were painted red to match.

Riverton noticed how the woman clutched Mayfield about the waist and held her other hand in his massive paw in front of the two of them.

They're lovers. Riverton was happy for the man. He noted it gave him actual joy. But then the young woman burst into another tirade, and he focused on the problem at hand.

The young woman launched into another string of epithets.

"In English," the older woman shouted. Mayfield hushed her.

"In English? Well fuck you, mama. Fuck all of you. How's that?"

"Mia, no one wants anything but the best for you. Armando is buying you a house, Mia. You will have a clean, nice place to live," the woman said.

"Well fuck Armando, too. He can't just decide where I should live. Who I should have as friends. It's my fucking life. I'm a mother now. I'm making all the decisions for me and my daughter."

"Mia, that's not what we're trying to do. Your mother is sick with worry about you, and we're only trying to help," Mayfield pleaded.

Riverton noted Mia had a knife in her hand. He saw Mayfield hold his palm out to him. It had been second nature to go for his piece, but Mayfield didn't

want to play it that way. But all bets would be off if she
went for either Mayfield or her mother.

"If you won't talk to me, Mia, talk to your brother.
Talk to Armando."

At this, Riverton's attention was piqued.

Armando? The SEAL Armando? That Armando?

"Of course. The good son, huh, Mama? Me, I'm the
screw-up, right? Poor Mia who can't fend for herself.
Well, you know what? I *am* fending for myself. And
part of this is I gotta get away from this fucking family.
Everybody has to make my business their business. Did
it ever occur to you I don't need it? I like the way I live,
who I am."

She lowered the knife, closing her eyes to wipe hair
from her forehead, briefly showing her exhaustion.
Riverton took quick advantage and wrested the weapon from her hand before she had a chance to come to.
Mia struggled, but he had her left arm held tight
behind her back and yanked it up until she stopped
moving. Without thinking, he grabbed her other wrist
and placed a zip tie on her.

Mia launched another string of expletives and attempted to kick Riverton with her pointed toe high-
heeled shoes.

"You wanna go for a walk with me, missy?" Riverton said, as he clutched her squirming body. It pissed
him off the girl had such a lack of respect for her

mother. "How about showing me you can be a good mother and calm the fuck down?"

A firm hand pulled him backward. The handsome SEAL, Armando, quietly took his place. Riverton hadn't heard him come in.

As Mia looked into the eyes of her brother, she collapsed into his chest, and sobbed. Armando held her, whispering things to her in Spanish. He rubbed his fingers through her jet-black hair and hugged her with a big arm covered in tattoos.

"You dumb shit, Mia. Don't you know we love you?" he said.

Riverton was struck with how tender Armando was with his wayward sister. Mia was built like a showgirl, he noted. Long, beautiful legs he tried not to stare at. Smooth, supple skin and—he had to look away. She would light up any convention or room of men anywhere on the planet. She was indeed a sexual siren.

And an emotional basket case. It was a shame.

Armando let her arch back and look up at him. He smoothed a hand over her cheek and chuckled. "You little spitfire. You can't keep doing this. You're biting the hand that feeds you. You need to learn who to trust."

"I want to do it my way. I don't want everyone's handouts," she whined. Her mascara had run down her cheeks and her bright red lipstick had smudged to the side of her mouth.

"You will, in time."

"But it's not what I want," she complained.

"Then make yourself want it, Mia, because there's no fucking way I'm gonna let you throw your life away. Start acting like a grownup, okay?"

Mia nodded. Riverton wondered if she'd been on something. She looked like she hadn't slept in a couple of days.

Armando turned, still holding his sister with her hands tied behind her back. His muscled arm was wrapped around her tiny waist as he swung her around to face her mother. "Why don't you start picking on people your own size, hmmm?" Armando said to the top of her head.

"Sorry, Mama," Mia whispered.

Before the little woman could come over to her daughter, Armando interrupted. "No. Not mama. I meant Mayfield, here." He winked at the big detective, who flinched and then chuckled. Armando's flashing eyes and handsome features were identical to his mother's. But hard and chiseled from pure steel. Riverton also saw that the trained killer was smart, and kind.

Armando took Mia to another part of the house, tenderly cutting loose her ties first. He nodded to Riverton before they disappeared from view.

"Thanks. Appreciate it," Mayfield said as he removed his arm from the little woman's shoulder and looked for a place to put his hands. He had pursed his lips and was frowning, looking down at his feet. Then he cleared his throat.

"I am Felicia Guzman, and you are welcome in my home," the petite Latina said, her voice wavering slightly.

"Thank you, ma'am," Riverton responded. "I'm so sorry, and can see you have your hands full."

"Indeed," she answered. "She has always been a headstrong child. Her brother too, but he—" She looked up at Mayfield as if to ask permission about a reveal she was compelled to make.

"I know about him, Ma'am." Riverton looked into Mayfield's weary eyes. "That's partly why I'm here."

Mayfield frowned. Felicia burst into the conversation, "Something is wrong? More trouble? Is Armando in trouble?"

"No, ma'am. Look, can I steal Detective Mayfield from you for a few minutes, please?"

"Sure. Sure. You want some coffee? I can make some?"

"No, thanks.

"Water would be great, Felicia," Mayfield said. He brushed his fingers underneath her chin and the little woman's eyes sparkled. "I need to talk to Detective

Riverton alone for just a few minutes." He looked back to Riverton. "And I don't think I'm going to like what I'm going to be told."

Riverton and Mayfield sat on a pink flowered couch littered with a bright hand-knitted afghan and an assortment of pillows Mayfield tossed into a nearby chair before he completely occupied half of the space. Riverton just had enough room not to physically touch him when he sat down. He retrieved the photograph of the dead cat from his breast pocket, along with his notebook.

"You seen this tattoo before?" he asked Mayfield.

"Geez," the giant said as his stiff fingers held the piece of paper between them. He held the photograph up closer to his eyes and examined it. "I've seen these tats on Kyle's group, mostly."

"Kyle's group?"

"Kyle is Armando's Team leader. They've been friends since BUD/S. I think their whole class got 'em, and then new members get them when they join up."

"You know who did it?"

"Sure. Daisy I think her name is, over at—can't remember the place, but Armando would tell you."

"Tell you what?"

Neither of the two men had noticed Armando had joined them. Riverton had chills up his spine because this was the second time Armando had moved to within striking distance of Riverton without his knowledge.

"The tattoo parlor where Daisy works." Mayfield turned his attention back to the photograph and then looked up at Riverton. "Can I show him?"

"Sure."

Armando whistled. "Fucking monster. You after a cat killer?" His eyes flashed as a little smile made a brief appearance.

Felicia Guzman brought two tall glasses of ice water and handed it to the detectives. "You want something, Armando?"

The SEAL grabbed his mother and gave her a bear hug. "No, thank you, mama. I'm going to go show Mia the house. She's getting a few things together." He was still holding the photograph in his left hand, but down at his side and away from Felicia Guzman's view.

"Good." The little woman retreated to the kitchen, and Riverton noticed Mayfield was focused on every step she took.

Riverton took several long gulps of the cold water and set his drink down. He accepted the photograph Armando returned to him.

"I have Daisy's number on my phone." Armando displayed it so Riverton could copy it down. "Seabreeze and Fourth, no Fifth."

Riverton was thankful for the information. "So, you

think she did this one, too?"

"Probably, Armando said. But look here, see how dirty the fingers are? And see that scar?"

Riverton looked at the photograph, ignoring the cat. It was hard to tell, due to its size, but yes, the fingers did look stained, or in shadow. He didn't see a scar. He cursed to himself for not noticing this detail.

"What scar?" Mayfield asked.

Armando leaned over and pointed to a spot on the wrist. Barely visible was a thin cross made from two lines bisecting each other.

"That a cross?" he asked.

"Not really," Mayfield said as he examined it over Riverton's shoulder. "That's the mark of a suicide attempt. At some point in time this fella was intent on taking his own life."

"Which means he isn't one of us," Armando said it as a fact.

"Why would you say that?" Riverton asked him.

"Don't you know, man?" Armando took a step back and held his massive arms out to the side. "We're God's gift to women. SEALs are way too conceited to off themselves and deprive the world, especially the lovelies, of the pleasure of their company."

Everyone chuckled.

Armando continued, "You know how it goes, gentlemen. Big egos, big—"

"Okay, that's enough. I get your point." Riverton frowned but was still laughing on the inside. "How about a former SEAL?" he asked.

"More than likely a wannabe. Someone who thought of himself as one, but never made it."

"A copycat SEAL."

"Oh, they're out there. You usually find them when they're trying to pick up girls in the bars. Actors. You call someone a Hollywood and that means he's a faker."

"Could he have been someone who washed out?"

"Could be," Armando said, nodding his head, thinking about it. "We weed them out. Hell, even some really great guys who would have been awesome wash out. This guy is a mental."

Riverton looked back down at the picture.

Mission accomplished. He discovered he was actually relieved to know SO Calvin Cooper was no longer a suspect. That eliminated one suspect just as he'd learned from Libby about Dr. Gerhardt. He didn't want to run up to San Jose, but if it was warranted, he would. The guy sounded like a creep, all right. Could he have had some kind of preoccupation with the Special Forces? Was that even sane?

Shit, no. But neither was hitting on your students. Riverton's stomach churned with revulsion. He hated to see innocent people get hurt.

But good news about Cooper. It always pleased him when his hunch matched up with the facts. He also liked it when he gained a couple more allies. Having a small force of SEALs to help him catch this bad guy wasn't a bad thing at all.

It rather made his day.

CHAPTER 35

COOPER PICKED UP Libby's bag in one arm, and wheeled out her mother's suitcase with his free hand. That didn't leave his hands free to touch Libby's ass as she sashayed down the hallway and then bent over to give Bay a pat on the head, encouraging the dog to go down the stairs.

He was beginning to lose track of how many times they'd fucked today, orally or otherwise. Like every true addiction he'd run across, the more he got inside her, the more he wanted her. He was going to have to talk to Timmons. Maybe he should sit out the next rotation until this fever died down.

Right. Like that will happen. That's when he knew he was screwed either way. But both ways were a heck of a lot better than his life had been just a little over a week ago. He'd have to tell Timmons it was all his fault, and then wondered if perhaps the man knew.

'Yeah, Cooper. Go over to Little Miss Hot Pants'

house and tell her you'd like to connect with her family.'
More like connect with his rod up her little jellyroll. He
chuckled, thinking about a new piece of equipment, a
duty pack so he could walk around all day and have her
strapped to his chest.

She turned and eyed him. "What are you thinking?"

"You've been bad. Very bad. I'm thinking of all the
ways I'm going to get back at you as soon as we get in
the water." He winked and wished he had a free hand
to adjust the monster coming to life in his pants.

Her laughter wafted up through the foyer and
slapped his heart mercilessly. That little laugh was so
devilish. Made him do all kinds of things. Think about
even more.

The bags were left at the front door.

"You don't want to put them in the truck?" she
asked with a pout.

Hell, he was looking forward to having an argument about it, just to see her get mad. Those lips of
hers, the way she curled them up and questioned him.
How dare she *question* him, a trained special operator,
and trained killer? Oh, she was gonna get it all right.

And they both were going to love every minute of
it.

"Libby, some day, I'm going to teach you some
manners," he whispered as he stepped to press her

body all down the front of his. He laced his fingers in her hair at the back of her head and pulled her towards him. She smiled and giggled again before he claimed her mouth. "Did I tell you to laugh?" he said as he kissed her neck. She was squirming like a schoolgirl. Like he was the big bad wolf.

She managed to wiggle away. "All of a sudden you don't like my laugh?" she asked. Her lower lip quivered and Coop sighed inside.

She'd pouted! Thank God she'd pouted. He closed the gap between them and buried his tongue in her mouth so she couldn't say anything further. He felt her melt as she gave in to her heat and allowed herself to be overtaken with desire. "I love your little laugh. But I love those little squeals you give me when you're coming," he whispered to her neck.

"Okay, but I thought we were going to go for a swim."

"I'm swimming now."

"Coop. We have a problem." She pulled away and straightened her clothes.

He sighed and waited, because anything she would say next he was going to enjoy. He placed his hands on his hips and cocked one knee forward. Bay sat at attention, right next to him as they both stared at Libby. His cock waited eagerly as well.

"The problem is, I don't have a swimsuit here."

"Oh, that is a very serious problem. You know what? I don't either."

"You can use your shorts. I'd have to use—"

"Think nothing of it," he said as he scooped her up in his arms and ran past the stairwell, through the kitchen and, unlocking the slider, out to the backyard. He flipped off his shoes as he carried her barefoot to the water's edge. Bay followed on his heels. Cooper held her over the turquoise water. "Say it."

"Say what?"

"You know, the magic word."

"What magic word?"

"The one you're supposed to say, or I'll throw you in, clothes and all."

She threw her head back, still holding on to his neck, and laughed. "I have no idea what you're talking about. You haven't taught me any magic word."

"Oh, yes I did. What could you say that would definitely get things in motion? What did you tell me earlier this afternoon?"

She looked like a child at Christmas with her bright eyes and the smirk on her lips. He pretended to lose his grip, but caught her. His heart was beating so hard in anticipation. He wasn't sure how much longer he could hold her.

"I want more," she breathed.

For just a second, Cooper faltered. It was the right

word all right, but the beaming face of the woman in his arms was saying way more than just she wanted a romp in the pool.

Yes, Miss Libby. I want more, too.

He began to set her down next to the pool, letting her slide deliciously the length of his torso. He recalled saying those words one day in the early morning in Nebraska as a boy, when the sun was barely visible on the horizon. He'd watched the golden ball creep up and he knew his life was more than getting up before dark and milking the cows, or riding back and forth on the tractor that tilled the rich dark brown earth in perfect rows. It was something about what he would become. And it wasn't about doing all these things, being all these things as a boy, as a teen, as a man, as a SEAL. It was all about doing it *with* someone. Having someone at his side. Was that someone Libby?

Coop, you know the answer to that. It sounded like his mother talking to him. He tucked the memory away in his chest and came back to the present.

Bay found a spot under a bush, lying down on the carpet of green lawn. Cooper scanned the yard. They weren't visible to any neighbors unless someone had a hot air balloon, or a camera mounted in the tall trees at the edges of the yard. Then it struck him that he should rig something like that up for surveillance, and he made a mental note of it.

Libby was standing there barely pressed against him, with her arms still crossed behind his neck, staring into his face. She said it again. She knew he'd gone somewhere else.

"I want more."

"Me too," he said. He saw an instant of regret there, as if she'd wanted him to repeat the words.

In time, baby. Trust me.

He bent and kissed her. She coaxed him with her tongue and they tasted each other. Her eyes looked glazed over slightly as she leaned back to say something, then thought better of it.

In time, Libby. Give me time.

He really needed the swim now. The sun was heating his back and he could feel beads of sweat form above his lip and on his chest.

She pulled his shirt off and kissed his nipples one by one. She laid her head against his left side and listened.

Can you hear the words I can't say yet, Libby? Do you feel what it is I feel for you?

She looked back up to him with her chin on his sternum. "Well, sailor, you want to swim nekkid?"

"Oh, most definitely," he said as his voice cracked.

He noticed the sprinklers had shut off. "Will the gardener be coming today?"

"No, tomorrow is his day. Not today." She tapped

her temple as if to say she had figured everything out.

They shimmied out of their clothes. He took her hand and they waded into the shallow end of the pool, walking down the semicircle steps in the corner. She sat on one step, the pool waist high, splashing water on her front, her shoulders, and finally her face. Cooper ducked down underwater and shivered at the refreshing coolness.

He came up in front of her and between her legs. He spread her knees to the sides as he fingered her labial lips in long strokes under water. She leaned back and braced her upper torso on her arms, her breasts ripe and round, glistening in the afternoon sun.

He kneeled in front of her, his erection prominent and demanding succor, and drew her over to rest on his cock and pushed her down on him. She wrapped her legs around his waist and drew him in deep. He held her bottom in his hands as he walked around the pool until he was headed toward the deep end. With one arm reaching out and along the surface, sculling, he kicked to keep them afloat as she rode him. She braced herself on his chest and shoulders to raise her body up and then down on him. She kissed him, and then leaned back and he felt the backward pull of her arch.

It was several stolen minutes in the sunlight in the beautiful pool surrounded by birds and sounds of life all around. The humming of the world doing its job.

He leaned back and she straddled him like a thin raft as they floated as one.

"I love how you move through the water, like you were meant to spend your life there," she said.

Here. Inside you.

"The view," he said as he took his sculling arm and brushed his thumb over her nipples, took another stroke and did the same again, "is awesome."

He brought her over to the steps again and sat her delicately down on the top step, raising her legs up and over his shoulders. He leveraged his knees and leaned forward to push into her as he kissed the breasts that had been squeezed between their bodies. He had access to her deep as he started slow and then worked up to a faster rhythm. Her face transformed as she bit her lower lip, wrinkled up her nose and moaned. Then she opened her eyes wide and showed him how she wanted all of him, accepted him fully, not holding back. When her eyes rolled back and she began to spasm, he let his orgasm fly.

"Enough?" he whispered to her ear.

"Never." She sighed. "But enough for now."

CHAPTER 36

RIVERTON DIDN'T LIKE tattoo parlors, because he didn't like seeing people violating their paroles. Even with the increased popularity of tattooing, inking their skin was still something the underworld crowd habitually did with their spare change. Some were excising demons, and others were decorating or memorializing their bodies. It was impossible to tell, just from the size, color and subject matter of the tattoos what statement they were aiming for.

But now he had a pretty good idea about this frog footprint tattoo. He needed confirmation of his hunch.

Daisy was quite the stunner, just like Armando had told him, and side-by-side, Riverton probably would have chosen her over Libby. But he could understand why Cooper had made his decision. On Riverton's radar, a woman with lots of worldly experience was way more valuable, and probably more able to deal with his personal demons, not that he ever wanted to show them.

He knew Daisy could pick up on it, so he tried to just look like a middle-aged cop who wasn't very good at his job, and see if he could snag something when she was unaware. He had a feeling this little lady knew the perp.

She asked him if he wanted a seat in her chair.

"No, thanks. Do you have a room we could sit in for a private conversation?" he asked.

Immediately the buzzing all around the shop stopped, which confirmed that the artists really could hear over the noise. He imagined they stoically over-heard all kinds of stories every day. Kinda like in his work.

Riverton followed her down the hallway and, in spite of himself, he noticed his dick had risen from the dead, where it was unsafe, and since it wasn't Saturday night with his favorite girl. And without the use of those blue pills she always offered him. Daisy was doing what Mia had started, making him feel like a man more than just a cop.

Okay, that's a good thing. Let's move on.

She pulled back a beaded curtain and took him to a break room sort of place with a coffee pot that had been fresh about six hours ago.

"You want some?" she pointed to the sludge in the pot.

He must have wrinkled his nose because she giggled. *Why do they train women to giggle? So fucking distracting.* He liked her loose, easy gait and the way her flesh hung on her frame. He envisioned a thorough interrogation with handcuffs and some sex toys, someplace much more private than this.

Geez. Would you grow up? He hadn't thought about those kinds of visions for years. So, maybe he was waking from the undead after all. Maybe it can happen.

Daisy leaned forward a little too obviously and showed him her butt cheeks as she surveyed the minefield of contents in a small white refrigerator. "We got water, and Red Bull."

He didn't know what to say at first. He was still thinking how nice her ass looked. She swung her head around, focused on the ground and very slowly drew her eyes up his body until she smiled when their eyes connected.

Have I just been flirted with? Holy shit. Someone actually flirted with me.

"How about I buy you a cup of coffee?"

Was that coming from his mouth?

She shook her head slowly, still looking at him with lidded eyes. "No can do."

I can only imagine.

She sighed. "I guess it's water, then." She handed him a cold plastic bottle.

Riverton opened up the cap and guzzled half of the water down. She was seated at the little Formica coffee table, her legs crossed, sipping on the bottle, those luscious pink lips all over the top flange. She stopped the water from spilling out on her chest, which wouldn't have been a bad thing, but she did it with her tongue, and that definitely was a good thing. She pointed to the chair across from her.

It was painful to sit. Riverton cleared his throat, set the bottle down and fumbled to get the picture from his breast pocket. Before he could show it to her, he found himself staring at her open palm, halting him.

"First, I want some ID."

He reached into his back pocket and produced his badge. Daisy fingered the ridges on the gold shield.

"Okay, then. What have you got there?" She leaned into the table and he couldn't help but see her enormous breasts were resting on the Formica. They were bigger than he'd seen in quite a long time, and the lovely pink plastic of the tabletop lifted them gently.

What I've got here is a colossal boner. Riverton adjusted his legs, spreading his knees wide and to the sides and showed her the picture of the cat murderer.

All the color leached from Daisy's face. Her forehead furrowed, and she was clearly distressed. He could see from her reaction she knew she gave that tat. She turned the photograph over, placing it face down on the table.

"Do you have an idea who this is?" he asked.

"What's he done?"

"I can't tell you that. You know him, don't you?"

"Not sure." She was being careful. "I don't get to know everyone who comes in here, but every once in awhile someone comes in and just gives you the creeps, you know what I'm saying?"

Riverton nodded. He liked her honesty.

"I think this guy came in about two years ago. Alone. And that bothered me. Usually the Team guys—you know this is the tat all the SEAL Team 3 guys, Kyle's group, get, right?"

"Yes, I've met them. Some of them, anyhow."

"Usually they will come in with the new guy. Give him a hard time, you know. They ask me to sort of blow his mind a bit, you know, clean fun and all that."

She smiled and Riverton's dick lurched.

"They make his first tat an experience?" he said, noticing his voice had gone up an octave.

"Exactly." Her large white teeth were stunning. And she had a dimple in the middle of her chin.

"Sort of an initiation, a welcome to the Teams and all. These new guys are always like babies, you know? They are scared to death. Guys in this shop start talking about asking them to bring back severed body parts and shit, you know, just to scare them. It does."

She giggled and her breasts bounced.

Riverton took a quick intake of air. This was getting hard. *He* was getting hard.

"But not this guy?" he asked.

"No. Not this one. Came in all by himself. And he kept asking questions."

"What did he look like?"

"Well, first of all, he looked too old to be a new SEAL. I mean, he looked like he could be my dad."

"So did you question him, like you did me?" Riverton was glued to her blue eyes and the way her eyelashes batted up and down in a flutter that almost made his heart stop.

"I'm careful." She appeared to be thinking before answering. "I didn't want any trouble, so, when he appeared to know all about the tats, I just painted him."

"What made you think he was trouble?"

"His questions."

"About what?"

"Had I ever seen a Team guy go off the deep end, had any of them gotten violent with me? That sort of thing."

"I can see why it gave you the creeps."

"Wouldn't have worked on him if I had been alone. He came back one other time and asked for something else. I was just closing and I *was* alone. I told him me and my boyfriend were closing for the night and to come back another day. He never did."

"So you have a boyfriend?"

"Had."

"He a SEAL too?" Riverton wanted to hear her say it.

"That one? Nope." She leaned forward again, mercifully. "A cop."

"Ah," Riverton managed to get out, despite the fact that his lower brain was making plans.

"I go for the uniforms. And I love equipment."

Riverton was sweating profusely.

"Recently, I was dating a guy on Kyle's Team. He's had a run of some pretty bad luck and hasn't been the same since."

Riverton guessed she'd not been happy with Cooper's departure. He didn't want to let on he knew all about it. Armando had warned him not to bring it up or he'd not get any cooperation. Well, maybe he could make it up to her for causing her a little distress this afternoon. "How about I pick you up for dinner when you close, and you can give me a thorough description of what this guy looked like?"

She thought about it for a minute, checking her fingernail polish. "Okay. I'm done at 5:30."

"Perfect." One thing was still niggling in the back of Riverton's head. "I don't quite follow something, if you don't mind. You were so careful speaking with me, checking me out and such. And yet, you didn't question this guy at all. How come?"

Daisy leaned onto the tabletop again, this time pressing her breasts into delicious pillows of flesh that made Riverton's mouth water. He'd get his lips on those tonight if it killed him.

"Because." She smiled as she noticed Riverton was transfixed on her boobs. "Giving someone a tat is one thing." She pushed the picture in his direction with one finger, polished to a bright pink. "Wanting to get naked with someone is something else entirely."

CHAPTER 37

COOPER WAS ON his way to drop Libby off at the Hotel Del. Armando called him during the trip over. Cooper had pulled over to the side of the road to listen. Libby could hear Armando squawking on the other end of the line, telling Cooper about a confrontation with someone named Mia, and the visit with Riverton. She remembered hearing somewhere that Mia was Armando's sister, and that made her feel a little better.

Libby stared out idly, leaning against the passenger window. Bay sat tall in the back seat and observed his humans.

"Honestly, Coop, don't think you have anything to worry about," Libby could hear Armando say on the other end of the phone. "But wanted you to know he'd be talking to Daisy. The tat was definitely hers. But here's the thing. The guy had scars on him, like he was a nut job."

Libby froze in place. Nut job? Who was Daisy?

"Scars?"

"Southern Cross."

Libby saw Cooper stiffen at first and grip the steering wheel. "I don't know anyone with one of those who's on any of the Teams. Do you?" he asked his friend.

"Not a one. Not possible, I'm thinking." Armando's voice was tinny. Armando ended the call by telling Cooper that Fredo had a package for him.

Cooper hung up, and pulled out into traffic. Libby wanted in the worst way to ask him about who Daisy was. She bit her tongue and continued to watch the shops glide past them as they wound through the commercial district along the strand. She twirled her hair and tried to think about anything else, but hearing the name of someone Cooper had obviously been involved with bothered her. She didn't like the immediate wave of jealousy that threatened to ruin her day.

Finally, Cooper cleared his throat. "I used to date this girl named Daisy. She owns a tattoo parlor on Coronado where a lot of us get our tats done."

Libby could tell there was more to it. "Uh huh. So why did he call, then? How come she's involved in all this—whatever this is?"

"The picture of the arm holding Noodles had tats on it like these." He rolled up his sleeve and showed her the frog footprints going up the inner side of his right forearm.

"The guy who killed Noodles had these?"

Coop nodded.

No wonder Riverton had considered Cooper a suspect. Thank God she'd never seen that picture. She had no idea. She'd seen these frog prints, of course, as he'd reached up to her while lying in bed, when he'd pressed his forehead to his arm while his hand rested at the top of a doorway, and while he pulled his shorts up and over that flat abdomen and those non-existent hips. They were as much a part of him as the dusting of light brown hair on his tanned chest.

Libby touched the little prints with her fingertips, as if checking to see if the ink was three-dimensional. "She did these?"

"Yes." Coop exhaled.

"And you think she gave a tat to the man who killed my cat?"

"I'm fairly certain, yes."

Libby didn't like thinking about Cooper with another woman, but she had a hard time removing the vision of his long lanky frame in bed with another anyone else. It wasn't possible to be casual about this, but she really tried.

"So, Cooper, was it serious?" She didn't look at him, but stared straight ahead.

Cooper's head whipped around and Libby felt his eyes on her profile. "No," he said. "Never. Not like—"

Libby turned to face him. "Us?" She hadn't wanted to ask, but she had to.

"No. Never serious. She didn't expect much from me. It was uncomplicated." Cooper's eyebrows squinted together. He was barely moving his head as he shook it back and forth. Traffic forced him to turn back to focus on his driving.

"It was just sex, then?"

Cooper didn't answer, which spoke volumes. She could see he was thinking about how to answer her. *Do I really want to know?*

Cooper grabbed her hand and kissed it, keeping his left hand on the steering wheel. He continued to grip her fingers as he shifted gears. Libby didn't pull away. He kissed her cupped palm and then released her.

"It's never just about sex with me. I'm not that way."

This was going to hurt. Libby braced herself.

"But it was what I needed at the time. And I found I just grew out of it. I changed. I consider her a friend still, but I have not seen her since I met you. That's the truth, honey." He reached out his right arm. "Come here."

Libby scooted beside him and rested her head against his shoulder. She concentrated on the raising and lowering of his chest and the sound of the wind fluxing through his lungs. With his arm around her, she did feel safe.

And yes, loved.

THEY HAD AGREED to talk later that night. Cooper would be spending the night at the Brownlee house, and Libby would stay at the hotel with her parents. She begged to come join him there, but he insisted she stay out of his way until he got everything set up at the house and finished working out his plan. He explained he had a lot to do and needed to concentrate. She reluctantly agreed.

On the way to the Hotel Del, Cooper stopped by Fredo's and picked up a large black plastic case that looked like a keyboard carrier. Bay, sitting in the back seat, looked as interested in it as Libby was. Cooper removed a metal panel from the front of the bench seat down by the floorboards and slid the case under the seat cushion. Then he replaced the metal strip and snapped it in place.

"What is it?" she asked.

"What?" Cooper smiled.

"That," she said as she pointed to the floor at their feet.

"I didn't see anything." Cooper leaned over the steering wheel and stared at the floor. "Gum wrappers and a toothpick."

"No, the thing—"

"First of all, you didn't see anything, okay? I mean it, Libby. You don't need to know what's inside that case. You don't want to know."

She sat back and considered her options. She didn't like secrets. She'd already learned about an ex-girlfriend, but for some reason, the black case beneath her butt bothered her more.

"Is it a weapon?" It wasn't a wise question, but she had to know.

"No. It is most definitely not a weapon."

"Then why can't you tell me what it is?"

"Can we just leave this alone for now?"

"But you would tell me if it was a weapon, right? I mean, wouldn't I have a right to know if a bomb or something could explode underneath me and blow us both to high heaven."

"It's not a weapon or a bomb."

"If it was, would you lie? Would you tell me a lie?"

"No, honey. I am not lying to you." He pulled up into the Hotel Del parking lot, parked and leaned over, pulling her into his arms. "It isn't anything dangerous. Equipment. But I can't show you and I can't talk about it, okay? Just leave it be, Libby."

His expression also contained that resolve she knew so well. There wasn't any way in hell she'd be able to find out what was in that case until he was good and ready to tell her.

What was he up to?

COOPER NEEDED TO gather some things he kept in a ministorage locker near the base. He'd bought some used surveillance equipment on eBay several months ago, and he befriended an ex-intelligence officer who was freelancing in civilian life and having difficulty making ends meet. Cooper managed to buy some sensitive recording devices and paired them with spare parts he had on hand, as well as some little microphones Fredo had gotten hold of.

Those little flag pins had worked successfully the last time they needed them in the states, when Armando and Mia had been kidnapped. They had Kyle wired up while they monitored everything from several hundred yards away.

He picked up one of the little pins and admired it. Unless you were trained in this sort of equipment, the average person would never notice the little black dot mounted on the underside. The dot was barely larger than the size of a beauty mark on a model's face.

All he had to do was set up the recording devices in central locations.

He brought his two large, black duty bags into the foyer of the Brownlee home. Bay had followed him and began casing the whole downstairs. He set the bags down on the granite tile and listened to Bay's tap-tap-tap on the polished stone floors. Outside, the sun had begun to set, bestowing a glow like dripping honey on the leaves in the back yard. He could still see water on the deck next to the steps where he and Libby had dripped after leaving the pool, flush from their love-making and completely naked.

Bay came back and sat next to him. "Everything okay, kid?" He padded the dog's head. "Good boy. Now, you stay here while I work upstairs."

Bay didn't obey, and instead climbed the steps with Cooper, who began work in Libby's bedroom. Libby had left one of her black panties on the floor and her underwear drawer was still ajar. He almost felt like she'd be making her entrance at any moment. The bed was straightened, like they'd left it, but the fact that they'd missed putting away the panties bothered him for some reason.

He heard a sound out front and saw Kyle drive up in his small SUV. He brought several more black cases of equipment Cooper had planned on going over to pick up later. His LPO entered and called out to him.

"I'm up here," he called.

Seconds later, Kyle set the bags on Libby's bed, surveyed the room, and whistled.

"So this is how the other half lives, huh? Can you imagine growing up in a house like this, a room like this?" He fingered the dotted Swiss canopy and leaned over to sniff the lacy fabric.

"No. Don't want to." Cooper was unzipping one of Kyle's bags. He was trying to push out of his mind the afternoon's caper, the vision of Libby riding his cock as he bounced on the white coverlet top.

"You bring the boosters?"

"If they were in the bag, they're there."

Fuck. "No, they were in a FedEx box next to the bag. You even look inside?"

"Nope."

"Ah, hell. Nothing I can do until I get those." Coop stood with his hands on his hips, looking down at the bed covered in black zipper bags of various sizes and shapes.

"C'mon, lover boy. I'll take you over there, and we can grab a bite, then I'll come back and help you," Kyle said.

Coop did admit he was completely starving, for food this time. He hadn't eaten anything since break-fast. He nodded his agreement and the two came down the stairwell, followed by Bay.

"Can you leave Bay here?"

"Nope. I'm not leaving him alone in *this* house."

"Gotcha. Everything out of the truck?"

"Yessir."

The two of them left the green beater where Cooper had parked it in the street.

CHAPTER 38

THE CALL CAME in to Riverton just as he was about to suggest he and Daisy might be able to retire to the Pink Slipper or some other hotel. She'd had two margaritas, and much as he hated to admit it, even to himself, he liked his women drunk. Besides, it took some of the pressure off if they didn't remember his performance. Not that he was ashamed, but he wasn't used to having lots of sex with more than just a couple regulars. He wanted to make sure Daisy had a good time, so he could have another.

"This better be good." He had recognized the number from the dispatcher at the precinct.

"All good, Clark." She insisted on calling him by his first name, even though he had reprimanded her several times for doing so. She did seem to be pleased with herself. "You're gonna love this news."

"Oh yeah?" he looked at Daisy, who had just begun her third margarita.

Christ. Hope I'm not going to have to miss anything. He wondered if he would have to be staring at a dead body instead of Daisy's luscious breasts. But he was a cop, and this wasn't a real date, and if the office was calling at 6:30 at night, it was important.

"Go ahead," he said as he watched Daisy lick the salt off the rim of the glass and then smile at him, with a few flecks of the white granules at the edge of her upper lip. God, he wanted those lips on his pecker something fierce. Salt and all. He wanted to taste that margarita second hand and needed to smell the perfume between her legs. He adjusted his pants with his right hand and Daisy smiled again.

"I think we caught your cat killer."

"You're fucking with me," Riverton said before he could edit his thoughts. Daisy looked up at him with wide eyes.

Stella was all cool and proper. "We got a call, a complaint, from a parent this afternoon. Officers went over to check it out. Seems that one of Dr. Brownlee's doctor friends is a pedophile. Goes for young girls. Patients of his."

"How do you figure he's the cat killer?"

"They went to his home. His housekeeper let them search his office, and they found a closet papered with pictures of Libby Brownlee, along with what could only be described as a shrine to his daughter. Candles and everything. They found semen everywhere."

"They got permission to do this?"

"Apparently the housekeeper had found it earlier, one day when he forgot to lock it up. She volunteered the information. She was creeped out by it."

Riverton was fully back into cop mode. "You getting an arrest warrant?"

"The uniforms are laying low down the block. The housekeeper expects the doctor any minute now. I think if you stop by you can pick up the warrant before you head over. It should be here within minutes."

"Thank God," Riverton said before he hung up.

THE THREE BROWNLEES got the call from Riverton while they were having dinner downstairs in the coffee shop.

"That's great news." He cradled the phone and told Libby and his wife that the police had arrested Dr. Dolan on sex charges and were prepared to charge him also with the death of Libby's cat.

"Dr. Dolan?" Libby was shocked. She had never thought of him as a sexual predator. He was wired tight, especially after the deaths of his family, but not leaning that far to the sexual deviant scale.

Her father snapped his cell phone shut jubilantly. "Let's celebrate! Champagne, shall we?"

"Thought you were going to stop, Austin," Carla reminded him.

"But this is a celebration. This is a special day."

"Are they sure, Dad?" Libby asked.

"I think so. There will have to be a trial, of course. They found your pictures everywhere. He had a full-on fetish about you. You were Stephanie's best friend, you remember that, don't you?"

"Of course."

"He transferred his feelings—" Brownlee stopped. "Oh, my God! I never thought about this. When she came to see me, I knew there was something going on at home that she didn't want to tell me. I didn't recognize the signs, but now—"

Libby's stomach was starting to turn.

"Who are you talking about, Austin?"

"Stephanie. I think she was having an inappropriate—"

All thoughts of celebration flew right out of the room. Libby thought about the pretty girl she had called friend, who apparently had had demons she'd been wrestling with all alone. How awful it would be to have the one person in your life you thought would protect you be the one who haunted your dreams at night?

In a small way Libby knew how Stephanie had felt. She had trusted Dr. Gerhardt. She knew what it was like to have to run from someone you trusted completely.

If only I'd known. She wished Stephanie had reached out. Perhaps she could have helped. But, if her father hadn't suspected, how could she?

Just the same, she felt partly responsible, and very sad.

LIBBY COULDN'T REACH Cooper to give him the news. She decided she'd go over to the house and tell him herself. The idea that they would have the whole place to themselves all night long filled her with excitement. She could hardly wait.

Turning down the familiar, tree-lined street, she was heartened to see the green truck parked in front of the house. She was delighted Cooper was there. Perhaps she'd sneak in and surprise him.

But she knew he probably had already heard her car pull into the driveway. She grabbed her bag and danced up the pathway to the front door.

The door was locked, which seemed odd at first, but then she realized Cooper was probably not wanting to be interrupted while he got his surveillance equipment up and in place. Looking into the foyer through the glass and metal front door, she couldn't see any sign of him. Her finger sat atop the doorbell but, at the last minute, she decided not to ring it. She still wanted to surprise Cooper if she could. Perhaps he was doing something wonderful like showering. Yes, that must be it.

Libby ran to the side of the house and went through the unlocked gate to the rear yard. The garden shed door had been blown ajar, as usual, and leaves had scattered over the concrete decking area around the pool. The water looked crisp and azure blue and contrasted with the bright orange of the sunset. She couldn't wait to be naked with Cooper, swimming, playing, loving the way they had earlier this afternoon.

Stepping carefully on rounded stepping stones, several of them with her childhood handprints embedded in the concrete, she hopped up to the concrete patio and headed toward the rear kitchen sliding glass door. She expected it to be locked as well. But it was not.

Inside the kitchen she expected to hear water running, but the house was silent. She decided to quit trying to surprise him and called out to Cooper. Her nerves were getting a little frayed.

"Cooper? Where are you?"

A strong arm with frog print tats grabbed her from behind and a large hand slammed over her mouth. At first she thought Cooper was trying to scare her on purpose, and she didn't resist. But then she felt the roughness of his skin. Something smelling like acid hit her nostrils. Confused, she started seeing black splotches before her eyes and realized, as her world was tunneling down to one small pinhole of light, that she had been drugged.

And the arm definitely did not belong to SO Calvin Cooper.

"Coop—" she croaked just before she passed out.

CHAPTER 39

D R. BROWNLEE CLICKED the TV on to see if there was any breaking news about the arrest of Dr. Dolan. He was disappointed to find nothing. Then he decided to check for a news update on his computer.

Scanning through local live feeds, he still came up short.

"Let it ride till morning, Austin," his lovely wife said as she walked into the room and stood behind him.

"Well, I guess it takes a few hours. I just expected it to be here, since Riverton told me Fred had been arrested this afternoon."

"It'll be there tomorrow," Carla said. "Come on, Austin. Let's go to bed."

He wiggled his eyebrows at his wife, who had walked backward into the master bedroom and waved to him from the doorway. He was about to close his laptop when he noticed a new email.

Something compelled him to take a look at what the email contained. The subject line of the email said, "Thought you might like this." The sender had some kind of numeric moniker he'd never seen before. He knew better than to risk getting a virus, but he couldn't help it. His middle finger pushed down on the square pad in the middle of his Mac, which highlighted the line of email. He waited while his computer worked on uploading an image.

The first thing he noticed was that there was music coming from his computer. Etta James was singing her signature song, *At Last*. Slowly the pixels on his monitor filled in the screen from top to bottom. What came into view was a picture of something fuzzy in white and peach tones. His stomach cramped when he realized it was a picture of Libby's canopy bed. He recognized the two bodies on that bed: Libby and Cooper. In the center of the screen was a black circle with a white triangle pointing to the right.

This was a video he knew he didn't want to watch.

But he had to.

He glanced up at the doorway, and mercifully, Carla had gone into the bedroom. His hands were shaking. He felt sweat stream down from his armpits. The back of his shirt was drenched. He was also about to lose the dinner he'd just eaten. He couldn't concentrate on anything except the single white triangle beckoning him. Very slowly his fingers positioned the black cursor on the screen and let it hover over the image.

The sound of his own ragged breathing filled his ears as if he was wearing a headset. The dull tympanic boom of his heartbeat echoed in his vacant chest. He pushed the silver pad and he watched a windmill design complete a few revolutions, and then disappear.

What he heard next was breathing. Brownlee tried to focus on the sides of the picture, trying to figure out what was causing the blackness at the border. Then he figured it out as he heard his daughter call out Cooper's name and saw the young sailor's thighs rhythmically slap against hers, the famous song playing in the background.

The video was being taken from Libby's closet. The man who took this was in her room.

Might still be in her room. And Libby had left several minutes ago to go to the house to find Cooper, to give him the good news.

Maybe this was taken earlier. Maybe Dolan did this before he got arrested.

He replayed the video and saw Libby's bedside clock, reading 3:30. That was after Riverton said they had the guy. It was obvious the police didn't have the right man. They'd arrested that scumbag Dr. Dolan, but the man who was terrorizing his family was still out there. Out there, hell. He was probably still in their house. And Libby was on her way there.

He jumped to his feet, raced to the phone and dialed Libby's cell. It rang four times and then went to voicemail. Her chipper voice brought tears to his eyes. He slammed the handset down with a very loud, "Fuck!"

Carla was at the doorway in an instant, wearing a nightie, alarm written all over her face. She looked at the handset as if she expected it to be smashed to pieces. She then ran over to him.

"What is it?"

Austin Brownlee pointed to his computer. Carla sat down without a sound, tapped the keypad with one finger and watched the images on the screen. Brownlee saw the colors flash on her lovely face, reflecting on glistening tears streaming down her cheeks. She brought her hand up to her mouth, squeezed it into a fist and held it against her face just under her nose. She closed her eyes and then opened them again, as if she would see something else. Anything else.

Brownlee tried Libby's phone again from his own cell this time. The call went to voicemail again after four rings. Then he dialed Riverton.

The detective answered on the second ring. Brownlee was going to say something to his wife who sat staring at the now frozen screen. He knew she was beyond shock as the significance of this video sank in.

"Brownlee, what can I do for you?"

"I—I have something else. You. Must. Come. Over. You have the wrong guy."

"What the hell's going on? Someone hurt?"

"I don't know." He put his hand up to his forehead at the hairline. "I don't know if she's safe. She went over—Oh God, Clark. You have the wrong man."

"No fucking way. We've got the right man all right. The guy is a certifiable weirdo. Wait till you see some of the stuff we've gotten from his house."

"Someone sent me a video clip this afternoon. It was taken today at 3:30. Libby and C—they were on Libby's bed. In Libby's room—"

"You mean that fuckin SEAL taped them together and sent you a clip? That what you're saying, Austin?"

"No. I don't think it was Cooper. Someone was holding the camera, adjusting it, making it focus on—body parts—" he could hardly get the words out.

"Who? Who took the video?"

"I don't know. But I know it's him. The one who's been sending the photographs. I just know it is. That's how he got Libby's pink stationery. He's been inside the house, Clark. He's been going and coming inside our house."

"You still at the Hotel Del?"

"Yes."

"Stay right there. I'm sending a squad over to the

Brownlee residence. Stay the hell away from there, you hear?"

"Yes."

"And Austin, try to get hold of Libby."

"All I get is voicemail. I've tried twice."

"Keep trying. I'll be right over to get your computer."

COOPER AND KYLE wound their way up the street towards the Brownlee house. A pickup truck almost scraped the driver's headlights on Kyle's SUV as it took the angle of the corner too steep, traveling at a high rate of speed. Kyle hadn't had a chance to downshift from high beams, so the lights flashed on the face of a man behind the wheel wearing a Padres baseball cap.

The Brownlee's gardener. "That's strange."

"What?" Kyle asked.

"The fuckin' gardener. Libby said his regular day was tomorrow. He's about as good a driver as he is landscaper." Coop snorted.

"Something wrong about that, Coop," Kyle replied.

Cooper turned and looked toward the rear of the truck that was smoking, picking up speed as it barreled down the hill to the commercial district. Something was definitely wrong. He started having that feeling like he did sometimes when he was in an unfamiliar neighborhood overseas, when they didn't know what was around the corner, when they were looking for bad guys in daylight or near daylight. This was the most dangerous time of day for them. They preferred working dark of the night assisted by their night vision gear.

Dusk was known as the killing time.

When they pulled up to the Brownlee home, Cooper saw Libby's car. It was locked. He and Kyle dashed to the front door of the house and found it was also locked. Kyle was going to kick it in when Cooper stopped him.

They tore off toward the side gate and quietly ran through the yard to the kitchen door and stopped. The slider was still open, and on the floor of the kitchen was Libby's purse, the contents spilled all over. Her cell phone had been ringing, and the light had just gone out.

"Libby?" Cooper shouted. They both listened as they searched the rooms downstairs. They sacrificed stealth for speed while Cooper shouter for Libby.

Upstairs nothing had been touched. They ran from room to room, and then met in the hallway.

"I think she's in that asshole's truck," Cooper said. "They've got a head start on us."

The two sailors dashed down the stairs and out to the back yard, and through the wooden fence. Cooper got out his keys.

"Hey, let's take mine. It's faster."

"Something I need." Cooper unlocked the driver's door, pulled the metal plate loose and pulled out the black case. He also a black duty bag over his shoulder. Kyle had already started up the SUV by the time Cooper inside, the case on his lap. Kyle took off down the street.

Cooper flipped open the two spring-loaded clasps and raised the lid. Kyle started to whistle. Pressed into charcoal grey packing foam were two white plastic pieces of a drone, controller unit, tail assembly and propeller mechanism.

Cooper pulled out the pieces he needed, threw the case in the back, and held the body of the drone in his left hand. He inserted the wing into the slot in the middle until it clicked in place. He screwed the propeller unit to the device's nose, clicked the tail unit in place and turned it on. He heard a slight whir of the props.

"Pull over for a second, would you?" he said to Kyle.

Cooper opened his door, held the drone in his left hand while he adjusted the toggle switch controller box until a small computer screen lit up. He arched his arm behind him, then thrusted the drone the direction they were traveling and they watched it take off.

"Go, go, go," Cooper shouted. Kyle took off down

the road.

The black and white monitor was not as clear as Cooper needed. The picture was fading in and out because night was beginning to fall. He directed the drone by adjusting two dials on the unit aiming for an elevation of two hundred feet. The monitor showed it had flown over the busy road that led to a string of businesses. He spotted the truck immediately and directed the drone to hover over it.

"No infrared?"

"Didn't get a chance to mount the camera. This will have to do for now."

Cooper punched a button and street lines formed on the screen.

Cooper's cell phone went off. He passed it over to Kyle.

"Hey Fredo," Kyle said.

Cooper heard Fredo shout at the other end of the line, "That detective dude is looking for him. Some urgent shit about Libby."

"I think we already know. Trying to locate her now."

"You guys over at the house? I want to help."

"Nope. Just came from there. We're following someone."

"That's what the dick said—" Cooper couldn't make out the explanation.

"We know this," said Kyle.

Fredo was asking for their position and Kyle gave Fredo some street names and descriptions of buildings.

The monitor showed the truck turning. "Take a right up there about three blocks," Cooper directed Kyle.

He was fairly certain the truck would go towards the freeway, which pleased him because he could see on the monitor commuter traffic ahead was at a near standstill.

"Fredo, we're barreling down South Morrison, I think headed toward the freeway."

"Fuck it," Cooper said as the truck turned in the opposite direction. "He's going back down the other side, parallel to the freeway."

"Okay, now we're headed south on—" he looked for a sign, crossed a set of railroad tracks, and still couldn't find any. "We just crossed some tracks, back on South Morrison. Have Riverton call us, okay?"

"Will do. Malcolm and I are gonna try to find you, too."

"No. Stay out of it," Kyle said.

"Not a fucking chance," Cooper heard Fredo shout back to his LPO.

Kyle hung up and placed Cooper's phone in the center console.

They tried to catch up to the truck, but traffic was

all over the place. For several minutes they followed and continued to fall further and further behind.

"Talk to me, Coop," Kyle demanded.

The truck had turned off the main road. "I think you go right at the next street."

Kyle did as he was told, and they hit a dead-end cul-de-sac. They quickly recovered and continued down the previous route, and then turned at the next intersection. For a second, the picture went black.

"Come on. Come ooooonnnnn, sweetheart! Don't fade on me now. Just a little longer," Coop was coaxing the machine with everything he had. The screen lit up again, and they spotted the truck turning into an industrial yard that looked like a graveyard for old semis.

Coop could see the chain link fencing coming up on their right. An automatic gate was just closing a few yards ahead of them. The sign out front said Corsi Bros. Transportation and Salvage. Several large hangars big enough for a cruiser sat in abandoned rows. Between them stood several two-story buildings with broken windows.

Kyle came to a sliding stop.

Coop's cell phone chirped again. This time, Coop picked it up just as Kyle hopped out of the van and ran towards the closing gate.

"Where are you?" Riverton shouted.

"Corsi Salvage Yard, off Morrison—South Morrison, down by the inlet."

"I know it. Don't try to approach."

"He's got Libby."

"Probably, but we can't say for sure. Did you get a good look at the guy?"

"Absofuckinglutely. The Brownlees' asshole gardener."

"Good. Look, you got to wait for us. No vigilante justice here, catch my drift? You'll get yourself killed, or, even worse, get her killed."

"Sorry, but I gotta run."

"Coop, do not interfere, do you—" Coop hung up the phone.

The picture on Coop's monitor was fading fast, and at this point was more out than in. Kyle had gotten through the gate before it closed all the way, hitting the reset button on the opposite side. They were rewarded when the gate slowly swung open again and Coop drove through.

"Where are they?" Kyle asked.

Cooper was trying to get a decent picture. "We might be too far away."

"Not possible. The inlet is only a few hundred yards in this direction. He's here somewhere in this fenced area."

For just an instant, Cooper saw an image on the

screen of the truck parked in a garage structure with a metal rollup door that was closing behind it.

"He's in one of those bays. One of those buildings over there." He pointed and Kyle drove to a row of warehouses and paused. They were looking at a cluster of buildings, each with similar roll-up doors, all closed. There must have been at least fifty of them.

Cooper's heart sank as he realized he might not find the right one in time to save Libby.

He called the drone back and flinched as it made a hard landing on the dirty asphalt storage yard just next to Kyle's van.

"So now we just have to find the needle in the haystack," Cooper said to his LPO.

"I'm guessing you brought equipment?"

"Fucking A." Cooper picked up the drone, placing it carefully in the back of Kyle's SUV without taking it apart. He set the controller next to it. He pulled out the black zipper bag and extracted another polyethylene case and flipped it open. His H&K MP7 was tucked into the black packing material, but Cooper was after the thermal scope.

He had small IED charges in another smaller bag, which he pulled out and attached to his belt as he joined Kyle.

"It was an interior garage, with doors on both sides," Coop said.

"So that rules out about eight of them. About forty to go." Kyle chuckled.

They put on their night vision gear. Cooper saw Kyle strap on a utility belt similar to his own, but not as customized. Coop had made a cottage industry of sewing specialized belt pockets and vests for other Team members. Each man had his preferred equipment in addition to the standard issue.

The two started creeping down the first row of storage units as Cooper scanned them with his thermal scope. He was picking up some small images toward the bottoms of the units.

"Rats," he whispered. They got to near the end of the first row when they saw headlights from a vehicle approaching around the corner of the building, stop and heard the idling of a gurgling motor.

Kyle and Cooper flattened themselves against the row of warehouses on the opposite side and took what few inches of cover they might have in one of the doorways.

The springs on the truck groaned as a very large man extricated himself from the driver's side and, in the light from the truck saw heavy lace up combat boots stomp on the ground. A flashlight clicked and light flooded out as they quickly flipped up their goggles to avoid getting blinded. He held something heavy in his hand, which wobbled the flashlight briefly.

Shotgun.

A gravelly voice bellowed "Hold it right there. Don't even *think* about farting, or I'll blow your asses into the bay."

CHAPTER 40

L IBBY WAS BEING hauled from a truck that smelled of gasoline into a chilly, dark covered space, perhaps a garage. As her feet dragged along the floor-boards, they snagged a gasoline can and tipped it, sending it crashing to the concrete below. She heard a man's voice swear. The gasoline smell was almost overpowering.

With his arms under her chest, her kidnapper dragged her through a doorway and into a carpeted small space. The room was done up in pink, complete with a set of Barbie Dolls on a French Provincial sideboard that looked like it came out of a little girl's room.

And then it hit her. It did look just like a little girl's room. A single bed with a hot-pink, fuzzy bedspread, dotted with stuffed animal pillows was in the corner. An overhead chandelier in pink had lit up automatical-ly as they entered the room. The massive arms hoisted her up and onto the bed. She was left in sitting position. She couldn't feel much of her body below the neck.

Her eyes were beginning to focus better and she turned her head in time to see the man's back, dressed in the same khaki clothes the gardener had worn every time she saw him. His hair fell loosely in ringlets as he removed his baseball cap. He quickly tied the ringlets back with a rubber band. Then he began searching for things in a makeshift kitchen consisting of a deep utility sink, a microwave and a hotplate.

He disappeared into what sounded like a small bathroom, bringing out a plastic glass of water. He sat and held it out to her. She saw his frog print tats, just like Cooper's. That's when she realized her hands were tied in front of her with green plastic tree staking ties. She took the water without looking into his eyes.

"You don't look much like my Callie, but then no one could ever be as beautiful," he said as he brushed the hair back from her forehead. She moved her head to the side and wrinkled her eyes and nose in disgust.

"Ahh. We are a little scared, and feisty. Don't worry, we have plenty of time to get acquainted."

She wouldn't look at him, but handed him back the water without taking a sip.

"Very smart, but no, I don't want you drugged. Nothing's in there but our horrible San Diego water."

Don't want me drugged? The impact of what that could mean sent a shiver down her neck.

He took the cup from her and placed it on a make-shift countertop in the kitchen. Bringing up a chair, he sat next to the bed, elbows on his knees, and rested his chin on his folded hands.

"You know, Libby, I've watched you. Watched you for several days now. You are such a beautiful girl, and I can see how fond your father is of you. I frankly don't blame him."

Libby looked at three Twilight posters pinned to the wall along the bed. There was a white collapsible dressing room divider in the corner. A pink flannel nightgown was thrown over the top. What she saw next to it frightened her. A studded dog collar and riding crop dangled from a hook secured by the top of the divider, along with a pair of handcuffs.

She looked at his face in shocked reaction but then wished she hadn't as he smiled back to her.

"Yes, my dear. We're going to have some fun. I intend to deflower you."

She didn't understand. *Deflower?*

"Well, you are more experienced than my daughter was. I watched you and that big SEAL having sex. I could hardly hold the camera up, it was such a turn-on."

Libby found her voice. "You are completely sick.

My father has only been good to you. Why are you doing this?"

"Your father?" He leaned back and stared to the side. "Your father didn't save my little Callie. She promised me she wouldn't tell." He turned and focused his brown eyes on Libby's lips. "I believed her. Still do. She went to her grave with our little secret. Your father's partner found out about it, and took advantage of her. Your father should have stopped it."

"How could he have known? You blame my father for what that cretin did to your daughter?"

"He's a useful idiot. I think Dolan will take the fall for what I'm going to do to you."

Libby thought perhaps her greatest chance of survival would be to delay whatever sick scenario he had planned out in his twisted mind. "I'm not following you. Dad gave you a job."

"Which is what I'd begged for because I wanted to get even. You see, I had other plans, but then—" he rubbed his fingers against Libby's cheek and she fended him off with her shoulder, turning her face around and back. "I feel I should be perfectly honest with you, Libby. We are going to have a wonderful time together. If you pleasure me enough, if you can convince me you like it, perhaps I'll let you live. But you must be very convincing," he said as he leaned over and tried to plant a kiss on her mouth.

Libby shook her head violently.

"That really isn't a very good start, sweetheart."

"I'm not your sweetheart. I'm not your daughter. And I'm *not* going to have sex with you." Her chest was heaving. Bravado and anger were taking over. All the things that had happened between her and Dr. Gerhardt came flooding back. She was angry for having to give up school, angry that he had tried to hold her grades over her head to gain sexual favors.

This monster had used her father's trusting side, their vulnerable side, to his sick advantage. She even found it in herself to be angry with her father for this.

The gardener stood, and began removing his shoes. She knew what was going to come next. His eyes were flashing like roman candles as he reached up and began to unsnap his shirt. As he tossed it to the ground, she watched with horror as he flexed his forearms when he fisted and released his hands.

The frog print tattoo, just like the Cooper had, danced on the skin covering muscles underneath.

CHAPTER 41

COOPER AND KYLE raised their hands, partly to protect their eyes from the disruptive bright light. Cooper saw smoke billowing around the massive legs and boots of the giant.

"So, what the hell are you guys up to?"

Cooper put his fingers to his mouth to indicate he wanted silence but the man wasn't having anything of it.

Kyle whispered, "He the gardener?"

Cooper shook his head, *no.*

The man raised his voice further. "I said, I want some answers, and quick, or I'm calling the cops."

Not a cop? With the boots and the gun, Coop figured he was either a bad guy or a security guard trying to do his job.

"They're already on their way," Kyle said as a test. His voice was commanding but not threatening. Cooper hoped they were not within earshot of the man who had Libby. The man with the shotgun didn't move, so Kyle continued. "We're looking for a guy in a pickup. We think he has kidnapped a girl and brought her here. Need your help."

The giant stepped back. "So you're not cops?"

"No, but we're working with them," Cooper said. "Look, we don't have a whole lot of time. We just saw him come in here," he continued in a low voice. He wished they could step closer so they wouldn't give away their location.

"I didn't see no truck. There's usually no one here at night. Besides, the gate's locked," the man said.

"Well, someone got in. We saw the gate closing right before we arrived," Cooper added, his impatience boiling over. He respected authority, but this man was wasting precious time.

"So how'd you get in?"

"I got there first," Kyle added.

The man scratched his scalp, lowering the shotgun. "That would be my clicker, then. It was stolen two months ago, right outta my truck."

A security guard. Much better. But they were still losing time they did not have.

"Please, we need to find out where he is." Cooper was sweating. A distant siren put his nerves on edge. If the cops came in blazing with lights and noise, Libby might pay the price.

"You look military."

"Navy," Kyle volunteered.

"Special forces, I'm guessing."

They both nodded. "You're security, then?" Kyle asked, and got a nod from the hulking stranger.

Cooper ventured a question, "You know a dark-haired guy, say in his late forties, drives a light tan Ford pickup king cab?"

"I know a lot of dark-haired guys that drive pickups. We got over 200 units here, plus some of the storage hangars. I don't remember everyone's face, or their vehicles." After a pause, he continued, "As a matter of fact, I get paid *not* to remember faces or vehicles, you get my meanin'?"

Cooper was angry at the holdup and wished they'd acted quicker, perhaps immobilizing the guard so they could complete their vital and increasingly urgent mission. He considered grabbing the man and wresting the weapon from him, but Kyle put a hand to his chest and stopped him. Cooper heard his cell phone chirp in his pocket. He stared into the light.

"I gotta get this. It might be our backup," Coop said and waited.

Kyle tried to be convincing. "Look, we're not here to bother anyone. Just want to catch this guy before he harms her. We'll explain everything later," He said in his usual velvet tones.

"You get that phone, then," the man said.

Cooper recognized Fredo's number. "Where are you, Fredo?"

"Right outside this fucking gate. Got razor wire all over the top or I'd already be in. Can you buzz us through?"

"I'm working on it. Hey, you have anything thermal on you?"

"Wish I did. No. Just the night gear."

"I'm going to send a security guard over to let you in. We're trying to find the garage and we only have one scope."

"Okay. Sorry I can't help you with that one. Malcolm is with me, though."

Cooper hung up and came back to the guard, who was shaking his head.

"You gotta let the rest of my Team in, sir. Someone's life depends on it," Kyle stepped toward the guard, who didn't object. He gripped his arm. "Please, I need your help."

That seemed to have done the trick. The guard climbed back into the truck and, before backing out, rolled down the window and handed something out to Kyle. "You might need these."

Kyle took a huge set of bolt cutters from the guard, and looked up at the man.

"Keys would be less expensive," he said.

"No. I can't do that. Everyone has their own padlocks, you see?" He flashed a light on one garage door and ran it down the first five or six units. Every one had a different kind and size of lock.

"Thanks, man."

Kyle and Cooper resumed their scan, starting down a fresh row of doors as the guard drove off to let in Fredo and Malcolm.

They thought they heard talking but couldn't make out from where. The scope detected blackness with an occasional hot spot where something was plugged in to a wall socket. Multiple targets showed up on the screen, all of a sudden in front of one door. Kyle cut the bolt and slid the door open, as quietly as he could. The metal squealed unless he lifted it slowly, and that got Cooper nervous. He dropped to his knees and immediately a rodent smell hit his nostrils. With his night vision goggles multiple cages along two sides of the storage unit held breeding mice. Then he noticed there was a door leading to a small room off to the right. He backed up and noticed there was an extra space with no roll up door between the two openings. As he looked down the line, he occasionally saw this extra space.

"Fuck."

"What?" Kyle stopped and hooked the metal chain in place, which secured the door in open position. "Oh shit, pee-ew." Kyle waved his hand in front of his nose.

"Kyle. There's a room off some of these units. Has no direct access to the outside."

Still using his night vision gear, Coop ran toward the small door and pulled a KA-BAR out of his utility belt. He kicked in the door, which splintered into several long pieces. He flipped up his goggles and felt for a light switch on the wall and flipped it on.

Nothing. Bags of feed were stacked waist-high. There was a plastic sink on metal legs and a toilet.

Coop ran outside, worried they'd been at this for too long, and if the gardener was intent on murder, he'd already had ample time.

They entered all the garages that registered heat until they came to one that definitely had a heat source large enough to be two humans.

The images were bouncing around as the heat source was obviously moving. Cooper guessed it could be a couple. He stiffened as Kyle looked over his shoulder and slapped a hand on his back. The door had a keyed lock installed in the door itself.

"Hey boss," Fredo ran up behind them. "I got this." Fredo attached a small explosive device to the locking mechanism and everyone retreated several bays to the right and left for protection, plugging their ears. A sharp explosion blew a two foot hole in the metal door.

Cooper hoped to God they were in time. Kyle

rolled up the metal quickly and the other three SEALs entered. A light under the doorway to the adjacent room was quickly extinguished.

Kyle slapped the concrete wall with the flat of his hand, indicating it would make good cover in case anyone inside was armed. He kicked the door in as Cooper flipped on the light.

An older Mexican man and a younger woman were disheveled and only half dressed. But clearly Libby wasn't there. Cooper soon realized they'd just scared the daylights out of a couple that was living in the diminutive space, never expecting to be bothered by intruders.

Fuck, where are you?

Cooper took the scope and now trotted down the row of garages. No time to go after anything other than human size. He made a mental note to keep his other scope in the bag in the future.

Malcolm and Kyle jogged behind, ready to remove any locking devices.

Again Cooper thought he heard talking, arguing even. He smiled. It warmed his heart when he realized it was Libby, he was sure of it. He'd recognize that righteous indignation rising in her voice any day. This time it appeared the noise came from the line of garages on the other side. They dashed over there.

The large orange shadows appeared so fast that it

almost caught Cooper off guard. Although faded, there was the unmistakable outline of two people. Neither body was moving, but lay side by side, in prone position. The shadows were further away from the wall, indicating this was a much larger room.

Libby. His heart nearly leapt from his chest.

Again Fredo placed the explosive charge on the keypad entry box, and, as soon as Kyle opened the door, Coop ducked under and was on the flimsy wooden door. He set his thermal scope down and, with one shattering kick, the door shattered. He flipped on the light switch.

What they saw drew an instant retching reflex. Kyle started to cough and backed up. Like a strange set out of an Alfred Hitchcock movie, the room had been decorated like a young girl's bedroom. In pink. It was decorated with Barbie dollhouses and lamps. The bedspread would have been pink, if it hadn't contained a nude woman's body covered in blood. A pillow had been placed over her face. Cooper was frozen where he stood. Was this what was to be their fate, after all this? Did he spend his whole life looking for this one woman, only to get there just as she'd been taken away from him forever? He didn't want to look, but he knew he had to.

He heard Fredo mumbling something behind him in Spanish. The little SEAL backed up and left him alone with her for a private farewell. The stench of death was strong. He expected her spilled blood to smell metallic. This was the smell of decay.

Something else began to kick in. Instinct. The room was too small. He stepped back, surveying the death scene and noticed the pool of blood on the floor was deep burgundy, almost brown and had nearly hardened into thick goo. He heard muffled voices.

Next door! Kyle stepped up and removed the pillow. The graying eyes and chalky white face of the once-beautiful young woman who had her neck slashed from ear to ear was not Libby's.

"Coop, you better look at this." Fredo handed him his scope and through the wall he could barely make out the two original heat patterns, still very much alive.

"Through the next one," Malcolm whispered.

Cooper watched in horror that the images next door were standing, and it appeared an arm was bent out to one side.

They put on their masks and night vision goggles and blew the lock, then Kyle kicked in the door, throwing a small flash bomb inside. Coop kept the light off. They all heard coughing, but couldn't see a damned thing. Malcolm didn't have a mask, so they pointed for him to go outside. The thermal scope showed them Libby's body was near the ground and was not moving.

Coop said a little prayer. *No. No. No.* He hoped he could get there in time.

The gardener was leaning against the wall near the doorway. If he didn't have a mask, he wouldn't last very long in the smoke, but any delay was too much. He had to get to her within seconds.

Then the gardener burst from the room with his arms up, stark naked, his dick dangling in front of him. Fredo promptly kicked him in the groin and the man fell, hitting his head hard on the concrete floor. Fredo spat epithets in Spanish at the man, who was groaning in pain as Fredo continued to kick him. Cooper and Kyle rushed through the doorway and found Libby on the bed. Cooper had her shoulders and Kyle had her feet. There wasn't time to check out what her injuries were. They brought her outside the garage.

She was completely naked.

Fredo had located a roll of carpet and had it spread outside near the entrance. Cooper lay her down carefully. Rolling smoke poured from the garage, but harmlessly dissipated into the night above them. He removed his vest and laid it under her head. Holding his small penlight in his mouth he checked her vitals. Kyle laid his jacket over Libby for privacy. She was pale, except for a large welt forming all around her left eye where he must have hit her. Her eyes were dilated. She had a pulse, although it was rapid. He was about to give her CPR when he saw the most wonderful sight of his lifetime. Her chest rose as she gasped in a deep breath.

CHAPTER 42

COOPER WOULDN'T LEAVE Libby's side. Paramedics came and tried to push him away, but he almost got heavy with the larger one and barked a "no" they would not soon forget. As usual, Kyle was making nice with the local authorities, including Riverton, who looked rather pissed.

"We caught the guy, Clark. I'd have thought you'd be a little more grateful," Kyle said. The two of them walked off into the night to have a private conversation.

Cooper helped the paramedics remove Libby to the gurney for transport to the hospital.

"I'm fine," she kept on saying. "Really, I'm fine. You guys don't have to fuss over me."

"Baby, that was so close. I'm never going to leave you alone again."

Libby giggled.

God, how I love that sound!

"Cooper, come here." She raised her head up and Cooper kissed her. He would have climbed on top of the gurney if the paramedics hadn't objected. They started pulling him away carefully. No one was going to be able to stop him, but he knew they'd try.

Libby placed her hands on his cheeks as he bent over, following along, hovering over her and the wheeled transport. She rubbed her thumbs over his lips. "I was so stupid," she whispered, searching his eyes.

God, how he loved this woman.

"No. No baby. You were smart." Cooper looked at the red and white stiff blanket covering her body, and focused on her bare shoulders. "Did he hurt you in any way?" He'd asked her this question several times and she'd said no. Cooper just wanted to be sure.

"No. No, and no. Stop asking me that." She smiled, her eyes sparkling with tears that began to well up. Cooper's heart lurched. "There was no way in hell I'd let him get that far."

"That's my girl, so stubborn. Never met anyone like you before."

"Thank goodness. You arrived just in time. Coop, I was hoping you'd find me. If I hadn't been so stupid—"

"Shhh. Be still, baby." He couldn't help but kiss her again.

The gurney hit the back end of the ambulance and

abruptly stopped.

"Sir, you are interfering with our transport. I'm going to have to ask you to step aside." The voice was far from friendly. That's when he realized one of the paramedics was a woman. A very large African American woman.

The other paramedic whispered, "He's a SEAL, Clojean."

"I don't care what the fuck he thinks he is, he's interfering with my patient. I've turned tougher Marines over my knee, stripped down their panties and had a needle in their butt so fast they was still thinking it was Saturday night. Don't you give me any trouble."

In the light coming from the rear of the transport, Cooper could see she wasn't smiling.

He had no intention of giving her any trouble. Co-op smirked and allowed her insult to roll off him like water off a duck's back. He wasn't in fighting mode anymore. He couldn't remember a day when he was happier, and he had other things on his mind right now.

RIVERTON WATCHED MALCOLM and Fredo trash talk each other, racial slurs that would cause a fight anywhere else. A tiny bit of regret bubbled in his stomach as he watched their quiet demeanor, while Kyle directed what things to pick up and where to put them.

He wished he'd thought enough of himself to try out for the Teams way back when. These were guys he'd wanted to meet his whole life. Real men. Not political hacks and guys afraid of their own shadow, working toward their pension. Doing the safe thing. These were all-or-nothing guys, and he might have enjoyed it. If he could have made it.

He watched the thermal scope go back into a polyethylene case that held, unless he was totally mistaken, an assault rifle. He drooled over the equipment they had. State of the art everything. And Kyle said Cooper had bought a lot of it on eBay, or overseas in the black markets.

Kyle didn't open the case very wide, just slipped the scope into its designated spot and fastened the clips silently.

Everything had a spot, Riverton noticed. He watched them even wipe down their goggles. The bottoms of the cases that had been strewn around the asphalt were even wiped clean before they were put back in the BMW. Kyle polished a KA-BAR Riverton was grateful never got used, cause then he'd have had to make a report, and he didn't want any of these weapons, or these guys' names, in his report.

Kyle looked up at him, as if answering a question he might have asked if he had been braver. "We don't do this sort of thing very often, you know."

FALLEN SEAL LEGACY

"Fortunately, neither do I. Of course, San Diego would be a safer place to live if I could get more of these bad guys off the street. But it's *my* job, not yours."

Kyle laughed and replaced the knife in its holder attached to his utility belt. "Come on there, Clark. Are we ever really off the job? You think if something happened to this great country we'd all claim retirement and let the same people who hired us to defend them perish without a fight?"

Riverton thought about that for a while. "It'd be one hell of a fight," he murmured.

"That it would. But not today. Today we go back to the Scupper and sit back and have a few brews."

Riverton raised his eyebrows.

"We get our women to come pick us up so we get home safely." Kyle's white smile glowed in the moonlight.

"Actually, I was thinking I might ask you if I could join you. You'll be one short, with Cooper otherwise occupied."

"That can be arranged. You sure?"

"As a heart attack." Riverton watched Kyle laugh. "What's so fuckin' funny?"

"A SEAL ride-along. That's a first." He could see Kyle was feeling very pleased with his comment as he went to load up the remaining equipment.

Fredo was pissed off he had ripped his pants on one

of the shards of door and half-heartedly blamed it on Malcolm, who protested the affront.

"Well then I won't fix you up with my sister, Fredo. Besides which, she's only about a foot taller than you are."

"That doesn't bother me in the slightest. There aren't many pretty girls my size. None of my dates complain, either."

The security guard was laughing at the two of them. He'd brought a pedestal lamp that plugged into his cigarette lighter, making the area bright as noon. In addition, the police photographer was flashing pictures of the corpse, the room where Libby was held and the surrounding area.

The guard turned to Riverton. "I like these guys."

"What guys?" Riverton asked.

"These SEAL guys."

"Son, you saved the day, didn't anyone tell you that yet? You're about to become a hero."

"Excuse me? What about these guys?"

"They were never here."

CHAPTER 43

COOPER COULDN'T REMEMBER being so nervous. The sun was setting on the ocean from atop the grand master suite that had cost him a month's pay. But this was going to be an important night. The rest of the Team had their celebration last night. Cooper had sneaked into the hospital room and spent the night in bed with Libby. He'd been tossed out twice, but still managed to get back in. Finally the nurses let him stay.

She was just being held for observation, and Coop talked them out of needing a monitor, telling the nurses a lie that he was an intern, on his way to becoming a Naval physician.

She had asked him afterwards if that was what he wanted to do, be a doctor.

He said, no. He wanted to get naked and inside her as soon as possible.

She seemed to like that idea just as much. Maybe better.

But tonight was the candlelit dinner he had never done before. He wanted everything to be how she would like it, just for one night. He would have to be honest with her, that his salary didn't allow for these kinds of extravagances.

But tonight he wanted to show her what he could do. How he wanted everything in her life to be perfect. How he loved her.

Room service brought strawberries dipped in chocolate and a bottle of lime mineral water. There were chilled shrimp salads in the refrigerator. The rare steaks were in their heated cart, along with the twice-baked potatoes with cheese and the veggies. He knew all these things were her favorites. He'd have liked cornbread and some fresh peas, like at home, but some day. Maybe they'd go back to his home and build a little house on that land he loved. Raise a ton of kids.

If she'll have me.

This suite had a fireplace he'd lit. Bay was stretched out in front of it. He noticed the dog seemed to be comfortable no matter where they were together. Just being together was all he wanted. If Coop were a beach bum, Bay would sleep outside on the sand under the stars right along with him.

He hoped Libby would feel the same way.

There was a light knock on the door. He lit the candles he'd bought, dimmed the lights and opened the door.

Libby stood in the hallway, wrapped in a velvet coat buttoned all the way down to below her knees. Her black eye had gotten bright blue and he had to laugh inside, but didn't want to show it.

"Well, madam, I can see you like it rough." He was about to bust a gut not to burst out laughing.

She gave him that wide smile he loved so much.

"You said you liked long kisses and great sex, sailor. That's why I'm here."

"Is it, now?" He stepped forward and led her into the room, closing the door behind her. "Can I take your coat?"

"You can try," she said winking at him as she walked into the room.

Even from behind, and underneath the cloak of velvet he could see her hips move, the beautiful, round curves of her perfect ass sliding against the fabric, teasing him. Cooper's reaction was immediate. He walked up to her, drew her into his arms and sank into the wonderful scents of her flesh, the taste of her neck, the way her hair brushed against his cheek. They swung back and forth, looking out over the shining bay, while he rubbed his hands up and down her thighs and bottom, needing to feel her warm skin under his palms.

He was wearing jeans because Libby had said she

liked him in blue jeans and white shirts, so that's exactly what he wore. No shoes. She turned around and looked up and down his body and dreamily smiled back at him.

"I'm not as formally dressed as you are, I was just thinking we'd be staying in—" he couldn't finish his sentence because she had reached over and grabbed his balls and squeezed them through the blue denim.

"It's perfect." Her other hand unbuttoned his shirt, carefully spread it to the sides and she lay her head against his bare chest.

"It *is* perfect, isn't it, Libby?"

She turned her face up and rested her petite chin on his sternum. "Yes, Cooper, it is. About as perfect as it gets."

He hesitated and inhaled.

"What's wrong?" she frowned.

"Come here for a second. We need to talk." He brought her over to the couch, sat her down, and noticed she'd kicked off her heels. "You want some strawberries?"

"Feed me," she said as she leaned back into the couch and looked at him with half-lidded eyes.

"My pleasure," he said as he unscrewed the cap on the mineral water and poured some into the two champagne glasses. Holding the chocolaty strawberry in his right hand, he eased it between her plump lips and onto her tongue. She bit down, and he was left with a green stem. Watching her eat the strawberry was making him so hard he could hardly stand it.

And she knew it. One of her fingers idly ran over her own collarbone and down. He could see that whatever she was wearing underneath her coat was low cut, and he was thrilled.

"So, what did you want to talk to me about?" she purred as she accepted a bubbling flute from him, pressed the cold glass against her swollen eye, then clinked her glass against his and sipped.

"You want a cold towel for that?" He asked with a sympathetic squint.

She shook her head, *no.*

Cooper barely sipped the bubbly before he set his glass back down. He adjusted his pants, straightening his pockets and moving closer to her. He picked up her errant hand and kissed the fingers and her palm, which she'd turned outstretched. He was so hungry for her he could hardly stand it.

"I said I never wanted to leave your side. I'm afraid I've lied to you."

She stilled and tried to take back her hand. He wouldn't let her.

"I can't be with you 24/7, like I told you that second or third day we met. I go away on deployments for several months at a time. I go on training sessions for months at a time. You'd be home alone—"

Libby covered his mouth with her fingers. "I don't care."

"A lot of couples in the community have a hard time."

"I know."

"I probably make less than your father's secretary."

"It doesn't matter."

"Kinda cramped in my little home."

"I like being slammed up against the walls and bumping into you all the time, Coop." Then she smiled, rubbing a finger over his nipple. "Would you consider an apartment with a real bed and a shower that wouldn't go cold in five minutes?"

"Anything, honey. You do know it's hell on couples when they are apart for so long. The odds aren't in our favor, Libby."

"Shhh," she said as she put her forefinger over his lips. "I already told you. I don't care. They don't have what we have."

"No, honey, they don't." Coop actually began to tear up, and he could see she had the same reaction. He took a big gulp of air and then let it out. "I've never said this to anyone before, well, not to a girl—a woman."

She cocked her head and smiled, observing his awkwardness.

"Tell me. Tell me, Cooper."

He was overtaken with a wicked thought. "Okay, here goes. Libby, would you let Bay live with you at your parent's house?"

At first she jolted as if she'd been slapped. Her beautiful warm eyes got wide as she searched his face, and, sure enough, he couldn't hold back the lie that was making him bust up inside with laughter. He'd never be able to lie to this woman. Ever. They both smiled.

"No, that wasn't what I wanted to say." He leaned over and planted a long, lingering kiss on her soft mouth, and heard the little groan deep in her throat. To her lips he whispered, "I love you."

"Tell it to me again," she said between kisses.

"I love you, Libby."

"And again?"

"I love you. And I want to marry you." She leaned back and stared at him. He added, "if you'll have me."

"If I'll have you? I've wanted you from the first day I met you at our doorstep. You are and have always been the one I wanted. Nothing would please me more than to spend the rest of my life here, with you."

"Well, it can't be here. I mean, I can't afford this all the time. But I'll never leave you. I'll always be with you."

"I would wait forever for you. No matter how far

you have to go, I will be waiting for you to return to me. Always, Cooper. Always."

Cooper fiddled in his pocket for the ring he'd bought that afternoon. It was all he had left in his checking account after paying for the room. "It isn't much, but it's yours."

"And I will cherish it forever because you gave it to me." He slipped it on her finger and kissed it there, relieved it fit.

"Some day—"

"It's perfect. What we have is perfect, Cooper."

How could he be so lucky? How could this beautiful woman want to spend her life being his partner? He couldn't believe his tremendous good fortune. He knew his mother was looking down on him right now. He thanked her for being the first woman he loved. He thanked his dad for being the plain man with a heart of gold who had taught him more about being a man than even the Navy had. He would miss them. But he had to quietly ask them to turn their backs. And he mentally explained.

I'm going to love her with everything I've got tonight. And I don't want you to watch.

THEY'D SAT ON the couch, watching the sun pour itself into the ocean's horizon while they finished the mineral water. Libby could barely touch the steak and everything else he had laid out for her so carefully. But she just wasn't hungry. She was fully satisfied. The strawberries, on the other hand, enhanced something deep and erotic which was building between them. Something she was looking forward to. Tonight she was spending the night with the man of her dreams, who was going to be her man forever, would be her husband, would wear a ring on his finger telling the whole world he belonged to someone, in a honeymoon suite he'd picked out and planned.

"You must be hot," he turned and said to her.

"I am." She gave him that wicked smile and she saw his eyes glaze.

He unbuttoned the velvet coat and did a quick inhale when he discovered she had nothing on underneath the coat but panties.

He chuckled.

She explained. "I like how you take my panties off, and sometimes I need help with them."

"Very happy to be of assistance."

"Was hoping you'd see it that way." She so wanted the feel of his hands on her body.

Cooper peeled the coat off her shoulders. The red satin lining fell open against the couch cushions. She matched his movements by removing his opened shirt. She even loved the feel of the stiff white cotton smelling of fabric softener, and the scent that was uniquely her man.

His forefinger rubbed the top of the bandless white lace panties. She was massaging his temple and down along his ear. At last, he bent over and covered her breast with his mouth, sucking and then ending with a little bite before he attended to her other nipple. His hands slid underneath her and squeezed her buttocks. She parted her knees and he slid up over her.

He kissed a trail down to her belly button, then explored with his tongue under the flange of the panties, then down further. His finger hooked the thin fabric below her waist and he pulled, sliding the panties down her thigh, revealing her swollen, eager sex. He bent to insert his tongue into her, and Libby felt the immediate spasm of pleasure his tongue bestowed. She arched back and twisted her fingers in the hair at the top of his head, loving the way he laved her, the way he kissed and tasted her most sensitive, secret place.

He inserted two fingers into her, twisting them, and kissing the swollen lips at the sides. He kissed the little hollow between her peach and her upper thigh. His thumb smoothed over her clit. He pressed and squeezed it, causing her to jerk. He sucked the little nub and massaged it slowly with his tongue.

She was close to orgasm as she squeezed the tops of his shoulders, digging her nails into his flesh. He eased up, and rose to look at her face. His fingers continued their ministrations and she showed him how it felt—showed him with her eyes.

"I love watching you when you're like this. I will think about this all the time, baby," he said hoarsely.

She lifted her hips to meet his fingers and push against him, wanting him deeper. She closed her eyes, and when she opened them, he was still looking back down on her, his head cocked, that half smile on his face, his hair mussed and his lips wet with their combined juices.

Yes, I will always remember you this way, too. "I love you, Calvin Cooper."

He slid his arms around her waist and lifted her off the couch, carrying her to the bedroom. He'd set candles all around the room and the scent of jasmine was everywhere. The warm flickering glow made everything seem surreal, like it was from a wonderful, erotic dream. He lay her down on the bed, stood and slid his pants down.

Coop's erection rubbed against her inner thigh as he climbed up on the bed and crouched over her. His cock nudged the little hollow and kissed her peach, spreading her lips and rubbing her wetness all over his tip. Libby raised her knees to give him better access. Cooper arched, found her opening and slowly began to fill her with his girth.

They stared at each other. He kissed her swollen

eye, as if that would heal it. "I love you, Libby. With all my heart. Forever."

"Yes. Forever."

Cooper slid in fully in one slow, deep plunge. Libby felt like she exploded into a million stars as he carefully moved inside her, giving her time to adjust to him. He was still watching her as he moved his beautiful hips in a fluid in and out movement. She squeezed him with her internal muscles, feeling the wonder of his flesh against the walls of her insides. She could have remained this way all night.

He demanded to be deep, and she relaxed to give him all of her. The pace of their mating picked up. She pulled him inside her, clutched his buttocks and begged for deeper penetration. He was kissing her neck, under her ears. She put her teeth on the top of his shoulder.

Her orgasm was forming like a thunderstorm. He must have seen it. She had his face between her hands as he stopped, lurched inside her so deep it almost hurt, the blunt force of his cock against her felt so incredibly wonderful. He plunged in once, twice more and she exploded.

Her body shook as she threw her head back against the pillows as she dug her heels into the coverlet and pushed against his strength, needing him, wanting him, and craving him with every ounce of life force she had.

He slowed just long enough to bring her back to the room, tipped her chin with one large hand, kissed her and then groaned as his body released inside her.

It was what she'd always wanted. She knew that she would spend her whole life devoted to this beautiful warrior who had given her his full heart.

* * *

Continue reading the first chapter of the next book in the SEAL Brotherhood Series…

SEAL Under Covers (Book #3) is available here.

Book 3 in the Band of SEAL Brotherhood Series: SEAL Under Covers

sharonhamiltonauthor.com/SEALBro3

CHAPTER 1

GINA HAD ROLLED her ankle twice as she hobbled along the wet sidewalk in her red patent leather four-inch heels. She was already flustered since she was running a good twenty minutes behind schedule, but she wouldn't run. The last thing she needed was to fall and end up walking in there with skinned knees or a bloody nose. She really needed to settle her nerves—now—in order to survive the night.

She was determined her first undercover assignment would be a success. She'd made the connection with the girl, Mia, and her gangland friends. The two of them had hung out together a few times, but Gina was about to raise the bar. She was going to get up close and personal with Carlos, the infamous Scorpions of San Diego leader who had taken over for Caesar during his incarceration.

The distinctive, unhealthy bar smells assaulted Gina's senses before she saw the dim lights and the flickering neon sign advertising "Babes." She'd not been to this particular part of town before, and wasn't used to meeting the men who frequented the bar—men who paid to watch topless dancers gyrating on poles way too close to the customers.

At least that's what the guys in the Department had told her. She could tell they had gotten off on it. Straight as an arrow Gina. By the book Gina. Going under cover on her rookie mission in her red heels. Well, she'd prove them all wrong. She had assets they didn't possess, and she was convinced she was made for such a caper.

It still scared the daylights out of her, though.

Gina hoped Mia was there tonight; otherwise, it would be a quick cab ride home after a text to the team. No sense hanging around a place like this unless there was a reason for it. She was glad she'd left her car at home.

On any other Friday night she'd be in sweats and T-shirt, in her LL Bean slippers or lavender moisture socks, wrapped in the lap blanket her grandmother had crocheted for her in college, reading one of her favorite romance novels. She'd be sipping hot tea, not downing pink umbrella drinks like she was planning to do tonight. She hoped she had it in her to keep her wits tight.

She smoothed her palms down the form-fitting, low-cut, red mohair dress, then put a wad of gum in her mouth and shook her head, which released a few of the curls piled high in a clip. Idea was to give her the "just fucked" look her handler had said she would need.

The irony wasn't lost on Gina. She hadn't been with a man for six months, not since her detective hunk she'd been down and dirty with told her about the wife he'd left back in New York. He wanted to continue as coworkers with benefits—and his version of benefits was pretty intense, since he was into all kinds of experimentation.

"We're separated," he'd said, as if that made it better, as if it didn't count that they'd spent the week prior to this reveal together, naked more than not. The memory of it sent a dull ache to her abdomen.

And before Sam? Well, there was her high school sweetheart, the soccer player who went off to war and never came back. It took some time before she could even think about dating. Then it became just dating for sex, uncomplicated sex. It helped take away the pain.

Her college days were unmemorable, romance-wise, since she'd thrown herself into her studies and made the Dean's list every semester.

Tossing her head back and licking her lips, now tasting of cherry bubble gum, she felt the little glass heart earrings she'd purchased this morning tap against her neck. The feeling was somehow comforting. As if the part she was about to play wouldn't consume her. Those hearts reminded her that she did have a soul, and it was good, unlike the slutty sexual siren persona she was about to play. She was nothing more than bait on a hook. She knew her place in the department. This was her chance to move up.

Her cab disappeared into the night air. She was left without a lifeline as she stepped through the opened doorway of the dark little dive.

A gasp came from several corners of the bar, making her panties bunch and sending shudders down her spine.

Showtime.

Mia was at the bar, just like she'd said she would be. Nestor, the greasy-haired Scorpions enforcer, had his arm around Mia as she was arching her back and raising her shoulders, trying without success to shake him off.

"Hey there, Mia," Gina said as she plucked the black sweatshirt-covered arm off her shoulder.

"Why don't you fuckin' mind your own biz, sweet cheeks?" Nestor stood up, huge muscles making him look like a stubby version of an already stubby Michelin Man.

"Thanks for the compliment," Gina said in her most direct way. She liked that she had a Smith & Wesson 642 Airweight .38 special strapped to her inner thigh, even though it would be a mistake to use it right now. "I'm her date for this evening, if you get my drift."

"I smell some female-on-female sex, and I wanna watch."

"Then go watch your mom in the bathtub. Or, better yet, go jerk off in the men's room and look real deep into those bloodshot eyes of yours." Mia snickered at this.

Gina saw the twitch in his cheek, the slow tilt of his head and narrowing of his eyes. Nestor was going to hit her, so she kneed him in the nuts before he could get himself properly positioned. He immediately bent forward, protecting his groin, nearly falling into her. She pushed him backwards with both hands, easily dropping his intoxicated ass to the floor. He landed on the ground spread-eagled, cracking his head on the concrete floor. Gina flinched.

Did anyone notice? She hadn't wanted to hurt the creep. Gina was relieved when he shook his head and was pulled away by a couple of his buddies.

"Gina, you gotta be careful. Those guys are part of Caesar's, gang," said Mia.

"Like I care? Notice how many of them were going to rush over to protect your virtue?" Gina said as she watched the crowd in the corner carefully. A tall, caramel-skinned man glared at her from under the bill of a red baseball cap as he shoved Nestor into a chair in front of the little stage next to him. He didn't hide that he was perusing Gina's every curve, daring her to show the smallest bit of fear.

Carlos.

Gina sucked in her gut and tried to calm her nerves. He was every bit as scary as they'd told her in the briefing. She stared right back at him and tried not to blink.

"Let's get out of here," Mia muttered, picking up her enormous red purse.

"You planning on staying overnight?" Gina said as she turned a shoulder to Carlos and pointed to the bag. "Come on, let's have one drink and let these guys drool a bit. It will do them some good."

Hope to God backup gets here soon.

Mia was nearly off the stool. "No, Gina, I mean it. They're bad news. Meeting here was a dumb idea."

While it was good Mia was starting to show some common sense, it would mess up the mission.

"Which makes me wonder," Gina studied Mia's heavily lined, gold-sparkled eyes. She could see her new friend wasn't nearly as tough as she wanted the world to believe. "Of all the dives in San Diego to hang out in, why here, if you're trying to avoid the Scorpions?"

Mia repositioned herself on the barstool, turning forward and focusing on the lighted bottles over the bar as she sighed. "That's a good question. I guess I thought I'd be safer here. And I have you to protect me, Gina."

This tugged at Gina's heart. It was true, Gina was a cop, and so she was able to protect the innocent from the lowlifes of society. Mia was able to somehow figure that out without knowing it consciously. But she was also still putting her faith in men, the wrong men, even though she'd been knocked around by several of them. Caesar's gang had even kidnapped her, thinking they could force Mia's brother, the SEAL, to sell them specialized military equipment and firepower. Only reason Mia was alive was because of her hunky brother and the rest of his SEAL Team 3, who saved the day and helped break up a ring that included some dirty law enforcements and regular Navy guys. All of them were serving time now.

The present operation was considered a cleanup detail, an attempt to eviscerate the rest of the gang, and perhaps catch the guys who were trying to take Caesar's place. "You come in here on Valentine's Day, and you're like candy on a string. Begging for trouble," she shot back to Mia.

The Department is using her, too. Gina wondered if she'd ever get used to it.

"None of them are supposed to touch me. Caesar's orders."

"Except you told me you never visit him. So are you

still his property?" Gina saw Mia flinch.

"I'm not his fuckin' property."

Gina took her seat next to the beautiful Latina. "Women are always some guy's property, honey. I'm sure your mother has told you so. That's the way of it, I'm afraid." Gina didn't want to look at Mia for fear she'd see it was a lie. Part of her wanted to cheer over the streak of common sense her friend was beginning to develop, though.

They ordered strawberry margaritas. Gina left a generous tip for the bartender, who gave her a friendly wink. "Pleasure doin' business with you," he said. He turned to serve another customer, then stopped himself and came back. "Say, you gals aren't here to try out, are you?"

"No." Gina said before she Mia could answer.

The bartender leaned on the counter and gave Mia a wolfish grin, his head barely clearing the pink and red paper hearts that hung from the ceiling in a ridiculous display of gaiety. "And what about you, little lady? I'd like to see you up on the stage, showing your stuff. You could make close to a grand a night, did you know that?"

Mia sat up straight. "A grand?"

"I never lie," the bartender said in a low, sultry voice. Gina could tell he'd been a handsome man at one time, but years behind a bar, and years of indulging in god-knows-what, had left his face ruddy and tired, and his gut flabby. His aloha shirt was buttoned one button too low to accommodate his thick neck, but it exposed a hairy chest with several gold chains buried in the fur.

Gina glanced at Mia and could see her friend was actually considering it.

"You're joking. You're not thinking of taking your clothes off in front of this crowd?"

"What kind of protection do I have?" Mia turned and asked the bartender.

The bartender pulled something from under the counter with both hands. He held it just high enough that the girls could see it but not so the other customers could. It was a Mossberg Persuader. Gina hoped the man had some training, or he'd be as likely to kill the dancer as protect her from an overbearing customer.

"You rated on that piece?" Gina asked before she could stop herself.

The bartender scowled. "You got a smart mouth, missy. You got friends in law enforcement or something?"

Gina went rigid. Blowing her cover on the first job in the big leagues was not what she wanted to do. "Hell, no. I thought maybe you were some kind of sick cowboy. I hate guns and what they do to people." It was true enough for her to follow her comment with a stare she hoped he'd feel all the way to his toes.

The bartender's hairy arms, covered with tats of naked women, fumbled behind the counter out of sight, replacing the shotgun. He scanned the gang in the corner, as well as some of the customers at the bar.

He was back on Mia. "If I were in your shoes, little one, I'd be wiggling that cute little ass all over the stage and taking home that grand three or four nights a week. Could do a lot for you and the kid. I doubt Caesar will be very good with child support. None of the rest of that lot would be, actually." He nodded to the corner.

Gina followed his direction and saw the boys taking seats as the music was turned up. All except the tall one with the baseball cap. His arms were crossed as he leaned next to the stage, not bothering to pretend that he wasn't checking them out, making a clear threat out of his continued slow, insulting perusal. Gina felt her pulse quicken and her hands start to sweat. She was sure the top of her chest was red and blotchy. Her stomach lurched.

The lights dimmed and thankfully, Gina could no longer see the guy's face, but she still could feel his eyes on her flesh.

A spotlight shone on the bright pink stage curtain. A prerecorded voice announced the first act.

"Put your hands together for the Sensual Shannon

and her pot of gold!" the announcer bellowed. Out walked a tall redhead wearing a short, green plaid, pleated skirt. She bent over and exposed her red satin panties.

Movement to their left caught Gina's eye.

Finally.

Three of the Department's finest sauntered through the door, followed by a fourth who wore a cap that concealed his face. Everyone was dressed in the black leathers they'd been talking about so much. Thanks to the heavy beat of the music, she'd missed the noise of their Harleys arriving. Devon, the first one in, gave her a wink, and Gina turned her back to them. She heard a low whistle and didn't want to see who'd done it. She was fairly sure she was blushing.

The bartender was studying her. She knew it was important not to let on she knew them, but she had to admit she was thankful they'd arrived.

A familiar scent crowded close to her right ear. Her body instinctively softened for just a moment before reality set in.

Damn it. Sam. This wasn't supposed to happen. He was the last one she'd expected to be on the team.

"I'm remembering all the sheets we tussled in. I'm getting hard just thinking about it. Miss you, hot stuff," he whispered tenderly, so no one else could hear. A chill went down her spine while she couldn't help but remember those lost days and nights with him.

She forced herself to stay focused on the mission and what she was there to accomplish. It pissed her off that his casual attitude was throwing a monkey wrench into an already difficult situation, so it wasn't difficult for her to turn around and slap him. Then she picked up what was left of her drink and threw it in his face. He didn't move a muscle, but she could see his was furious with her, blinking through the strawberry liquid staining his face and dribbling down his light blue shirt. Little red paper hearts hanging from the ceiling twirled all around him.

The bartender handed him a clean towel and Sam quietly wiped his face, his eyes riveted on Gina.

The rest of the guys whistled, whooped and chuckled. They grouped around the two girls. That's when Gina figured out the guys had brought him along on purpose to rattle her.

That's right. I'm outside the network. I got the fuckin' message.

"You going to introduce me to your friends, Gina?" Mia was giving them long, thirsty looks.

At least that part of the plan was working.

"This one, he has a bad memory. Like the fact that he has a wife," Gina said jerking her thumb toward Sam, who still lurked behind her. "The rest of them, if they're his friends, I wouldn't bother." She ignored all of them, hoping they'd think twice before deviating from the plan again and fucking trying to upset her. She ordered another drink.

Little Shannon was keeping the boys around the stage busy. She was down to her panties, her kilt and small white schoolgirl blouse discarded on the stage. She swung her long legs around the brass pole, turning, writhing and riding it with her thighs, leaning backwards air-kissing the men closest to the stage.

Not that Carlos was watching. He hadn't taken his eyes off Gina, and it made her skin crawl.

Sam leaned into the side of her head, carefully. "You've drawn the right kind of attention, G-spot."

Gina's loathing for the situation flared into anger. "Keep your fuckin' distance or I'll have him call the cops." She shot a glance to Devon as if to say, *'What were you thinking?'*

The reference to calling the cops was supposed to be the safe signal, but only used in a blown operation. The group got quiet. The bartender spoke up.

"You boys want something, or are you just gonna ogle the customers for free?"

"Yeah, I'm not on stage yet," Mia turned around, leaning back, to make the most of her lush breasts temptingly exposed by a mostly-unbuttoned black satin blouse. The boys responded appropriately, giving Mia the reaction she wanted. Sam whistled as he brushed past Gina, making sure that they had a thigh-on-thigh experience on his way to snaking an arm around Mia's waist.

He thinks he owns me. She had fallen really hard for him, and fast. That was the part that hurt the most. She'd thrown caution to the wind. No questions, just a couple of nibbling kisses, and *wham*, she couldn't wait to get naked with him. And because he was a cop, she'd thought she could trust him.

Mia was cooing and enjoying the attention of four really big leather-clad guys. Gina noticed the long looks she gave the corner, like giving the gang the finger. Mia was going to be a big problem when she found out the guys she was getting cozy with were cops.

Little Shannon was really working her buttock muscles, shaking them faster than Gina thought was humanly possible. The dancer backed up closer to the face of one of the front row crowd and Gina felt herself shudder again. The gentleman had his forefinger rubbing up and down Shannon's rear, as he inserted dollar bills in the lacy string that held her panties together. When the supply of bills dried up, she moved on to the next customer, revealing a little more each time, letting the customers get a little closer, touch a little more inappropriately.

Gina wondered what it would feel like to do that

onstage for strange men. Could she do it if it was required? For the good of the mission? She decided the answer was a definite *no*. What difference would it make if you debased yourself for a paycheck from the Department or from a bar?

It was still wrong.

SEAL Under Covers (Book #3) is available here.

sharonhamiltonauthor.com/SEALBro3

ABOUT THE AUTHOR

NYT and USA Today best-selling author Sharon Hamilton's award-winning Navy SEAL Brotherhood series have been a fan favorite from the day the first one was released. They've earned her the coveted Amazon author ranking of #1 in Romantic Suspense, Military Romance and Contemporary Romance categories, as well as in Gothic Romance for her Vampires of Tuscany and Guardian Angels. Her characters follow a sometimes rocky road to redemption through passion and true love.

Now that he's out of the Navy, Sharon can share with her readers that her son spent a decade as a Navy SEAL, and he's the inspiration for her books.

Her Golden Vampires of Tuscany are not like any vamps you've read about before, since they don't go to ground and can walk around in the full light of the sun.

Her Guardian Angels struggle with the human charges they are sent to save, often escaping their vanilla world of Heaven for the brief human one. You won't find any of these beings in any Sunday school class.

She lives in Sonoma County, California with her husband and her Doberman, Tucker. A lifelong organic gardener, when she's not writing, she's getting *verra verra* dirty in the mud, or wandering Farmers Markets looking for new Heirloom varieties of vegetables and flowers. She and her husband plan to cure their wanderlust (or make it worse) by traveling in their Diesel Class A Pusher, Romance Rider. Starting with this book, all her writing will be done on the road.

She loves hearing from her fans:
Sharonhamilton2001@gmail.com

Her website is:
sharonhamiltonauthor.com

Find out more about Sharon, her upcoming releases, appearances and news from her newsletter, **AND receive a free book** when you sign up for Sharon's newsletter.

Facebook:
facebook.com/SharonHamiltonAuthor

Twitter:
twitter.com/sharonlhamilton

Pinterest:
pinterest.com/AuthorSharonH

Google Plus:
plus.google.com/u/1/+SharonHamiltonAuthor/posts

BookBub:
bookbub.com/authors/sharon-hamilton

Youtube:

youtube.com/channel/UCDInkxXFpXp_4Vnq08ZxMBQ

Soundcloud:

soundcloud.com/sharon-hamilton-1

Sharon Hamilton's Rockin' Romance Readers:

facebook.com/groups/sealteamromance

Sharon Hamilton's Goodreads Group:

goodreads.com/group/show/199125-sharon-hamilton-readers-group

Visit Sharon's Online Store:

sharon-hamilton-author.myshopify.com

Join Sharon's Review Teams:

eBook Reviews:

sharonhamiltonassistant@gmail.com

Audio Reviews:

sharonhamiltonassistant@gmail.com

Life is one fool thing after another.
Love is two fool things after each other.

REVIEWS

PRAISE FOR THE
GOLDEN VAMPIRES OF TUSCANY SERIES

"Well to say the least I was thoroughly surprise. I have read many Vampire books, from Ann Rice to Kym Grosso and few other Authors, so yes I do like Vampires, not the super scary ones from the old days, but the new ones are far more interesting far more human then one can remember. I found Honeymoon Bite a totally engrossing book, I was not able to put it down, page after page I found delight, love, understanding, well that is until the bad bad Vamp started being really bad. But seeing someone love another person so much that they would do anything to protect them, well that had me going, then well there was more and for a while I thought it was the end of a beautiful love story that spanned not only time but, spanned Italy and California. Won't divulge how it ended, but I did shed a few tears after screaming but Sharon Hamilton did not let me down, she took me on amazing trip that I loved, look forward to reading another Vampire book of hers."

"An excellent paranormal romance that was exciting, romantic, entertaining and very satisfying to read. It had me anticipating what would happen next many times over, so much so I could not put it down and even finished it up in a day. The vampires in this book were different from your average vampire, but I enjoy different variations and changes to the same old stuff. It made for a more unpredictable read and more adventurous to explore! Vampire lovers, any paranormal readers and even those who love the romance genre will enjoy Honeymoon Bite."

"This is the first non-Seal book of this author's I have read and I loved it. There is a cast-like hierarchy in this vampire community with humans at the very bottom and Golden vampires at the top. Lionel is a dark vampire who are servants of the Goldens. Phoebe is a Golden who has not decided if she will remain human or accept the turning to become a vampire. Either way she and Lionel can never be together since it is forbidden.

I enjoyed this story and I am looking forward to the next installment."

"A hauntingly romantic read. Old love lost and new love found. Family, heart, intrigue and vampires. Grabbed my attention and couldn't put down. Would definitely recommend."

PRAISE FOR THE
SEAL BROTHERHOOD SERIES

"Fans of Navy SEAL romance, I found a new author to feed your addiction. Finely written and loaded delicious with moments, Sharon Hamilton's storytelling satisfies like a thick bar of chocolate." —Marliss Melton, bestselling author of the *Team Twelve* Navy SEALs series

"Sharon Hamilton does an EXCELLENT job of fitting all the characters into a brotherhood of SEALS that may not be real but sure makes you feel that you have entered the circle and security of their world. The stories intertwine with each book before...and each book after and THAT is what makes Sharon Hamilton's SEAL Brotherhood Series so very interesting. You won't want to put down ANY of her books and they will keep you reading into the night when you should be sleeping. Start with this book...and you will not want to stop until you've read the whole series and then...you will be waiting for Sharon to write the next one." (5 Star Review)

"Kyle and Christy explode all over the pages in this first book, *[Accidental SEAL]*, in a whole new series of SEALs. If the twist and turns don't get your heart jumping, then maybe the suspense will. This is a must read for those that are looking for love and adventure with a little sloppy love thrown in for good measure." (5 Star Review)

PRAISE FOR THE
BAD BOYS OF SEAL TEAM 3 SERIES

"I love reading this series! Once you start these books, you can hardly put them down. The mix of romance and suspense keeps you turning the pages one right after another! Can't wait until the next book!" (5 Star Review)

"I love all of Sharon's Seal books, but *[SEAL's Code]* may just be her best to date. Danny and Luci's journey is filled with a wonderful insight into the Native American life. It is a love story that will fill you with warmth and contentment. You will enjoy Danny's journey to become a SEAL and his reasons for it. Good job Sharon!" (5 Star Review)

PRAISE FOR THE
BAND OF BACHELORS SERIES

"*[Lucas]* was the first book in the Band of Bachelors series and it was a phenomenal start. I loved how we got to see the other SEALs we all love and we got a look at Lucas and Marcy. They had an instant attraction, and their love was very intense. This book had it all, suspense, steamy romance, humor, everything you want in a riveting, outstanding read. I can't wait to read the next book in this series." (5 Star Review)

PRAISE FOR THE
TRUE BLUE SEALS SERIES

"Keep the tissues box nearby as you read *True Blue SEALs: Zak* by Sharon Hamilton. I imagine more than I wish to that the circumstances surrounding Zak and Amy are all too real for returning military personnel and their families. Ms. Hamilton has put us right in the middle of struggles and successes that these two high school sweethearts endure. I have read several of Sharon Hamilton's military romances but will say this is the most emotionally intense of the ones that I have read. This is a well-written, realistic story with authentic characters that will have you rooting for them and proud of those who serve to keep us safe. This is an author who writes amazing stories that you love and cry with the characters. Fans of Jessica Scott and Marliss Melton will want to add Sharon Hamilton to their list of realistic military romance writers." (5 Star Review)